VALLEY OF SHADOWS by Candace West is the breathtaking sequel to this talented author's debut novel *Lane Steen*. So often as I read this story following Lane's star-crossed parents I was so taken with the emotion and beauty that I would sigh and savor the moment. But don't let the lyrical writing fool you into thinking it is all just pretty window dressing. Depths are mined and in such a genuine way that it would seem there was no remedy. And that is where this book shines. Your heart will be pulled with gossamer strings as you follow these beloved characters through love, loss, hope and redemption. It is a journey you will not want to miss.

— KATHLEEN L. MAHER, ACFW GENESIS AWARD WINNING AUTHOR OF *THE ABOLITIONIST'S DAUGHTER* AND *THE CHAPLAIN'S DAUGHTER* (SONS OF THE SHENANDOAH SERIES)

Valley Creek Redemption • Two

Forgiving is far from forgetting.

Valley OF SHADOWS

CANDACE WEST

Scrivenings PRESS
Quench your thirst for story.
www.ScriveningsPress.com

ACKNOWLEDGEMENTS

Without the love and support of my parents this writing journey would never have happened. Mama and Daddy, thank you for the loving home you gave me. Sometimes preachers' kids grow up hating the experience (I had those seasons), but you shielded me from many pitfalls. You never made me the example. You gave me the freedom to be an ordinary, mischievous child, to never be a people pleaser. Most of all, your walk with God spurred within me the desire to know Him for myself. Thank you for teaching me that Christianity is not a religion, but rather a relationship with the Living God through His Son Jesus. To Him alone does all glory belong!

To my husband and son, I owe thanks for supporting and loving me every step of the way. Thank you for not minding those piles of laundry while dust bunnies gathered under the furniture. And I appreciate all those times you pitched in while I followed Lorena and Earl through Valley Creek.

I owe a huge thanks to my beta readers Kathleen, Becky, Lynn, and Patsye. Your feedback was amazing. Thank you for taking the time to read this story and help it through its growing pains! You're the best!

Thank you, Jolene, for allowing me to use your beautiful photograph that inspired the background in the first two editions of this book cover. Your God-given talent for capturing the beauty of Arkansas blesses so many. And most of all, thank you for your friendship! Everyone be sure to check out her Living Every Moment Facebook page where you can follow her photography!

To the other ladies of the Arkansas chapter of ACFW, thank you for always encouraging and upholding one another. Tonya, Kathy, Jolene, Jenny, Cindy, Debbie, Shannon, Linda, and Suzanne, keep letting your light shine!

Kathy, Jerry, Diane, and everyone else at Mantle Rock Publishing, I thank you for taking a chance on me. You make your authors feel like family. Getting to work with you has been an amazing experience. May God bless each of you!

Thank you, Linda and Shannon, for taking this series into the Scrivenings Press family. Your enthusiastic support for the folks of Valley Creek keeps these stories alive. I treasure your friendship and tireless work to make these stories shine for God's glory.

Stories never happen by themselves. They spark the imagination and spread through the writer's fingers. But it doesn't end there. Readers open their hearts to new characters and carry them within forever after. Even more wonderful is when readers share those stories with others. The story lives on.

The best thing about the writing journey is befriending readers and other writers. Since my debut, I've been blessed by all of you who took the time to read Lane's story. Thank you for your words of encouragement, your reviews, and your friendship! You've made this journey worthwhile!

*Yea, though I walk through the valley of the shadow of death, I will
fear no evil for Thou art with me.*

September 2, 1910

The torrent swept away Lorena's well-devised surprise into the muck. Coal-black clouds hurled sheets of rain upon the surrounding Ozarks and against the little train station huddled under the trees.

Stranded. Lorena was five miles away, but she might as well be five thousand miles from Valley Creek. No one knew she was here. Father told her to wire first, but she wanted to surprise her daughters. Lorena shook her head.

Edging back farther on the covered platform, Lorena winced as rain thundered down the tin roof, splattering mud on the bottom step as it pounded the ground. A burst of lightning swept across the sky and the hills. A sudden flood of color assailed the next moment with gray. Thunder crashed and rattled the station's windows.

"Ma'am." The stationmaster poked his whiskered head around the door. "You ain't got no one to pick you up?"

"No, I was planning to walk to Valley Creek. I guess it'll have to wait for now."

The stationmaster stepped further through the doorway. "I reckon this rain will be here for a good spell, but I don't get off work 'til after the nine o'clock train comes this evening. I can take you then, if you don't mind. Even when it quits raining, the road won't be in no condition for your feet." His eyes dropped to Lorena's cream leather button-up boots, very fashionable in New York City but not in the Arkansas Ozarks.

A weak smile curved her lips. Nine o'clock. Five more hours. "Thank you. I guess I'll have to wait then."

The old man lifted his cap and ran a weathered hand through his white hair. "I'm right sorry, ma'am. Would you like to come in and set fer a spell?"

His kindness brought sudden tears to Lorena's eyes. "Perhaps later. I really appreciate your offer to take me to Valley Creek. I think I'll sit out here and watch the rain for a while."

"I'll be right here if you need anything."

"Thank you."

With a nod, the stationmaster backed away and closed the door. Sighing, Lorena wandered down to the other end of the platform where a crude wooden bench squatted in the shadows. Just as she settled down, the man poked his head through the doorway again.

"Ma'am, I don't know where my mind is. There's supposed to be a young feller from Valley Creek bringing me a crate of squash this afternoon. I'm sure he'd take you there, if you don't mind."

For the first time since stepping off the train, Lorena beamed a true smile at him. He raised his bushy eyebrows and grinned.

"Now, ain't that a welcome sight!" Seeming embarrassed, he cleared his throat. "Of course, that young feller may not be coming with the rain pouring like it is, but he might."

"I hope he will. If you think it would be all right to go with him."

"A few years ago, no. But now," he nodded, "I'd trust him with one of my own."

Mud splattered against the buggy while the rain pelted the canvas above Earl's head, a constant thundering in his ears. Good thing the wind wasn't blowing, or he'd be drenched. Just another mid-fall downpour that might last a few minutes or a few hours. Underneath the seat, a crate of squash creaked with each rut that the wheels crisscrossed.

Earl yanked the hat farther down on his forehead. When the downpour started, he almost turned around, but he promised to bring the squash. And he was determined to be a man of his word once more.

"Lord, I guess the earth needs a good drink of water, but I wish it could've waited until tonight." He chuckled. At the sound, Crockett twitched his ears back and shook his head. Earl chuckled again, a rare thing. Learning to laugh again didn't come easy.

As Earl pulled in front of the depot, he pulled the reins and stopped the buggy. Grabbing the crate, he swung down and hurried to the steps.

"Well, well, you brought 'em after all!" greeted the old man, rounding the countertop as Earl opened the door.

"Yessir. It came quite a storm, didn't it, Mr. Henry?" Earl set the crate on the floor.

"It sure did!" Henry bent and picked up one of the squash, turning it over in his calloused hands. "Boy, they look good, and they'll sure smell good on my stove tonight! Cain't wait to sink my teeth in them. How much do I owe you?"

"Nothing."

Henry raised his salt-and-pepper eyebrows. "No, son. I have to pay you something. It ain't fair that way."

Earl smiled with a wink. "I don't see what's so unfair about it. Just keep the squash and enjoy them. That's pay enough for me ... unless you want to give me one of your prize watermelons next year."

Henry leaned against the counter, eyeing Earl carefully. "Well! I guess religion is good for something after all. Was a time when I'd never thought it of you."

Something tight squirmed in Earl's gut and wound its way up his throat, suddenly making it hard to smile. Like a horse sidestepping a rattlesnake, his mind balked at unbidden memories. Memories, a lifetime of them, he wanted to forget. "I guess I'll be going for now. I ..."

"Wait a minute, son. There's a little favor I'd like to ask. It ain't for me. It's for the little lady out there."

"Little lady? I didn't see anyone." Earl glanced over his shoulder at the door.

"Oh, she's there at the end of the platform sittin' on the bench. She came in on the train about an hour ago and was planning on walking to Valley Creek."

"No one was here to get her?" Earl shook his head, imagining some careless, forgetful relative sitting by their fireside in Valley Creek.

"Nope. Not a soul. Just ain't right, I said to myself. But anyhow, she ain't got a way there, and she can't walk in this rain. Would you mind giving her a lift?"

"Not at all. I'll take her right now." Earl turned toward the door.

"I'm obliged, Earl."

Taking off his hat, Earl stepped onto the porch, the rain thundering against the tin roof. At the end of the platform in the shadows sat the lady, turned toward the nearby hills. Earl took a step, unsure of how to let her know he was there without startling her. No use clearing his throat. She wouldn't hear it over that racket.

Earl stepped closer. Lightning blazed through the grayness and lit her profile. He froze, his mouth running dry. No matter if it had been a hundred months or a hundred years, her profile was seared into his memory. Of all times, of all places.

"Lorena." The word escaped before he knew it.

THOUGH HER MIND was a million miles away, though the rain crashed against the roof, that voice called her back. That same voice that haunted her dreams at night and filled her soul with anguish.

Lorena felt the color drain from her face as she whirled around. "Earl!"

Earl twisted the hat in his hands, wordless. Stiffly, Lorena rose and stepped back until she bumped the wet porch railing. Her heart pounded as she scrutinized him.

Auburn hair flecked lightly with gray. Sturdy, broad shoulders. Tanned face suddenly ashen. Same blue-green eyes. Strong chin.

For the first time in sixteen years, husband and wife faced each other.

The blood roared in her ears as Lorena's heated gaze scorched him. The minutes stretched silently. The bitter years rose up between them—the deceit, the pain, the wrongs, and the sins.

Trembling, Lorena dug her fingernails into her palms. "You? You're the young fellow?"

Earl nodded, twisting his hat even harder.

"I came to see my daughters."

Earl nodded again, this time clearing his throat. "Will you come?"

Lorena gritted her teeth. What a way to bridge years with

words like that. "Are you daft? I'd rather wait until nine o'clock when the man inside closes for the day. He'll take me."

Earl tore his eyes away from hers. "I can't leave you here."

Hot words rushed to her tongue before she could stop them. "Since when?" Sixteen years of buried feelings overtook the roar of the rain and thunder.

"Lorena, I ..."

Unwilling to hear another word, Lorena held up her hand and shook her head. "No! I'll stay right where I am. I'd rather die than go with you anywhere."

Moments passed while Earl stood like a statue, twisting only his hat. At last, he stepped back and put it on his head. "I'll be going."

Lorena's hands covered her face. "Please do."

As Earl turned away, she crumpled onto the bench, her shoulders shaking with sobs. She rubbed her throbbing temples, fighting a losing battle as anger boiled higher and higher. She swiped at the tears with the back of her hand. What was wrong with her? She thought she had given all her anger to the Lord years ago.

Those lost years planted themselves firmly before her in the person of Earl Steen. He had robbed their family, never once caring about the heartache he caused. In fact, he deliberately planned it.

Lorena struggled for control. She fumbled within her pocket, pulled out a flowery handkerchief, and wiped her face. She inhaled slowly, deeply. In. Out. In. Out. The practical side of herself seized her emotions and crammed them deep down inside.

Well, she just had to deal with it. One day at a time. No one said it would be easy. And as for Earl ...

Lorena shuddered. She didn't dare finish the thought.

Tears wedged in Earl's throat. They wouldn't go up, and he couldn't swallow them down. He took a deep, ragged breath before hurrying down the steps into the rain. If he could just disappear. The irony of the thought stabbed his heart. He did once, and he had never been able to return.

Muddy water sloshed with every step and soaked into his overalls, but he hardly felt it. The sting of rain slapped his face as a burst of wind collided into him. Overhead, thunder cracked.

Tossing his head, Crockett stamped his feet and whinnied. Earl snatched up the reins and jumped into the buggy. Against his will, his eyes sought another glimpse of his wife huddled on the bench. Her face was buried in the handkerchief.

"Oh, my Lord, help her! Forgive me!" The wind snatched away his prayer.

Earl slapped Crockett's back harder than he intended. Deep-seated regret pressed down against his heart. No, more than regret. Something deeper that had no words. Sorrow, agony, hopelessness, and a thousand other feelings. Earl's sins rose up in the rising mist and pursued him along the road. Guilt shook him.

Time to pay up.

2

Though the ride to his daughter's house was not too far, the miles stretched much longer than usual. Once more, though gentler, Earl flicked the reins. Crockett sloshed quicker through the puddles as though sensing the memories chasing them. Above all else, Lorena's face hovered in Earl's mind. How it hardened to stone as soon as she saw him. The girlish face he remembered no longer held the expectant gaze, love, and trust. Rightfully so. Despite that, her beauty hadn't dimmed. Time had only deepened it.

At last, the five miles passed, and Earl stopped at Lane and Guy's place. Before he lifted his hand to knock, Lane opened the door. Light from a lantern streamed through the opening and puddled around their feet.

"Father." Lane widened the door for him to pass. "It's a dreary afternoon to be out."

Earl stayed rooted to the spot. "I can't stay. Sorry. I've something to tell you."

A frown furrowed across Lane's brow as she peered at her father. "What's wrong?"

"Your mother. She's here. Down at the station."

"Mother?" Lane brightened. "How? She isn't supposed to be here for a few weeks yet."

"I know, but she is. I saw her myself when I took that squash to Henry. She wanted to surprise you." His eyes latched onto Lane's deep blue-green ones, just like his, unspoken things passing between them. "She was planning to walk here, but the rain ..."

"Evenin', Mr. Steen." Guy came to stand by his wife. "Don't worry. I'll go fetch Mrs. Steen."

"Me too! Can I go, Papa Guy?" Their adopted son Jimmy bounced into the doorway.

"If it's all right with Mama." Guy smiled, ruffling Jimmy's blond head.

"Mama Lane? I'd like to go, please."

"Yes, you may." Lane patted his shoulder. "Run along and get your shoes."

"Yippee!!!" The eight-year-old disappeared into the house.

"I'll go hitch up. Mr. Steen, come on in and grab yourself a cup of coffee. Lane just made a fresh pot." Guy pulled his hat from a peg behind the door.

Earl's head throbbed. "Thanks, Guy, but I best be going. I'm obliged." As he turned, Lane's voice caught him.

"Are you sure, Father? There's plenty here for you, and it'll warm you up."

Like balm to a burning wound, Lane's simple words held more promise than Earl ever dreamed possible. A tear escaped and trickled down his cheek, but the gathering twilight hid it. "Thanks. I reckon I could use a cup after all." He cleared his throat, swiping the tear away.

Lane stepped aside to let him in, a small smile touching her lips.

Moments later, as Earl settled down at the kitchen table, Lane's words poured over his wounds once more. "There's plenty here for you, and it'll warm you up." Once, he possessed everything but, like Esau, he had traded the best for a bowl of pottage. Now just sharing a cup of coffee with his daughter meant everything.

"I can't imagine the shock both of you had seeing each other." Lane handed over a steaming cup and poured one for herself. Though her face remained calm, the cup trembled slightly in her fingers as she sat across from him.

"It's been about sixteen years."

"A long time."

Earl stared into his cup. "Been a lifetime, and not nearly long enough." He squirmed as though it might ease some of the pain.

"Father, I'm listening."

Earl blinked at his daughter, the link that bound and divided Lorena and him. In Lane's eyes, he beheld the guarded trust just as he did the day he snatched her out of her mother's arms and disappeared. Her trust had turned to hate, rightfully so, but the Lord was healing the breach. Was it enough?

"Maybe it's better if I just leave Valley Creek."

"What?"

"I figure Lorena will stay until after your sister has her baby. That's quite a while yet. We can't be runnin' into each other all the time."

Frowning, Lane traced the rim of her cup with a finger. "You're not seriously considering it?"

"I am."

"Where would you go? You can't get too far on sawmill wages."

"I don't have to go far. Just far enough to give Lorena the space she needs. There's plenty of sawmills in these mountains."

"For better or worse, Valley Creek is your home. Running away won't help, you know," Lane's gentle reminder softened her frown.

"Yes, I do know, but Valley Creek ain't never been my home. I gave my home up when I left your mother. It's best for Lorena if I go."

"I'd pray on it first, Father. Don't make any rash decisions." Lane sipped her coffee, studying Earl's face. "You have more roots here than you realize."

Earl shook his head. "If you'd seen Lorena's face, you'd understand."

"Just promise me you'll pray on it, Father. Let the Lord guide you. He's brought you and Mother this far."

A yearning filled Earl to reach across the table and grasp Lane's hand, but he clutched the cup instead. For so many years his hands had terrified her, bruised her body, and scarred her heart. His hands had shown her his rage but never his love. The Lord had changed all of that. Though she no longer hated him, could she ever learn to love him with a daughter's love?

As she watched him, Lane swallowed, her gaze faltering from his.

Her battle wasn't lost on Earl. He watched it struggle across her face. The longing, sorrow, hesitation, and worst of all, fear.

He set the cup aside, pushed the chair back quietly, and stood. "I'll pray, Lane. You have my word. Thanks again for the coffee. And the talk." He tried to smile, but the lump in his throat halted it.

Before she could reply, he was gone.

"MY DARLING GIRL! I wanted to surprise you!" Lorena framed Lane's face in her hands as she drew back from their embrace.

"You have! I'm so delighted you're here!"

"Me too!" Jimmy threw his arms around both ladies while Guy stood aside and beamed.

"I've missed you, Jimmy." Lorena kissed his freckled nose.

"I've missed all of you so very much."

"Come sit by the fire, Mother. You're chilled through!" Lane tugged Lorena toward the hearth while Guy added more firewood. Sparks scattered up the chimney as the wood popped.

Lorena lowered herself into a rocking chair. "Oh, it's so good to be out of the rain and wind!"

"You could've sent a telegram," Lane fussed, tucking a patchwork quilt around Lorena.

"I know. I know. Father told me to send one." Lorena drew the quilt up under her chin.

"Speakin' of your pa, how is Mr. Wallace?" Guy rubbed his hands together above the fire.

"He's anxious to leave New York. After he sets things in order, his partner will handle the business while he takes time off to come here. It'll do him good to get away."

"And I imagine he's not about to miss the birth of his first great-grandchild," Guy grinned, his hazel eyes twinkling.

"Not hardly. How is Edith doing? She said in her last letter that she wasn't feeling well."

Biting her lip, Lane shook her head. "She's been sick quite a bit, mostly all the time. Doc says that some women have the sickness worse than others. I go over there every day after I'm through teaching."

"Then it's good I came early. She should be over the sickness by now, but some have it the whole time. I'll do all I can to help." Lorena held her arms open and clasped Lane close to her heart once more. "I'm so happy to be together with my two girls again."

Later in the evening as the firelight flickered into the shadows across the room, Lane settled on a stool at her mother's knee to talk privately. Across the room, Guy's chestnut head bent over Jimmy's sandy one as he taught him how to carve a horse. Their voices blended together in whispers as light danced off the knife's blade. Love rose and brimmed over Lorena's heart. The dearest things in the world surrounded her, now. How different it was only a few years ago.

"Mother," Lane ventured, fingering the quilt across Lorena's knees, "How was it? Seeing him?"

Lorena's sigh stirred the auburn tendrils curling around Lane's forehead. "Awful. I was so startled and angry. So very, very angry. Lane, I truly thought I put those feelings to rest, especially when I heard that Earl came to Christ. But when I saw him, I wanted to shout at him, slap him, make a scene."

"But you didn't."

"No. But I wanted to make him pay so much that I trembled." Wearily, Lorena rubbed her arms.

"That doesn't sound like you. You've always been so strong and poised."

A wry smile tugged Lorena's lips. "That's what you think."

"You're stronger than you realize, Mother. I only wish I was."

"You are. The Lord has brought you through."

"And you too." Closing her eyes, Lane laid her head in Lorena's lap.

"Yes, He has, but I must pray about this. It'll be difficult."

"I know how you feel. The journey I've made hasn't been easy, but I'm still learning. Father and I are getting to know each other with God's help. At one time I would've hated to admit it, but he *is* different. I don't hate him anymore, Mother. I feel like I'm a baby learning how to walk all over again. At first, I couldn't without God picking me up. Then I began to crawl a little, bumping into my past and my hatred. Now, I'm making little steps, and Father is too. And it feels right. I still have hard moments, but no one knows how much he's changed more than me. You'll come to see it too."

"Listen to you." Lorena stroked her daughter's hair. "Talking like you're the mother and I'm the child. I know Earl has changed, and I'm glad of that. But I want as little to do with him as possible. The scars are too deep, for him and me."

"Your thinking is keepin' me awake." Guy rolled over and faced his wife.

"How'd you know I was awake?" Lane shifted the pillow underneath her head.

"I just know." He reached out and drew her to him.

Smiling in the darkness, Lane wrapped her arms around him, marveling how much she loved Guy.

"What's the matter?" His lips moved against her forehead.

"I can't get the thoughts of Mother and Father out of my head. Do you realize I have no memory of them together?"

"I know. You and Edith are the link between them."

"A link that reaches across the miles and years. I'm both afraid and curious to see them in the same room. Does that make any sense?"

"Yeah. You're their daughter. You've never known what it's like to have a ma and pa under the same roof. It's natural." Stroking her back, Guy's embrace tightened around Lane. "Wouldn't it be something if you're the one who drives them back together?"

"Matchmaker," Lane teased softly, then sobered. "No. Too much rough water under the bridge."

"You know, Lane, I'm a believer in second chances. My life proves that. Me and you, we're proof of that. I never thought you'd love me."

"Neither did I, but you sure didn't act like you thought it."

"I had to keep up a good front." With a low laugh, Guy kissed his wife.

"I believe in second chances, too, but ..."

"If you don't get some rest, you'll be a mighty sleepy teacher in the morning."

Rows of eager, young faces filled Lane's mind. "You're right." She yawned, nestling her head against Guy's chest. "Now is not the time for working out problems."

ACROSS THE HALL in Jimmy's room, Lorena turned over and stared out the window, feeling guilty that Jimmy had to sleep on a makeshift mat in front of the fireplace. But Jimmy, sweet child that he was, didn't seem to mind. Even if he had to sleep on the floor, he didn't care as long as he was with Lane and Guy. Ever since his mother's death, they were his home.

Yet Lorena's trouble went far deeper. In vain, she scrubbed Earl's face from her mind and begged sleep to come.

Beyond the window, moonlight splashed against everything it touched, bouncing off the barn's tin roof and spilling over into the rain barrel underneath the eaves. A far different scene than the noisy city streets. Though the view filled her eyes, Earl's face did as well.

Even though he was only in his early forties, the lines around his eyes and mouth told of the hard, wasted years he'd lived. His blue-green eyes, though not bleary with alcohol, didn't snap with ambition. His mouth was solemn, almost mirthless, but it no longer twisted with bitterness. Underneath his mouth, the chin was still firm, no longer proud.

Though warm under the covers, Lorena shivered. His mouth once said cruel things, and his hands had hit her. He had stolen their daughter and poured out the violence of his anger on her. And he had lived years with another woman who pretended to be Lane's mama.

Lorena loathed him. Yet, against every part of her will, deep down inside, love remained as well. Anger stirred once more.

"Oh, Lord," she groaned, whispering. "I wish I could reach

inside my heart and take away these feelings, but I can't. Only You can help me."

Reaching underneath the collar of her nightgown, Lorena drew out a hidden, gold chain. Her wedding ring dangled from it, captured within its hold. She fingered the cold metal.

The years had made her strong, but she was not formidable. No one else knew it better than she did. She had to get through this. She must. Sighing, Lorena squeezed her eyes shut against the memory of Earl's face and turned over again.

As Lorena tossed and turned, a light gleamed through a window of a small house across the woods. The glow pierced the darkness and cast Earl Steen's kneeling shadow across the floor. With folded hands and bent head, he sought guidance and grappled against guilt.

"Lord, forgive me. Forgive me of all the harm I've caused, of all the sins I've done. Help me now to do the right thing. Lord, I need Your help."

The prayer was simple but as fervent as Jacob's prayer when he struggled with the angel. For a long time, Earl didn't speak. God knew his heart. It was open for His eyes to see.

Finally, he lifted his head and rubbed his hand across his eyes. "I'm like Esau. I've sold my birthright, my wife and children. Lord, take them and keep them always in Your care. They're Yours, not mine."

Slowly, he rose from his knees and sat on the bed. Despite his trouble, peace slipped into his soul. The Lord was near and would anchor him. It wasn't going to be simple. He loved Lorena. He loved her the way he should have from the beginning.

Pulling back the bedcovers, he sank onto the pillow not realizing that a few miles away Lorena was praying too.

3

___

"You don't know how happy I am you're here!" Delight shone on Edith's pale face as she sat near her mother the next morning. "I only wish Lane could've stayed too."

Brushing back some loose raven strands from Edith's face, Lorena pasted on a smile, her chest tightening with concern. "You never told me in your letters how sick you were."

Edith smiled, rubbing her stomach. "Doc says some women have the sickness the whole nine months. I guess I'm one of those."

"That may be so, but you still need help. And I'm here to give it."

"Lane has been helping me, Mother. And Harley Ray helps as much as he can when he comes in from work. Really, I'm fine."

"An extra pair of hands never hurt anything. Lane can't be here all the time since she's teaching. When harvest is over, Harley Ray will be working long hours at the sawmill." Lorena leaned forward and placed her hands over Edith's. "You're as pale as a sheet, and you have dark circles under your eyes."

"Thanks. I feel better already." Edith scrunched up her nose.

"I know you're a grown woman and very capable. You've embraced life here in Valley Creek after growing up in the privileges of the city. You'll never know how proud I am of you. But I'm still your mother. I feel helpless so far away knowing I can't reach you if something were to happen. I want to be here for you and Lane."

"What about Grandfather? You've both taken care of each other for so long."

"He needs time away. His partner agreed to take care of everything so that he can visit here. The only thing I don't like is crowding in on you all." Lorena grimaced.

"We don't mind at all, but I've been thinking. What if Lane and I talk to the school board about the teacherage. It's been sitting empty since Harley Ray and I married. If you offer them a reasonable price, I'm sure they'll let you rent it."

Relief washed over Lorena. "It would be perfect. Grandfather and I don't want to be any trouble."

"You'll never be that, Mother. You and Grandfather have always been good to me, raising me and living your faith in front of me. I wish there was more I could provide."

A soft smile lifted Lorena's lips. "Daughter, it's more than enough. We'll be very content there."

"I'm glad." Abruptly, Edith dropped her gaze and fingered a button on her sleeve, as though an unwelcome thought troubled her. "But what about Father?"

Lorena stiffened. "What about him?"

"You won't be able to avoid him. You'll see him often."

"I already have." Lorena frowned as she explained their meeting. "But I'm not letting that stop me. We'll have to learn to get along for your sakes. I've prayed about it and decided that I'm not going to hide or run away from him. That's useless."

"Mother, I just want you to be happy while you're here.

Lane feels the same way. We want you to be comfortable, and we're going to see to it."

Heartache squeezed Lorena. How fragile Edith looked. "Dear, as long as I'm with my daughters, I'm happy."

"I think Father wants to stay out of your way as much as possible." Edith squirmed against the stiff back of the chair, rubbing her side. "He really has changed. The Lord has done a wonderful work in his life."

"I'm glad. I hope he'll spend the rest of his life serving Him."

Suddenly, Edith groaned and laid her head back.

"Are you getting sick?" Lorena sat up straight.

Edith closed her eyes, nodding. "There's a pail beside the bed. I'm going to need it."

In an instant, Lorena rushed to the bedroom and returned with it. "I'm going to get a washcloth." She set the pail in Edith's lap.

Outside, a footstep creaked across the porch and a hand tapped at the door.

"Come in." Edith's listless voice sent a shiver through Lorena as she snatched a cloth from a nearby washstand.

Earl Steen stepped inside, a cool breeze stirring the room as he shut the door. Immediately, his eyes darted to Lorena. Wringing out a washcloth at the basin, she mustered enough frost into her glare to freeze his insides. At least she hoped it did. Earl took a step backwards.

"It's all right, Father. I'm just feeling a little sick."

"I was stopping by to see how you were."

"I could be better, but then again, I could be worse. Ohhh!" Edith leaned over the pail while Lorena rushed over and pressed the washcloth to her forehead. The sickness seized her, shaking her shoulders as she gasped for breath. Wisps of black hair fell loose and swept across her cheeks.

"Take slow, deep breaths," soothed Lorena, rubbing Edith's back with her free hand.

Tossing his hat aside, Earl strode across the room and stood on the other side of Edith. Several tense moments passed while she battled with the nausea.

Gasping, Edith leaned her head back. "I'm okay now."

Wiping Edith's face, Lorena jerked her head toward the pail, her eyes snapping at Earl. "Empty that and wash it out."

Taking the pail, Earl headed outside. Several moments later, he returned, pausing in the doorway as Lorena bent over Edith, whispering comfort. From the side, Lorena felt him watching the tender scene. She snapped herself ramrod straight and forced herself to meet his eyes.

The warmth in them thinned her breath. Her eyes faltered to the pail still clutched in his hand.

"The pail, Earl."

Earl blinked. "Oh. Of course." He hurried across the room and handed it to her. "I'm going now, Edith. I hope you'll feel better." He reached for his hat where it had fallen near the chair.

"I hope so too. Thanks for stopping by, Father." Though she tried to smile, it trembled on her weak lips.

Glancing at Lorena, Earl touched the tip of his hat, but she busied herself wiping Edith's forehead and face. A moment later, he was gone.

Long, silent moments passed as Edith regained some of her strength. Standing over her, Lorena hummed and bathed Edith's face with the cool, refreshing rag. The melody drifted gently through the room, soothing her soul. "When other helpers fail, and comforts flee, Help of the helpless, oh, abide with me!" Glancing down, Lorena discovered Edith studying her, the brownblack of her eyes like a shining sea.

"Your faith, your strength has taught me so much through the years."

Yet Lorena sensed there was more behind Edith's words. "What is it, darling?"

"Nothing."

"You're wanting to ask me something."

"It's not important."

But Lorena knew her daughter too well. "It's something to do with your Father, isn't it?"

"This isn't the time for questions like that." Edith shifted her head away.

Lorena read it, however, in her face. "You want to know if I love him still. Edith, you're so young, and hope is easier to come by when you're young. There are some things that can never be worked out. I must be honest with you. It doesn't matter what I feel. Forgiveness is one thing. Forgetting is another. It's best for things to remain as they are."

"You never cease to amaze me. When I was a little girl, it made me so mad when you knew what I was thinking. How did you know?" Edith lifted her head.

"The same way you'll know with your child." With a knowing smile, Lorena laid a hand on Edith's round stomach.

VALLEY CREEK FOLKS shuffled into their pews Sunday morning to hear Reverend Crandall, the new preacher, untried by those who professed to know the Gospel better than the ministers or the Lord Himself.

After a round of hearty handshakes and greetings, the service began. The singing spilled once more through the empty street and echoed up the hillsides. Glancing around, Lorena filled her lungs, aware of a nervous distraction thrumming over the congregation. All eyes involuntarily veered her way as she sang with her daughters and sons-in-law. Perhaps the center of the room was the worst place to sit.

Curious smiles met her self-conscious one. A few whispers trickled down the aisle between songs. Swallowing, Lorena wished she could loosen her collar.

After the singing, Reverend Crandall stepped to the pulpit and cleared his throat. The attention pivoted away from her.

Releasing a slow, relieved breath, Lorena folded her hands and listened to Reverend Crandall's words. From one of the windows, the sunlight streamed into the room and glowed across the congregation. A breeze from one of the open windows stirred a few loose curls framing her face, tickling her cheek.

The service passed, and afterward young and old vied for a chance to talk with her.

"Mrs. Steen, it's so good to see you again," gushed Eliza Huitt. "I hope you had a safe trip here."

"Oh, yes, thank you ..."

"I wish we'd known you were comin'." Mrs. Watkin scolded, patting Lorena's hand. "Lane, next time, you'll be a dear and tell us, won't you?"

"If Mother tells me to, I will." Lane's voice sounded a little too sugary to Lorena, but she understood. Only a few years ago, they never acknowledged her existence. As Lane turned away, she rolled her eyes. Then, catching Lorena's, Lane covered a chuckle with her hand.

"It's such a pity that Mr. Steen wasn't here. He never misses a service." Mrs. Huitt cast a shrewd glance at Lorena as they went down the steps outside.

"Oh?" Lorena flushed, her collar tight once more.

"Yes. He really has shocked us all, you know." Mrs. Watkin dipped her head, lowering her voice. "He was such a drunk."

Returning to her side, Lane reached out and drew Lorena away. "No one knows that better than she." Her eyes flashed between Mrs. Huitt and her friend. "Now, if you'll excuse us, our dinner is waiting."

Before the offended ladies could reply, Guy whisked Lorena up into the wagon. Lane climbed in behind her.

"Lane?" Lorena turned slowly. "Were they telling the truth? Has Earl never missed a service?"

Lane gritted her teeth. "No, he hasn't. I could just wring Eliza Huitt's neck!"

"Lane! I'm surprised at you. Surely they meant no harm."

"Mother, I've known those women ever since I can remember. They were being nosy and rude. I *know* them. All they wanted was your reaction so they could talk about it over dinner."

"She's right, Mrs. Steen." Guy nodded, grabbing the reins and releasing the brake. "As much as I hate to say it, there ain't a charitable bone in their bodies."

Lorena chewed her lip. "Do you think he stayed at home because of me?"

"There's no telling. He may not be feeling well," Lane suggested.

"Maybe, but I don't believe it." Lorena waved away a fly. "I won't have it. If I'm going to be here until Edith's baby arrives, we can't spend the whole time avoiding each other."

"What are you going to do?"

"Take care of it."

Later, after dinner, Lorena's clammy palms grasped the reins as she jostled along the rutted road to Earl's place. Her arms ached as the mules pulled against them. Looking upward, she sucked in a deep breath. "Lord, help me to say the right words."

Everything within her wrestled against her conscience. But Earl was a child of God, and she wasn't going to stand in his way.

The mules clipped along at a steady pace, and Lorena's heart kept time the closer she drew to Earl's house. Not a breeze stirred the trees. Sweat beaded across her forehead, trickling down her neck. When she was within several yards of the place, she pulled the wagon to a stop and whipped out a handkerchief. Taking a few deep breaths, she dabbed away the sweat. If only her heart would stop racing.

An old, familiar sound filtered through the hedgerow. Blinking, Lorena leaned forward and strained her ears. Through the leaves, almost a mere whisper, drifted the sweet strains of a violin. Grieg's *The Last Spring*. The notes dipped and rose, carrying Lorena back to those lost years. The stage, the lights, the hum of the audience gathering in their seats. Her fingers flying over the ivory keys of the grand piano. The sudden hush as Earl drew his bow across the strings with a masterful hand. The breathless audience, always the audience, carried away to another world. Her husband had been the best, the most talented of anyone in that orchestra. No one on that stage could match him. His music had plunged them to their ruin.

A sharp pang drove her back into the present. Pressing her lips together, she flicked the reins and drove into the yard.

Shielding her eyes against the sun, Lorena scoured the object of her nightmares and her futile efforts to find Lane. Before her stood the house where Lane spent her childhood, never dreaming that she had a mother desperately searching for her. Music now filled the void where hateful shouts once filled the air.

Lorena stopped the wagon and climbed down. In a nearby tree, a mockingbird twittered.

Abruptly, the music stopped. A few seconds later the door flew open as Earl's tall, broad form filled the doorway.

"Lorena?" Earl stepped forward, a worried look drawing his brows close together.

Lorena lifted her chin. "I came to talk to you."

"Would you like to come in?" Earl's throat bobbed as he swallowed.

"No, no, thank you. What I'm going to say won't take long." Oh, if only her pulse would stop roaring in her ears.

"Well, here. At least have a seat on this swing." Earl nodded at the porch swing.

"Thank you. I'm fine right here."

Earl eyed her in silence, waiting as he leaned against a porch post.

"You weren't in church this morning."

"I thought it was best to stay home today."

The open, honest way he looked at her stole her breath away. Lorena's heart thundered with resentment. "Why?"

Earl grimaced, looking down at the toe of his shoe. "It would be a little awkward for you. For both of us. It's best if I stay out of the way for the time being."

"Earl, I'm going to be here until Edith's baby is born. We can't go around avoiding each other all the time. We have the girls to think about. I don't want them uncomfortable every time we happen to be around each other. And let's face it, we're going to be around each other whether we like it or not."

Hooking a thumb around his overalls strap, he glanced up. "I've thought about that too. I've been thinking about leavin' Valley Creek."

To hide the trembling in her arms, Lorena crossed them. "That's pointless, Earl. We might as well face this thing here and now."

"But—"

Lorena plunged ahead. "God did a work in your life, and I don't want to keep you from coming to His house. It isn't right. Don't let me stand in your way."

"But you—"

"I'll be all right." Lorena held up her hand. "Come and go as you please. Valley Creek is your home, and you belong at God's house. Please don't stay away on my account."

A long minute passed while neither of them spoke. Finally, Earl raised his head. "You mean it? Are you really sure?"

"Yes."

Earl let out a pent-up breath. "I've prayed about it, and I knew the Lord would work it out somehow."

Lorena looked straight into Earl's blue-green eyes. "I've prayed about it too." She stepped back. "Well, I've said my peace now, so I'll go."

"I haven't."

"What?"

"I haven't said my peace."

Lorena stifled a sigh. "There's no need. You wrote a letter to me. That's enough."

"No, it's not. I've got to tell you—"

Lorena turned to climb back in the wagon. "There's no need, really."

"Don't go just yet, please."

The plea in his voice halted her. Without a word, she turned and waited, crimping her lips together.

"Saying I'm sorry is not enough. I can't undo it, but the Lord knows how much I wish I could. Lorena, I'm sorry, so very sorry. I just want you to know that."

Grinding her heel into the ground, Lorena whirled away to hide the stinging behind her eyelids. "I know you are, Earl." She grasped the seat and pulled herself up into the wagon, her mouth quivering. With her slap of the reins, the wagon lurched forward.

Damp, oval spots darkened her navy skirt as tears dripped from her chin.

ORANGE and red leaves drifted past the library window of the Wallace home in New York City. Across Mr. Wallace's desk,

George Curtis settled himself on the leather chair, the supple cushion creaking under his weight. "Have you settled your affairs before you go to Valley Creek?"

Mr. Wallace nodded, his iron-gray mustache curving with a smile. "I'm leaving in two days." He shut his Bible and laid it on the desk.

"That's good. You need the rest, and I know you're anxious to see your granddaughters. Have you heard anything from Lorena?" Though George schooled his voice to sound casual, his heart listened for the answer.

"I received a telegram yesterday. She's doing just fine. Edith has been pretty sick even though she's past three months now."

"I wish she was here so that I could tend to her. Is there a good doctor around Valley Creek?"

"Dr. Brown is there, and he's one of the best in that area."

"I hope Edith gets plenty of rest." Dr. Curtis swallowed, working his jaw. The next question dug like a burr in his side, and he couldn't hold it back any longer. "Has Lorena mentioned anything about him?"

Him. Mr. Wallace raised his brows and leveled dark, gray eyes at George. Pressing his palms together, Mr. Wallace tapped his fingers.

"Not a word, not even a hint."

"That's like her."

"I have a feeling that they're trying to stay out of each other's way."

"But that's rather hard to do in a small place like Valley Creek."

Mr. Wallace nodded, his British accent unruffled. "I've no doubt Lorena will manage."

George frowned, twisting in the chair. "Maybe, but it's bound to be hard on her. He's still not drinking?"

"Not to my knowledge. I'm very anxious to see it for myself. I pray he has the strength to stay away from it."

The memory of his former best friend stung like a blindsided slap. "For Earl's sake, I do too. For Lorena's, I hope she steers clear of him."

"I'm sure she will." Mr. Wallace leaned back, his gaze never wavering. George resisted the urge to shift his eyes away.

"Tell me, why are you so concerned?"

A bright flush scalded his face, and he gritted his teeth, hoping the truth didn't show. "Mr. Wallace, I've known Lorena since childhood, and I'll always be her friend. I don't want her to get hurt."

"You've seen some of her darkest hours, and you've been a good friend to me as well. Like a son. I can't begin to express what it meant to me all those years we searched for Lane. You always helped in every way you could." Mr. Wallace paused, rubbing his chin. His chest lifted with a sigh. "But I must ask you to be fair to Lorena."

The air thickened between them, and for the first time, George's gaze faltered. "What do you mean, sir?"

Mr. Wallace cleared his throat. "I've been aware for a long time of your feelings for my daughter, and I know you've tried to keep it a secret from us. As far as I know, Lorena doesn't suspect anything. I hope you'll keep it that way, George. She isn't free to return your love."

Though George winced under the blunt words, he plunged forward with the intention of his visit. "That may be for her to decide."

"I'm asking you not to interfere. You know as well as I do that Lorena will never divorce Earl."

"He stole their daughter. He lived with another woman for years. Surely Lorena can't forgive that? She has every right to move on."

Mr. Wallace blanched. "That is Lorena's business, no matter how painful it is for us. Please be reasonable. Let the Lord guide your life instead."

Bitterness rising in his throat, George shook his head. "I gave up on that when my wife died years ago. I've stood by in silence, watching Lorena suffer because of Earl Steen, and I'm not going to stand by any longer. I'm sorry, but I have to do this. Now or never."

Mr. Wallace stood, his eyes thundering. "I forbid it."

George stood also, keeping his answer soft. "I know, sir, and I'm sorry. But that is Lorena's choice."

"You intend to go to Valley Creek?"

"Yes, sir. You'll see me there."

"For how long?"

"For as long as it takes." With a brief nod, George excused himself and left the house. Inside the study, Mr. Wallace sank down in his chair and lowered his head. A long time passed before he moved again.

4

"The school board says they'd be glad for you and Grandfather to stay in the teacherage. All it needs is a little cleaning up, and it'll be ready." Lane sank down into a chair at Edith's table after a long day of teaching.

Relief filled Lorena. The aroma of vegetable stew swirled around her head as she lifted the lid of the iron pot. She stirred the thick, bubbling liquid. "That's wonderful! Father and I will thank them as soon as we can."

"If we work tomorrow and the next day, it'll be ready by the time Grandfather gets here." Edith glanced up as her knitting needles clicked together.

Lorena added a pinch of salt to the cast iron pot, listening to Lane's answer.

"Not you, sister-mine. You can watch us, but that's all. Doctor's orders."

Casting aside her knitting, Edith groaned and reached for the pail while Lane snatched up the washcloth draped over the arm of the chair. Whispering a prayer, Lorena thrust the spoon aside and rushed to rub Edith's back.

After the sickness passed, Edith pushed her wobbling arms

33

against the table and rose. "I think I'd better go lie down for a while."

"Here. Lean on me." Lane circled Edith's arm around her shoulders. Edith's steps trembled as she shuffled to the bedroom.

Rushing ahead of them, Lorena folded the quilts back and waited as Lane lowered her onto the bed.

Small and white under the covers, Edith looked more like a child, her dark eyes too large for her face. "I don't know what I'd do without both of you."

"Oh, I'm sure you'd keep that husband of yours busy if you couldn't boss me around." Lane's sunny smile seemed forced. "Rest now. You'll feel better later."

With Edith in bed, the women gathered at the stove and kept their voices low. "I'm worried about her, Lane. She's so sick." Lorena scrubbed off a splatter on the counter as though it might scrub away the fear knotting in her stomach.

"I hope Doc is right. I hope it's normal."

"So do I. I wasn't sick like that when I carried you and Edith. It's too severe. Perhaps I'm just worrying too much." Lorena stirred the stew once more.

"Perhaps. At least you're here to take good care of her. You're the only one she'll half-way listen to."

"She gets it honestly."

"Just wait till she has one of her own." With a droll grin, Lane turned to gather her books. "It's getting a little late, and I've still got supper to cook before Guy gets home." She reached over and embraced her mother. "Try not to worry."

Lane opened the front door to the sight of Earl catching Jimmy from a tumble. Lorena's throat constricted.

"Whoa, there, fellow." Earl dusted Jimmy's overalls. "That could've been a nasty fall."

"Thanks, Mr. Steen. I wasn't watchin' where I was going."

Looking up, Jimmy grinned at the ladies standing in the doorway. "Are we fixin' to go home, Mama Lane?"

Lane nodded. "Go get in the wagon. I'll be right there."

"Bye, Mr. Steen. Bye, Mrs. Steen!" Jimmy waved as he bounded away.

Frowning a little, Earl watched Lane come down the steps. "My shift's over, so I thought I'd stop by and check on Edith. How is she?"

"She's just gone to bed for a while. She's pretty sick."

Earl's frown etched lines around the corners of his lips. "I was afraid of that."

His glance shifted to Lorena still standing in the doorway. Lorena steeled her features to brook no comment from him, a hidden warning. His eyes veered back to Lane.

"Mother is taking good care of her. We just have to be patient until it passes."

A somber smile weakened Earl's frown. "I was never one for patience."

"Then I get it honest. May I give you a lift home?"

Earl raised his eyebrows. "Are you sure?"

Lane nodded. "It's on my way. There's no need in walking if you don't have to. I'll let you drive."

Once more, Earl glanced at Lorena and tipped his hat with a nod. Stepping back, Lorena turned and snapped the door shut, slashing any further communication between them.

THE AIR in Earl's lungs whooshed out as he climbed into the wagon and took the reins. The frozen blue stare of Lorena chilled him all the way to his bones. If he could just stay out of her way somehow.

Settling on the seat beside Earl, Lane brushed the dust from her skirt. He sensed her sideways peep at him, her shoulder brushing his. She shifted slightly away. Their awkwardness stifled them like a heavy blanket. Earl knew she struggled at times with her feelings about him. And he didn't blame her a bit. Any time she reached out filled him with wonder all over again.

In the wagon-bed, Jimmy stretched out, arms behind his head, and stared at the orange-streaked clouds trailing across the sky.

"He's a good youngin'," observed Earl in a low voice.

"The best."

"It's a shame about his ma."

"Yes. He misses her."

"At least he's got you and Guy."

The late afternoon breeze wiggled the brim of Earl's hat and swept the curls away from Lane's face. Earl cleared his throat. "Looks like we're having a warmer fall than usual."

"I don't think I ever remember a fall being this warm." Lane dabbed her throat with a handkerchief.

"This kind of weather brings storms. Late summer mixed with sudden cool weather can brew up all sorts of trouble."

Lane twisted her hands together in her lap. "Speaking of trouble, you and Mother are having your share of it, aren't you?"

"That's only to be expected."

"Yes."

Earl squinted at his daughter. "I reckon you feel somehow caught in the middle."

Lane nodded. "Well, I *am* the cause of it."

Sighing, Earl rubbed his chin. "That's not so, Lane. I am the cause of it. I lost sight of the most important things in life, faith and my family. When I forgot them, I no longer cared about anything but my success."

"I used to think I knew you, but I don't know you at all."

"I hardly know myself. God's grace is an amazing thing. I

thought it was impossible for a person to change, and it is, unless the Lord does it."

"I've found that to be true too. I know where I've come from."

Wordlessly, Earl nodded. No one knew it better than he did. He had plunged her into that world. The rest of the ride to the Steen place was quiet except for an occasional tune whistled from Jimmy's lips. When they arrived, Earl pulled the mules to a stop.

"I appreciate you giving me a ride home." His clear blue-green eyes held Lane's.

"Anytime." A gentle, soft smile brightened her face, easing the turmoil within Earl's heart.

Stepping down, Earl said goodbye to Jimmy and headed toward the house.

As they drove away, Jimmy crawled over the seat and plunked down beside Lane.

"He shore is a quiet man, Mama Lane."

"Very quiet. A far cry from what he used to be."

"Why don't your mama like him?"

Lane sighed. Things like that were hard to explain to an eight-year-old. "It's a long story, Jimmy. There are things that Father did to her a long time ago."

"Bad things?"

"Yes. She's trying very hard to be nice to him because he isn't like that anymore."

"What did he do?" Jimmy's blue eyes widened, his mouth forming an "o."

"Well, for one thing, he stole me away from her when I was little. She didn't know where to find us for a long time."

Jimmy whistled. "That's pretty mean. Mr. Steen really did that?"

"He really did. But the Lord changed him. He's very sorry now for what he has done."

"Do you like him?"

Lane tightened her grip on the reins as she looked down into Jimmy's searching stare. "I'm learning to with the Lord's help. With time, I'm learning that healing is possible. There's a lot of hope for the future."

"I remember my mama sayin' that your pa was one of the worst men on God's green earth."

Despite herself, Lane chuckled. "He was, Jimmy. He surely was."

"I wonder where my pa is. Mama said he just up and left when I was a baby. She never saw him again." Fumbling with an overall strap, Jimmy nestled his head on Lane's shoulder.

Lane's heart pricked as she circled an arm around him. "There's no telling. You know, that might be a hidden blessing."

"I figure it is. I got you and Papa Guy. I'm mighty lucky."

"Blessed," corrected Lane softly.

"It's certainly good to be back." Mr. Wallace released Lorena from his embrace and stretched his arms. "The teacherage, though small, is more spacious than a cramped railroad car."

Lorena laughed and gestured around the room. "How does it look?" She watched as Father viewed the fruits of their hard work.

Two beds, one on each side of the room, stood against smooth, pine walls. The scrubbed floor planks gleamed, filling the air with a fresh, clean smell. Begging to be filled once again, the narrow bookshelf stood beside the kitchen doorway. In the center of the room, a newly braided rag rug exploded in a rainbow of color on the floor.

"Very nice indeed. And restful." Though his mustache hid his smile, his eyes twinkled at them.

"Mother and Lane really worked hard to get it ready," Edith said, sitting on one of the rocking chairs by the fireplace. "They wouldn't let me do anything."

Mr. Wallace came up behind her and placed his hands on her shoulders with a gentle squeeze. "And I don't blame them. You're much too pale and weak, Edith."

"She's trying hard to mind us, aren't you, dear?" Lorena masked the worry from her face.

"They're letting me supervise," Edith rolled her eyes, teasing.

"I should think you'd make an excellent supervisor."

"You don't think it's too small, Grandfather? The winters can be long here."

Mr. Wallace shook his head. "As long as that bookshelf stays, I'll be fine. I can't tell you how much I've been looking forward to getting away. I'm ready for some peace and quiet."

Edith reached up and laid a hand on her grandfather's. "I'm so glad you're here. I've missed you."

A tremor passed over his face. He pressed a kiss on the top of Edith's raven hair.

"Now, that's the first real smile I've seen on your face in a while." Lorena winked.

"When Grandfather is around, I can't help it."

Once school was dismissed, Lane and Jimmy soon joined them. As Jimmy scampered inside, Mr. Wallace held out his arms and wrapped him in a solid hug.

"Jimmy, my good man, it's good to see you again!"

"I'm sure glad to see you, too, Mr. Wallace. Was the train ride fun?"

Mr. Wallace laughed. "For an old man like me it was too

long, but for a young fellow like you, it would be a lot of fun." He reached into his pocket and pulled out a long, fat piece of red swirled taffy. "I brought this all the way from New York for you."

Slowly, Jimmy reached out and took it, his eyes round and sparkling. "New York? Thanks a whole bunch, Mr. Wallace! Mama Lane, it's all the way from New York!"

"You don't say?" A saucy grin tipped Lane's lips. "Take care that it won't spoil your supper. I think I'll have my hug now, Grandfather."

Mr. Wallace gathered his granddaughter close, planting a kiss on her ruddy hair. "I've never seen you look so well. Marriage must agree with you."

"It does."

"I trust all is well at school?"

Her saucy grin changed to a wry one. "I have my days, but I enjoy it anyhow."

"And how is your father?" His question, though quiet, grated on Lorena's ears.

Lane's gaze skittered to Lorena, seeming unsure how to answer in front of her. The pleasant look on her face stiffened as she nodded for Lane to answer.

"He's all right. I think you'll be pleasantly surprised."

"I hope so. Our last meeting wasn't so pleasant. I must go see him soon."

"He leaves the sawmill late in the afternoons."

"And he stops by my house every day to check on me," Edith chimed in. "Can you believe it?"

Mr. Wallace's iron-gray mustache twitched. "Indeed?"

"You'll have plenty of time to see him, Father." Lorena spoke a little too cheerfully, twiddling with the end of her sleeve.

With a final squeeze, Mr. Wallace released Lane. "Quite true. Now, Edith, tell me everything Doc Brown has told you."

Dipping her head, Lane snagged Lorena's glance, and they

shared a silent look of understanding. After that, no more mention of Earl Steen brooked the conversation. Once Lane took Edith home, however, Lorena picked up the matter once more. As she watched them drive away, she turned from the doorway and folded her arms.

"You look rather stern, Lorena." Mr. Wallace's gentle, British accent filled the space between them, his gray eyes unblinking.

"I'm rarely, if ever, angry with you, Father, but I am now." Her voice quaked. Snapping the door shut, she bit back the hasty words rushing to her tongue.

"You don't want me to go and see Earl."

"I can't stop you. Besides, you're bound to run into him sometime whether you go or not."

Mr. Wallace stepped forward, studying Lorena's face. "It's been years since I've seen you this angry."

Squirming under his perusal, Lorena brushed past him and kept her back to him. "It's been years since I was this angry." Grasping the back of a rocking chair, she dug her nails into the wood.

"I'm sorry, Lorena. If it means this, I won't go."

His compassionate tone swept over her, dousing the fire blazing within her spirit. She kneaded her temples as his footfall neared. Father had every right to seek out Earl. "No, no, Father. I'm sorry. I know you must. I ... I don't know what's the matter with me anymore."

"Lorena."

"I don't!" Unshed tears threaded her words. "Ever since I saw him, all of it has returned, all those terrible feelings. I believed I was rid of it, I truly did, but when I saw his face for the first time after all these years, I thought I could kill him and not be sorry."

Mr. Wallace's strong, large hands clasped her shoulders, turning her around. "My dear girl, you didn't mean that."

"Oh, but I did. I never knew I could really feel that way about someone. Not even Earl." Gasping, Lorena's voice broke.

"Then cry it out, my dear, on your father's chest. Don't keep holding it in."

Clinging to him, Lorena pressed her head into his solid, firm chest, allowing the storm to drain from her heart. After a little time, her father's quiet voice quelled her sobs as she realized he was praying for her.

"Your capacity for love has always amazed me." Lorena gulped, feeling like a young schoolgirl unable to fend for herself.

"It wasn't always so, Lorena. It took years of the Lord's teaching to help me, and even now sometimes through my weakness, I falter."

"Apparently mine has never grown."

"You will overcome this. You forget I once hated Earl too. I hated him as much as I had loved him. When he took Lane and disappeared, he silenced our home. Your mother faded away and died a few years later." His solid chest heaved against her cheek. "We've come down a long, long road, but the Lord has been with us all the way."

Lorena pulled in a deep, ragged breath. "Why can't it just go away?"

"Only God knows the whole reason. For some people, forgiveness seems to come easy. Perhaps that's because they haven't much to forgive. I don't know. For other people, like you and me, forgiveness is hard to come by. But rest assured, Lorena, when forgiveness does come you will appreciate it all the more because of the hard struggle you had with it. When you are finally able to forgive someone for a grave wrong, you'll understand just how much God has forgiven you too."

"I haven't the power to forgive, Father. I've tried and struggled with it, but I can't." A sob shook her shoulders.

Holding her slightly away from him, Father smiled down at

her, sad and wise, halting the fresh tears. "Then you've learned the first and greatest secret about forgiveness. No one has the power to forgive except God. If we truly forgive someone, it's because He gave us the ability. Tell me, Lorena, do you want to forgive Earl?"

Lorena sighed. "Part of me does, and another part doesn't."

"That's only natural. Let me tell you a secret." For a moment, he paused, his jaw clenched as his own emotions rippled across his features. Like a little child, Lorena waited, knowing how hard it was for him to share his deepest thoughts. "For a long time, I wanted nothing more than to find Earl and punish him, whatever it took. I knew it was wrong to hate, but I couldn't help it any more than I could help breathing. And then, one evening, your mother and I had an argument."

"You did? But you both rarely argued." Lorena glanced up and beheld the pain in his eyes.

"It was some trifling matter, like most arguments. I can't remember anymore, but I remember I became very angry. And then your mother accused me of becoming a bitter man. The moment she said that, I felt like she held up a mirror before me, and I saw myself. I didn't say another word. I went down into the library and fell on my knees."

Tears pricked his eyes, and for another moment, he paused. "I said, 'Lord, You know what I am. I don't want to hate anymore. I want to forgive but I can't. I haven't the power in myself, but You, Lord, can forgive. You have the power. Please help me to forgive. I no longer want to hold onto these feelings, but I can't get rid of it. I leave it in Your hands to help me. I'm willing, Lord.' His peace came to me then, but He still had a lot to teach me. After that moment, I still had difficult times, but when they came, I would pray, 'Lord, You know I don't want to feel this way. I won't hold onto it, if You'll help me.' And He did, with time and patience. But you must be willing, Lorena."

Lorena stirred from the strong shelter in his arms and

wiped her eyes. "I promise I'll try. I don't want to be destroyed by this. I'm glad you told me. I know it wasn't easy for you."

"It'll take time, and you'll still have days and moments when you feel you've made no progress at all. But you have and you will. Just trust in Him. He's the only One who can fight our battles."

Subdued, Lorena sank down into the rocking chair. "Ever since my marriage fell apart, trust has never been my strong point, but I'll do my best."

"It's strange how hard it is sometimes for us to put our trust in God. After all, He created the universe and holds it in His hands, and still, we can't trust Him with the smallest matters."

For the first time, Lorena smiled, albeit a wobbly one. "I feel like a child again, a lost little child."

"'Suffer the little children to come unto Me, and forbid them not: for of such is the kingdom of God.' You'll find your way again, dear."

Lorena nodded, running her fingers along the smooth, unvarnished arm of the chair. "Well, I don't want to stand in your way when it comes to Earl. I know you want to see him, and I ... I won't make a fuss if you do."

5

L ate the next afternoon, the muffled clopping of a horse
pulling a buggy reached Earl's ears. Pausing, he wiped
the sweat from his brow and surveyed his work. For the past
month, he had been building a cellar in his spare time. Finally,
after all the dirt and grit, he had completed it. Nothing fancy by
any means, but it was solid.

The rattling wheels grew closer. A horse nickered. Laying
aside his toolbox, Earl emerged from the dark opening,
shielding his eyes from the bright sunlight. A man was
climbing out of the buggy. Slowly, the man turned, as though
carefully inspecting his surroundings. The yard, the barn, the
fall garden, the house. Then he turned toward Earl.

Earl blinked, his eyes coming into focus, a wave of
recognition crashing over him. A tall, older gentleman. A
pressed navy suit out of place in those parts. Iron-gray hair,
mustache. An uneasy expression shadowing his face. The man
retrieved a pocket watch from his trousers, snapped the lid
open with a hasty glance, then snapped it shut and tapped it
across his palm. Earl remembered his father-in-law's habit of
doing that whenever they played chess together. An age ago.

Pain shook Earl's heart as he remembered their last meeting. What could he say?

After a few more taps, Mr. Wallace slid the watch back into his pocket and straightened his shoulders. Several long, tense moments passed. The silence stretched almost beyond endurance. When he could stand it no longer, Earl sucked in a deep breath and stepped forward.

"Mr. Wallace." Earl nodded.

"Earl."

Another heavy pause. "I see you're back in Valley Creek."

"I'll be here until Edith's baby comes." Mr. Wallace peered at his son-in-law. "You're sober."

"Yes, sir."

"Good."

Earl cleared his throat, fighting the urge to rub his hands together like a nervous little boy. "Mr. Wallace." He cleared it again, the words clogging up his windpipe. "I'd like to apologize for my behavior the last time you came."

"I accept." Simply put, simply meant. Clasping his hands behind his back, Mr. Wallace took a few steps toward the house. "It has changed quite a bit since last time. Looks more like a home should. You've done wonders with it."

Earl let out a silent breath. "Thank you. A lot has changed since then."

Once more, Mr. Wallace peered at him, his eyes missing nothing. "So I've heard."

Earl held his direct gaze though a cold tremor tingled down his spine.

Mr. Wallace turned, scanning the pile of dirt near the house. "You're building a cellar."

"Yes, sir. I just finished it, as a matter of fact." Earl brushed a grubby sleeve across his damp forehead. "Would you like to take a look?"

"Don't mind if I do." Striding across the yard, Mr. Wallace

approached the opening. Stooping down, he followed the steps down into the dim, earthy room. "This is good work. Looks solid. You'll be able to store plenty of food."

Earl ducked his head through the opening. "The idea came to me one day as I was walking home from work. Mostly, it was just to keep my mind busy."

"From thinking about Lorena?"

Her name was like a bomb shattering the stillness. Earl scrubbed the back of his neck with his palm. "From everything."

"I see." Climbing up the steps, Mr. Wallace brushed past him back into the sunlight. "You've got a garden, too, a fine-looking one."

"Thank you."

"Like I said, you've done wonders with this place. You've put a lot of time and energy into it."

Cramming his hands into his overall pockets, Earl scrambled his mind for a reply but failed. Instead, he nodded.

"Have you picked up your violin?"

"I play it whenever I don't have anything else to do. It passes the time."

"Any of the old ambition stir inside you again?"

"None whatever. It died a long time ago."

With a sigh, Mr. Wallace surveyed a flock of geese flying overhead, a torrent of emotions clouding his face. His jaw tensed. "A lot of things died then, didn't they?"

"Yes. The ambition was the last to go."

"Too bad it didn't die first."

Weariness swept into Earl's soul. "True."

"We can't go back and undo it, no matter how much we want to. We must move forward and make the best of what we have now." Mr. Wallace pinned Earl with another stare. "We're still a family, no matter how broken we are."

Tears blurred Earl's eyes and squelched any words that he

might have spoken. If only he could ask Mr. Wallace to forgive him. But asking didn't go far enough. No one else deserved forgiveness less.

As if reading his thoughts, Mr. Wallace reached out and gripped Earl's shoulder. "By God's grace, I forgave you a long time ago."

Stinging, unshed tears swarmed his eyes and trickled down his sunburned cheeks. Mr. Wallace's tears followed, dark round spots splotching his navy jacket. For a long time, neither one moved or spoke. Little by little, peace settled over them, quieted the storm.

Finally, Mr. Wallace removed his hand from his face and pulled in a shuddering breath. "I had to see you, to see if it was true. You were like a son that had been lost to me. Then you took my granddaughter. You took everything, and it gave you nothing. But God, in His goodness, has restored."

Powerless to control his trembling lips, Earl only nodded.

"I'm going now, but we'll talk again." A smile touched his eyes. "It's good to see you at last, Earl."

Earl watched as Mr. Wallace returned to the buggy, climbed in, and drove away with a wave. Amazement dawned in his spirit. Acceptance from Mr. Wallace was one of the things he never hoped or expected. Was this how the Apostle Paul felt as he experienced forgiveness from those he had injured?

As the buggy disappeared from view, Earl's mind drifted to the past. Before everything fell totally apart, Mr. Wallace tried to council him, to show him what he was doing to himself and his family. Mastered by his addiction, Earl had refused to listen, believing he was in control. He remembered the worry and devastation on Mr. Wallace's face each time he failed to help him see the truth. And he also remembered Mrs. Wallace's grief-stricken face after he and Lorena had separated. Her words drifted to him as they often had. "Earl, if you don't stop, nothing good will come of it." She passed from life knowing the worst had come. He could never apologize to her.

Shuddering, he shook himself back to the present. With more spirit than he felt, he straightened his shoulders and went to fetch his toolbox in the cellar.

"Doc, if you could spare some time, you need to come take a look at Edith." Harley Ray shifted from one foot to another, his six-foot-three build filling the doorway.

Doc Brown pushed back from his supper, his sharp eyes alert. "I can come now. What's the trouble?"

Running a hand through thick, wavy brown hair, Harley Ray frowned. "She didn't want to trouble you at supper, but I came anyhow. She's hurting, Doc. Sharp pains."

"I don't care what time it is. You come." Doc snatched up his bag from a side table.

"I know, Doc."

Jumping into the wagon, they jostled down the road at double-speed, never feeling the jolts and bumps. After a mile, the wagon rattled into the yard. While Harley Ray threw on the brake, Doc Brown jumped down ahead of him and rushed up the steps. Without knocking, he twisted the doorknob and strode inside.

Wrapped in a blanket, Edith rocked in her chair, rubbing her stomach.

"Now, what's this I hear?" Doc approached, opening his bag. "Harley Ray tells me you're hurtin'."

Behind Doc, Harley Ray entered and shut the door.

"It started a few hours ago." Edith winced.

"Have you been up doing too much work?" Doc rummaged in his bag and pulled out his stethoscope.

"I haven't felt like doing anything. I can't even cook for my own husband." Tears edged Edith's voice.

"There, there. We'll have none of that," Doc scolded gently.

"I'm not worried about meals, Edith, just you." Harley Ray came over and cupped her chin in his hand.

"I'm going to listen to you, Edith. You just sit quietly and breathe." Sticking the earpieces into his ears, Doc listened to Edith's heart first, then moved the stethoscope to her middle. Slowly, he moved it across. High, low, sides, every spot in between. He listened again and again. Repeated the examination, his brow furrowing deeper at each place. The young couple's eyes never strayed from his face, their breaths bated.

Finally, Doc straightened, his dark eyes focused everywhere but on them. Deliberately, he folded the stethoscope, returned it to the bag, and pulled out a bottle of medicine.

"I want you to take a dose now. Then another at midnight. And another in the morning, first thing. It'll help ease the pain. Has there been any blood?"

"No, no blood. Doc? Is there something wrong?" Alarm raised Edith's voice.

Doc pushed a smile across his weathered face. "I don't want you worryin'. A woman can experience a lot of upsets during this time. Bringing babies into the world is the hardest work there is. I want you to rest. No work, Edith. None."

"I won't, Doc."

"Good girl." Doc snapped his bag shut. "I'll be looking in on you tomorrow."

On the ride back to Doc's house, Harley Ray broke the stillness.

"Something's wrong, Doc, and you're not telling us."

The bright, clear moonlight bounced off Doc's silver head as he bowed it. "You let me do the worryin', and you do the praying."

"I've known you all my life, and you're not bluffing me, Doc." Harley Ray turned to his friend. "I'm asking you to be straight with me."

Doc's eyes searched the stars. He frowned, the lines furrowing across his forehead. "I couldn't hear the baby tonight."

Harley Ray flinched.

"Now's not the time to assume anything just yet," Doc rushed on. "I've seen it happen before ... just like Edith ... and everything turned out fine. That's why I don't want you and especially her worrying."

Rubbing his hand along his chin, prickled from missing a shave, Harley Ray shook his head. "How long before we know?"

"Might be tomorrow. Might be several days yet." Doc turned to face the young man, his voice lowering to a growl. "Not a word of this to Edith. And if there's blood ... you get me right away. If her pain gets worse ... unbearable ... you come. Is her mother still coming every day?"

Harley Ray nodded, unable to speak as he struggled with Doc's words.

"Good. Tell her privately so that she'll know what to do if something happens." Doc's stern face softened as he watched Harley Ray. "It's not time to lose heart, son. When a woman carries a child, lots of things can happen and still turn out right."

Harley Ray scanned Doc's face and saw the truth behind the brave words. Doc no more believed it than he did.

SATURDAY DAWNED BRIGHT, fair, and unusually warm. A steady breeze swirled through the valley, stirring the dust along the roads and gradually gathering clouds overhead. Smells of sawdust from the mill spiced the churning air. In the teacherage, Mr. Wallace and Lorena sat at the table for an early supper.

"How's Edith faring today?" Father spooned his potato and onion soup.

"Not much better. She's still hurting, but the medicine Doc sent helps. Harley Ray left work early to be with her. He's very worried." Although Lorena lifted the spoon to her lips, the savory meal tasted like the sawdust hovering in the air, her mind churning with Harley Ray's warning.

Taking a sip of water, Father nodded, unaware of Doc's words. "I'm praying for her. I'm sorry that she is so sick." He wiped his mustache with a napkin. "There's a matter I want to discuss with you."

Lorena lifted her brows. "About?"

Father coughed a little and fumbled with a button on his collar. "I think you ought to know, Lorena, that George is coming to Valley Creek soon."

"George? Whatever for?"

He took a deep breath and released it slowly. "It's a little difficult to explain. You see, he came to see me a few days before I left. He's coming to see you, Lorena."

"To see me?" She frowned. "I hope there's nothing wrong."

"Oh, there's a great deal wrong." Pushing back his chair, Father whipped the napkin from his lap and smacked it on the table.

Confusion rising, Lorena gaped as he rose and clasped his hands behind him. "Father! What is it?"

"My mind hasn't had a moment's rest with trying to decide how to tell you." He shook his head. "I don't know how to say this, but George is coming ... to win your hand."

"Win my hand?" A horrible realization crept into her chest and seized her heart. Her spoon clattered into the bowl. "Why, he can't! I'm married!"

"That apparently doesn't matter to him. He confessed

plainly that he has loved you for a long time. I hoped it wouldn't come to this."

She felt the color drain from her face. "What exactly did he tell you?"

"He wants you to divorce Earl."

"Is that so?" Lorena stood on wobbly legs and paced the floor. "I am married, and he must respect that."

After a few moments, Mr. Wallace halted his daughter's pacing with an outstretched hand, his grip gentle. "Do you love George?"

Lorena's eyes clashed with his troubled ones. "Of course not! He has always been my friend, ever since childhood, and he was married to my best friend. He seemed devoted to her memory."

"That was a long time ago, Lorena." Sighing, Father squeezed Lorena's arm then released it. "Well, I thought you should know. Forewarned is forearmed, they say. I forbade him to come, but he respectfully defied me. He said it was for you to decide."

"For me?" She splayed a hand across her chest, feeling the tiny lump she once wore on her finger. "There's nothing to decide! If he can't be my friend, then he can be nothing at all." As she squeezed her eyes shut, the load from the entire day cumbered her mind. "I think I need some air. I'll take a little drive to settle myself, if you'll excuse me, Father."

"What about your supper?"

"I'm sorry. I couldn't eat it if I wanted to."

Gathering her skirts, Lorena flung open the door and whisked outside. Ever since she returned to Valley Creek, her carefully constructed world had toppled, and emotions she had mastered surged back like a tide over the rocks. And she was trapped by the swell.

The wind tugged at her tresses while she hitched the horse

to the buggy. Tossing her chestnut mane, Grits whinnied and stamped the dirt.

"I know, girl, you'd much rather be in the stable, but we won't be gone long. I promise." Lorena stroked her velvet neck and breathed in her scent. "You're a good girl, Grits." After hitching the horse and one final check, Lorena climbed into the buggy, the tempest of her thoughts blinding her to the storm brewing over the hills behind her. The buzzing of the sawmill sliced into her thoughts. "It's all Earl's fault," she murmured, flicking the reins. "None of this would've happened if he hadn't turned his back on our family. On us."

With another flick, Lorena tossed her head and focused on the road as they whizzed out of town, chased by the rising breeze.

6

Earl slumped against a porch post at Huitt's store, his neck and shoulders throbbing after a long shift. His eyes blurred then cleared when a familiar buggy sped past. The teacherage buggy. Blinking, Earl glimpsed the fury brewing on Lorena's face. Without doubt, he was the cause for the turbulence in those dark blue eyes. Part of him longed to go after her, but he stopped himself. He couldn't help her.

"Lord, help her," he muttered. "And, Lord, please help me too."

Thunder rumbled behind the hills, an angry warning as the wind picked up. Earl scanned the clouds for several long moments. A streak of lightening flashed. Somewhere beyond town, a black cloud lumbered low.

Earl stepped forward, still straining his eyes. How far was it from Valley Creek? Goosebumps pricked up his arms. Suddenly turning on his heel, he dashed into the store.

"Huitt! I need a favor. Can I borrow your horse?"

Mr. Huitt shoved the register door shut with a clang. "Whatever for?"

"My wife's driving toward Lane's." Earl strode over to the

counter and leaned across, his glare burrowing into Huitt's. "There's a tornado coming. You'd best spread the word. Now."

"Take it!"

Both men dashed outside. Earl ran into Huitt's stable and bridled the horse, leaving the saddle behind. In mere moments, man and horse were galloping down the road.

Minutes passed. The sky blackened, the wind growling. Up ahead, the horse and buggy jogged away from him. Digging his heels a little deeper into the horse's flanks, Earl closed the distance. As he pulled up alongside Grits, he reached over and pulled her to a stop.

"What's the meaning of this?" Lorena glowered at him.

"There's a tornado comin'. You can't go any further, Lorena."

Swallowing, Lorena stuck her head around the buggy's canopy and glanced back down the road. Dread coiled in the pit of Earl's stomach. The black cloud cast its shadow across the valley, a steady advance.

A gasp escaped her lips. "Since it's coming, I need to make it to Lane's in time." She flicked the reins, but Earl jerked the bridle back.

"You won't make it, Lorena. It'll catch up with you."

"Take your hands from that horse, Earl. I mean it." Lorena's face flushed.

Earl shook his head. "I'm sorry. I can't do that. I've seen enough storms in these parts to know what a cloud like that means. You've got to come with me."

"I'll do no such thing!"

"Lorena, there's no time to argue. I have a cellar. For the girls' sake, come!"

With another glance toward the swirling cloud, Lorena nodded and turned Grits toward his place.

"Let's hurry!"

When they reached his place, Earl leaped from the horse,

stripped off the bridle, and slapped its hindquarters. "Get!" With deft fingers, he unhitched Grits and did the same.

"I'm giving them a chance to find a safe spot. They won't go too far."

As though frozen in a horrible dream, Lorena stayed rooted in the buggy. "My daughters, my father, the town!" The terrible blackness loomed like a predator, rumbling steadily now, echoing through the valley.

Earl reached up and grabbed Lorena's arm. His eyes clashed with hers as they blazed to life. "I'm sorry, but you've got to listen to me. We haven't got much time."

"Let go of my arm. Now." Lorena's voice was deathly quiet.

Earl dropped it as if it were a piece of hot iron. "Please listen to me. Come."

Her face crumpled into defeat, searing his heart with guilt. She sprang to the ground and followed his swift steps to the cellar.

Opening the door, Earl stepped aside for her to enter. Lorena glanced back at the sky. Sawdust swirled upward, an eerie mix of light and dark.

"Oh, the sawmill! Earl!"

Plums of sawdust towered above Valley Creek. Beside him, the wind ripped at Lorena's hair. The rumbling echoed toward them as the trees dipped and swayed. Without a glance at Earl, Lorena clambered down the steps. Earl followed, holding the door cracked open to allow just enough light for her to see.

"Over on that shelf is a box of matches." Earl nodded at the shelf. "I'd be obliged if you'd light that lamp in the corner while I latch the door."

Fingers quaking, Lorena fumbled with the box and pulled out a match. After striking it, she lit the kerosene wick and replaced the globe while Earl latched the door. Light filled the small, dim room.

Earl turned around. "There's a stool behind you if you care to sit down."

Lorena sank down and clutched her hands in her lap. Jamming his hands in his pockets, Earl leaned against the wall and tried not to look at her.

"I hope I didn't hurt your arm," he ventured. "I wasn't trying to. And I know you feel forced into coming here."

Silence.

Earl cleared his throat, concentrating on the wall across from him. "I was only concerned. There's no way you would've made it to Lane's in time."

Silence still.

Stifling a sigh, Earl lowered his head and closed his eyes. All he could do was wait and pray.

THROUGH LOWERED EYELASHES, Lorena peeped at Earl. Shock jolted her. He was praying. Not a word he spoke aloud. Only his lips moved. Shame washed over her. In her dismay and anger, she had forgotten to pray.

The wind died and silence pierced the noise. Both of them listened. Nothing moved, not a bird, not a twig. The muscles in Earl's jaw clenched. Sweat prickled around her neck.

He looked at Lorena then. "It's almost here." Earl double-checked the latch then backed away from the door.

As soon as he moved, a rumbling shuddered the air, intensifying with every second. The door danced hard against the latch, clicking with every throb of Lorena's heart. The rumbling transformed into an angry roar above them, rattling the shelves in the cellar. Earl shut his eyes.

Reading the worry on his face, Lorena sprang from the stool. "Oh, Earl! The girls, Guy and Harley Ray! Father!"

"I know, Lorena. I know."

"Oh merciful Father, keep Your hands over them! Over everyone!"

Outside, a loud groan exploded followed by a crash. Trembling, Lorena buried her face in her hands. What was happening to their family? Were they all right? If only they were all here in the cellar.

The roaring shrieked and pounded on the cellar door. Squeezing her eyes shut, Lorena rocked, breathing silent, frantic prayers.

Then strong, firm hands rested on her shoulders. Her eyes flew open. She waited for anger to boil to the surface, but his compassionate, anxious gaze quelled it. For the first time, Lorena realized Earl shared her feelings. Edith and Lane were his daughters too. Who would've believed that the man who once distressed her would now try to comfort her?

Again she lowered her head, listening to the howling wind rage. She tried to ignore the pressure of Earl's hands, steeling herself against any softness toward him.

Her mind turned again to her girls, their girls. Were they safe? Tears choking her throat, she once again asked the Lord to keep them.

Moments crawled as the storm subsided, rumbling further away. Thunder clapped. Stepping back, Earl dropped his hands from Lorena's shoulders and went to the door. Unhooking the latch, he shoved against it and climbed to the top of the steps. His feet froze.

From below, Lorena saw Earl's ashen face. "Earl? What is it?"

For a second, Earl said nothing. His throat bobbed, eyes wide. "My house. It's gone."

Lorena clambered up past him. "Oh my! Oh my!" Her hand flew to her mouth.

Scattered in piles across the yard lay the remnants of Earl's house, the chimney toppled across the foundation. Boards and furniture speckled across the grass, as though a giant lost his temper and kicked the place to pieces. Oddly, the barn still stood as if it had never been touched.

Lorena stepped up into the yard and surveyed the damage further, awestruck and horrified at the same time. "The barn is still there."

"It happens that way sometimes." Earl followed her, his voice numb.

"I'm so sorry, Earl."

He set his jaw. "I'll just have to rebuild."

Scanning the yard, Lorena gasped. "Earl, look!" Against one of the stripped trees lay his violin case unharmed.

Earl picked his feet across the debris and lifted it from the ground. "Almost like the Lord set it aside while the cloud destroyed everything else."

Lorena shivered and rubbed her arms, fear crowding in. "If it did this to your house, there's no telling what it may have done to the girls'." Glancing toward the road, she saw Grits and Huitt's horse in the next field, stamping near the buggy which lay twisted and crumpled into the brush as though made of paper, tossed aside.

Earl followed and whistled for the horses. "It's a good thing you weren't in that buggy."

Lorena tasted dust on her lips. "I must get to the girls."

"That's exactly what I'm going to do." He reached out to the approaching horses and patted their necks. "Woah, there. I'll saddle her up and go to Lane's first. She's the closest."

"All right." Biting her lip, Lorena followed him to the barn. As they picked their way over boards and pieces of furniture, Lorena shuddered. How terrifying that a cloud could flatten everything in its way. The remaining shreds of wind tugged at her skirts.

Inside the barn, shadows brimmed the corners, spilling onto the floor. Dust still hovered in the air, temporarily suspended by the storm. After laying aside the violin case, Earl plucked a saddle from its rack and heaved it over Grits' back.

A little later, just as Earl tightened the cinch, they heard a horse galloping up the road. Lorena rushed outside.

"It's Guy!" Gathering her skirts in one hand, she plucked her way through the mess, waving wildly.

Guy pulled the horse up beside her and was on the ground before she could speak.

"How is everyone?" Lorena grasped his arm.

"We're all fine. It blew a few shingles off the roof and downed Lane's favorite tree, but that's all."

"Thank God!"

"Y'all weren't so fortunate, I see. I'm sorry, Mr. Steen." Guy surveyed the damage. "Lane is wild with worry."

"We're here. That's what counts," Earl swung up on Grits while he held Huitt's unsaddled one by the reins. "I'd better go check on Edith and the rest of the family."

Tossing the rest of her pride aside, Lorena stepped forward. "Take me with you."

Earl removed his foot from the stirrup, allowing her foot a step. "Give me your hand."

Lorena complied, trying to ignore the strength and warmth of his hand. Earl pulled her up behind him as if she were no larger than a child.

"Since you're goin' to town, I'll go back to tell Lane y'all are fine. I'll be along." Guy turned his horse and tapped his heels into its sides.

"Hold on to me, Lorena." Earl's quiet voice seemed to fill everything.

Gritting her teeth, Lorena wrapped her arms around his waist and linked her fingers together.

THE BUILDINGS of Main Street littered their path. Huitt's store, the post office, the school, the sawmill, the blacksmith shop, the boarding house, and Doc's office. All gone. Pieces of tin roofs screwed around tree trunks and stripped limbs. Broken glass glittered the road. Only the church and the teacherage stood almost unscathed. A large oak limb stuck through one of the church's windows like a javelin. Except for some missing shingles and a shattered window, the teacherage stood, an island surrounded by a sea of wreckage. Earl breathed a prayer of thanks.

Mr. Wallace was picking through the yard as they stopped. Releasing him, Lorena slid off and ran toward her father.

"Father! Father!" She flew into his waiting arms, sobbing.

"Thank God!" A little color returned to Mr. Wallace's face. "I feared the worst. The storm followed you."

"Earl caught up with me and took me to his cellar."

Mr. Wallace nodded to Earl over the top of Lorena's head. "Thank you."

Earl shifted in the saddle. "I'm happy you're all right."

"The town. Father, there's almost nothing left."

"I know, dear heart. It's the most horrible thing I've ever seen or heard."

They watched as some folks slowly emerged, stumbling through the debris as though lost.

"It's gone. Gone." Mr. Huitt's stunned voice broke the stillness as his wife buried her face in her apron and wept among the scraps that was once their store. Earl chewed the inside of his cheek, the sounds of her cries punching him in the stomach.

Lorena pulled herself away from her father's arms, glancing across the street. "How awful! Father, we're going to check on Edith and Harley Ray now."

"I pray all is well."

"I'll let you know as soon as I can." Earl noticed how Lorena avoided his eyes as he lifted her behind the saddle. Carefully, he navigated through the rubble, watching for anything that might injure Grits.

He felt Lorena's hands trembling around his waist. He resisted the urge to cover them with one of his. "Try not to dread the worst before you know, Lorena."

"I can't help it. Something's wrong. I can feel it."

As they approached Watkin's sawmill, shock rippled through Earl. Where it once stood, nothing remained. Wiped clean save for one engine belt swaying from a tree limb. The lumberyard strewn in every direction like scattered leaves.

"Oh, Lord, help us all." Lorena whispered into his back, her forehead coming to rest against the scratchy fabric of his shirt.

Edith's place was on the other side of Valley Creek, beyond the sawmill about a mile. When they arrived, Earl reined in the horse, relief almost making him dizzy. The house was still standing.

"Thank the Good Lord, Lorena. It's still here."

As his feet hit the ground, Earl turned and reached for her. His hands lingered just a fraction of a second around her waist before releasing her.

Without a backwards glance, Lorena rushed up the steps of the house and burst through the door. Earl's quick steps followed.

"We made it through." Harley Ray stepped forward and embraced them both. "How did you fare?"

"My house is destroyed. I stopped Lorena as she was headed toward Lane's, and we stayed in the cellar." Earl didn't bother to mention the buggy. The dark glint in Harley Ray's eyes stopped him.

At the same time, Lorena noticed it too, her hand grasping her throat. "Harley Ray, where's Edith?"

"Edith's in the bedroom, lying down. During the storm, she started hurting bad ... worse than ever before. As soon as it moved past, I rode to Doc's." He chewed his lips, tunneling fingers through his wavy, brown hair. "She's in labor, Mrs. Steen."

"No, no!"

Once more, Earl gripped her shoulders. Dread curled up around his heart and seized it.

"Doc's with her. He's doing all he can."

Shrugging off his hands, Lorena pushed through them and scuttled to the bedroom. Earl trailed her, pausing in the doorway to find Doc standing over Edith, checking her pulse. Doc glanced over and motioned them nearer. Hiding a shudder, Earl crept up to the bedside and choked back a breath as he scrutinized Edith's colorless face, eyes closed.

"Edith, dear." Lorena bent and caressed her shoulder.

Edith's eyes fluttered open, brown and murky. "Mother." She moaned, grief etched on her face. "I'm going to lose my baby."

Lorena took Edith's hand, her tone calm and anchored. "I know, dear. I know." She sat down on the bed and pressed a kiss on Edith's brow. "Heavenly Father, help us now."

"Stay with me."

"I promise I will."

At that moment, Edith cried out as sharp pain contorted her face. The sound weakened Earl's knees.

Lorena leaned over her daughter. "Put your arms around me and hold on."

Crying, Edith gasped for air and hid her face on her mother's shoulder. "I don't want to lose my baby! I don't want to!"

Doc rounded the other side of the bed, his voice gentle but firm. "You must stay calm, Edith. I know it's asking a lot, but it's important. Focus only on having the baby. Nothin' else."

"Shhhh. Shhhh." Lorena stroked Edith's hair, murmuring prayers and comfort.

Harley Ray shadowed the doorway, watching helplessly. When the pain passed, Edith lay back against the pillows once more. Slowly, Earl approached the bedside and took Edith's hand in his own.

Edith turned her head toward him. "Father." Tears choked any further words.

Earl gnashed his teeth, unable to speak as well. On the other side of the bed, Lorena grabbed a washcloth from the washstand and dipped it in the bowl of water. After wringing it out, she bathed Edith's face.

"You must calm down, dear. Please try."

"She must be kept as quiet as possible. I need everyone to leave the room except Mrs. Steen." Doc listened to Edith's heart.

After pressing her hand to his lips, Earl followed Harley Ray from the room, too stunned by the sight to speak. How could life change with a blink? Harley Ray dropped into a chair, burying his face in his hands. Unable to sit, Earl paced the room instead.

His breath thinned. He needed some air. He needed out of there. He strode to the window and peered out. Far in the distance, those dark clouds causing so much havoc receded further over the Ozarks. How could a day start so beautiful and end so ugly? Wincing against the sunrays piercing the retreating clouds, he stared until the colors mingled together. His home, the town, his family. His gut churned. The baby would be lost. What of Edith? He was only just beginning to know her. Toward the west, the sun slipped through the last thread of clouds and warmed Earl's face. Closing his eyes, he gripped the window seal. *Lord, please don't take her too.*

LANE AND GUY came a little while later and found the scene much as before. As Guy waited in the front room with the other men, Lane helped her mother nurse Edith through the ordeal. As Lorena watched Lane clamp down on her grief to tend her sister, she breathed a prayer of thanks.

Except for Edith's occasional sobs and the gentle instructions from those around her, a grave silence shrouded the bedroom, bearing down on everyone and filling the rest of the house. The kerosene lamp, now lit since the sun's departure, cast an eerie, yellow light on Edith's face. Shadows pooled in the hollows of her cheeks and under her eyes. She chewed her lips until they nearly bled.

Doc Brown pulled Lorena aside. "The baby will come soon."

Lorena swallowed and asked the question plaguing her for the last few hours. "Will Edith make it?"

Doc paused before answering, looking deep into her eyes. "I don't know yet. If the complications ain't too severe, she should." He laid a weathered hand on her shoulder. "Let's keep our chins up for her sake. She's gonna need it."

Lane, watching from the bedside, took Edith's hand and clasped it to her cheek. "Oh, Heavenly Father," she whispered, "bring her through this and give her Thy strength." With her other hand, she swept Edith's black tendrils from her face.

"I ... I don't know if I can do this."

"You've got to. I've come too far to lose you now. You hear me?"

"I'm tired."

"I know, but you've got Harley Ray to think of and the rest of us. You've got to fight hard."

Lorena rubbed her hands together, their words almost too much to bear.

Another sharp stab of pain wracked Edith's body.

"I need you to push, Edith, just once more. This is it." Doc's calm tone belied the trepidation on his face.

Edith gritted her teeth and pushed for the final time. The baby came, silent and still. Gently, Doc whisked away and laid the baby on a table behind him. As Lorena rounded the bed, he held up a hand.

"Not now." He wrapped the tiny form in a towel. "Right now, we've got to take care of Edith."

Lorena shut her mind to the silent form and focused on her daughter. Across from her, Lane gulped back the tears glistening in her eyes and followed Doc's instructions.

"Now, Edith girl, I need you to stay calm and quiet. Your health depends on it."

Closing her eyes, Edith turned her face toward the wall, away from Doc, away from the tiny bundle on the table. Her lips trembled but no cry escaped.

For the next several minutes, they followed Doc's composed, unhurried commands as he worked and cleaned. Droplets of sweat trickled down his forehead and face. Once he looked up and caught the anxious, unasked question on Lorena's face.

"She's lost a good deal of blood, but I'm doing what I can. The rest is in God's hands."

More long, anguished minutes passed. Finally, after what seemed like an eternity, Doc straightened and washed his hands in the water bowl on the table. "The bleeding has slowed. Normal now. Your girl is gonna be all right with rest and care."

Relief swept over the women. Lane squeezed her mother's arm. Leaning over, Lorena brushed Edith's cheek with her lips.

"Doc says you're going to be fine, darling."

Edith turned her head toward her mother and nodded, her dark eyes muted. Pain constricted Lorena's heart. How could she feel such joy and agony at the same time? The deliverance of her daughter, the loss of her grandchild. The soft swishing of water interrupted her thoughts. Doc's unhurried, tender movements washing the baby.

With a thundering heart, Lorena approached Doc as he wrapped the baby in a clean towel. "Is it a boy or a girl?" She whispered in a shaky breath.

"Girl," he muttered through pinched lips.

Lorena's eyes roved the miniature face. She was tiny, very tiny like a porcelain doll. Tiny yet perfect. Everything present except life. Lorena turned away, hands clenching her stomach, unable to look anymore.

"Doc, I want to see." Edith's weak voice rasped from the bed.

"Go get Harley Ray," Doc urged Lorena. "Let 'em know that Edith will be all right."

Numbly, Lorena left the bedroom with Lane following. The walls and furniture blurred together as she crossed the floor and reached Harley Ray's side.

"Edith will be fine."

A great gust of air rushed from Harley Ray's lips as he wrapped Lorena in a bear hug. After returning the embrace, Lorena stepped back and patted his shoulder.

"Go to her, now."

He was opening the bedroom door before she even finished.

Across the room, Lane collapsed in Guy's waiting arms and sobbed as she hadn't dared earlier. Blinking against his own tears, Guy rested his chin on her hair and closed his eyes.

EDITH WOULD BE ALL RIGHT. Thank the Good Lord! Head down, Earl leaned against the mantle as Lorena edged closer to him.

"It was a girl."

A pain that Earl never knew existed tore through his chest

and escaped as a low sob. This coming child had meant more to him than he'd realized. Shuddering, he turned his back.

A moment later he felt a light touch on his arm.

"Are you all right?"

He couldn't look at Lorena, not then, or he would surely crumble. "I've got to be. That's all there is to it. I can't tell you how glad I am that Edith was spared."

Her hand left his arm, the warmth where it rested vanishing. Lorena turned to Lane and Guy. "She was beautiful. I'll always remember her face as long as I live."

"Me too." Lane lifted her head from the security of Guy's chest. "I've never seen anything like it."

With sagging shoulders, Doc Brown shuffled into the kitchen and poured himself a cup of coffee from the stove. He lifted the cup to his lips and sipped. Though he glanced their direction, his eyes stared through them.

"Lord, it's times like this I hate bein' a doctor," he murmured.

7

———

They buried the baby the next morning, a cloudless day with a sharp, cool breeze sweeping through the mourners. The news had spread throughout Valley Creek, and all of the town gathered on the hillside beyond the church to pay their respects to the little one who would never know those neighbors gathered around her tiny grave.

The small pine box lay in the narrow gap of earth, a cluster of black-eyed Susans and rose verbenas swaddling it. A colorful quilt of flowers offered with loving hands. With bowed head, Harley Ray stood beside it, his wife absent from his side. Although she had begged to come, Doc refused to let her. She was far too weak and fragile. Lorena stayed by her side.

Earl's foggy thoughts tried to focus on Reverend Crandall's words. This was only the first soul that would be put to rest in Valley Creek that day. The tornado had ravaged several families as well. Five men from the sawmill were gone. The postmaster and his family were gone as well. Several homes had been wiped out. The town lay in shambles.

From the hillside, Earl viewed the destruction along with

his neighbors. A river of boards, shingles, broken glass, dishes, and smashed furniture littered Main Street, hardly a patch of bare earth to be seen. Sunlight spilled over the church and teacherage, the remaining symbols of their community.

At the sight, hope dwindled from the faces around Earl, their unspoken thoughts obscuring the preacher's words. How could they start over? Was this the end of their town? So many livelihoods depended on the sawmill. Right that moment, Mr. Watkin lay injured on a makeshift bed at his in-laws, his home and sawmill gone.

Heads bowed for the final prayer. Afterward, everyone offered words of sympathy to the family. As the mourners filed from the graveyard, Lane turned to her father. Purple shadows, ringed red from weeping, circled her eyes. "Stay with us until you rebuild your place."

Earl was too numb to feel surprised. "Are you sure?"

Lane nodded. "Come home with us." Beside her, Jimmy leaned into her as though seeking comfort. No doubt memories of his mama's funeral clouded his face.

"I'm obliged to you, Lane. It would leave more room in the church. Three families are staying there now. Nowhere else to go."

Behind them, Harley Ray approached. Earl turned and shook his hand. His brown eyes glimmered with the tears he had shed, his tanned face wan from the sleepless night spent at Edith's side. Lines creased his forehead as the morning sun struck his face.

"We'd like y'all to come for supper. Several neighbors will be bringin' food later. Doc says he might allow Edith out of bed this afternoon to sit up for a spell. I know she'd like to see y'all, and I wouldn't mind the company myself. The house is too quiet."

"We'll come," Lane promised. "Give Edith my love and tell her to do as Doc says."

Harley Ray nodded and headed for his horse.

Touching Lane's elbow, Guy cleared his throat. "Mr. Steen and I have some things to take care of, Lane. Don't wait up dinner for us."

"Helping with the cleanup, I imagine."

"There's time for that. We," he lowered his voice, "we're helping make the coffins. Have ten to do." Guy swiped a hand across his jaw. "The more that helps, the quicker we can be finished."

Shutting her eyes hard, Lane wobbled, staggering into her father's broad chest. Earl's arms caught her.

"There now." His voice near her ear popped Lane's eyes wide open. She blinked up into his face.

Earl gave her a ghost of a smile. "Haven't held you like this since you were a little thing."

Lane smiled back, the corners of her lips quivering. "No. I don't mind this, though."

"Nor do I."

BY LATE AFTERNOON, Earl sat on the porch steps of Lane's house and mulled over the whole ordeal. The memory of Harley Ray lowering the little wooden box into the earth sank his heart all over again. The thud of dirt splattering against it panged within his chest. He remembered the fierce urge to yank it out of the ground, battling the utter helplessness of knowing there was nothing he could do to change it. To wind back time. To change yesterday. That child was his flesh and blood, his grandchild. God's blessing. And now she was gone.

Earl raked a hand through his auburn hair. He felt old. He felt tired.

He and Guy worked almost wordlessly with other mourners making coffins. Men like John Mansfield, Thomas and Andrew

Ray, Ben Watkin, and Edward Huitt brought their hammers, saws, and nails to put more souls to rest. One by one they gathered stray boards from the street. Each stroke of the hammer, every groan of a saw pierced the hush of Valley Creek. Pressed down with grief, they worked as one.

The smell of death still clung to Earl like a spider's web. Ten neighbors gone. Eleven counting the wee little lady. One by one they bore their coffins up the hillside to rest near the fresh, small one. Friends, enemies, neighbors, and family followed behind them, no one speaking as the long line proceeded up the grassy path.

Reverend Crandall spoke comforting words over them all, his voice swallowed up by the heavy silence of the graveyard. Folks strained to listen, tried to let the words soak deep within, but their hearts were already too full. Earl racked his brain for the reverend's words, but the memory failed him. All he could see was those ten boxes joining the little one.

Rubbing the back of his neck, Earl squeezed the tension knotted there. He shuddered. Utter helplessness. The past couldn't be changed. Death only pounded that fact home with cold cruelty. It was done. Over before it had hardly begun.

To have a precious baby ripped away so suddenly mind-numbed Earl. Now he fully realized what he did to Lorena when he took Lane away.

His hands scrubbed his face. "Oh, God, forgive me! Is this my punishment? To have this child ripped away?" Earl choked on his prayer and shook his head. "What a selfish thing to say! Who do I think I am? This is Edith and Harley Ray's child, not mine. I've no right, no right at all."

"Hey, Earl. You busy?"

Earl's head flew up. At the edge of the yard stood Robert Sims who had been an old drinking buddy at one time. Rising, Earl groaned and went to meet him.

"What do you need, Rob?" The pungent smell of whiskey tinged Earl's nose.

"I hated to hear 'bout the girl."

Earl sucked in a deep, steadying breath. "Thanks. I appreciate it."

"Yeah, anytime," he slurred. His bleary, hazel eyes squinted at Earl. "You look like you could use a drink."

Earl stiffened, alarm searing his spine. "I'm doin' fine."

"Liar." Rob thrust a hand into the deep pocket of his overalls and extracted a half-full whiskey bottle. "Thought you might could use this." He shoved it into Earl's hand, closing his fingers around it. "It'll help calm you some."

Panic raced up Earl's arms and tightened his chest. He held the bottle out to Robert. "I don't want it. Take it back."

A surly grin stretched across missing bottom teeth. Rob backed away, holding his hands up. "Naw. Keep it. What are friends for, anyhow? It'll do you some good. Ever since you got that religion, you've had more an' more troubles. You didn't have none when you was drinkin'. Remember?"

Fire leaped in Earl's blood, his face burning with anger as he glowered at Rob. "Get out."

"Suit yerself. Just trying to help ya." Wobbling, Rob staggered out of the yard and down the road. Further away, his off-key voice began wailing *When the Roll Is Called Up Yonder,* an unwelcome, haunted sound filtering through the hazy air.

Wincing, Earl stared down at the bottle in his hand. The amber-colored liquid called to him. Just one drink. Just one to make him forget everything for a little while. That's what he needed, just to forget a little. Feel a little better.

Even from inside the glass bottle, the burning of that liquid tingled up his arm into his suddenly hot and parched mouth. A blinding thirst. He could almost taste it. His grip tightened on the bottle.

Another voice, though, warred inside his head. What would happen if he did? Everything he'd gained would be destroyed with one swig. What of Lane, of Edith. Of Lorena. What about his own soul?

Earl's hands quaked. "Just one drink. It wouldn't have to be the whole bottle. It wouldn't have to be any more ever again. Surely I can handle that. Just this time."

Lord, help me! With stiff fingers, Earl unscrewed the bottle. The sharp smell snaked up and filled his nostrils, enticing his senses. Drink it, drink it. Earl closed his eyes and lifted the bottle.

And emptied it onto the ground.

The bottle slipped from his fingers and hit the grass with a hollow clunk. Earl stepped back. Peace and strength flowed into him, a hard-fought victory won.

Behind him, the door screeched on its hinges as it swept open wide. "Father!" Lane's anguished voice cut through him.

Earl whirled around, fresh tears filling his eyes. "I didn't do it, Lane." With hunched shoulders, he moved toward the porch and sank down on the steps, his broad shoulders shaking.

"I know. I saw everything through the window. I was so frightened!"

Her noiseless footfall neared. Earl sensed her hesitation as she wavered at his side, but then she sat, the slight dip of the step shifting with her weight.

"I've never seen you cry before."

Not knowing what to say, Earl shook his head and wiped his face.

"What you just did, I can't tell you how much it means to me."

Though Earl craved to earn Lane's confidence, he understood her battle. Despite God's miracle in his life, she still held him at arm's length, afraid to let him too near the one place she shielded. Her heart.

"It's the first time I've ever seen you turn a drink away."

The scenes from that day and the temptation had almost been too much. Lifting his head, Earl gulped air. "It's the Lord's doing. Not mine. All I know is that I can't go back to that."

Gingerly, Lane reached out and laid her hand on his shoulder, the first time she had ever reached out first to touch him.

"I love you, Pa."

Like glimpsing the flicker of light in a dark place, Earl turned and stared at his daughter. Trust shone in her blue-green eyes. The last time she looked at him that way, she was toddling across the floor to him during happier times. Times she couldn't remember. Times he had stolen from her.

Her unguarded eyes told him that her heart was open to him once again.

"My girl, my girl!" Earl gathered her close to his heart as she gathered him close to hers. Fresh, restored love bloomed in the gathering twilight.

Like the gentle lapping of a stream against a rocky bank, something within washed their souls and swept away the remainder of their doubts. A verse rose in Earl's mind. "He leadeth me beside the still waters. He restoreth my soul."

A little later, when Earl lifted his cheek from the top of Lane's head, he noticed a long shadow stretching across the porch.

From the doorway, Guy brushed a work-worn hand across his eyes and smiled.

FOR THREE DAYS, Valley Creek held its breath, as though suspended between life and death. Heavy silence shrouded the town, seeming to dare anyone to disturb the grief. No whirling of the sawmill, no smells of freshly cut timber drifted through the street. No clattering wagons, no pounding of hooves, no voices of working men, no clanging school bell resounding through the hills, no children shouting in the schoolyard. Nothing.

The quiet grief crowded around every supper table like an unwanted guest. Not a soul could toss it out or demand it to leave. It clogged every throat that dared talk about the loss. And every evening, as the sun slipped away, the shadows snaked over and down the ridge, drawing their hearts toward the eleven fresh mounds of earth fading in the dusk.

The next afternoon Lorena and Lane sat on either side of Edith's rocking chair just as they had every day since the wee one had departed. On the floor at their feet sat a cedar box, its lid folded back on its hinges. The spicy sent of the cedar hovered in the air around them.

"Harley Ray says it's a blessing we had a good harvest … with the sawmill now gone." Without looking at her mother or Lane, Edith stared down at the baby blanket in her lap. Her fingers stroked the snowy crocheted rosettes before slowly folding it.

Lorena watched the wave of sadness crash over Edith's face and struggled to mask the anguish that threatened to crumple hers. Beside her, Lane's voice wobbled.

"Guy is really happy about his crop too. He said it's enough to get us through the winter and lay aside some for planting in the spring. It's a blessing that all the families had their crops or gardens. Even though the sawmill is gone, they have food to see them through."

"That's good." With a final caress, Edith lowered the folded blanket into the box. For a moment, her face lingered over the box before she reached into the basket across Lane's lap and pulled out another item, this time a baby's dress.

"Edith, why don't you let me and Lane put those things away for you? If Dr. Brown knew …"

"What Doc doesn't know won't hurt him." Edith turned the dress over, tucking the tiny sleeves in place.

"Yes, but—"

"No." Edith's eyes snapped up and collided with Lorena's, a flicker of rebellion glinting. "No," she breathed, a little more softly. She finished folding the dress and placed it on top of the blanket.

"There's going to be a prayer meeting at church this evening." Lane swallowed, glancing at Lorena. "They're going to discuss how to rebuild the town and replace the sawmill. If it can be done."

"That ought to be interesting." Edith picked up a tiny violet bonnet and fingered the ribbon.

"Is Harley Ray going?"

As if trapped in a slow-moving dream, Edith laid the bonnet in the box. "He says he is. I suppose he will."

Lane chewed her lower lip as Edith pulled a rattle from the basket. A gift from Lorena. The beads rolled and plinked inside the silver, shattering the brief silence. The once cheerful sound mocked them now.

Edith paused, her thumb tracing the quaint little etchings of flowers and leaves. Lorena wanted to snatch the toy away. But Edith was a woman with a woman's sorrows, and she must deal with it in her own way. Lorena could protect her no longer.

Quietly, Lorena rose and excused herself.

The rattle jingled down into the box before dying away in silence. As Lorena opened the door and stepped onto the porch, Lane's comforting tone reached her. Motherly pride filled her soul despite the hurt. Lane's years in the Ozarks had made her strong, able to bend with the storms.

Lorena wrapped her arm around a porch post and drew in a deep breath. "Lord, just when things are beginning to fall into place, something else happens. Please help us all and give us strength. I don't understand. I may never understand.

But help me to accept it. Strengthen Edith and Harley Ray, I pray."

Her eyes roved over the changing countryside. Tinges of scarlet, yellow, orange, and mauve speckled the trees, a promise of beauty in the coming weeks. A scripture came into her mind. "I will lift up mine eyes unto the hills from whence cometh my help. My help cometh from the Lord, which made heaven and earth." Everyone in Valley Creek needed help.

A fresh breeze played with her collar and sleeves, feathering over her cheeks. Winter would come before she realized it. Winter and no baby. Lorena rested her head against the post.

Muffled through the door, Lane's and Edith's hushed voices mingled together. The sound soothed the raw edges of Lorena's spirit.

Not far away, a horse gave a short snort and a rider soon appeared. Lorena shielded her eyes with her hand, squinting for a better view.

Earl rode Crockett, loosely gripping the reins in his tanned hand. Dust covered his hat and face, all the way down to his worn boots. Tired circles darkened his eyes from full days of cleaning his place.

Heart beating quicker, Lorena's throat tightened. Despite the grime, he posed a striking figure. Ruggedly handsome, the boyish charm that she remembered was gone. She narrowed her eyes as he approached, showing no hint of her feelings on her face.

Earl's eyes fastened on hers as he dismounted. A ring of dust rimmed his forehead when he removed his hat. As he neared the foot of the steps, his gaze never faltered from hers. Lorena's ribs jammed against the stays beneath her dress, clipping her breath.

Weariness creased his forehead. "How's Edith?"

"Grieving. She won't let us help put the baby's things away. I think she has shut us out for a while."

"It'll take time." Earl paused, his fingers turning his hat around the brim. "Your father sent word that he would sit with Edith this evenin' while we're at the prayer meeting. Are you coming?"

"I don't know why I should. Edith needs me here."

"It'd give you a little break. Why don't you let him stay?"

"I'll think about it."

A faint smile curved Earl's lips. "Besides that, you never know what might happen at one of our meetings. Might give you something to talk about all winter."

Heat rose in Lorena's cheeks. "Earl Steen!"

A tiny twinkle lit his blue-green eyes. "That's good to see. A little spark will keep you going." The twinkle faded. "I know there's nothing funny at the moment, but sometimes a little smile makes things more bearable. I reckon I'll go wash up at the pump and then see Edith for a bit."

With a little grunt, Lorena watched as Earl stepped back and disappeared around the corner of the house without a backwards glance, his steps unhurried.

"That man!" She shoved away from the post and brushed her arms. After several moments, Earl's voice emerged through the wall. He must have entered through the backdoor.

Without realizing it, Lorena slid her fingers underneath the lace of her blouse and plucked at the ring hiding below the hollow of her throat. A moment later she caught herself. What on earth was she doing? Shaking her head, she groaned.

INSIDE, Earl laid aside his hat and surveyed his daughters. Edith was closing the lid of the box while Lane watched. Both of them glanced up.

"Afternoon." Earl stepped forward.

Lane smiled her hello while Edith nodded, her face void of expression. "It's nice of you to come." She held out a pale hand.

"Are you making it?"

"I don't know yet." Edith shrugged.

Stepping closer, Earl grasped her hand, his large one swallowing up her dainty one. He gave it a slight squeeze. "Your grandfather told me he was going to sit with you while we're at the meeting."

Her hand remained limp. "He doesn't have to, but if he wants to, he can."

Her listless voice tugged his heart. He met Lane's glance, and she shrugged with a slight shake of her head. Earl cleared his throat. "We'll be praying about the future of Valley Creek. No one knows what to do, but I believe the Lord will provide. And He'll provide the comfort you need, too, Edith."

Edith's eyes swam as they lifted to his for the first time since he came inside.

"I won't keep you. I just wanted to look in on you for a minute." Releasing her hand, Earl turned, grabbed his hat, and headed for the backdoor, anxious to avoid Lorena.

As he crossed the threshold, he heard Lane's footsteps padding behind him.

"Well?" he turned as she clicked the door shut and leaned back against it.

"I don't know what to say to her, Pa." Ever since the night they embraced each other, she had reverted back to calling him *Pa*.

Earl picked up a wayward stick and tossed it into the yard. "There's not much you can say right now. Just keep on letting her know you love her."

"It's just hard, especially when she doesn't respond. She doesn't even respond much to Mother."

Pent up air escaped Earl's mouth as thoughts whirled

around inside his head. How could he answer when he wasn't sure of the answers himself?

"Maybe she doesn't need words now. Just be there, doing little things to help. When she feels like talking, then talk. When she doesn't, then don't. She knows that you and Lorena love her."

"Do you think she'll come around?"

"Yes, I do. There's a lot of people that love her. Sometimes love is enough. And the Lord. I learned that lesson a little late."

"But not too late, Pa."

Earl gazed at his daughter, still amazed at her courage and strength. "Almost, Lane. Almost. You of all people know it." A slow, sad smile spread across his face. "Edith is strong ... like her plucky little sister."

Lane laughed quietly. "That sounds like something Guy would say."

"He has a bad influence on me." In spite of everything, it felt good to share a chuckle with his daughter. Fresh healing abounded in it. Earl briefly touched her cheek.

"Father?" Edith's voice reached them.

"We'd better get back to your sister."

When they returned, Edith's head rested back against the blue afghan draping over the rocker. Her waist-length black hair rippled around her shoulders, making her look like a child. Her closed eyes fluttered open.

"I've been curt with both you and Mother. I didn't mean to be. I'm sorry."

Compassion mixed with regret anew. Earl had missed her childhood, but he would watch over her adulthood. Tenderly, he reached out and laid his weathered hand on her head. His lips moved in silent prayer. Beside him, Lane bowed her head and placed a hand on top of his.

Edith squeezed her eyes shut, tears dampening her lashes. She reached up and covered their hands with her own.

Across the room, the front door opened almost soundlessly. Earl glanced over his shoulder. Lorena paused mid-step, transfixed at the sight, a tide of mixed emotions battling across her lovely features without resolution. Joy, sorrow, love, and disgust.

She backed away, clicking the door shut between them.

Earl's heart sank.

8

Late afternoon brought the residents of Valley Creek to the church. Purplish-silver clouds unfurled overhead while the sun blazed golden fire behind them. Lorena wondered if anyone else noticed the splendor, however, as folks almost wordlessly filed inside, shuffling to their pews. Glancing over her shoulder, she saw Earl take his place behind her pew. He caught her eye and nodded.

Reverend Crandall, after a few words of greeting, encouraged them to find a place of prayer. Some knelt at the wooden altar in front of the pulpit while others knelt at their seats. Their murmured prayers drifted upward, an outpouring of hearts uniting as one before their Heavenly Father. At one corner Jimmy Tackett knelt, expressing his heartache for the eleven on the hillside. Mr. and Mrs. Mansfield swiped at tears at their places before the altar. Close to the pulpit, Harley Ray whispered through trembling lips, but the Father understood what the young man's heart was saying. A bittersweet ache struck Lorena.

Against the wall, the pot-bellied stove radiated heat as the wood popped and crackled inside. Misty beads of moisture slowly veiled the windows as the crisp outside air filtered through tiny gaps and collided with the warmer air inside.

Time seemed to melt away within those simple, whitewashed walls. Almost without notice at first, a peace descended over those country folk, a mantle of comfort wrapping every heart and quieting the turmoil of every mind. The murmured prayers dwindled one by one until a different silence filled the place. The silence of tranquility. Heavenward, Lorena lifted her thanks.

Reverend Crandall rose without hurrying and stepped behind the pulpit, his red-rimmed eyes grazing the congregation.

"I'm thankful we serve a Heavenly Father who knows every need." He gripped the top edge of the pulpit. "As you all know, we're here to figure out the way forward, especially since the sawmill is gone. Brother Mansfield is going to speak now, since he's the foreman. Keep Brother Watkin in your prayers as he recovers. I know his family is devastated by the loss of his sawmill and home."

Standing at his pew, Mr. Mansfield shuffled from one foot to the other. "The steam engine was damaged considerable ... beyond repair. We found it mangled in a gully. If we rebuild Watkin's Sawmill, it's gonna need a new engine, and they ain't cheap. We got word from Watkin's brother-in-law. He's got a used one that he's willing to sell for 1,000 dollars."

A rumble skittered through the congregation. Some gasped while others shook their heads.

Mansfield grimaced. "That's not countin' the supplies we'll need for rebuilding the mill. We've got lumber scattered all over. Some of it we can re-use, but it's not nearly enough."

"One thousand dollars!" Mr. Huitt crossed his arms. "We couldn't scrape up that much money even if we all emptied our pockets."

"And that's not counting Huitt's store, the post office,

blacksmith shop, or the school." Thomas Ray scowled, shaking his head.

"What about the families that's lost their houses? There's four of them." Andrew Ray, Harley's brother, leaned his shoulder against the wall.

"My pa said he'd sell the good lumber for a quarter of the price to the ones that lost their homes." Eighteen-year old Ben Watkin suddenly stood. Every head snapped in his direction. "He asked me to speak for him tonight."

Another rumble from the congregation echoed off the walls.

Reverend Crandall cleared his throat. "Those families should have the first choice for the lumber."

The congregation murmured again, heads close together before finally nodding in agreement.

"Well, Brother Crandall, beggars can't be choosers, so I'll take Watkin up on that offer. Give 'em my thanks, Ben." Thomas Gillham, one of the homeless families, hooked his thumbs around the straps of his overalls. "I've got to get a roof over my family's head before the cold comes."

The other homeless families agreed. Yet how would Earl afford even that price? Lorena frowned. Behind her, he remained silent. As if sensing his worry, Guy turned around.

"It's all right, Mr. Steen. You've got plenty of trees on the back of your place. We can build a log cabin, and it'll be nice and tight through the winter. Sound okay to you?" He held out his hand.

Against her will, Lorena strained to hear every word.

"You bet it is, son!" Relief gushed through his voice. "I thank you."

What a far cry from the life Earl once knew as a youth. Early in their marriage, she and Earl had visited his parents at their plantation in Georgia, a sprawling farm with acres of rich soil and orchards. Every detail of the pale-yellow home flickered through her memory. All seventeen rooms delighted her senses. The oak, mahogany, and rosewood furnishings polished until they gleamed. Gilded chandeliers imported from France. As the youngest, Earl had the most privileges, a fine education, a private music tutor, and a scholarship to the music conservatory in New York City.

A far cry from a sawmill worker living in a cabin with hardly a penny to his name.

Mr. Huitt's voice barged into her thoughts, dragging her back to the present. "The thing is this: No money, no Valley Creek." His knuckles rapped the back of the pew. "That's the long and short of it. I don't see how we can start over."

"We can raise the money!" The pews creaked as everyone whisked their heads around to Mrs. Mansfield. She crimsoned. A hand fluttered to her chest. "Well, why ever not?"

The room hummed to life, doubtful and excited whispers mingling together. Huitt eyed Mrs. Mansfield and held up his hands.

"A fine idea, but that's all it is, folks. We can't make enough to rebuild the town and pay for a sawmill. This ain't the city, and most folks do good to scrape by."

"As much as I hate to say it, he's right," Guy whispered to them. The sudden hope on all the faces vanished like a snuffed-out candle.

"I was only trying to help." Mrs. Mansfield ducked her head, her chin quivering.

Lorena leaned forward and patted her arm. "It was a fine idea."

Mrs. Mansfield smiled through trembling lips, unable to speak. With graying flaxen hair and blue eyes, she was the older image of her daughter Tabitha, Lane's best friend.

Lorena's heart warmed as she thought of Tabitha. She had spent a school year with them in New York, attending McLaughlin's Ladies Academy with Lane. Earlier in the summer, Tabitha had married their pastor Frank Calloway. At the end of the year, they would be moving to a new church in Georgia.

"Just a moment!" Mrs. Watkin lifted a hand. "We could do it!"

Folks sat in stunned silence. If she had suggested hiring a circus, it would've been no different. Mrs. Watkin lifted her chin and peppered them with a scowl.

"Well, don't look at me like that! It can be done. And I know just the thing. A benefit concert." She clasped her hands together, her look daring anyone to argue.

Mansfield cleared his throat loudly. "Well, all of us like music. I reckon we could round up some of the boys and have people pay to hear 'em."

Mrs. Watkin scrunched up her nose and shook her head. "That's not what I had in mind. I meant a concert with classical music. Something folks would want to pay to hear."

Gawks met Mrs. Watkin from all sides. Alarmed, Lorena darted a glance over her shoulder at Earl and slid down a little in her seat.

"No one around here is going to pay money to hear music ... not the kind of money we need. 'Specially to hear classical music." Mr. Huitt sighed, thumping the pew.

"Speak for yerself!" Someone in the back chortled. Crimping his lips together, Huitt plopped down beside his wife.

Mrs. Watkin sprang out of her seat. "Wait! Brother Huitt has a point." Her chest heaved as she took an excited breath. "Suppose we took the concert to the city. You all know my cousin is a congressman in Little Rock. I could ask if he would help us find a way to hold a concert in one of the theaters there. People love classical music! I'm sure we could make enough to pay for a new sawmill and get a good start on rebuilding the town." She paused, turning toward Lorena, a smile lighting her face. "All we need is for Mr. and Mrs. Steen to agree to be our performers. You all know they once played for an orchestra."

All eyes shifted toward them. An expectant hush settled over the crowd. Behind her, Earl groaned. The collar of Lorena's blouse tightened, her breath trapped in her lungs. Her head whirled. Grimacing, she peeked at Earl. The color drained from his face, panic settling in the lines around his eyes and mouth. Beside her, Lane choked back a gasp. Guy laid his hand on her arm.

"I think that's fine!" Andrew Ray grinned. "A real concert! I've never been—"

Harley Ray silenced his eager young brother with a look. Andrew tucked his chin into his collar.

Mrs. Watkin must have sensed the folks' growing excitement. "It's for a good cause. We would be obliged if y'all would. I've heard how talented you both are and how successful you were in New York. In Little Rock, you'll be sure to draw a crowd."

Huitt squirmed out of his seat. "Now wait a minute! I mean no disrespect to Mrs. Steen or her talent, but I ain't about to depend on Earl Steen to save my skin."

Quite a few people murmured with nods.

"Mebe Brother Huitt's right." Mr. Gillham leaned forward. "I know Earl is trying to do better, but what if he gets drunk and can't do it?"

Sympathy tremored with anger along Lorena's spine as her eyes collided with Earl's. His face masked whatever feelings were going on inside, but scarlet was darkening the skin around his collar.

"Do you have any better ideas?" Mrs. Watkin jammed her fists on her hips. Mr. Gillham lowered his head.

"I ain't about to hang my last hope on Earl." Huitt glared across at her. "And most folks here feel the same way."

Had Earl turned to stone? He stared straight ahead at no one.

"Now hold on!" Reverend Crandall gritted his teeth. "There's no call for that kind of talk about one of our brothers. God can use anyone He pleases, and He doesn't need your approval. I think it's a fine idea myself, though why Mr. and Mrs. Steen would consent after all this, I don't know. If they do it, they have all the support and prayers I can give them."

"It's for a good cause, Mrs. Steen. Earl." Mrs. Watkin gestured her hand toward everyone around them. "We've lost nearly everything."

Blinking against old, unwelcome memories, Lorena forced the words out, her voice taut. "I truly am sorry. I truly am. I, we simply cannot do it. It's been too many years since we performed on stage. It requires hours of practice. Neither of us are suited to it anymore."

Lorena heard Earl's sharp intake of breath as he stood, deflecting the attention fixed on her.

"We know how you feel. We've had our losses too. I still have my place to rebuild." He rubbed his chin. "Truth is, I don't know what to say except that Lorena's right. It's been too long for us. She has no place to practice—"

"There's a piano right here."

Pain shot through Lorena's tightly clutched fingers as she twisted them deeper into her lap. Her pulse throbbed in her neck. She couldn't do it. She absolutely couldn't.

As her gaze darted around at the faces, some beseeching, some doubtful, her heart plummeted. How could she refuse them? To perform in public was something she promised herself she would never do again. They didn't realize what they were asking of her. Or Earl.

Mrs. Ray spoke up. "Oh, please do it. It would be so wonderful for our town."

With a set jaw, Earl shook his head. "I know, but I've been

working at a sawmill for years. My hands are ruined for that kind of playing." He held up his thick, muscled hands for everyone to see. "It just isn't possible."

A mix of displeasure and angst snuffed out the hope on Mrs. Watkin's face. "I'm sorry to hear that, Earl. I'd hoped that you, of all people, would want to do your part."

Lorena whirled around in her seat, her eyes pleading with Earl not to relent.

Earl reddened at the jab from his boss's wife. He clenched his jaw, as though tempted to remind Mrs. Watkin of a few things he remembered through the years. Then his eyes caught Lorena's. "Mrs. Watkin, I just can't do it. I'm sorry."

In the front, Reverend Crandall stepped around the pulpit and called their attention to him. "Folks, let's not put undue pressure on our brother and sister. I'm certain with time and much prayer, the Lord will provide a way."

Squaring her shoulders, Mrs. Watkin sat as her brown eyes glinted at Earl.

Chewing her lip, Lorena saw the look and knew what it meant for him. No job. Lorena felt incredibly selfish and cowardly. Repressing a shudder, she smoothed her skirts and stood.

"I'd like to say something, please." As every face turned to her, she gripped the pew in front of her to steady her trembling knees. "I understand what this means to you all. And Mrs. Watkin is right. A concert would help tremendously. But please understand it's no small thing to do. It will take a lot of arranging. Earl is right about his hands, and I'm horribly out of practice. You all may regret asking this of us because we can't guarantee success."

"Are you saying yes?" Reverend Crandall asked.

Oh, Mighty Father, help! Lorena dared not look at Earl's face. "Only if Mr. Steen agrees."

A long, silent moment charged the air as everyone waited for his answer.

"If Mrs. Steen is willing." The words came out clipped and taut.

"Mrs. Watkin, will this suit you?" Lorena's calm tone belied the quaking in her stomach.

A grateful smile mollified Mrs. Watkin's features as she nodded. "Yes. Thank you, Mrs. Steen. Thank you, Earl. My son will go to the train station to send a telegram first thing tomorrow."

"Suit yourselves." Glowering, Huitt gestured for his wife to stand. "I, for one, won't pin my hopes on Earl Steen. Not today or any day for that matter. As far as I'm concerned, you might as well let Valley Creek dry up and die for all the good he'll do."

With wife in tow and head held high, he marched down the aisle and into the gathering darkness. People stirred in their seats. Stunned, Lorena watched as over half of them followed suit, their expressions bleak and disgusted. Reverend Crandall's mouth gaped open.

"I've never wanted to punch a man so bad in my life." Guy rubbed his hands together.

THE COOL EVENING air prickled over Lorena's clammy forehead and cheeks as she dashed down the church steps. What a horrible meeting. All she wanted to do was collapse into her bed and hide. Filling her lungs, she stepped toward the teacherage.

Quick footsteps approached behind her. "Lorena, I didn't want this to happen." Earl's long stride fell in step beside hers.

Lorena rubbed her temples and quickened her pace. "I know, Earl. We can't control everything."

"I don't want to play in public any more than you do. I want you to know that. I know how hard it is for you."

"Do you?" Lorena raked him with a glance.

Earl swallowed hard. "I do."

"I doubt that."

Earl fell silent. Against her will, Lorena stole another glance at him. The darkness shaded his eyes, hiding the emotions that played through them. Here he was worried about her when he had been humiliated in front of the whole town.

Her fingers itched to push his hat up out of the way so she could read his expression. She folded her arms instead. "I'm sorry. That was harsh."

"I understand."

His ready compliance exasperated her. Her mind scrambled for something else to say.

"The last few days have been rough for everyone. There's so much to do. You'll help me pray about this, won't you?"

Earl shoved his hands into his pockets. "I'll be praying. I'm sorry you're in this position."

Lorena sighed. "I appreciate that. I feel so terrible for everyone. I truly want to help them but not this way." Remembering Huitt's harsh words, she winced. "I'm sorry you're in this position too. Huitt certainly didn't help matters. He was awful."

"This isn't our first tangle. He has his reasons." Earl dipped his head. "My reputation, after all, is rotten."

The stark, unvarnished words twisted like a knife in Lorena's heart. "Maybe when things get back to normal, it'll be better."

Earl stole a glance then. The moonlight drove the shadows from his face, blurring years away. He almost looked twenty again.

"Do you think it'll ever get back to normal?"

Something in his voice made her heart waver and then race. "I don't know." She veiled the breathlessness in her chest.

Earl turned his head. "We'll have to practice over at the church after the families move out. With everyone pitching in building, it won't take long."

Unable to think of a reply, Lorena held her tongue.

"Too bad your piano's not here. It was a beautiful piece."

"It wouldn't matter. I got rid of it years ago," Lorena blurted out. How foolish of her. Inwardly berating herself, she clamped her mouth shut.

A twig snapped under Earl's foot as he halted. "Got rid of it? Why? You loved it."

The night air played with the loose strands of Lorena's hair. She swept them back. "Never mind. Father bought a new one for me last year after Lane returned."

Frowning, Earl was not to be sidetracked. "It was because of me, wasn't it?"

Silence.

"Tell me, Lorena."

"Let's just forget it, Earl."

Earl shook his head, stepping closer. "You know as well as I do that'll never happen. Neither of us will ever forget. I'm asking you to tell me. Please."

Wrenching her gaze from his, Lorena linked her fingers behind her back. "All right. It *was* because of you. After you took Lane, I quit playing. It hurt too much, brought back too many memories. I told Father to get it out of the house. I didn't touch a piano again until Lane came back, and even then, she had to beg me."

For several long moments, silence enveloped them. The wind in the trees moaned through the hills, whispering around them of things they both yearned to forget. The ease in one another's company, heartfelt conversations, secret dreams. Moonlit walks together. Nights like this one.

The present, however, stood between them.

Earl shuffled his feet. "I stopped playing a few years after I left and didn't play again until the Lord came into my life." He breathed deeply. Without warning, he reached out and tipped her chin up with his hand. "Dear heart, I destroyed a lot, didn't I?"

Brimming with tears, Lorena's eyes flew to his face. His old nickname for her, spoken in that miserable way, rattled her defenses. "Please, please don't call me that."

As though burned, Earl snatched his hand back. "I'm sorry, Lorena. I didn't mean to say that." His fingers kneaded his forehead. "I'll see you on home."

"No, I prefer you didn't." Gathering her skirts, Lorena scrambled away, away from him, away from their past. If only she could keep on running.

When she reached the steps of the teacherage, she hesitated and glanced over her shoulder. His broad-shouldered silhouette stood out amidst all the wreckage, unscathed through the path of the storm.

"Yea, though I walk through the valley of the shadow of death, I will fear no evil: for thou art with me."

Lorena dashed through the door and snapped it shut. Shivering, she leaned back against it, yearning for its strength and hardness.

Hours later, as Lorena lay wide awake, Earl's touch still burned along her chin.

9

Voices and footsteps rumbled through the train station as a man stepped from the train. Resisting the urge to rub his stiff knees, he paced the length of the platform, grateful to stretch his travel-weary legs. Beyond him, the land sloped upward, houses dotting the streets as spires and chimneys jutted through the treetops. Telegraph lines dipped between poles spaced along the tracks. On one of the nearby streets, an ice wagon jostled along the cobblestones.

The smoke of a cheap cigar wrinkled his nose. Sitting on a nearby bench, an older gentleman perused a newspaper, his black top hat jutting over it as smoke curled upward. An overloaded cart of luggage clattered past, a teenage boy huffing as he tugged it.

The man retrieved a gold pocket watch from his gray vest. Eleven o'clock. He snapped the lid shut and skimmed the skyline of the city. An hour before the train resumed the journey.

"You look a little lost, mister." The older gentlemen folded his paper and laid aside the cigar.

"If this is Little Rock, I'm not lost." The man held out his hand in greeting.

"It's Little Rock, all right. My name's Thompson." The gentleman's thick hand gripped his with a robust shake.

"I'm George Curtis. Pleased to meet you."

"You're from back East. I can tell by your voice." Thompson chuckled. "Sticks out like a sore thumb in these parts."

George's face relaxed in a grin. "I'm sure it does. I'm from New York."

Thompson whistled. "A long way from home indeed! If you don't mind my asking, what brings you here?"

"I'm only passing through. I'm headed to Valley Creek."

The smile evaporated from Thompson's face. "Valley Creek? Do you have family there?"

"Not family. I'll be visiting some friends of mine."

"I guess you haven't heard the news then."

"What news?"

Grimacing, Thompson handed the paper to George. "A tornado hit Valley Creek almost a week ago. Nearly destroyed the whole town. It's in the paper ... there." His stubby finger pointed to the headline. "I'm a congressman. Valley Creek is in my district. I'm headed there today to view the damage."

The bold, black print clashed with George's eyes. *Small Ozark Town Wiped Out.* His breath clenched his throat. Afraid to read further, George looked up.

"Any deaths?"

The grimace lengthened the lines around Thompson's mouth. "Ten people and one baby stillborn after the panic."

Immediately, George's thoughts veered to Edith, alarm piercing through him. Oh, let it not be her. What of Lorena, Mr. Wallace, and Lane? "I've got to get there! I've got to see if my friends are all right!"

George spun on his heel toward the puffing, idle train, but Thompson caught his elbow. "Hold on, son! It's not going anywhere for an hour yet. There's a place nearby where we can get a cup of coffee. You come on with me, and we'll talk until time to board the train. Don't assume the worst. From what I understand, the people killed were trapped in town unable to get to shelter. Your friends may be all right."

His well-meaning words did little to alleviate the fear rolling in George's gut.

A few hours later, the train chugged through the Ozarks, deeper away from the clatter and bustle of the cities. Amazed, George stared out of the window at the deepening beauty of the trees and rocks jutting here and there from the mountainside. Hints of orange, gold, crimson, and deep mauve fused together, promising to drape the hills in a coat of many colors.

For the past two miles, a bubbling stream tripped and swirled a short distance from the tracks, a turquoise highway cutting through the untamed land.

So Earl fled here all those years ago with two-year-old Lane. No wonder he vanished so easily. All their efforts to find them had been in vain.

George tried to picture his former best friend, a cultured young man from Georgia well-suited to life in New York City, disappearing to such a place. No conveniences, no connections, no wealth, no friends, no family. No fame.

Just him and his craving for whiskey. His thirst for it had shattered their friendship, his future, and worst of all, his family. Everything.

Beside the stream, a doe raised her head above the long, golden grass as the train approached. She twitched her ears and vaulted into the trees. Swift. Elusive.

George's heart wrenched as he thought of Lorena, his lifelong friend. Together they had both grieved when his wife died, and though he had buried himself in his practice, the passing years dulled the pain and stoked another feeling altogether. He didn't know when or how it even happened, but one day it was there, brimming with each beat of his heart. He loved Lorena.

His fingernails dug into the wooden windowpane. He had fought it. He had hidden it under a brisk, gruff demeanor. Yet it burned inside, eating away at his conscience year after wretched year. Enough was enough.

It was now or never.

If Lorena had to face Earl, then she also must face him. George swiped a hand over his aching eyes. The train swayed slightly as it slowed its trek. They must be nearing the depot. He dreaded what he might find in Valley Creek. Would they be all right? Though he lost all heart to pray long ago, he hoped with every fiber of his being that they were unharmed.

Next to him, Thompson's chin drooped further into his vest. His steady, deep breathing was undisturbed by the slowing train. George smothered a sigh. When was the last time his sleep had been so undisturbed?

GEORGE STARED AT HIS SURROUNDINGS, a small town scattered between the mountains. The tornado's path ripped right through the heart of it, lumber, shattered glass, tin, and tree limbs strewn from one end to the other. His eyes followed the length of the main street, much shorter than a New York City block and without pavement.

With a low whistle, Thompson shifted his suitcase from one hand to the other. "Mercy, what a sight! It's a wonder anyone survived!"

Fear churned within George once more. He had never seen anything like it.

Some of the men clearing the rubble of Huitt's store straightened and narrowed their eyes at the two newcomers.

One of them plucked up a rifle from a stump and clutched it in his hand.

Another of them, a short, bald man, picked his way through the piles of litter toward them, thrusting out a gritty hand. "Hello there. I'm Edward Huitt. Y'all walked from the train station?"

"We did. My name is George Curtis." George gripped the offered hand with a firm shake.

"Obliged." Mr. Huitt turned to Thompson. "And you're?"

"I'm Congressman Thompson. Mrs. Watkin, one of your neighbors, is a cousin of mine. I've come to see the damage and talk to you folks."

Dabbing his face with a stained kerchief, Huitt puffed out a breath and gestured for the men to follow him. "We're starting to clean things up, but as you see, it's going to take a while. Four of our families lost their homes, so some of our men have teamed up to build those first. We're scraping together all the lumber we can."

Thompson nodded, his expression hidden under his mustache. "You've got a huge task ahead of you."

"Yes, sir. We're still sorting that out." Mr. Huitt turned to George. "What brings you here? I can tell you're not from around here, are you?"

"I'm from New York. I came to visit some friends of mine."

"Wouldn't happen to be Mr. Wallace and his folks, would it?"

"The very ones. I didn't hear of the storm until I arrived at Little Rock. Are they all right?"

Huitt nodded, kicking a piece of screen out of the way. "Yes, they are, but Miss Edith lost her baby." His voice trailed off as his eyes lifted toward the cemetery on the hillside.

Bittersweet relief swept through George, but he schooled his face to remain calm.

Thompson set his luggage against a bedraggled oak. "Well,

I'll worry about accommodations later. Looks like you fellows could use some help. Just point the way."

"Thank you, Congressman. You can come over here with me." Huitt cut his glance toward George. "Speaking of help, there's Mr. Wallace over at the school helpin' clean up what's left of it."

Following where Huitt pointed, George gaped as he saw Mr. Wallace untangle several boards and toss them on a nearby pile.

Indeed, Mr. Wallace looked very much in his element. George had never seen him without a suit before. With his shirt sleeves rolled up past his elbows, he shoveled through the debris as if he'd been doing it all his life. Even more amazing, he looked like he was enjoying it. His once immaculate iron-gray hair toppled past his forehead, making him look younger. As he swiped an arm across his forehead, Mr. Wallace straightened and saw George approaching.

"George Curtis!" He moved forward, kicking past the rubble.

For several long moments, they clasped each other's shoulders without speaking, eyes locked with unshed tears.

Mr. Wallace finally broke the silence. "My boy, you've caught us in difficult circumstances."

"I heard of it when I reached Little Rock. I'm terribly sorry for all of you, especially Edith."

Mr. Wallace's eyes darkened. "She's taking it hard."

"I can't imagine. I'll see her as soon as I can." George tried to smile and lighten the mood. Taking a step back, he surveyed the dusty, sweat-streaked shirt and pants. "Mr. Wallace, if our friends could see you back home, they wouldn't believe it."

"It makes me feel good inside working with these men. I only wish it was for different reasons. These folks are the most resilient people I've ever seen. They ask for no help and expect none, yet they all pull together." Mr. Wallace paused and worked his jaw, concern edging his tone. "I suppose I don't have to ask what brings you here."

George's smile stiffened. "No, sir. The reason is the same."

Mr. Wallace nodded, leading him away from curious ears. "I want no trouble stirred up in my family, George. I'm asking you to respect that."

George kept his voice low. "And I don't want to stir any trouble up."

Like a swirling cloud across the sun, a dark frown rippled across Mr. Wallace's face. "I won't go to the trouble of repeating our last conversation. You're timing, to say the least, is unfortunate."

Wincing, George looked at his feet. "I'm sorry, Mr. Wallace. While I'm here, I'd like to help in any way I can."

Sighing, Mr. Wallace rubbed the lower muscles in his back. "We do need the help, and I appreciate it. I'm sorry for being curt with you. None of us have had much sleep. Lorena's anxious about Edith. We all are. It's going to take some time for Edith to get over this, not to mention Harley Ray."

"How is Lane?"

"Doing fine, doing fine," Mr. Wallace answered, his voice growing lighter. "She stays busy, that girl. She'll be teaching school at the church once we can move those families into their new homes."

George couldn't help but grin when he thought of Lane. During her stay in New York, she had managed to get under his tough skin. "I'm glad she's happy."

"So am I. Tell me, George, where are you going to stay?" Mr. Wallace eyed him curiously.

"I was hoping there would be a boarding house or an inn of some sort in town, but that was before I heard the news."

"Never come to the Ozarks unprepared." A hint of amusement flickered in his dark eyes.

"I can see that."

"I'll see what I can do. Someone might rent you a room. Dr. Brown has a house on the edge of town, and I hear his wife is an excellent cook."

"Dr. Brown?"

"Yes. I'm sure you two would enjoy talking over new medical procedures and such. Is that your luggage over there under that tree?"

"No, sir. I couldn't carry my trunk. That's Congressman Thompson's."

"I heard he might come." Mr. Wallace motioned toward the teacherage. "We'll fetch yours at the station later. That's the teacherage where Lorena and I are staying. If you want, go over and rest a little while. There's a pitcher on the table with water. When I'm finished here, we'll go have a talk with the doctor."

"Lorena ..."

Mr. Wallace's brows lifted. "Is at Edith's."

George sighed, shrugging out of his jacket. "Thank you, Mr. Wallace, but I don't need rest at the moment. I'll just lay this inside and be right out to help."

After hanging his jacket on one of the pegs beside the door, George dusted his slacks off. His eyes roved over the small but neat room. If those walls could only talk, what would they tell? Over on a small table sat the cream-colored pitcher. Mouth dry as sawdust, his throat twinged, aching for a cool drink.

After rummaging through the cabinets, he found the cups and filled one. The cool water slid down his throat, soothing him inside and out. He sat down in the chair and gulped another slow, long drink. For something with no taste, it was the best he'd ever tasted. He propped his head back against the wall. The swaying motion of the train still vibrated within his body.

Eyes sliding shut, he thought of Lorena. Somewhere, in the midst of his musing, sleep claimed him.

LEGS ACHING from the walk the long way around town, Lorena paused at the teacherage door to watch the men working. Piles of lumber lined the street while they loaded wagons. Sweat shone in the afternoon sun and splotched their clothing. The waiting mules flicked their tails, their ears twisting at the loud voices. At least, the street would soon be clear.

Weary, Lorena drooped her head and went inside. As the door clicked in place, she lifted her eyes and froze.

"George!"

Her voice stirred him from his slumber. George bolted upright and hopped to his feet, almost upsetting his cup.

"Oh!" He stepped towards her. "I'm sorry to barge in like this. I didn't mean to doze off. Mr. Wallace is probably wondering where I am."

Lorena shook his proffered hand and stepped back, eyes traveling no further up than his loose necktie. His voice was the same, brisk, impersonal. Perhaps Father was mistaken.

"It's good to see you, Lorena." His tight voice filled the space between them.

Lorena felt a deep flush creep over her cheeks. "What brings you here?"

"I know it's a little surprising, but I wanted to see all of you. New York City is a pretty lonely place without the Wallaces."

"I'm sure New York City is managing nicely without us." Lorena tossed him a pointed stare.

The navy color of his eyes darkened. Reaching up, he tugged his necktie. "I didn't know what had happened until I arrived at Little Rock. I can't tell you how sorry I am, Lorena, especially for Edith and her husband."

Pain shriveled Lorena's heart. "Thank you. We're just trying to make it through one day at a time. Everyone has lost so much, some more than others, yet they're so brave."

"Now that I'm here, I want to help as much as I can."

"How were you able to leave your practice?"

"I've been training a new graduate from medical school. I thought it was time to let him manage things for a while. He's very capable, has a brilliant mind. This opportunity will be a good test for him."

"I see." Lorena fingered a button on her sleeve. "How long do you plan to be gone?"

"Perhaps a month, maybe more." He stepped a little closer. "I told your father for as long as it takes."

The air in the room stifled her breath, robbing her voice of an answer. She clinched her hands together behind her back.

"Aren't you going to ask me why?" he pressed quietly, searching her face.

Pulling in a deep, quivering breath, Lorena lifted her chin, meeting his warm, blue eyes. Why had she not seen it before? "There's no need to ask why because the answer doesn't matter. You've wasted a trip, George. Go back to New York."

"That's for me to decide, Lorena." He took a few steps back and leaned against the kitchen doorframe. "This isn't easy for me either. We've been friends nearly all our lives. You stood by me when my wife died. I stood by you when your marriage fell apart. The years have been hard for both of us."

Shaking her head, Lorena fought against unbidden memories. "I haven't forgotten, George. I've always been your friend, but that's all it can be. Don't waste your time here."

"Is that what you want?"

"Yes."

George knit his brows with a scowl. "You can't mean that, Lorena."

"I do."

"You would rather throw your life away because of a man who betrayed you in every possible way?"

Lorena's face flamed, anger shaking her voice. "I'm not

throwing my life away. Nothing can change between us." She folded her arms. "I can tell by your face that you don't believe me."

"You know me well. No, I don't believe you, and I'm not going to leave until I'm sure."

Lorena opened her mouth to say more, but the door opened, cutting off the words that blazed to her tongue. Father stepped over the threshold. His eyes darted from one to the other.

"And not a moment too soon, I see."

Suddenly, she could breathe again. "Father, George has come."

"Yes, I know." He nodded, unruffled. "Well, George, are you ready to pay Dr. Brown a visit?"

"Dr. Brown?" Lorena lifted her eyebrows.

"We need to see if Dr. Brown will rent George a room. And we'd better get moving because the sun is going down. I heard the Congressman will be staying there too." His cheerful British accent eased the tension in the room. "The school board's buggy was destroyed in the tornado, so I'm borrowing an old one from Harley Ray's family. It's rickety, but it'll do."

In spite of herself, Lorena clamped down the smile threatening to melt her angry expression. Her father knew how to turn an awkward situation almost into a pleasant encounter. No one else was better at rising to the occasion. Ever since Lane returned to their lives, something within him had revived.

"That sounds fine, sir." George fetched his jacket from the peg. Turning, he sought Lorena's eyes. His were vibrant, alive with feelings that she believed had died long ago within herself.

Something sharp and bitter struck her heart. She wasn't free. She could never be free to love anyone else.

Or could she?

10

Lorena watched as Edith's arms wrapped around George in a tight embrace, her dark curls spilling over one of his shoulders.

"Dr. Curtis, I'm so glad you've come." Her weak voice, laced with tears, murmured against his strong shoulder.

His arms tightened around her. "There now, honey. I'm glad to see you too. I've missed you. I see that you have a beautiful place here. Harley Ray did a wonderful job building this house."

Edith sniffed and nodded. "He's a talented carpenter. I couldn't ask for a better husband."

"I'm looking forward to working with him today. I wanted to see you first, though." He leaned back and cupped her chin in his hand. "You know, things will get better. With time."

Two big tears rolled down her cheeks and dripped onto his hand. "I don't know. I hope so."

"It will. I promise you. I hear that Dr. Brown is taking good care of you too."

"He's very much like you."

"We have quite a bit in common. I'm staying with him. Good man."

As George glanced up at Lorena, she turned her head away, rubbing her arms to ease the taut muscles. She had spent a wakeful night while thoughts of Earl and him had bobbed back and forth. And they were the last ones she wanted to see so early this morning.

"You don't look as though you rested very well, Lorena."

"No, I didn't, but I'll manage."

"Mother." Edith turned. "You should've slept in for a while. I would have been all right."

Lorena's face relaxed into a smile. "I'm sure you would've, but I wanted to come." When she looked back at George, the smile dwindled. His eyes had never strayed from her face, soaking up every detail. His open, unabashed perusal burned deep color into her cheeks. She whirled away on her heel.

"Let me make you a pack lunch before you go," Edith offered.

"Thanks, but Mrs. Brown already made one for me. How about I take you up on that offer tomorrow?"

"That would be just fine." Edith's skirts swished across the floor as she joined Lorena near the window. Her hand rested on her mother's arm. "Are you sure you're all right?"

Unwilling to turn around, Lorena could only nod.

A knock rapped at the door. Glad for a diversion, she crossed the room and answered it. Earl stood in the doorway, just as he had every morning before joining the other men.

In one hand, he grasped his hat. Looking over her shoulder, Earl's blue-green eyes collided with George Curtis's.

Clenching her teeth, Lorena stepped aside. Former friends faced each other as a heavy silence descended in the room.

A moment later George crossed the room. "Earl Steen. It's been a long time." He scrutinized Earl from the top of his combed hair, his faded overalls, all the way to his dusty shoes.

A faint sneer played around his lips. "A far cry different from what you used to be."

Earl crossed the threshold, his eyes never wavering from George's. "That's so." He stepped past him, laid aside hat and lunch pail, and approached Edith.

"Morning, Edith."

"Good morning, Father." Edith smiled and held out her hands.

Leaving them to speak privately, Lorena stepped onto the porch. George followed, pulling the door closed behind them.

"What's he doing here?"

"He comes by early every morning to check on Edith."

"I see. Just like he owns the place."

Lorena folded her arms as George's face clouded. "It isn't like that."

"You dare defend him? After all this time?"

"I'm not defending him!"

"It sure sounds like it."

Lorena drew her brows close together, fighting a stream of hot words on the tip of her tongue. "George, you know better than that. You asked a question, and I answered it plain and simple. Don't start looking for things that don't exist. To be perfectly clear, I have no more interest in defending him than I have in changing our friendship."

George flinched, her words finding their mark. "I'm sorry, Lorena. I'm a fool. After all these years, seeing him, knowing what he did to you all, it's as though he gets to pick right up where he left off."

"I must confess I've thought the same thing. I know that Earl has paid in so many ways, though. He is having to rebuild the relationship and trust he broke with his daughters. He has lost everything that matters, and he knows it." She pulled in a trembling breath. "Yet it doesn't quell my anger. I, I've failed God. I've failed my faith."

Before she could step aside, George's arm circled her shoulders. How many times had he done that through the years? A month ago, she would've given it no more thought as if it had been one of her brothers. But he wasn't her brother.

The front door opened and Earl stepped outside. Lorena darted away. Earl halted, his gaze bouncing back and forth between them. George narrowed his eyes.

The air sparked between them. No one moved.

Averting his eyes, Earl fixed them on the nearby hills and stepped between them, down the steps. Without a backwards glance, he put on his hat and strode toward town.

EARL'S THOUGHTS TICKED FAST. What was that about? Lorena looked like she wanted to crawl under the house. And what would bring George all the way to Valley Creek?

The first blaze of orange and crimson maple leaves glided along lazy wisps of damp, earthy air and strewed in the path. The early sunrise fingered shafts of light through bare limbs while dewdrops speckled across patches of black-eyed Susans. A slight chill tinged the air, but the sun was quickly warming it.

Yet it did nothing to calm the rising turbulence within him.

Where was Lydia, George's wife? Had she stayed behind in New York? Earl shook his head. He never dreamed he would ever meet his old friend again. Tangled memories, distant laughter rose and crumbled in his mind. Small wonder George was unhappy to see him. Like everyone else, he had a right to be angry.

"Lord, I need Your help facing this. I ask for Your strength." His voice was a whisper among the rustling leaves. "I don't deserve his forgiveness, nor Lorena's, but I crave it. More than anything."

Unbidden, unexplained peace crept into his heart and

soothed the ache. As long as the Lord was with him, he could muster the courage to face them knowing he deserved nothing in return.

Shaking the thoughts away, he quickened his pace. For now, he had houses to help build.

The midday sun shone down on sixty men as the clattering and hammering of boards filled a small clearing. Not far, another group of sixty men worked on another home place. Hardly a stone's throw away another group of sixty worked as well. Back in Valley Creek, about fifty men still worked to clear the damage and salvage as much as possible.

The sound of a dozen saws' teeth cutting boards mingled with the pounding of hammers as they worked together. Rather than silence, the talking and hammering filled the valley, sounds of life stirring once again.

A deep gratitude filled Earl. As he glanced up from hammering a new wall for the house, he marveled at everyone's generosity. Even people from nearby little towns had come to lend a hand.

The smell of fresh baked bread and smoked ham tickled his nose. His stomach suddenly gnawed as the sweet smell of peach cobbler followed it. Just a few yards beyond the framework of the house, a few dozen ladies bustled around a couple of wagons, arranging the food on the beds. In a few more minutes, the men could line up and take their share.

Earl spied Lorena's dark hair at one of the wagons, the sunlight threading gold through the waves. Swallowing hard, he turned his attention back to his task. The sight of her plunging right in to help the other ladies did things to his heart he would rather ignore.

"Looks like we're almost done with this wall, Mr. Steen." Harley Ray smacked a nail into place then wiped his shiny brow with a sleeve.

Earl nodded, trying to jostle it, testing its stability. "The best wall in the house if I do say so myself."

Earl was glad to see the grin spread across Harley Ray's face, the first in days.

"It might be, at that. With all this help, we'll be done in a few days."

"Then on to rebuilding Valley Creek and the sawmill."

The grin just as quickly waned. Harley Ray slipped the hammer into his belt loop. "Do you think it can be done?"

"I'll admit, it's going to take a lot of hard work and pulling together, but it can be done. With God's help."

"Speakin' of help, did you take a little of that help I gave you the other evening?"

Clenching his hammer, Earl twisted around. With a smirk, Rob Sims tipped his hat up with a pluck of his finger. Several men paused at their task, tools suspended in their hands.

"Nope."

Rob turned his head and speckled a stump with brown tobacco juice. "You don't expect me to believe that, do you?"

"Not a bit."

Guffawing, Rob slapped his knee. "You was always one for a good laugh, Earl."

Earl pulled in a calming breath and turned back to the wall. Flames of temper kindled around the edges of his spirit.

"Just a minute!" Thomas Gillham squeezed through two wall studs and faced Earl. "This here's my place we're working on. You'd best be sober here."

Earl looked down at the shorter man whose fists clinched at his sides. "I'm sober. I haven't had a drink since the day I came to the Lord."

In the next room, Huitt laid aside his saw and dusted off his hands. "You expect us to believe you turned down a drink? From your old pal? Just like that?"

"Yeah, Earl. Just like that?" Rob smirked, cramming his hands into his pockets. "Almost a whole bottle?"

Heat rushed into Earl's hands. It would be so easy to knock both of them flat on their backs, but then, what would it prove?

"Just the same, I didn't."

The looks on most of the faces told Earl that they believed otherwise. To explain was a waste of time.

"You expect us to think you can hold a concert and raise money for our town?" Thomas wagged a finger under Earl's nose. "Who do you think you are, anyhow? You ain't never done nothing for anyone."

"Back up, Gillham." Earl kept his voice low and calm like waters just before they toppled over rocks.

Though he scowled, Thomas backed away, almost bumping into Harley Ray.

"You have a strange way of showing your thanks, Mr. Gillham. He's here helping you when his own place is gone."

"I didn't ask for his help. Mind your own business, Harley Ray." Thomas brushed past him and hopped down into the yard.

Earl glanced around. One face after another shuttered. None of them believed him. Anger and helplessness burned in his chest. He ground his teeth.

"You're setting this whole town up for disappointment. Why don't you do the right thing, for once, and call the whole thing off? None of us want your help."

In one long, quick stride, Earl stood inches from Huitt's nose. "Like it or not, I'm here. And I'll not do any answering to you."

As Huitt's face blotched, the veins bulged out on the sides of his neck.

"Dinner's ready! Y'all come on!" Mrs. Mansfield's apron fluttered in the air as she waved.

The men didn't have to be told twice. From all corners of

the house frame, they scattered. Shaking his head, Harley Ray whistled low.

"Almost came to blows."

The weight of the hammer filled Earl's palm. He had forgotten he was still holding it. No wonder everyone else scrambled. In spite of himself, he chuckled.

"I was just letting them know they're not going to run roughshod over me. I wasn't about to hit anyone."

A grin fringing his mouth, Harley Ray eyed the hammer as Earl laid it aside. "It sure didn't look that way."

Earl clapped a hand on the young man's shoulder. "No, I reckon not. I was tempted to. I've done my share of it, and as long as I'm breathing, I'll not raise my hand to anyone else again."

As they joined the line at one of the wagons, Mr. Mansfield strode over and slipped into place behind him.

"Fine work you've been doing on the house." He brushed sawdust from his overalls.

"Thanks. I'm glad to help."

Mansfield smiled, his leathery tan crinkling like brown paper around dark eyes. "You've certainly pulled your own weight and then some! It's helped more than you know."

Earl cast aside the ready pride that passed through him. "Well, it's not more than anyone else here. You've had your work cut out organizing and leading these three teams. Between the three houses, you haven't stopped all day."

"I like the work. I always have, but I'll admit, I'll be glad when I get in my bed tonight." Mr. Mansfield chuckled then sobered. "I think you're done here, though."

Earl's eyebrows arched. "Say again?"

"I've been thinkin'. We've got enough men here to finish these houses sooner than I planned. I think if I sent, oh maybe around forty-five men, that's fifteen men from each team, to help you build your house, you'll be sitting by your own hearth in no time. What do you think?"

Shock flashed through Earl as he tried not to gape. "You sure do know how to take a man by surprise, Mr. Mansfield. That's beyond generous of you. But Guy is going to help me build a cabin from my timber as soon as we're finished here."

"No need, Earl." Mr. Mansfield shook his head, picking up a tin pie pan. He grabbed a piece of cornbread. "I've thought it out. There's enough lumber to spare to build you a house. Nothing big, mind you. It'll save you time from cutting and splittin' that timber, not to mention chinking the place. What do you say?"

"I can't afford the price."

Chomping a bite, Mansfield waved aside the comment, one side of his cheek bulging. After a few more chews, he gulped it down. "The Lord provides, Earl. You've helped these past days without a thought to your own place. For as long as I've known you, you've never once asked for any help, even when you sorely needed it." He plunked a piece of smoked ham in his plate. "Besides, I've a feeling Valley Creek will be owing you and Mrs. Steen before it's over."

THE LAMPLIGHT FLICKERED shadows across four exhausted faces gathered around Doc Brown's table later that evening. The faint, spicy scent of kerosene dizzied George's senses. Perhaps because he was accustomed to electric lights. From the small parlor, the mantle clock chimed seven o'clock.

They had squeezed every bit of daylight clearing and stacking lumber, burning anything else that couldn't be salvaged. The smell of smoke, earth, and sweat clung to them like chimney soot.

Yet George had to admit, all that back-breaking work made him feel clean inside, a feeling hard to describe.

Either ignoring the smell or holding her breath, Mrs. Brown poured cups of coffee for each one of them before retreating to fresher air in the parlor. George stifled a chuckle. They must be a sight, smells aside.

Thompson lifted the steaming cup to his lips and sipped the bitter liquid. He smacked his lips. "Now, that's coffee! Can't get my housekeeper to make a decent cup like that." He took another sip. "Gentlemen, I don't think I've worked so hard in years."

"We're obliged, Congressman." Doc Brown sampled his own cup.

"Piffle tosh! Don't forget I grew up not far from here. Just a few hollers over. I'm glad to do what I can. Which is what I want to speak with you men about right now."

George rolled a small sip over his tongue. It was good. It slid down his throat and warmed him. Across the table, Mr. Wallace and Doc waited.

"There's a matter that my cousin, Mrs. Watkin, was telling me. I must say, I really like the idea, and with the right arranging, it might just pay for the sawmill. So, tell me more about this benefit concert idea. I hear you have a concert pianist and violinist right here in Valley Creek."

Smacking his cup down harder than he intended, George gulped down a mouthful of the scalding coffee. It seared down his throat. Blinking hard, he bit back the yelp that rushed to his lips.

Three sets of eyes fixed on him.

"Are you all right, Dr. Curtis?" Doc Brown asked.

What a question? How in blazes could he be when he wanted to yell to the rooftop? And it had nothing to do with his aching throat. George could only nod.

Doc turned his attention back to Thompson. "We do, but

Mr. Wallace can tell you more about that. It's his daughter and son-in-law."

"Indeed? I'd love to hear more." With a congenial smile, the congressman folded his hands together and waited.

The blood ran hot through George's veins. He, for one, had heard enough, but it wasn't his place to say so. He clenched his jaw, catching Mr. Wallace's glance.

"My daughter was once a very accomplished concert pianist. She performed in the most prestigious orchestra in New York as did my son-in-law. He was a violinist. Very renowned. "

"Do you mind my asking how they ended up here?"

"A long story for another time, perhaps?" Mr. Wallace's voice, though pensive, brooked no argument. "Earl and Lorena agreed to practice and help. It's been a long time, years, in fact, since they've performed in public, but they're willing to try."

Thompson rubbed his chin. "I like the idea, and I think it could work. I've friends. I'll have no trouble booking a theater, advertising. And then there's the story behind the benefit concert. With the right campaign, word will spread like wildfire. People love to give to a good cause, and they're already familiar with the tragedy in the papers."

"And how much will all this advertising cost, along with everything else?"

"Not a penny." Thompson turned the cup in his hands. "Like I said, I have friends. The question is, can your daughter and son-in-law pull it off?"

Looking up at the ceiling, Mr. Wallace heaved a long sigh. "They'll do all they can, and it will take weeks, long hours. I don't know, Congressman. So much depends on it."

Several silent minutes ticked past as the men thought. Each tick of the clock seemed louder than the last. Finally, Thompson leaned forward, his face intent.

"What other choice is there? No money, no sawmill, no

money to rebuild. As it stands, y'all don't have much to lose. I say let's do it."

"I think that's just fine." Doc leaned over and nudged Mr. Wallace. "What say you, Wallace?"

"It's more than fair. Thank you, Congressman."

Reaching across the table, Thompson burst into a grin, pumping Mr. Wallace's hand. "Call me Thompson. I'm happy to oblige, but I have one request. Will you come back with me to Little Rock and help with the arrangements? Your presence will put a face on this endeavor."

"I'll be glad to do whatever I can."

George could take no more. Pushing back from the table, he cleared his throat. "If you'll excuse me, I think I'll get a breath of air."

Before they could say good night, George shoved the screen door open and disappeared outside. The crisp, night air cooled his burning face. Jamming his hands into his pockets, he rounded the house, crossed the yard, and stepped onto the road.

Aloud banging on the door rattled the windows of the teacherage. With a gasp, Lorena looked up from the book in her hands. Laying it on the table, she hurried to the door.

"Who is it?"

"Me." George's muffled voice came through the thick door.

Lorena twisted the latch, but before she could open the door, George let himself inside. He strode past her and whirled around, his face ablaze.

"Whatever is the matter?" Lorena pushed the door shut but dared not move further into the room.

"So, what's all this I hear about a benefit concert?"

Sweat broke out on the back of Lorena's neck. "I ... Mrs. Watkin asked us if we'd be willing to help the town."

"Is that so?"

"The town had a meeting. Everyone was there. If you only could've seen their faces—"

"You must be joking! You, *you* would agree to something like that? Working with Earl?" His taut voice rose.

Lorena held up her head. "It's for a good cause. They've lost everything."

"Why drag Earl into it?"

"I didn't! Mrs. Watkin suggested it. Believe me, Earl certainly didn't want to."

"Don't defend that wretch."

"I'm not! George Curtis, you're behaving like a spoiled child. I've never seen you this way."

In almost one bound, George crossed the room and seized Lorena by the shoulders, his grip firm but not harmful. His navy eyes flared into her startled ones.

"Me? What do you expect? After all these years, the very man that nearly ruined your life walks right past you this morning as if he has the right, as if nothing had happened. Did he see you all those terrible days, weeks, and years after he disappeared with Lane? No, but I did. And now you're actually going to work with the man!"

"George, please don't be angry."

"Angry? Lorena, I love you."

Lorena twisted herself from his grasp. "That's quite enough," she snapped.

George's hands fell to his sides, his breathing heavy.

"I can't expect you to understand. I prayed about it, and I believe if I turn these people away when it's in my ability to help them, then I'll commit a grave sin against them. Against my Lord. How can I turn them away?"

"Why does it have to be you?" George took a shuddering breath. "I don't want to lose you."

"You can't lose what you don't have." Her words, though spoken gently, caused pain to ripple across his face.

"Are you so sure of that, Lorena?"

Silence suspended between them, both of them scrutinizing the other. Anxiety twisted in her chest. Striving to keep her voice even, Lorena glanced away.

"Yes."

"I'm not sure I believe you."

"I think it's time for you to go, George. Good night."

"Good night, Lorena. But know one thing, I'm not leaving until we're both sure. One way or the other."

Balling her fists, Lorena whirled away from him. A few moments later, the door opened and shut softly behind her. Her trembling legs carried her over to the rocking chair. She slumped down onto it and covered her face. Ever since coming there, trouble dogged every step she took, and there seemed no way out of it. Where had her peace gone?

It had fled into the shadows.

EMOTIONS WITHIN GEORGE loomed as dark and suffocating as the blackened countryside. As he trudged back toward Doc's, his eyes darted through the gloom, desperate for something to calm his churning thoughts. Of all times to be blunt about his feelings. The words had bolted out like a prisoner wrestling a captor and breaking free. To say that he loved her. The timing couldn't have been worse.

Up ahead, barely distinguishable, a form moved toward him on the path. George stiffened. It moved closer, unhurried.

"George, is that you?"

At Mr. Wallace's voice, George relaxed. "Yes, sir."

Mr. Wallace drew closer and stopped. "Getting that breath of fresh air?"

"Something like that."

"I see. Went to see Lorena, did you?"

Although George couldn't clearly see his face, he heard the frown in Mr. Wallace's voice.

"I did."

"Do you think she owes you an explanation?"

George rubbed the back of his neck. "No, I don't, but I want—"

"You want to stand in the way." Mr. Wallace thrust his hands behind his back, his mustache a dusky, hard line above his lips.

"Sir, this is between Lorena and me."

"No, George, it isn't. It is between all of us."

"Earl—"

"Earl is the least to consider!"

His sudden anger slashed across George's conscience. Since his boyhood, he had never known Mr. Wallace to raise his voice.

"You must consider the girls as well. You must consider this community. Lorena is a married woman. I'll not have you trifling with her heart, especially in front of everyone."

"I'm not trifling, sir."

"Lorena gave her heart to Earl and made her vows to him. You may confuse her, but you won't win her."

George worked his jaw, striving to keep his tone even. "I'm not so sure of that. And neither is she."

Only then did Mr. Wallace break his rigid stance, rubbing a hand over his face.

"Have it your way, then. But know this: I'll use every bit of influence I have over Lorena to stop you."

George thrust his hands out at his sides. "Whatever for? Why would you, of all people, ruin our chance at happiness?"

"Believe me, I empathize with you and Lorena, but you're taking advantage of her while her heart is hurting. I'll not let you do it. It's not fair to her. Can't you see that?"

George brushed past his mentor, his lifelong friend, unwilling to hear another word.

"I'll do what I have to do."

"And so will I."

THE NEXT MORNING, the rosy flush of dawn crept above the hills while the starlight dwindled, the greater light snuffing out the lesser lights one by one. Perched on a split-rail fence, a meadowlark trilled, its song dipping low and high. High then low. A trail of buggy wheels in the dew led to Lane's front porch. The deep aroma of percolating coffee seeped from under the front door and filled George's nose.

He raised his hand and knocked. Footsteps thumped across the floor and the doorknob turned.

"Dr. Curtis." Guy smiled, stepping aside. "This is an early surprise. You're just in time for a cup of coffee."

George managed a stiff smile. "Thanks, but I'm here to see Earl. Can you ask him to come out?" He stepped back. "I'll wait here."

A guarded look came into Guy's eyes. "Sure."

After he closed the door, low, indistinct voices broke the stillness of the morning air. A moment later the door opened and Earl stepped outside.

Their eyes clashed, each one summing up the other, years of unspoken words simmering between them. Old, forgotten feelings and happier memories surged in George's mind, but he steeled himself against them. Those days were dead and gone. Forever.

"What can I do for you?" The words were as still and calm as the morning air.

George bit back his initial thought. How about step out of the way? "I came to have an understanding with you."

Earl crossed his arms over his chest, waiting.

"You've made Lorena suffer enough. I've stood by and watched all this time, but no more. I intend to make her happy."

Confusion knit Earl's brows together. "What do you mean? Where's Lydia?"

Her name, spoken aloud after so many years, split the scar across his heart. Unexpected pain seeped through his being.

"She's dead."

With a sharp intake of air, Earl unfolded his arms. "I'm sorry, George. I, I didn't know."

"How would you?" George swallowed down the ache. "Save your sorrys. I'm here about Lorena."

"You want me to set my wife free."

"Yes."

Deep anger blazed across Earl's face. His pupils grew large and dark, almost obliterating the blue-green of his eyes. His palms turned white where his fingernails dug into the flesh.

"You don't deserve her. You betrayed her. And you have no right to her any longer. She deserves to be happy and loved."

Grinding his teeth, Earl stepped forward. With narrowed eyes, George met him, their faces a hand-breadth apart.

"Get out, George. Get out before I ..."

"Before you what? Going back to the old ways so quick?"

Though the flames glinted, Earl spun away and planted his fist into his palm. The smack silenced the meadowlark. It spread its wings and darted into the trees.

"You're tempting me mighty hard." Earl blew out a long breath, lowering his hands to his sides. "I'm asking you to leave."

"Not until I have your word you'll let Lorena go."

Slowly, almost methodically, Earl pivoted to face him again, this time the fire in his eyes damped. "I'm not giving you my word on anything. I owe Lorena. Not you, George."

Though the years separated them, George knew when Earl's word was final. He backed away and turned toward the buggy. Before climbing up, he paused. Earl was still anchored in place, watching.

"From now on, it's Dr. Curtis to you."

THE STING of George's words jabbed Earl with every hammer strike on the framing of his new house. Around him the men worked and talked as usual, but his thoughts pounded louder than the racket. The joy of this day was ruined. Rightly so.

Another nail pierced the wood clean through to the board adjoining it. As Earl drew back the hammer, he noticed the dent, a little deeper than normal. He ran his thumb over it. What was he trying to do? Hammer his guilt away?

He held another nail in place. Every time the hammer struck its head, it forged the words echoing within his heart. Right. Right. Right.

George was right.

Bitterness he hadn't felt in ages bled into his spirit, so strong he could almost taste it. He had no hope, no chance of ever winning Lorena's love. He was a broken man who had shattered the love of his life. She deserved better.

Right. Right. Right.

Earl stepped back, brushing a coarse sleeve over his forehead, everything around him a mangled blur. He had to step away. Just for a moment.

Blindly, he wormed his way through the other workers to the water bucket hanging from the limb of a sweet gum tree. Turning his back, he reached for the dipper and lifted it to his lips. The crisp spring water soothed his crackling throat. His eyes roved over the hills, the autumn colors deepening.

Just breathe. Try not to think.

"Lifting your eyes to the hills?"

Earl flinched. The dipper dropped into the bucket with a dull thunk.

"I'm sorry. I didn't mean to slip up on you like that." Reverend Crandall flushed under the tan collar of his homespun shirt.

"That's all right, Reverend." Earl smiled despite himself. "I didn't hear you, that's all. I'm obliged to you, coming to help out today."

"Not at all. I just wish I could do more." Reverend Crandall tipped his head toward the mountains. "You seem troubled today. I hope you don't mind me sayin' so."

Earl sighed. "I'd mind if it were anyone else, but not you. Just got a lot of things going on in my head."

The Reverend reached down, plucked up a prickly sweet gum ball, and twiddled it around his palm.

"Worries are a lot like this: full of sharp barbs no matter which way you turn 'em. We roll them around back and forth, but all they do is stick and sting. You can look at it from any direction, and it's still the same. Can't change it."

He handed it to Earl. "Close your hand over it tight."

Earl shook his head. "I know what will happen if I do."

"When you clamp down on your worries instead of turning them over to God, the same thing happens."

Tears clogged Earl's throat. The strain of the past few weeks pressed harder upon him. He opened his mouth, tried to speak, but crimped his lips together instead. After all the death, the insults, the suspicious, hard glares, the compassion on Crandall's face was almost too much.

The young man must have sensed it. He shifted his eyes away, rubbing the toe of his shoe in the grass.

"When I was praying this mornin', the Lord brought you to mind. I don't know why. He gave me a scripture in Psalm 121. 'I will lift up mine eyes unto the hills, from whence cometh my help.' He knows, Brother Steen, what you're facing, and He cares."

Clearing his throat, Earl struggled with his voice. "I thank you, Reverend."

"I don't think anyone will miss you if you were to slip into the woods for a bit to find some time with Him."

Yes, that was what he needed. With a strong hand, Earl gripped Reverend Crandall's shoulder and nodded.

In the shadow of the woods, twigs snapped and leaves crackled under his feet until he reached a stump, mottled with lichens. The canopy above him muted the noise and soothed the throbbing in his head.

He sat, pressing his face against the palms of his hands. Warm, stinging tears dampened his wrists and flowed until they dripped onto the ground.

"Father forgive me. I don't deserve it from You or anyone else. I can't fix the past."

I will guide your future.

Earl lifted his head. Who had spoken? At that moment, he realized the words had been spoken within his soul.

"Lord, guide me to do the right thing about Lorena. I only ask that she would somehow find it in her heart to forgive me. Grant her the peace and love she deserves." He pulled in a deep breath. "Help me not to lose my temper with George. Lord, whatever happens, give me strength to do what's right."

A perfect stillness surrounded Earl, a stillness unlike anything he'd ever known, calming the turbulent thoughts and emotions that threatened to overtake him.

"He maketh me to lie down in green pastures: he leadeth me beside the still waters."

Amazed, Earl rose and swiped his thumbs underneath his eyes. Nothing, no one else in the universe could calm the storm so swiftly.

"He restoreth my soul."

Restore. Jesus restored health to the sick, restored strength to the lame, restored sight to the blind. He restored innocence to the guilty.

And Earl Steen was as guilty as they came.

"Earl! Earl!"

The voice of his wife propelled his feet forward.

12

The shuffling in the woods caused Lorena to clench the reins tighter. Just in front of the horse, Earl stepped into the clearing.

His gaze immediately locked with hers. Lorena caught her breath, noticing his bloodshot eyes and ruddy cheeks.

"Have you been drinking?" The accusation slipped out before she could stop it.

"No, Lorena." His gaze didn't waver, only deepened.

His calm tone pierced her conscience. Of course, he wasn't. If she had just waited a moment longer, she would've known. Tear tracks lined the dust on the sides of his face.

Beside her, Edith stirred, the first time she had ventured out since the tornado. Dusky circles traced her cheekbones and rounded her eyes.

"It looks more like the flush of prayer to me." Edith extended a hand to her father. "How are you?"

Mortification chilled Lorena's cheeks. Here was her daughter acting more like a lady should.

Earl reached up and took Edith's hand. "I'm fine. And you?"

"Well, I'm out of the house. At Mother's insistence."

"Your mother is right. Fresh air and sunshine will do you good. When winter hits, you'll be wishing you could get out."

Lifting her chin, Lorena mustered courage. If only she could start this conversation over. There was nothing to do but plow ahead.

"Andrew Ray brought the mail from the depot. There was a letter for you."

"A letter?"

Lorena reached in the pocket of her skirt and drew out a stained, ragged envelope.

"Evidently it's had a hard journey." She smiled softly, hoping it conveyed her regret. Careful not to brush her fingers against his, she set it in his hand.

Turning it over, Earl saw the fine, cursive script with the words "Steen" in the upper left-hand corner. A frown rumpled his forehead.

"It's from Ella. Surely you recognize her handwriting."

"It's been too long. Why on earth would she write me?" Earl tunneled a hand through his auburn hair.

"You're her brother. She has written me all these years, waiting for any word of you. She loved you, you know."

Loved. Earl glanced up, his eyes melding into her blue ones, expressing things she was terrified to discern.

"Thanks." Earl crammed the letter into the pocket of his overalls. "I better be getting back to work."

With a nod at both of them, he took wide, quick strides as though he couldn't get away fast enough.

"Do you think he'll read it?" Edith asked as Lorena turned the buggy around and headed toward Valley Creek.

"Yes, he'll read it."

"I wish I could read it." Edith ran her fingers along the frayed seat cushion.

Lorena didn't miss the longing in Edith's voice. "So you can know him better?"

Biting her lip, Edith nodded. "He shows so little of himself, as if he's afraid of hurting us again. I want to tell him that it's all right. I'm not afraid." Her dark honey-colored eyes blinked. "Does it make you angry?"

For a brief moment, Lorena stroked her daughter's cheek, so soft and young. "No, Edith. Your feelings are natural, and I understand. I am angry at Earl, I'll admit, but it has nothing to do with you."

"I wish I could help you."

She felt a bittersweet smile touch her lips. "I'm very proud of you. You put me to shame. You have no malice in your heart."

"You taught me well, Mother. I owe it to you." Like a child, Edith laid her cheek against Lorena's shoulder.

Lorena shook her head. "I guess I forgot to teach myself."

Only the murmuring breeze whispered between Edith and her on the way home.

"Did Grandfather say how long he would be in Little Rock?" Lane passed a plate of fried potatoes to Guy then reached for a jar of green tomato relish to spoon onto her plate.

Firelight danced with lamplight across the faces at Edith's supper table that evening. The days became shorter and the cool, evening air grew sharper.

Lorena shook her head. "He didn't know exactly." Focusing her eyes on the platter of cornbread, she took a piece, avoiding the eyes around her, particularly George's across the table.

"You mean the concert?" Jimmy grinned. He swished a fork in the air. "Boy, I wish I could see it! Mama Lane was tellin' me about how y'all will practice and—"

"Jimmy." Guy raised his eyebrows, his voice quiet.

Grimacing, Jimmy ducked his head.

"It's all right." Lorena forced a smile at Jimmy. "Mr. Steen and I will need a lot of practice so we'll know exactly what to do."

"How long will you need?" Edith passed a bowl of black-eyed peas to Harley Ray, her voice listless.

Lorena cut a glance at her, concern tightening her chest. Edith was only going through the motions, everything else an afterthought. She lifted a quick, silent prayer heavenward.

"Hours, weeks. Even then, it may not be enough."

"We're praying, Mrs. Steen. The Lord will help you both." Harley Ray took a sip from his cup.

George plopped his napkin a little too hard beside his plate. Fork mid-way to her mouth, Lane's eyes snapped up. No one else seemed to notice.

Oh dear. Lorena watched her daughter's eyes narrow a little. Surely she didn't suspect. But then, Lane was very much like her perceptive father.

"Before it gets too cold, you should try out Guy's fishing hole, Dr. Curtis." Lane said, guiding the conversation to safer ground. Her stare never wavered from George's face.

George caught Lane's look and his stern expression gentled. Lorena knew he had always carried a soft spot for Lane.

"I've never fished a day in my life."

"Well, there's always a first time for everything. But I give you fair warning. I'll have to hog-tie you if you tell anyone where it is!" Guy pointed a butter knife, his hazel eyes twinkling.

Laughter bounced off the walls, easing the tension around the table. Tossing his head back, Dr. Curtis joined in.

Lifting a cup to her lips, Lorena hid a relieved sigh.

WHILE THE LADIES washed and dried the supper dishes, Dr. Curtis leaned his shoulder against an oak tree. Behind him, on the porch, Guy strummed a guitar while Harley Ray plucked a banjo, a soft, lazy tune improvised while one took turns following the other. The song meandered through the evening air.

New York City felt a million miles away on a night like this. Above him, the stars glimmered like jewels in an infinite, black ocean while the moon spilled light on the surrounding countryside.

"Miss the city?" From the shadows, Lane stepped beside him and looked up into the sky.

"No, I can't say that I do." George looked down at his young friend. "It's a welcome change, for once. You miss it?"

"I learned quite a lot while I was there. But this is my home, for better or worse." Lane turned her face to his.

George fought the urge to squirm under her probing stare. She knew his secret. Had discovered it months ago, shrewd lass that she was. And worse than that, he couldn't even be annoyed with her.

"You told her, didn't you?"

George remained silent.

"After you asked me not to." Scowling, Lane crossed her arms.

Frowning, George shifted his eyes back to the stars and clenched his jaw. Yes, he'd asked her not to tell. It was true. He'd made up his mind being near Lorena was enough. But Earl had found religion. What if Lorena found Earl as well?

"You have nothing to say, Dr. Curtis?"

"I have plenty to say, but not to you, Lane."

"Why would you do such a thing? To torture her?" Although she kept her voice low, anger shook it.

"You know better than that."

"And you know she isn't free." Clutching his arm, Lane tugged it. "Dr. Curtis, please."

Only then did George look back at her, so lovely, so young.

So very dear to his cynical heart. Her eyes glistened up at him. He enveloped her hand with one of his and squeezed tenderly.

"Forgive me, Lane, but I must. I can't expect you to understand."

"It isn't about understanding. It's about what's right and wrong."

"You don't think I realize that? I'll tell you what's wrong. Lorena and I were cheated. My wife died and Earl abandoned Lorena. We've spent years alone. Now, I'll tell you what's right. She and I deserve to be happy. Maybe my sense of right and wrong doesn't match yours. I'm frankly past caring anymore what anyone thinks."

In the moonlight, Lane's face paled, the narrow bridge of freckles across her nose standing out.

"Even if it means ruining her self-respect? You can't mean that."

George ignored the unease tightening his chest. "I do."

Lane pulled her hand from George's and stepped back. "I can't tell you how I wish things were different for you and her. I love you both so much. Mother will never change. You're only hurting her more by being here." A tremor rippled across her lips. "I'll tell you something else that's wrong, Dr. Curtis. It's wrong for you to hurt Mother this way. Just as it was wrong for my father to hurt her."

Heat blazed up George's spine. "Don't dare compare me to him."

Lane's features became stone. "I will. Father's selfishness was no different than yours. His desires came at a high price. Mother paid in full. You want what you want no matter what. You would have her pay in full too?"

Lane turned on her heel and marched back to the house. The soft music swallowed up the sound of her footfalls in the grass.

The chill of the evening air swept over him. He suppressed

a shiver. That young woman knew how to cut to the heart of a matter.

To cause Lorena pain, to strive against her family gnawed at him like acid eating away at iron. His resolve weakened.

Only but a moment.

She was the only thing left that he had to believe in. Without her, he would be cut adrift, alone. To give up now was out of the question.

George squared his shoulders. He stepped from under the tree and strode out of the yard into the darkness.

EMBERS PULSED orange-red on the hearth as the flames licked upward, the only light in the room. The firewood popped and crackled as Earl laid another stick across the dog-irons. The rest of the house was quiet while slumber claimed the family one by one.

He settled down on a nearby stool and reached into his pocket. A slight tremor shook his fingertips as he drew out the letter. Staring at the handwriting, he hesitated, both afraid and curious.

Ella. Just thinking of her brought the taste and smell of their mama's freshly baked apple pie. The afternoons he and she swiped one from the pie safe, eating more than their fair share, scandalizing the rest of the family. Oh, the bellyaches afterward.

A slow smile curved Earl's lips before sadness overtook it. With his thumb, he pried the envelope open and pulled the letter out. The scent of lemongrass struck him like an invisible slap across his cheek. Ella's favorite scent.

He'd forgotten. It was the scent of home.

Earl unfolded the stationary. Several dollar bills slid into his lap. Frowning, he set them aside and angled the letter toward the firelight.

> *Earl,*
>
> *I hardly know what to say. I have started a dozen letters only to discard them. Since I have never been one to beat around the bush, I will get straight to the point.*
>
> *I want to see you. Although I heard about your conversion, I need to see for myself. May I come? You need not bother writing back. Enclosed is enough money for you to wire an answer.*
>
> *Ella*

With one hand, Earl kneaded his forehead as his thoughts swirled like the dust in a funnel cloud.

"Pa?"

Earl's head jerked up. In the doorway stood Lane. Her bare toes peeped from underneath her flannel nightgown.

Thoughts still whirling, Earl bent his head again. The sound of her gown grazing the wooden floor came close. Across from him, she sat cross-legged as though still a child. Thick, coppery waves of hair flowed past her waist barely skimming the floor.

"Bad news?"

Shrugging, Earl shook his head. "I don't know. It's from my sister Ella. She wants to come see me."

"Your house will be finished soon. I never even knew you had a sister ... until recently."

Although Earl tried to swallow, his mouth felt as though someone stuffed it with cotton. He didn't even want to think about the secrets he had hidden from her. Best to talk of something else and leave that one alone for now.

"Havin' trouble going to sleep?"

If Lane noticed his abrupt change of subject, her face never showed it. But then again, she knew well how to conceal emotions. He had taught her. To his shame.

"I had a dream that woke me up. It always does, and I can never go back to sleep afterward."

"You've had it before? Is it a bad dream?"

Lane hesitated, nibbling on her bottom lip. As she scrutinized his face, it took everything within him to hold her gaze.

"I've had the dream for as long as I can remember. It used to be a bad one, but not so very much now."

Earl didn't like the sound of it, yet he had to know. "What about?"

Hugging her knees to her chest, Lane shifted her eyes to the fire. "For years I didn't understand. The dream is a song, a violin playing the tune, and a man's voice singing."

Earl's eyes slid shut. "My voice."

"Yes. And your violin. You sing *Lorena*."

Lane chewed her lip once more, seeming to gauge his reaction. Before answering, Earl folded the letter and money, then slid them into the envelope.

"Your mother's favorite song. Mine too. The first time she ever heard it was when I sang it to her. We were courting ..." The beautiful, haunting lines threaded through his mind, cutting off his words.

Earl pulled his gaze away from hers, focusing on the fire as he grappled with emotions besieging his heart.

Lane sighed. "I used to hate that dream, but I don't anymore. It's my only memory of better times."

Blinking hard, Earl wrestled for control of his voice. "That's a shame. I ... I am sorry I gave you nothing else." What pathetic, insignificant words.

For a little while the crackling fire made the only sound in the room. Even though the warmth enveloped them, the chill of Earl's past steeped his spirit. If only those things could be crumpled up like a piece of paper and cast into the fire. Transformed to ashes.

Yet those memories hovered and shadowed his every thought. They stalked his every move, and they stared back at him in the beautiful turquoise shimmer of Lane's eyes.

"You don't have to keep saying you're sorry."

Earl's breath hitched, yet he couldn't look at her. "It's not enough."

"That's true. But God's grace is." Lane scooted closer. "Pa, let's think of the future. Ours. I'm tired of looking into the past. We'll always have those memories, but there's so many more good memories we can make."

Tentatively, as though afraid he might break her, Earl reached over and stroked the top of her silky head. Unspoken words clogged his throat.

If only he could start over with Lorena as well.

Some things were just too hard to overcome.

13

A few days later, the early afternoon breeze twiddled with a few stray locks of Lorena's hair. Her navy skirt brushed back the ankle-deep grass of the graveyard as she wound carefully through the headstones. At least those fortunate enough to have one.

She paused, perusing the things she missed that awful day when they had laid so many to rest.

Stones, rough and jagged, marked many of the resting places. Near her foot lay a large gray one, striped narrowly with blue. She bent over and ran her fingertips over its smooth surface. Beside it lay a jagged, rose-pink stone, catching sparkles in the sunlight. Five more stones, smaller and plain, followed in a perfect row. Not a name to be seen. Their time on earth marked only by a piece of the valley itself.

Did a husband and wife lie there? Were the five smaller stones children? Only God knew now.

Lorena straightened. She remembered the family plot where Mother was buried in New York City, surrounded by hundreds of headstones and monuments. She thought of

Lydia's grave, not far from Mother's. Yards of marble and granite cold to the touch, names and dates carved for posterity.

Yet none of them moved her as much as these humble, silent stones placed long ago by loving hands. By someone who wanted to remember and honor the ones they loved. No monument was as beautiful as these.

Reverence filled Lorena's soul for these resilient people of the Ozarks. No wonder Edith had fallen in love and chosen to make her home here. Her daughter had become one of them.

She had laid her beloved to rest among them.

Lorena stepped forward, rounded a large pine tree, and faced the eleven unmarked mounds of earth. She halted. Her chin quivered.

On top of every resting place was a fresh bouquet of autumn wildflowers. Rosy and lilac-colored forked asters blended with black-eyed Susans. Star-like clusters of boneset peeped between them. A few shafts of goldenrod crowned each array. The wee one's grave had the most colorful spray.

Tears spilled down her cheeks as she crept forward as though afraid of disturbing the bittersweet beauty. The dry grass rustled around the folds of her skirt as she knelt in front of the nameless child's place.

"Who did this?" she whispered. Her fingers caressed a silky petal. "They are fresh, brought earlier today."

In every bouquet each flower was placed so that one color complimented the other. A perfect arrangement of tender love. Lorena's heart squeezed. Lifting her head, she scanned the clear, blue sky.

"Thank you, Father, for whoever did this." Was it Edith or Lane? It couldn't be. Lane was busy helping the ladies supply food to the men working at Earl's place. Edith never ventured from her home unless coaxed.

For a long while, Lorena listened to the breeze meandering

through the canopy of leaves overhead. At last, she rose and turned. Time to go back to the living.

As she picked her way along the path, she saw George heading toward her. Shaking her head, she sighed.

"Are you all right?" Concern filled his voice as he approached.

Lorena nodded. "Yes."

"I wish there was something I could do."

"Thank you." Her eyes looked everywhere except his face. "Only the Lord and time can help this."

George offered his arm. "May I?"

"I don't know." Lorena stepped back. A few months ago, she wouldn't have hesitated, but not so now.

A sheepish smile touched his lips. "Please. I promise I won't bite, Lorena."

"Well ..."

He reached out and gently linked her arm with his, keeping a respectable distance between them. The rough gray tweed of his jacket prickled her fingers. The scent of soap and English lavender drifted from him. Just under his firm jawline, a tiny nick marred his otherwise smooth skin.

Lorena focused her eyes forward.

"I need to apologize for my behavior the other evening."

As they stepped forward, Lorena racked her brain for a reply and found nothing.

"I didn't mean to lose my head like that. I'm sorry."

"I'd prefer not to talk about it anymore."

"I understand. I'd like to forget it myself and enjoy this walk."

"So would I."

A deep chuckle parted George's lips as he released her arm. He reached out and pumped Lorena's hand as if it were a rusted faucet. "Hullo, Ma'am, fancy meeting you here! Beautiful weather we're having, isn't it?"

Lorena laughed, feeling the sorrows of the past days melt away if only for a moment. With murky blue-gray twinkling eyes, George squeezed her fingers. "Well now, that's better." He nestled her arm within his once more.

"I have to admit, it does feel good to laugh again."

"It does. Friends?" He cast her a sideways glance.

Lorena met his glance, sobering. "Only friends."

THE SNORT of an approaching horse drew Earl's attention as he worked alongside his neighbors. He turned his head and saw Jimmy riding up, most likely from the depot. Until school resumed, he had taken a job at the depot delivering telegraph messages.

"Mr. Steen, I've got a message for ya."

Earl stepped over a pile of boards and patted the horse. "What is it?"

"It's from Grandfather Wallace. He's comin' in. Will be here in a few hours. He says you're to pick him up and bring the wagon when you do. No buggy."

Earl knitted his brows. "All right."

"They're 'bout done with your house. It looks real good, Mr. Steen." Jimmy bobbed his sandy head with a bright grin.

Earl followed his stare. The plank siding would be finished by the end of the day. The tin roof was on, gleaming in the sunshine. They were already paneling the walls. "Thanks. They're doing a fine job."

"I guess you'll be moving in soon." Jimmy's smile faded. "I'll sure miss playing checkers with you in the evenings."

"Well, now, then you'll just have to come over and play here." Earl patted the boy's knee.

Jimmy's blue eyes lit up, matching the cloudless sky. "Sure

thing, Mr. Steen! I'd better be getting back." He turned the horse and trotted back down the road.

As Earl returned to his work, Ella's letter rustled in his pocket. Well, today was as good as any to send an answer.

Later, Earl pulled up in front of the depot and set the brake on the wagon. As he climbed up the steps, the stationmaster opened the door and held up his watch.

"The train is due in 10 minutes. She hasn't been late a day all week."

"Good. While I'm waiting, I need to send a telegram."

"Come on in, come on in." Henry led the way. "By the way, how's that pretty lady doing?"

Earl ran a hand up and down his overalls strap. "Doing fine, I reckon."

"You reckon? That's all?" Henry eyed him, then shook his head. "Wasted on youngins." He walked behind the counter and grabbed a piece of paper. "What's your message?"

"Come."

Henry paused, pencil hovering over the paper. "'Come?' That's all?"

Earl nodded soberly. "That's all. Send it to Ella Steen." After giving the address, he paid the fee and stuffed the rest in his pocket, planning to return it to Ella.

Henry tapped out the message. "There ya go. Is there anything else?"

With a slight smile, Earl nodded toward a barrel by the window. "There's one more thing. How 'bout a game of checkers?"

Slapping Earl on the back, Henry tossed his head and laughed. "That's the first thing you've said that makes sense. I thought you'd never ask."

Right on time, the train chugged and puffed into the yard. As it slowed to a stop, steam spewed across the platform, hissing loudly.

As Mr. Wallace stepped off one of the cars, Earl's throat tightened. He and his father-in-law hadn't spoken very much in recent days, but then, they were both busy. His mind hearkened back to long lost days when he and Mr. Wallace were close like father and son. Inwardly, he shook himself and forced his eyes to meet Mr. Wallace's.

Hat perched on his iron-gray head, he was striding toward him, impeccably dressed in a charcoal suit with a matching striped waistcoat, his silk tie secured with a pin. An easy, relaxed smile lit his features as he reached out to grasp Earl's hand with a firm shake.

"Earl, I appreciate your coming. I've got quite a load to get to Valley Creek."

"I'll drive the wagon around. What is it?"

"A surprise." Mr. Wallace's gray eyes twinkled with mischief. "And I've hired several strong-looking chaps to help us with it."

Curiosity piqued, Earl hurried back to the wagon and brought it around to the loading dock. As he backed up to the platform, he noticed the five young men, fellow-passengers, who Mr. Wallace hired. Beside them stood a wooden crate, almost shoulder-high and not quite as long as he was tall at 6 foot 3.

Mr. Wallace was grinning broadly now, no doubt very pleased with his surprise. Earl set the brake and climbed down.

"That's quite a surprise, Mr. Wallace. Will it stand the rough road back to Valley Creek?"

"It's been packed extra carefully just for that very thing. Very thick padding all around. If you drive slowly, I think it will be all right."

Earl's curiosity deepened, and Mr. Wallace deepened it further. "Oh, and I have these parcels too." He plucked five packages from the top of the crate. One was shaped like a large, thick book wrapped in brown paper and tied with stiff yarn.

Two were striped red and white boxes, the kind that held store-bought clothes. A dress for Lorena perhaps or the girls. On top of it lay an unassuming gray shoebox. Behind it sat a hatbox.

Earl reached up and took them. "I'll put them under the seat."

"Thank you, son."

Afterward, with Earl's help, the young men slid the box carefully into the back of the wagon and helped tie it down. With hearty thanks and generous pay, Mr. Wallace shook their hands and bid them safe travels.

The brisk sound of Mr. Wallace's shoes clipped down the steps as he headed toward the wagon.

"Ready?" He climbed up and settled beside Earl.

Nodding, Earl flicked the reins and chirruped to his horses. The wagon jerked slowly forward.

"Are all of the arrangements made?"

Rubbing his knees, Mr. Wallace blew out a breath. "Finally. Congressman Thompson didn't exaggerate when he said he had friends. The concert will be around the end of November. He'll let me know the final dates."

A heavy, invisible weight pushed down on Earl's shoulders. Grimacing, he rubbed the back of his tanned neck.

"Will that give you and Lorena enough time?"

"I'm certain Lorena will do fine. I'll do my best, sir, but I can't promise anything." Earl flexed his fingers. "It's been too long." Dread throbbed with every beat of his heart. Everyone was counting on them. Suppose he let everyone down, especially Lorena? What if the concert was a flop? And all because of him. Valley Creek needed Lorena. They didn't need his failure.

He felt Mr. Wallace's gaze summing him up. Earl shifted away slightly, unwilling for him to read his doubts.

"I have confidence in both of you. I want you to know that." Mr. Wallace's British accent had an odd way of soothing him. "I believe with all my heart that God will provide what you both need."

Earl tried to make his tone light. "He'll have to, that's for sure. So, are you still not telling me what the surprise is?"

Mr. Wallace chuckled. "You never could stand surprises. You'll have to wait a little longer for this one, though."

Shaking his head, Earl gave him a lopsided grin. Deep inside, he was glad that Mr. Wallace remembered some things about him with fondness.

"Earl, there's another matter I must speak with you about."

He stiffened, not liking the sound of it. "Sir?"

The twinkle faded from Mr. Wallace's dark eyes as they probed deeply into his, never wavering. "Lorena."

Everything within him shouted no, but Earl held the stare without flinching. "I'm listening."

"You know why George is here?"

"I do."

"What do you intend to do about it?"

Earl's grip slackened on the reins then tightened, his knuckles turning white. "What can I do? I have no say."

"Don't you?"

"No, I don't. I forfeited that right years ago. It's up to Lorena."

"Is it?"

Face flushing darkly, Earl knitted his brows together as he swallowed a lump of heartache. "Mr. Wallace, I mean no disrespect, but I don't have much patience for this kind of talk. What's done is done. Lorena is free to make her choices."

Mr. Wallace leaned slightly forward. "That's just it, Earl. She isn't free and neither are you."

"A piece of paper can fix it. Is that it? I can tend to it as soon as I'm settled." Earl clipped off every word as though he were hammering those boards again.

A deep sigh rumbled in Mr. Wallace's chest. "You're missing

my point, son. You're both in limbo, have been for years." He rubbed his chin wearily. "I've never been good at this sort of thing, but I've got to do something."

Earl gentled his tone. "There's nothing you need to do. It's my place to do the right thing by Lorena."

"And it's my place to see that you do. I've looked after her all these years when you should've been doing it."

Earl drooped his head. "You're right." And it ripped his very soul in pieces.

"I'm going about this all wrong." Clearly frustrated, Mr. Wallace fidgeted with his gold watch chain. "Bear with me, Earl. When you get older like me, time grows more precious. I lost my wife, you know, and I've learned a thing or two. We only get the gift of time once. Every second that passes is forever gone. Do you love Lorena?"

"It doesn't matter what I feel."

"That's just the point, my boy. It does! A moment ago you said, 'What's done is done.' True. But time, yours and Lorena's, isn't done."

Earl lifted his head, suddenly intent.

"If I could have one more moment with my wife..." His voice trailed off, a tremor quivering his mustache. He drew in a ragged breath. "You've committed terrible wrongs, Earl. By God's grace, you're not that man today. The old Earl had no right. The new Earl, well, you have every right to pursue your wife."

Had his father-in-law lost his head? Did he realize what he was saying? "Lorena—"

"Lorena deserves the right to know once and for all herself. She deserves to know you. She deserves that chance. She's waited all these years, you know."

Shaking his head, Earl frowned. "Lorena hates me, Mr. Wallace."

"Does she?" Tilting his head, he quirked an eyebrow. "Anger and hate can be two different things."

"Not in this case. She deserves a better man. George would make her happy."

For a moment, heavy silence dangled between them. Only the creaking of the box and wagon spilled into their thoughts.

Finally, Mr. Wallace spoke. "You never answered me straight earlier. Earl, do you love Lorena?"

Why did the man press him? Clamping down on a groan, Earl squeezed his eyes shut. "Yes."

Though only one word, his entire heart and soul was in it.

Mr. Wallace sat back against the seat, seeming relieved. "You'll both be chasing ghosts the rest of your lives if you don't give one another a chance. It's up to you to do it. Only then will you both know."

Earl turned to his father-in-law in earnest. "Just one more question. Why? Why on earth would you want a man like me for your daughter?"

Sudden, unshed tears gleamed in the older gentleman's eyes. "Because I believe in second chances. I believe in God, I believe in redemption, I believe in my daughter. And I believe in you."

A sob ripped through Earl's chest, releasing a burst of tears boiling under the surface. They poured unchecked down his face in vast rivers of regret and gratitude.

Mr. Wallace's tears followed. He raised a trembling hand and covered his eyes.

Already knowing the way home, the horses paid no mind to the slack reins and plodded forward.

14

As the wagon approached the teacherage, George stepped outside, having said goodbye to Lorena after their tea. Lorena stood in the doorway listening as the wagon creaked over the ruts. Behind it, the sun was slipping lower toward the mountains. Long shadows stretched out behind the team. The low voices of two men reached her ears.

George paused, listening. Lorena squinted. Her father's soft chuckle drifted over the zesty breeze.

Gathering her skirts, Lorena scurried down the steps and waved. "Father! Father!" A smile parted her lips.

Mr. Wallace waved a gloved hand as the wagon drew closer. Lorena squinted harder at the man who was driving, broad-shouldered, sitting tall. Then she knew. Her heart stilled.

She took a step backwards right into George's waiting arm. His hand cupped her elbow protectively.

No expression troubled the calm in Earl's eyes as he looked from George to her. Lorena knew from experience, however, that Earl was quite adept at hiding his feelings. Not wanting to seem rude, she sidestepped George's hold and stood firmly on her own.

Earl reined the team to a stop, and Mr. Wallace reached out a hand to Lorena. His firm, warm grip encircled her fingers as he smiled down at her.

"My girl. It's good to see you." Mr. Wallace nodded at George then cut a glance at the crate. "I brought a little something back with me."

The large crate brought a broad smile to her lips. "I'd say you did. What is it?"

"You'll see soon enough. I need several men to help unload it at the church. Earl and I are going there now. Would you like a ride?"

"I'll walk."

"As you wish." An impish gleam lurked behind her father's smile.

Straightening his jacket, George stepped forward. "I can gather a few men to help, if you'd like."

Mr. Wallace nodded amiably. "That'd be fine, George. Thank you."

Before Earl could urge the team forward, George was gone. The horses pulled forward toward the church. Lorena matched her stride with them, easy, unrushed.

What on earth did Father bring in such a box? And for the church? Even Earl's presence couldn't hamper her curiosity.

In no time, Earl, George, Mr. Huitt, Andrew Ray, and Mr. Mansfield had the box unloaded into the church. A few crowbars made quick work of the wooden sides. As they popped loose, a sliver of something shiny and black peeped from under a corner of thick padding.

Lorena stepped back. It couldn't be.

Mr. Wallace swept back a layer of the padding, revealing half of his surprise. Forgetting his manners in the church, Andrew whistled.

"Wait 'til I tell the folks at home! A piano!"

Mr. Huitt rubbed his jaw, speechless along with the other men. It wasn't just any piano. It was a baby grand piano.

"Where are the legs?" Mr. Huitt sputtered.

"They're wrapped up. They're on the other side." Mr. Wallace ran his hand along the glossy surface.

Lorena cast a furtive glance at Earl. His hands drooped to his side, his eyes staring at the toes of his shoes. Motionless. As though turned to stone.

Then he looked up at her.

The breath in her throat caught.

"Why did you, Father? It's too much."

"To tell you the truth, I had my qualms about buying it, but you need it when you practice. You need the feel and tone similar to the one you'll play on stage. Only the one on stage will be bigger." He peered at her. "I didn't want to upset you."

They were standing alone outside as the men finished assembling the legs. Brilliant amber and mauve colors flamed up over the mountains as the last sliver of the sun sank out of sight.

Lorena hugged her arms against her chest and rubbed them. "I understand, and you're right. It will help. Seeing it makes it so ... real."

Mr. Wallace wrapped an arm around her shoulders and squeezed. "I know. It'll be all right."

Shuddering, Lorena closed her eyes and leaned into the comfort and strength of his sturdy shoulder. They stood in silence until the men came out one by one, finished with their task.

"I've never seen the like, Mr. Wallace. I can't wait to see you play, Mrs. Steen." Andrew shook their hands before going home.

"Thank you, Andrew." Lorena smiled.

While everyone said their good evenings, Lorena watched Earl slip unnoticed to the wagon.

"Excuse me a moment, Lorena. I need a word with Earl, then we can go home." After shaking Mr. Mansfield's hand, Father hurried over to catch him.

She would have given anything to hear their conversation.

IN HIS BEDROOM at Lane's, Earl stared at the two striped boxes, the gray shoebox, and the hatbox on his bed. With his hands on his hips, he thought about Mr. Wallace's words before he drove away from the church.

The boxes were his, a generous gift that rattled him. His calloused fingers reached and lifted the lid on the first striped box. Earl blinked as though in a fog. Awestruck, he ran a hand over a deep navy wool jacket, single-breasted with three buttons down the center. Very subtle gray stripes threaded through it. Underneath it lay a matching five-button waistcoat with a slash pocket. Earl pulled it out and laid it on top of the suit jacket to find a white, gray-striped dress shirt. Beside it was a small box.

Earl fumbled with the lid. Inside was a stiff, tall white collar to go with the dress shirt. In another narrow box was a pair of soft gray kidskin gloves. And then, of course, was a silk, dove gray tie as well. He pulled out the matching navy pants last of all.

Too stunned to think, Earl moved to the second striped box. Inside was a black, wool overcoat. Beside it, within the hatbox, nestled a gray Homburg, a black band circling it. Earl plucked it up and set it on his head. A perfect fit.

Polished black shoes lay in the shoebox, glossy under the light of the kerosene lamp sitting on the dresser.

Earl's throat tightened as he took it all in. He hadn't worn a suit so fine since he was a young man. He could see himself again, young and twenty, with Lorena on his arm as they strolled together in their neighborhood in New York City. He could feel her in his arms as they had danced together in a ballroom surrounded by friends and the drinks he once found irresistible.

Mr. Wallace meant well. He only wanted to help him find a starting place to earn Lorena's regard and possibly love.

How could he even hope to contend with George wearing old, faded duds, washing out into the background?

Earl caught his reflection in the dresser mirror, the Homburg still perched on his head. A mockery of the past. The clothes on the bed were wretchedly out of place in this simple, farmhouse bedroom.

Every piece shouted gentleman. And Earl was no gentleman. Not by a long shot. He ground his teeth. The urge to crush that hat flew over him like wildfire. Instead, he tossed it into the box.

The past was indeed the past. The present glowered right back at him. A plain, simple, sawmill worker who could barely rub a couple of dollars together. A terrible truth twisted round and round him. He would never be anything more than this.

Lorena could never share his life. It was asking too much of her.

Mechanically, Earl folded the suit, placing each piece perfectly back in place. He couldn't wear it.

"I won't pretend to be something I'm not. Lord, help me. I have to let her go," Earl muttered as his quivering hands replaced the lids on the boxes. He piled them up and set them in the corner.

Turning, he sank down on his knees at the bedside and wept.

⁂

THE TINY MANTLE clock struck midnight as the firelight dwindled. An arm over her forehead, Lorena lay in bed staring up at the ceiling. Across the room, Father's rhythmic, soft snoring broke the silence.

Dear Father wanting so much to help. As soon as they reached the teacherage earlier, he had handed her a thick package wrapped in brown paper secured with stiff yarn. After cutting it, she unwrapped it to find a stack of sheet music, all classical pieces, along with materials for composing the arrangements. Father had thought of everything, even buying duplicates of each one so that they both would have a copy.

She had thumbed through some of them until a terrible ache swelled within her. Memories of all their times working and learning until they played together as one crowded her mind. Hours upon hours until they both somehow knew what the other one was going to do. It bound them together in ways she couldn't describe. The music had enriched their love.

The red and cream snowball quilt covering Lorena rose gradually and fell with her sigh. No matter how hard she tried, she couldn't shake the image of Earl's expression when he looked at her tonight.

It took her back twenty years. She gently tugged the gold chain around her neck and brought the ring out from under the collar of her gown. Within the band, she ran her finger across the engraving. Bound Eternally to Thee. His choosing.

The once so beautiful sentiment between them had turned into a bitter, hard burden. In the years after Lane's disappearance, she felt those chains almost physically at times. During those moments, the Lord had been her only solace. Lane's return had released those chains.

Another kind, however, was closing around her heart.

Resentment bubbled up in the form of tears. Somewhere,

deep down, she knew she was powerless to erase him from her heart, but she refused to admit it even to herself.

How would she ever get through working with him again?

Hours later, the early, scarlet flush of dawn glowed through the trees as Lorena stepped from the teacherage. Stifling a yawn, she bound her coat a little more tightly around her and tugged her hat farther down. Sleep had eluded her all night. Dusky shadows hovered under her eyes.

She lifted her gaze toward the graveyard and stepped that direction. Perhaps a morning walk would do her some good. Lifting her skirts, she breathed in deeply, admiring the countryside so hushed at this hour. It was the time of day when the earth seemed to hold its breath.

Though troubled, God's peace hovered over her soul unexplained. The silence surrounding her felt like a comforting embrace. Far from the hustle and rumble of the city, God seemed nearer in this place.

Only the brightest stars still shone, fading one by one as the sky grew brighter. Ahead of her, a few deer stood in the path. Their ears perked up. The next second they leaped into the woods.

Lorena neared the resting place and reverently passed the rocks and headstones. As she approached the eleven, she froze.

On each grave lay a fresh bouquet of wildflowers. With a gasp, she rushed forward. Yes, they were new. Forked asters, boneset, black-eyed Susans, and goldenrod, wet with dew, unwilted. Yesterday's bouquets were gone.

Lorena whirled around in every direction, her eyes wildly searching for the giver. At her feet, fresh footprints in the dew dotted the grass among the stones. Forgetting her skirts, she stumbled alongside them until the trail ended at the edge of the tree line.

Whoever did this came through the thicket. And only moments before she arrived.

Lorena shook her head and turned around. She eyed the tracks as she walked back. She could tell where the person had come and gone, but the steps mingled together so that it was hard to tell the size.

The flowers lay perfectly centered on each lump of soil, and the wee one's again had the largest spray of all.

"Lord, who is doing this?" she whispered through fingertips on her lips.

As the sunlight burst over the hills, its warmth caressed her face and with it rose Lorena's profound gratitude.

"And there were new bouquets there early this morning."

Edith pulled the cup of hot tea from her lips as the steam rose and curled around her forehead. She swallowed. "You saw no one?"

"No one. I saw only the footprints. They ended at the thicket." Lorena watched a myriad of emotions pass over Edith's face.

"That is so very kind."

Edith's voice filled with unshed tears, and Lorena refrained from telling her about the baby's bouquet.

"Whoever makes them takes special thought. Each one is arranged so that one flower compliments the other. They're absolutely beautiful."

"I wonder if it's Harley Ray's mother. She is always picking flowers and arranging them on her table. And they live that direction." Edith took another sip.

"But to go through the woods?" Lorena's fingers wrapped around her cup, soaking in the warmth. She breathed in the fragrant aroma.

Edith nodded. "There's all kinds of trails. It sounds like something she would do." Her eyes clouded. "I haven't even gone there yet. Can't." She rubbed her forearms. "I'm a coward."

Lorena nearly dropped her cup. "Edith! You're most certainly not a coward!" Setting it aside, she reached across the table and laid her hand on Edith's arm. "I'm so proud of you. You are one of the bravest ladies I know."

A tremor shook Edith's lips. Then her face crumpled. "NO! I can't even put flowers on my own baby's grave! My baby's!" She shoved back from the table, the chair grating across the floor.

Rising, Edith darted from the room. Lorena rushed down the small hallway after her and stopped at the bedroom doorway.

Edith lay sprawled across the bed, face down, sobbing uncontrollably. With swift steps, Lorena crossed the braided rug and knelt by her side. Biting back her own tears, she stroked Edith's ebony hair.

"There. There. Edith, darling, you'll be sick if you continue."

Edith shouted into her pillow. "I don't care! I don't! Just let me die!"

Lorena gasped. "Honey, you don't mean that."

Edith lifted her blanched face, her eyes huge and dark. "You don't understand. No one does."

"Darling, yes, we do. I understand." Lorena soothed, still stroking her hair. "I know what it is to lose a child."

A tiny spark flamed in Edith's eyes. "Lane didn't die. My baby did!" Sobbing again, Edith buried her face into the pillow.

Pain seared across Lorena's chest. How could she console her daughter? Just then, in the front room, the door shut and footsteps plodded across the floor.

Lorena jumped up and collided with Earl's solid chest in the hallway. He gently grabbed her shoulders. Stunned, she stepped back and looked up into his face.

"What's wrong?" Concern lined his forehead.

"It's Edith." Lorena grabbed his arm and pulled him into the room. "She's grieving, but I can't calm her."

Earl hurried to the bedside and laid a hand on Edith's shoulder. "Edith. Edith. We're here. Let us help you."

"Please go away!" Edith's shoulders shook.

Lorena saw the heartache in Earl's face as he bent closer over Edith. "No, sweetheart. Your mother and I are not going away. We're going to get through this. Together." He reached down, his hands tender, and turned Edith over. "It's going to be all right." Without warning, he scooped her up in his arms.

The sudden movement silenced Edith. Her lips parted in surprise. Stepping back from the bed, Earl turned and carried Edith into the front room.

Dumbfounded, Lorena could do nothing but follow.

Earl, tall and broad-shouldered, carried Edith as though she were no heavier than a feather pillow. An old, buried memory intruded into Lorena's mind. A four-year-old Edith, fallen on the gravel drive of their weekend cottage, shrieking. Blood gushing from her little knee. Earl, who had been napping in the hammock, leapt up and reached her first. He had done the same thing then. He scooped her up, carried her inside, and held her while Lorena had washed and bandaged the wound. He had dried her tears then.

A different wound bruised Edith now. One not so easily fixed.

Lorena stifled the rest of the memory lest her heart soften and focused on the present. Edith was still sobbing but much quieter now. Carefully, Earl eased into a chair, still holding her. He said nothing. He seemed to know that talking would only worsen things.

Turning her head, Edith hid her face in his shoulder. Small hiccups quivered across her stomach. Lorena pulled another chair close and sank down onto it. Her heart throbbed with a mother's pain as she watched her child grieve.

Tears smarted her eyes. Earl rested his chin on Edith's head, but his eyes sought Lorena's and found them. Tears glimmered in his as well. For a long moment, Lorena held his gaze, then wrenched hers away.

She tried her best to harden her heart. Yet somehow, in that moment, she couldn't.

15

"Just tell us where to put 'em, Earl." Mr. Ray hopped down from his wagon along with his son Andrew.

After a husky thanks, Earl showed them where to carry the bedstead and mattress.

"No need to thank us. It's an old frame and mattress, but my wife thought you could use it." Mr. Ray's face reddened as he and Andrew lifted the mattress and carted it inside Earl's new house.

"Tell her that I'm much obliged. It will sure beat sleeping on the floor." Earl reached into the back of the wagon and lifted out a tall, pine headboard, plain and worn smooth from years of dusting. After bracing it against the side of the wagon, he plucked out the footboard, then gathered both pieces to carry inside.

Another wagon rolled into the yard carrying Guy and Lane while Harley Ray and Jimmy sat in the back.

"Mr. Steen, we got a little something for you here." Guy reined in the team and set the brake.

Earl turned and nearly dropped the head and foot boards. In the back of the wagon stood a table with four chairs.

"I, I don't know what to say."

Guy jumped down, then reached for his wife. "The look on your face says it all. Kind of looks like that time I punched you in the nose." He threw Earl a sly grin.

Earl flushed with a slight chuckle. "I reckon you winded me then just like now. How did y'all do it?"

"We worked a few extra hours at my place just about every evening." Harley Ray helped Jimmy out, then handed him a chair.

Earl struggled for the right words. "It means a lot, what y'all have done for me. I won't forget it."

"I hope not 'cause I'll need a place to go whenever Lane sends me to the doghouse." Guy winked while Lane swatted him on the shoulder.

A deep laugh shook Earl's shoulders. Chilly and refreshing, like a long, frosty drink of spring water. Clean all the way down.

"Y'all come on inside and have a look. I decorated it myself."

The yard echoed with the men's deep laughter. Lane's eyes widened in wonder as she watched her father's merriment. Reaching up, she pulled a familiar, worn case from the wagon seat and brought it to him.

"I thought you might like to have this," she said almost shyly. She cradled the violin case carefully in her hands.

If his hands weren't full, he would have hugged her. He gave her a tender smile instead. Stepping aside, Earl let Lane enter the new house. The spicy smell of cut lumber permeated the rooms, reminding Earl of the sawmill, of the loss they all suffered.

Several days had passed since he had held Edith in his arms while she cried quietly into his shoulder. After a long while, she had wiped her face, risen, and apologized to both of them for her outburst. Like a boarded-up house, she had shuttered her spirit. Lorena didn't seem to know what to say, but neither did he for that matter. Without a word, he had nodded his goodbye.

He had been finishing up here ever since.

Jimmy interrupted his thoughts, lugging another chair through the door. "We can have a fine game of checkers on this here table, can't we, Mr. Steen?"

Behind him, Guy and Harley Ray hauled the table up the steps and through the door. Shuffling across the floor, they set it in the middle of the room.

"I think we can have a bunch of games." Earl ruffled the blond head.

"Yippee!" The boy bounded outside, clearing the steps and landing flat-footed in the grass.

Lane perused the rooms, one bedroom, the living room, and a kitchen. "The men did a good job, didn't they?"

Nodding, Earl handed the head and footboards to Mr. Ray and Andrew. "It's good and tight. Maybe, in a year or two, I can add another room and a front porch."

Lane ran a hand over the smooth doorframe. "Maybe it's a hidden blessing, losing the old place." Her eyes spoke more than her words, but Earl knew exactly what she meant.

"There are no memories." Earl drew in a breath and let it out gradually. No shadows lurked here. Everything was new, untouched by either good or bad. No matter where he looked, the past couldn't visit these rooms with harsh, vicious scenes. Old words, smells, and sounds didn't whisper from these walls. Only his mind held them now.

"It isn't even laid out the same way. I like it." Lane wandered over to the fireplace and ran her hand along it as well. "A window in every room. Plenty of light."

"I like that best of all."

Mr. Ray clomped into the room. "Earl, I've got a small wood

stove that would be just right for this room. It's out in my barn. I'll bring it by tomorrow, and we can put it in."

"That's too much, Thomas. The tornado didn't carry off the cookstove. We set it up yesterday. It'll do."

"Naw. It'll heat the kitchen, but the rest of your house will be cold come winter." Mr. Ray jerked a gritty thumb over his shoulder toward his place. "That potbellied stove ain't helping nobody while it's in the barn. It might as well be here."

Loathed to say the words, Earl shuffled his feet. "When I can, I'll pay you."

A grin split Mr. Ray's face, showing a missing bottom tooth. "I reckon you can't do that since it was give to me. It wouldn't be right."

Unsure whether to believe him, Earl shook his head.

"Besides we're counting on you and Mrs. Steen to save Valley Creek, you know. It's the least we can do."

Earl opened his mouth, but Lane's moan stopped him. Whipping his head around, he saw her stumble over to a chair and sink down. She slid the violin case onto the table. Trembling, she slumped over it and laid her chalky face on its cool, black surface.

Earl rushed to her side. "Lane! What's wrong?"

"I, I don't know." She moaned again.

A scuffle of several feet hurried across the floor. Guy rounded the table, laying a hand on the small of her back. On the doorstep, Harley Ray whipped a kerchief out of his pocket and thrust it into Jimmy's hand.

"Pump some water on this and bring it back."

At the table, Guy leaned close to Lane's ear. "Honey, what's going on?"

Lane shook her head. "I hurt. Here." She rubbed low on her middle. "And I feel dizzy."

By this time, Jimmy pushed past Harley Ray and scampered

across the room. "Here's this, Mama Lane." He raised her head with his hand and laid it against her forehead.

Eyes fluttering closed, Lane groaned again.

"Do we need to get Doc?" asked Andrew, inching closer.

Lane shook her head. "Not yet. Just let me stay here 'till it passes."

Standing quietly, the men looked at one another then back at her as though not knowing quite what to do. After several minutes passed, the color ebbed back into Lane's face. Slowly sitting up, she pulled the kerchief from her forehead.

"I'm sorry." She blinked. "I don't know what came over me."

Unease flashed in Guy's eyes as he glanced across at Earl. His hand caressed Lane's shoulder. "It's all right. You just sit tight until we're done, then I'll get you home."

Earl said nothing, but he intended to have a word with Lorena as soon as he could.

EARL JOSTLED in the seat as the wagon crunched through dry ruts along the road to Edith's. Back at his house, everything was in order, the bed assembled and made, the table and chairs placed near the window, his few belongings laid in a crude box at the foot of his bed. Yet no suit. He had left it at Lane's, hoping to forget any reminder of things out of his reach.

Through the trees, Edith and Harley Ray's house emerged into view. As he pulled into the yard, he stopped and climbed down. Overhead several squirrels barked at him, no doubt annoyed by his interruption.

He was sure Lorena would be annoyed as well. He took a steadying breath and removed his dusty hat as he climbed the steps.

At his knock, he heard footsteps nearing. The door opened, and George filled the gap.

Mercy! Did the man follow Lorena wherever she went?

George's lips crimped together in a thin, hard line. If George thought he would ask his permission to go inside, he'd better think again.

"Excuse me, Dr. Curtis."

Earl took a step forward, but George stood rigid, his jaw set. Pausing mid-step, Earl locked eyes with him and steeled his tone with as much calm as a still, deep pool of water, the consequences hidden beneath.

"I'm not here to cause any trouble, and if I were you, I'd do the same. Excuse me."

George flushed a dark crimson and parted his lips as if to retort. He hesitated, clamped his mouth shut once again, and stepped aside.

No one was in the front room. Earl lifted his voice only a little. "Lorena."

In the hallway, a door clicked shut and Lorena came toward him, her face pale and weary.

"Edith is lying down. She has a headache today. Is Harley Ray finished at your place?"

Earl nodded. "He's gone over to his father's to help get a potbellied stove out of the barn."

Lorena rubbed her arms as if she were cold in the warm house. "I'm sorry you won't be able to see Edith right now."

"That's all right." He glanced over his shoulder at George still standing by the door. "I'd like to have a word with you alone, if you don't mind."

"Of course. Will you excuse us, George?"

With a brusque nod, he stepped outside, shutting the door behind him. Earl stepped closer, careful to maintain his distance.

"It's about Lane. I think you need to see her." He briefly explained what happened earlier. "Maybe you can persuade her to go see Doc. She almost fainted."

Alarm lit her eyes. "Yes, I'll go now. Let me tell Edith I'm leaving." She turned but Earl's voice caught her.

"Will you let me take you? It'll save time."

Lorena frowned a little, her lovely blue eyes growing dark as she scanned his face. "I don't know."

Earl held her gaze and his breath. "Please."

Sighing, Lorena nodded. "Very well. There's no use trying to avoid one another around here, is there?" Then, she surprised him by casting a wry smile his way.

Earl's heart warmed. "No, no I reckon there's not."

Steady, Mister. Just remember you don't have a chance.

Looking away, Earl turned and headed outside to the wagon, passing George as though he wasn't standing there. Deep down, the ache of their broken friendship stung him. He couldn't change it, though. He deserved every bit of George's contempt.

He heard Lorena's voice behind him, then George's.

"I see. I wish I had a way to take you." His tone was genial like the George he remembered. "Would you like me to come along?"

Putting on his hat, Earl turned and watched beneath the shaded brim. Lorena shook her head as she descended the steps.

"Thank you, but I'll be fine."

George accompanied her to the wagon, but she didn't take his arm. Once more, he fixed his eyes on Earl, a silent challenge simmering in them. Surely Earl wouldn't dare help Lorena into the wagon, would he?

Earl swallowed down a flash of temper and rounded the wagon instead. Grabbing the reins, he climbed up and waited while George helped Lorena. A perfect gentleman. He fixed his gaze ahead as though neither one of them were there.

Lorena settled beside him. It was the closest they had been in ages. Inches yet worlds apart. As Earl flicked the reins, he lifted a silent prayer upward. He felt Lorena shift as far away as possible on the seat.

For a long while, they rode in silence with only the sounds of the valley filling in the space between them. Earl opened his lips to voice the thing he dreaded most of all. He needed to let her know that he would set her free as soon as possible. His palms grew clammy.

He cleared his dry throat. "Lorena."

"Um."

"While we're here, I need to speak with you about something." He took her silence for permission to plow ahead. "It's about George."

Lorena suddenly sat ramrod straight. "What about him?" Her sharp tone held an unspoken warning.

"I understand that he wants to ..." He faltered, losing his nerve as her clear, beautiful eyes pierced his. Sunlight danced through the dark, golden strands of her hair.

"What?" she demanded.

His chest tightened. Every fiber of his being rebelled against telling her. As long as her eyes looked into his, he knew he couldn't do it. He steeled himself and turned his head away.

"I'll have papers drawn up to set you free." The words tumbled out in a rush.

Her sharp intake of breath almost physically hurt him. Against his will, he turned toward her.

Color flamed in her face before dying away to leave her features ashen. Lorena opened her mouth. Shut it. Blinked several times. Her hand pressed against her throat.

Earl caught himself just in time before he reached out to touch her other hand.

"Stop the wagon, Earl."

"What?"

"Just stop it." Her words clipped out. "I'll walk the rest of the way."

Earl knitted his brows. "It's still a quarter of a mile to Lane's."

"I don't care. Let me out."

Before Earl could completely stop, Lorena clambered down. She took a few steps, then stopped, keeping her back to him. She lifted her chin.

With all his might, Earl yearned to jump down and take that chin in his hand. To look deeply into her eyes beyond the past and future. To a place where they might forget only but a moment. But what then?

Lorena's voice came to him stern, full of tears. "Don't ever say that to me again."

EVERY FOOTFALL SEEMED to tread on Lorena's heart as she rushed away. Once, when she dared glance over her shoulder, she saw Earl still sitting in the middle of the path as though turned to stone.

Bitter tears spilled down her cheeks. She swiped them with trembling hands. To be free. They had been apart for so many years, Earl had dishonored his vows to her, and he had shattered their family. The choice should be simple. It was hers for the taking.

"Heavenly Father, please guide me. I don't know what to choose." Without thinking, her hand reached up and covered the hidden lump beneath her blouse where her ring rested. Bound Eternally to Thee.

Freedom with the stroke of a pen and a fistful of papers. Though trees and hills surrounded her, Lorena saw only Earl's stricken face as he uttered those words. She had never seen such a look in his eyes. Whether she accepted it or not, it shook her to the core.

Even with a piece of paper, would she ever really be free?

Collecting her skirts, she almost ran the rest of the way to Lane's, chased by a truth she refused to acknowledge.

A few hours later, Lorena sat at Doc Brown's, much more patient and calm than she had been with Earl. The visit and ride to Doc's settled the turmoil in her heart. She gazed around the tiny office, a small add-on to the main house. A polished roll-top desk with a chair sat across from her. Behind it stood a door to his examination room. Plain and unassuming like the man himself. The faint odor of pipe tobacco twitched Lorena's nose. She lifted a finger and stifled a sneeze.

The door opened and Doc's face appeared. "Mrs. Steen, you can come now."

Although Lorena tried to read his expression, nothing gave his thoughts away. She entered, eyes darting to Lane. Still a little pale, Lane sat on the examining table looking more like a little girl than a grown woman nearly nineteen. Deep, abiding love washed over Lorena.

Stepping beside her, she squeezed Lane's shoulder and gazed into her round, blue-green eyes. So like Earl's.

Doc gave a gruff, low cough, drawing their attention.

"What's wrong, Doc?" asked Lane, her voice small and tight.

Methodically, Doc plucked the spectacles from his nose and tapped the rim across the palm of his hand. "Not a thing." His sober eyes shifted from one to the other. "You're young, healthy, strong—"

"Then why?"

"Where are your manners, girl, interrupting me like that?" Doc leaned his hip against the corner of a small cupboard. "Now where was I ... oh ... you're young, healthy, and strong. A perfect candidate for a new mama." A grin crinkled around now twinkling eyes.

A stunned hush fell over the two women. Shaking his head, Doc plunked the spectacles back on his nose. "Ladies, now we all know it isn't in the drinkin' water."

Wonderment flushed Lane's face like a beautiful rose. "Me? A mama? Doc, are you certain?"

"Around next May, dear."

Lorena squeezed Lane against her heart. "Darling! I'm so happy for you! Oh!" Joy surged through them as they held each other.

Pushing away from the cupboard, Doc came over and touched Lane's elbow. "I heard yesterday that school will be starting over at the church soon."

"Yes. The school at Booneville is donating some of their old books. We're expecting them any day now."

Doc nodded. "Teaching requires a lot of time on your feet. As long as you're feeling well, that's fine. But I want you to give me your word that when you start feeling sick, you'll rest."

"But—"

"No buts. When you get further along, I'll meet with the rest of the board. Maybe we can persuade Edith to take over for you. The change would do her good." He patted her arm. "And I'd like to do everything I can to bring this one safely into the world."

Lane covered her mouth with a hand. "Oh, Mother! What about Edith? How can I tell her this?"

"We'll find a way, and we'll pray for the right timing." Lorena's eyes pled with Doc for the right answer.

"Lane, it's gonna be hard for Edith. There's no denying it, but one thing's certain. She's a strong woman, and when her body and mind heal, there will be more chances for her to have babies too."

After they left Doc's office and climbed into the wagon, Lane spoke. "I'd like to keep this a secret for a little while longer for Edith's sake. I'll tell Guy and Father, but no one else for now."

Lorena flicked the reins, and the wagon jerked forward. "I

understand. Lane, please take care of yourself. I pray you never have to ..." Her voice dwindled.

Lane shuddered. "I know." Straightening, she lifted her shoulders. "We'll take it one day at a time."

Lorena answered her daughter's brave smile with one of her own.

16

"Well."

The lady drew in a long breath, fingering the pearls that dangled around her neck. Rarely at a loss for words, she begged her mind to think of something to say, but the right words deserted her.

"Ella."

His voice had changed little over the years. A little deeper, a little more husky, yet still the voice of her long, lost brother. Her twin for one month out of the year. When they were younger, they savored the distinction in their family, born only eleven months apart. Every year, that one month eclipsed the rest. This was that month.

Earl held out a work-worn hand. For a moment, Ella hesitated before gingerly reaching out and curling her slender fingers around his. Though rough, his hand was warm. Her gaze traveled from the toes of his shoes, his washed-out overalls, his auburn hair, then to those blue-green eyes. Sudden, unexpected tears stung behind her eyelids.

He coughed a little, as though uncomfortable with her perusal. Flushing, Ella stepped back. Her hands fluttered up to straighten the wide, oblong brim of her hat trimmed with a floral, blue-gray scarf.

"Earl. I hardly know what to say." Her soft, Georgia drawl filled the space between them.

"That's not like you." Earl took his turn scrutinizing her appearance. Ella tipped up her chin just a smidge.

"No, although I have my reasons."

"And very good ones." Earl motioned to her trunk and other luggage on the depot's platform. "I'll load these up, and we can be on our way, if it suits you."

"Very well."

Once they were on their way, Ella's hat teetered wildly like a seesaw with each bump and rut. She reached up and pulled loose a golden beetle hatpin with jeweled wings.

"If I wear hats around here, I'll have to do a better job of pinning them." Setting the hat in her lap, she carefully jabbed the pin through it. The fresh rush of air fanned through her thick, wavy cloud of cinnamon hair. "And this is Valley Creek?"

Earl shook his head. "Not yet. We'll reach my place before we get to town. What's left of it." He then told her about the devastating storm. Ella listened as he told about the aftermath, noting the emotions he tried to swallow down. Her heart tugged, especially when he told her of Edith's baby.

"I'm so sorry, Earl. I wish there was something I could do."

"Thanks. It's just one day at a time."

An awkward silence spread around them. Ella's eyes roamed over the scenery. Beautiful, secluded, almost cut off from the rest of the world. Indeed, Earl had hidden well for fourteen years. Ella chewed her bottom lip.

"Why did you write me that letter ... the one that gave away your whereabouts?"

The Adam's apple bobbed in Earl's throat. "I wanted to get away from here, and I had no money. I needed just enough to start over."

Ella raised one eyebrow. "And disappear again."

Keeping his face straight ahead, Earl nodded.

"You were willing to risk being found?"

"I was pretty desperate and past caring at that point."

"Were you in debt, in trouble?"

"No debt but in plenty of trouble ... not with the law, just my own demons." He turned to look at her then. "I owe you a debt of gratitude for sendin' that letter on to Lorena. You helped save Lane. And you helped save me."

Ella blinked against that blue-green gaze like one gazing at the sun. She shifted away and clamped down on more tears.

"You don't owe me anything. I only did what I thought was right."

Another long pause followed before she heard Earl sigh.

"I reckon Mother and Father are gone?"

More tears thundered, but Ella gulped them down hard. "Yes. It's been about 10 years, almost a year apart." She noticed Earl tighten his grip on the reins.

"I'm sorry."

"I'd rather not speak of it." She cut a glance sideways at him, but the shadow from his hat hid his expression. His face remained fixed ahead.

"What about our brother Douglas?"

Thankful for the change in subject, Ella's voice lightened. "He married Barbara Hastings, and they have four children. Three boys and one spoiled but delightful daughter. He runs the plantation and bosses the rest of us from daylight 'til dark. Such a prig!"

"And what about you?"

Fresh sorrow squeezed Ella's heart. "What about me?" she shrugged. "I live in the cottage on the eastern part of the plantation ... my inheritance."

"What about Charles Gibson? You were engaged."

The gold locket brooch pinned above her heart seemed to grow heavier. "He died a few weeks before our wedding."

When Earl remained silent, Ella struggled to fill the gap. "I never had much heart for anyone else after that. I tried. I finally gave up and decided being an old maid suited me very well. Mother was devastated." She tried to laugh.

"And you?"

"I do very well."

Nothing but the chirruping of birds filled their conversation for the rest of the ride. Ella was tempted to pinch herself to make sure all of this was real. Thoughts of Mother and Father crowded her mind. Their sorrow over losing their youngest to the unknown. They had always hoped to see him once more, even on their deathbeds.

Ella shook her head. What would they be thinking now? The answer lay deep in her heart and had kept her awake many nights.

The wagon turned and jostled up a narrow, short path into a clearing. A tiny, unobtrusive house stood on a foundation of native stones stacked and spaced evenly on all sides. The few windows gaped at them, void of curtains.

"Here we are." Earl reined the horses in, set the brake, and stepped down.

Ella's jaw fell slack. "Gracious!"

A wry smile played around the corners of Earl's mouth. "Not quite like home, is it?"

Ella blinked, pinching her lips together. "Not quite." Shifting her eyes to Earl, she reddened as he read the thoughts on her face.

"If you'd like to go back to the station, I'll take you."

For one fleeting second, she opened her mouth to say yes. She had no business here. What had she been thinking?

"I never imagined this. I mean, I knew you were ..."

"Not far from the poorhouse? Knowing it and seeing it are

different things. This is my life, Ella, and I won't blame you if you want to cut this visit short."

Her russet brows drew together. "You had so very much. And to come to ... this?" She flung a hand toward the house. Incredulous, she searched her brother's face. He stood looking up at her, one hand resting on the seat, patient, unruffled by her words. An expression she'd never seen on his face smoothed the lines around his mouth and eyes. The ambition was gone. Peace had usurped it.

Earl nodded. "That's so, but I'm content most of the time."

"Most of the time? What happens when you're not?"

"I have to lean a little bit harder on my Lord."

Ella's violet eyes widened. Well, that certainly flummoxed her. Perhaps his change was true after all.

Earl started climbing back into the wagon.

"Whatever are you doing?"

"If we're gonna get back to the station, we'd best do it now."

"Hold it!" Ella pushed his shoulder and scooted forward. "I didn't come all this way after all these years to just turn around."

"Are you sure you want to rough it?" A challenge glimmered in Earl's eyes as his lips twitched.

"If my memory serves right, Earl Steen, I used to go camping with you in the woods for days on end much to Mother's horror. I can *rough* it when I have to."

Stepping back, Earl chuckled. "Have it your way. Still spunky, I see." He reached up a hand to help her down.

Ella resisted the urge to roll her eyes, focusing instead on the house. "At least it's not a tent. And it's a good thing I brought my sewing. The windows are begging to be covered."

Tossing back his head, Earl laughed deep and hard as he hadn't done in years.

———— ❧ ————

Mustering all the composure she possessed, Lorena grasped the heavy stack of sheet music as Earl topped the church steps with the violin case in his hands. The coppery tints of his hair glinted in the late afternoon sun.

She stood frozen in the center of the aisle as he filled the doorway and paused, his eyes searching hers. Then his gaze fell to the stack in her hands.

"Here," he said, laying the case on the back pew. "Let me take those." Before she could protest, he gently plucked them away, his fingers brushing hers. He gave no sign that he felt the touch.

After he laid them on the pulpit, he turned and rubbed his hands together. "Lorena, I don't like this any more than you do, mostly because it puts you in a hard position."

"I just hope we can get through it." She chewed her bottom lip. "I suppose we have little choice, do we? Everyone is counting on us."

"I've been thinking. Would it be all right if I write the arrangements? It might take a little of the pressure from you."

Lorena nodded with a wan smile. "You were always better at that."

"Good." Earl passed her to fetch his case. He smelled of fresh, dewy grass and open fields. As Earl picked it up, he hesitated, tapping his fingers on the dull, black surface. "I was also thinking that maybe for this first practice we ought to just forget the classical music."

Lorena frowned. "I don't understand."

Earl's chest heaved with a sigh as his eyes looked everywhere but at her. "Trying to play classical music together after all this time would be like trying to dance before learnin' to walk." He stepped closer, still avoiding her stare. "It might be easier if we just start playing some hymns first. To get the feel of things."

With her lips slightly parted, Lorena stared at him in shock.

Earl kept his eyes trained on one of the windows, his inner emotions masked.

"You've given this a lot of thought."

Earl nodded.

"Just improvise at first?"

He nodded again. "If it would suit you."

His thoughtfulness touched a place in her heart where she didn't want to feel. To hide a shudder, she turned toward the glossy, new piano and struggled to keep her voice even.

"I think that's a sensible idea." As she passed one of the pews, she grabbed a hymnal.

Behind her, Earl's steps followed. She pressed a hand against her churning stomach and sat on the piano bench. All eighty-eight of the ivory and ebony keys stretched out and seemed to mock her.

Remember, this is for Valley Creek, an inner voice reminded her.

Her fingers tentatively ran across the cool, silky keys. Laying the violin case on the first pew, Earl snapped the latches open and lifted the instrument out.

"It'll have to be tuned." He sounded apologetic.

"Of course."

Earl positioned himself near the rear leg of the piano, the farthest away from her and turned his back. A pent-up breath escaped Lorena. At least, he wouldn't be looking at her. Reaching into his pocket, he fetched out a tuning fork, tapped it against his knee, and laid the fork's point on the bridge. A perfect *A* pitch hummed through the soundboard.

Earl took it from there, stroking the strings slowly. A. D. G. E. The sounds melded together little by little until they blended in perfect agreement with each other.

Transfixed, Lorena listened. Her heart sped up, and she clenched her teeth. For pity sakes, it was just a violin.

Yet it was Earl drawing the bow.

"There," he said, his voice a little dry. "I'll adjust as needed. When you start playing, I'll join in."

Lorena thumbed through the pages without seeing a single hymn. This wouldn't do. She wedged a finger in a spot and opened. Placed it on the music rack.

She closed her eyes. Pulled in a slow, deep breath, filling her lungs. Exhaled as much tension as possible. Opened her eyes. Positioned her fingers. Began.

> When peace, like a river, attendeth my way,
> When sorrows like sea billows roll;
> Whatever my lot, Thou has taught me to know,
> It is well, it is well with my soul.

Earl lifted his bow and joined the piano. As the violin's notes sang, a sweet, sharp pain pierced Lorena. Her fingers stiffened and halted. Earl stopped as well.

"Lorena?" He glanced over his shoulder.

She inhaled again. Exhaled. "I'm sorry." Placing her fingers on the keys, she began once more.

They made it through the chorus. Lorena's emotions rose with each harmonious note. She tried to ignore the bend of his head over the instrument, a sight she once loved so well.

> My sin—oh, the bliss of this glorious tho't—
> My sin—not in part, but the whole,
> Is nailed to the cross and I bear it no more,
> Praise the Lord—

Gasping, Lorena pushed back and sprang from the seat. The hymnal crashed to the floor. Earl spun around, his eyes widening.

"I'm sorry! I can't do anymore!"

"Lorena, I—"

"NO!" Lorena sobbed. "Not now. I need some time to settle myself. We'll try again tomorrow."

Her scurrying feet echoed against the wooden floor as she rushed down the aisle. Down the steps she swept, taking wide strides toward the teacherage. At least Father was visiting at Lane's, and she would have time alone.

When she reached the teacherage, she thrust open the door.

At the table, George sat reading a book as though he belonged there. Lorena stepped over the threshold as he stood. Her heart plummeted to her toes.

He must have sensed it. "I'm sorry. I came to call."

Lorena shut the door with a little more force than necessary. "You mean you came to check after my practice with Earl."

With a dry smile, George spread his hands. "You know me too well."

"Perhaps you're just too obvious."

George's dark blue eyes studied her for a moment before answering. "Perhaps so. Things didn't go so well?"

Shaking her head, Lorena draped her shawl over a peg. George stepped back and gestured toward the table. "I took the liberty and made tea for us. I hope you don't mind."

Lorena looked at the simple, yet perfectly set table. A copper tea kettle sat in the center with two milky white cups. The thoughtful gesture eased the tension a little. George held the chair as she sat, then took his seat across from her.

"I'm sorry to sound ungracious. Thank you for the tea, George."

Before she could reach across to pour the cups, George poured them instead. Lorena fumbled with the edge of the tablecloth, unsure of what to say next.

"Do you want to talk about it? I'm sure Earl was on his best behavior." Sarcasm tinged his remark as he handed Lorena the cup.

"Earl did his best. He kept his distance. It was me."

"How so?"

"You remember. Music was so much a part of our lives. We loved playing together by the hour." Lorena sipped the tea, drawing comfort from its warmth. "Music brought us together."

"It also tore you both apart."

"His ambition did."

"And now?" George leaned forward a little. "What are you afraid of, Lorena?"

Snatches of melodies played through Lorena's mind. Shards of memories like broken china pierced her heart.

"The memories. I don't want to remember, but seeing Earl and playing the music ..." She shuddered. "I don't want to relive any of it."

George swiped a piece of fuzz from his knee. The minutes stretched long and quiet before he spoke. "It's hard to compete with memories."

Their gazes mingled across the table, unspoken thoughts whispering between them. Just one chance to discover if there could be something more. Freedom with the stroke of a pen. Did she really want to spend the rest of her life alone?

Sighing, George tapped the side of his cup. "You know, Lorena, memories are one thing. Reality is another."

"I know." Lorena's chin trembled.

"The here-and-now is all we have." He reached over and captured her hand in his. Tenderly, he stroked her knuckles with his thumb, his gaze never leaving hers.

Lorena resisted the urge to pull her hand away. It had been so long since she felt cherished.

"You're very quiet this evening." Sliding a tip of thread over her tongue, Ella threaded her needle. The crackling fireplace broke the chill settling over the house.

At the table, Earl nodded as he sifted through the pile of sheet music. "I have a lot to do. I've got to pick the music and write the arrangements."

"You used to be quite good at it."

"Used to be. That's not what Valley Creek is counting on." Earl grimaced as he laid a piece of music on a pile to be reworked. Closing his eyes, he leaned back in the chair, his mind far away from his task.

With his thumb and forefinger, he rubbed his eyes roughly. He understood how Lorena felt. Like stumbling back through time. When she started playing the music, it took everything he had not to run away too. Their reasons differed, but the feelings were the same.

"You can't avoid it, Earl."

Earl's eyes popped open as Ella stitched away on material Lane had given her to make curtains. She raised her eyebrows knowingly at him. He knew there was no need in asking what she was talking about. She still had the uncanny ability to see right through him.

"You might as well plunge right in and figure out if there's anything left between the two of you." Ella's violet eyes snapped a deeper lavender in the firelight.

Was Ella blind? Didn't she understand he couldn't hope for a future with Lorena? Not only did she rightfully detest him, he couldn't provide for her in the way she deserved.

"It's not that simple."

Once more, Ella put her deft finger on the thing that stung the most. "Why? Because of this?" She glanced around the room. "I'll admit, it takes some getting used to. The bedroom is tiny. Nothing here is convenient."

Earl raised a finger. "Ella—"

She rushed on as if he hadn't spoken. "But I think you misjudge Lorena if you think these things would stop her."

Her quiet words broke over him like a wave of icy spring water. Clenching his jaw, Earl started to rise, but she laid aside her sewing in a basket and stopped him.

"Don't go outside on my account. It's time I went to bed anyhow." An awkward smile warmed her eyes. "I know I'm too blunt at times. I guess it gets worse with age." She stepped near and laid a hand on his arm. "I loved and lost once."

He felt her hand tighten with an affectionate squeeze. A lump rose in his throat, cutting off any words he wanted to say.

Ella turned and headed to the bedroom, but before she shut the door, she paused and glanced over her shoulder.

"And if I could do it all over again, I would."

As the door clicked shut, Earl glanced over at his lumpy cot then back at the table. Works composed by Debussy, Mozart, Bach, Schubert, Beethoven, Grieg, and others littered the surface like fragmented pieces of his life. Each one was like an estranged friend.

He plucked up Grieg's "The Last Spring" between his

thumb and forefinger, rubbing it as though it might reacquaint him with his past performances. This had been one of Earl's best and most-loved.

The golden hue of the lights, the intense emotions filling him as his fingers coaxed the beautiful melody from the violin crept back into his memory. The melody rising, swelling, and filling the concert hall from floor to ceiling. Music sweeping through time and space. The rapt attention of the audience, the deafening applause and cheers hummed in his ears. A younger Lorena sat at the piano, her back arched with perfect posture, eyes shimmering with unshed emotion as he drew his bow across the strings. All of it intoxicating.

Earl closed his eyes. For the briefest of moments, he was there once more. He could almost step through the veil between past and present. So close. Then Earl opened his eyes and looked around.

Yet so very far.

With a shake of his head, he sank back down in the chair. He laid aside "The Last Spring" and sighed. He didn't want to relive any of it. Most of all, he didn't want to crave any of it again.

Folding his hands, Earl bowed his head. "Father, you know what I have to do. I don't want to do it. I'm afraid I'll want the fame again. It destroyed me once. There's no place for it in my life now. Help me, Father, to do what's right. Grant me the strength and ability to help Valley Creek. Grant Lorena the strength and ability she needs to get through it. I pray that you'll use us for Your glory and honor, to help our friends. Supply their needs. And I ask that when it's all over, please help me to walk away."

He swallowed the knot in his throat and reached for the paper for writing arrangements. He took a pencil, clenched it between his teeth, and pulled Beethoven's "Moonlight Sonata" closer. Taking the pencil in his fingers, he poised it over the paper, his mind ticking. He had to start somewhere.

With God's help, he'd start here.

GUILT WRAPPED around Lorena as snug as the long coat hugging her body. Her shawl enveloped her head, knotted under her chin, making it harder to swallow. Or perhaps it was her conscience making it harder instead.

Her breath misted into a translucent veil before her eyes as she climbed the path toward the graveyard. In the east, a deep ruby sky smoldered as the sun rose nearer to the horizon.

She thought of the conversation between her and George, the unspoken words, his touch. Lorena's cheeks warmed against the chilly air spiced with the scent of pine trees.

She had prayed long into the night, but no answer came. Earl's face hovered in her mind. A part of her, she was ashamed to admit, yearned to use George's attentions to hurt Earl.

The guilt squeezed.

Forgive me, Father.

As she stepped into the graveyard, she paused and listened. A twig snapped near the edge of the woods. The brush rustled and crunched as though something, or someone was hurrying away.

Hoping to hide, Lorena sprang into the shadows and tiptoed along the row of trees lining the graveyard. Curiosity drove her legs toward the sound, outweighing the fear. Whoever was kind and loving enough to leave such tokens surely wouldn't harm her.

The steps retreated further into the woods. Lorena halted in the darkness of the last tree along the row.

Silence. As though she had imagined it.

She leaned against the rough bark and wrestled to calm her

breathing. Across the graveyard, a silver sheen of frost glazed the headstones and rock markers, an ethereal beauty.

For a few minutes, she stood immobile. Ahead, the eleven mounds glittered as the first sunrays grazed them. A familiar scripture flitted through her mind.

I am the resurrection, and the life: he that believeth in me, though he were dead, yet shall he live.

Her knees quivered as she stepped toward them. What did the giver leave this time? The mist from her breath stilled as her eyes looked from one mound to the other.

There, side by side, stood a beautifully carved, wooden cross at the head of each mound.

Her hand flew to her mouth.

All that day, the image stayed with Lorena, the intricate carvings, the careful inscription of every name with the exception of the unnamed wee one's. Perhaps to be added later. Etched underneath the names, the date of that awful storm mirrored the one inscribed on Valley Creek's heart.

Her lunch tasted like sawdust. Pushing it aside, she spent time alone at the church, praying. Afterward, she sat at the piano wondering where to start. She stared at the ivory and ebony keys, fingering their glossy, smooth surface without pressing them. All melodies fled.

Why not let her fingers decide?

Without thinking, she pressed her fingertips on the keys and moved them, testing a few notes then forming a few chords. Her fingers did several scales as they warmed up, yet she still couldn't think of anything to play. Her hands slowed then and rolled a chord.

Out of those chords, the notes slowly rose and weaved together in a song. "What a Friend We Have in Jesus."

The melody rose and filled the church. Each note pushed back the aching of Lorena's heart and soothed it.

> O, what peace we often forfeit,
> O, what needless pain we bear …

The door creaked open. Gasping, Lorena pulled her hands back from the keys and looked. Sunlight streamed in behind Earl as he entered and shut the door, his violin case in hand.

"It sounds beautiful." Earl walked the aisle. "Don't stop on my account."

Lorena took in his easy, unhurried stride. Her mind clambered for something to say. "I was passing the time."

Earl said nothing as he laid aside the case, opened it, and pulled out the bow. He began to rosin it. "I've been practicing most of the day and arranging."

How perplexing yet how familiar it felt to be talking about music with Earl. Almost like peering into a window and watching herself.

"Are you having trouble?"

Earl turned and cast her a half-smile, his blue-green eyes flickering. Lorena's heart turned over. He opened his mouth to answer, but their eyes locked instead. For a long moment, no words were needed.

Realization dawned over Lorena.

"It's you, isn't it?"

Confusion knit Earl's brows as he shook his head. "Me? What do you mean?"

Lorena fumbled with the ring hiding at the hollow of her throat. "You're the giver. The flowers, then those crosses this morning. It's you, isn't it, Earl?"

A dark flush crept from his collar to his forehead. His lips stiffened. Lorena read the truth on his silent, immobile face.

"I know it's you."

Earl rubbed his jaw and let out a pent-up breath. "I'd appreciate it if you wouldn't tell."

Lorena nodded. "I won't." Earl snatched his gaze away from hers and turned his attention back to his bow.

He was the one who had filled her heart with such gratitude. He was the one who had soothed the ache of grief every time she found a new bouquet, brimming her cup of thankfulness to the full with those crosses that very morning. He was the one who had brought a glimmer of hope in the shadows of these past weeks. How could this be? He was her enemy.

He was her husband.

As though nothing had happened, Earl picked up the violin and cupped it under his chin. He kept his back to her.

"Would it be all right if we began with 'What a Friend We Have in Jesus'?"

Shaking herself, Lorena blinked and cleared her throat. "Um, yes. Of course." Positioning her fingers, she began the song, and Earl soon followed.

The sweet sounds reverberated between them. Silencing all thoughts, Lorena focused only on the music. First verse, second, third, then continuing on without hesitation. They played the melody once more. Only this time, they varied the parts. He led the first verse while she led the second. They blended the harmony together on the third.

Like learning to walk before trying to dance.

When the song ended, Earl lowered the bow. Still, he didn't turn around to face Lorena. "That went pretty well. Would you play another one?"

Lorena thumbed through the hymnal. "What pieces have your started arranging?"

"I worked most of the night on the *Moonlight Sonata*. I'm still not finished." He turned then, an apologetic frown on his face. "I'll need your help, Lorena. When I'm arranging your part, I need to hear you play it."

Of course. Even more time to spend with him. Resisting a sigh, she chewed her lip instead.

"You know I wouldn't ask if I didn't need to." Pulling his gaze from hers, he concentrated on the toes of his shoes instead. "Please."

"I know. And I understand. I'll do what it takes to make this successful."

"No matter how many days and hours you'll have to spend with me?"

Lorena wrestled with her voice. "No matter."

"Thank you." Keeping his eyes down, Earl seemed to struggle with his own husky voice. "It'll mean keeping Valley Creek alive if we can earn money for the sawmill. You're very kind and generous to do it. And it's the least I can do."

Humility from Earl Steen. Although she didn't want to acknowledge it, Lorena saw it all too clearly.

"Why did you do it? Bring the flowers, the crosses?" The question pried open her lips before she could stop it.

Blinking, Earl looked up as though he hadn't expected the question. He cleared his throat. "It was just something I had to do."

Lorena quirked an eyebrow. "Had to?"

"It was just my way of paying my respects. I couldn't do much, not really anything, but I wanted to do something."

"Trying to ease the debt?"

Earl's face clouded. "I can never hope to pay my debts, Lorena. Not to you, Lane, or anyone else. An entire lifetime isn't enough, and I only have today. That's what God has been teaching me. His gift is today. I gave the flowers and crosses to honor them. To honor their memory." His voice quivered. "There's no second chances for them."

As she looked away, Lorena's throat constricted and her eyes burned. "I know."

For a long while only the moaning of the wind around the

eaves filled the church. The clapboards rattled with each gust of the deepening autumn air. Lorena kept her eyes fastened on the fingers clutched in her lap.

"I am sorry."

Unable to speak, Lorena shook her head. One tear brimmed over, followed by another. Oh, that they would stop flowing. She couldn't bear to hear the sincerity in his voice.

"Lorena, I am sorry."

She knew he was speaking the truth. Whether she wanted to acknowledge it or not, she could see it in how he talked, how he carried himself when he walked, how he quietly and simply lived.

Then understanding dawned.

Earl would never ask her to forgive him. Though he craved it with every ounce of his soul, he refused to ask because he believed he didn't deserve her forgiveness. Her eyes rose to his steady, unflinching gaze. Yes, it was right there in his eyes. He believed his chances were the same as those buried in that churchyard.

Never.

18

___

"You mean you'd actually let this go to waste? Have you taken leave of your senses, Earl Steen?"

Earl groaned as his sister waved her hand over the clothes spread out on the bed, each one smoothed to perfection by her hand. "I can't believe you would leave these at Lane's. On second thought, yes, I can." Surveying each one, she put her hands on her hips. "She couldn't have brought them over at a better time."

"What do you mean?"

"You'll wear these, of course, when we go to the Mansfield's for supper this afternoon."

"I'm not wearing that suit."

Ella continued as if she hadn't heard him. "This is a generous gift! And wonderful quality!" Gasping, she spread her hand across her chest and laughed. "That's it!"

"What?"

"Since Mr. Wallace gave you these, it means he's giving you his blessing."

"Ella ..."

"I'm a hopeless romantic, I know. Spinster that I am, I'm still foolish enough to believe in second chances." Her violet eyes sparkled like a young girl's.

Shaking his head, Earl tried to smile. "Well, I don't ... not those kind, at any rate."

"If Lorena sees you in these, it'll take her back twenty years." She fingered the sleeve of the dress shirt.

All traces of amusement drained from Earl's face. "Ella, don't interfere. Lorena doesn't want to be reminded of those times, and I don't either. It would only hurt her."

A sympathetic smile touched her lips as she scrutinized his face. "Until both of you work through this, you'll never be able to move forward."

"Maybe. But it's not up to you to do the pushing."

Shrugging, Ella swept past him into the living room and sat down in the chair. Picking up her sewing basket, she pulled out an unfinished curtain.

Earl leaned against the doorframe. "Ain't you getting ready?"

"*Aren't*, brother. Have you forgotten your education?"

"I've slept since then." He watched her deft hands stitch the hem. "We'll have to leave in an hour."

Her hands kept stitching. "I'm not going."

Earl pushed himself off the doorframe and came around to face her. "Not going? This supper is for you and Dr. Curtis, to welcome you both here. If you don't go, you'll insult them."

Ella's russet eyebrows raised as she paused between stitches. "I'll not go with you looking like you just came out of the field."

"That's not the reason, and you know it."

"All right. Wear the suit, and I'll go. Don't wear the suit, and I'll stay."

Frustrated, Earl tunneled his fingers through his hair. "You're being childish, Ella."

A mischievous sparkle gleamed in her eyes. "Well, now, it's

been quite some time since I've been childish. I'm not too old to try it out every once in a great while."

"And if I refuse to play along?"

Though smiling, Ella narrowed her eyes. "Then I guess you'll have to give everyone my regrets."

Earl ground his teeth. "Still as stubborn as a mule."

"I have you to thank for that."

It was pointless to argue further. He knew that when Ella set her mind to something, she would stick with it regardless. Even if it meant being perceived as rude and arrogant, she would see her little scheme through.

"All right. Have it your way." Earl headed for the bedroom and firmly clicked the door behind him.

Ella's lighthearted voice came through the door. "Wearing a suit isn't the end of the world. It isn't a proposal of marriage either. Forget the past and future, and just enjoy the moment."

Scowling, Earl popped loose his overall straps, stepped out of them, and kicked them to the corner. The way he felt, he'd rather run through a briar patch barefooted than put on those duds. He began unbuttoning his shirt. Like shedding his real skin for something that no longer belonged.

His addiction had stripped him of everything. Wife, family, home, love, and his career as a successful violinist with a prestigious orchestra. He belonged in that world no more than those clothes belonged on him.

That fact cut raw and deep as he stepped into the well-tailored trousers.

Long minutes passed as he donned the rest of the suit, shrugging into the shirt, fastening his collar, straightening his tie, buttoning his waistcoat, fastening the cufflinks he hadn't noticed the first time. Then he slipped his feet into the glossy, black shoes.

Everything fit almost perfectly. Turning on his heel, he

opened the door and stepped back into the room where his sister waited.

With a small intake of air, Ella stood. "As I live and breathe. It's you."

"I reckon so," Earl grumbled, running his calloused finger around the snug collar.

Shaking her head, Ella's eyes misted into a violet sea while she surveyed her almost twin. "No, I mean, you look so much like you did when I last saw you ... only older. It's almost like coming home."

Almost but not quite. Earl cringed. "The last thing I need is someone in my family insulting my foreman and his wife by snubbing an invitation. Mr. Mansfield has always been fair with me. He gave the extra lumber for this house when he didn't have to."

Ella hesitated almost as if she were reconsidering her demand.

"I'm trying to prove myself here. I have a rotten reputation in these parts." There. Maybe that admission would soften her stubborn streak.

Resolve banished the mist from her eyes. Folding her arms, Ella lifted her chin. "All the more reason for them to see you in a new light."

No, no.

"Just a moment." Ella darted into the bedroom and came back with a comb in her hand. "May I?" On tiptoes, she reached toward Earl's hair.

Earl staggered backwards. "What are you doing?"

"Your hair needs combing." Said like it was the most common thing in the world for her to do. She tapped the comb against her palm, waiting.

"I'm capable of combing my own hair, if you don't mind." Impatient, Earl held out his hand.

A too sweet, too innocent smile parted her lips as she

handed it over. "Be sure to do a decent job. Your hair is as unruly as ever."

Not having a mirror, Earl stood in front of a window and peered at his reflection as he raked the comb through his thatch of hair. Behind him, he could see Ella's mind twirling while she watched.

"You know, the more I think about it, I think Mr. Wallace intended more behind his gift than just his blessing. I believe he intended for people to see you in a new light as well. To emphasize the change."

Scowling, Earl finished the job and tossed the comb without warning over his shoulder. Unruffled, she caught it and sauntered back into the bedroom to put it away.

"Good thing you taught me how to play ball all those years ago."

Earl, however, was not amused. "I'm a fool and a phony."

When she returned, she eased closer to him, all playfulness absent from her face. Gingerly, she laid her hand on his arm. Her lips quivered.

"Once you were a fool and a phony. But not now. You're my brother. And I've missed you."

The Adam's apple in Earl's throat bobbed against the stiff collar. He'd never expected to hear those three words from anyone. Almost like a language he'd forgotten. Something warm and pleasant seeped deep within his soul, a feeling both new yet once familiar.

A smile softened the stern lines around his mouth as Earl looked down at her upturned face.

"I've missed you too."

THE CRISP, late afternoon breeze shook the tendrils curling around Lorena's face as she sat beside George. His hands gripped the reins easily as he turned his handsome face to hers and smiled. In the seat behind them, Mr. Wallace coughed a little impatiently.

"It was kind of Doc Brown to offer his buggy." Lorena ventured, not sure how to feel accompanying George to the Mansfield's.

"A little too kind, if you ask me."

Shrinking inwardly, Lorena hoped George didn't hear Father's muttered remark. She could feel his eyes on the back of her neck.

George didn't seem bothered. "He and I get along well. I wish he had a practice in New York." Once more, George smiled, his admiring eyes roving her face. The feelings he had fettered for so long showed plainly.

Lorena turned her head. A flush heated her cheeks, yet it brought an uneasy, almost queasy feeling rather than a pleasant one. George was thoughtful and kind. She knew him better than most. What was holding her heart back?

Thankfully, Father took over the conversation and kept up a flow of words until they reached the Mansfield's.

Conversation hummed from the house like a busy hive. Mr. Ray and his son Andrew were wedging an extra table through the front door while Harley Ray pushed the screen door back as far as the spring would allow.

A toothless gap showed on one side of Mr. Ray's mouth as he grinned at them. "There'll be room enough for everybody today!"

The smell of fried chicken seasoned the air. After George climbed down, he reached up for Lorena. His hands around her waist were warm and steady as he set her on the ground. They lingered there only a fraction of a second longer than necessary.

Father climbed down, his face somber as he watched. Then,

without warning, it brightened as he looked beyond them. Lorena turned to follow his gaze.

Earl and his sister were coming into the yard. Rather than wait for him to help her, Ella's nimble feet found the ground as soon as the wagon stopped. With a swish of her skirts, she sailed across the grass and threw her arms around Lorena.

"Lorena! Lorena!"

Lorena clasped Ella tight as that familiar scent of lemongrass enveloped them. Clean and zesty. Thoroughly Ella.

"How I've missed you!" Lorena kissed her smooth cheek.

Half-sobbing, Ella laughed. "And I you. It's been too long. My, let me look at you!" She pulled back just enough to sweep her gaze over Lorena.

My! Those unforgettable violet eyes shone just as vividly as Lorena remembered.

"Still beautiful, inside and out, just as I knew you would be. I can't tell you how happy I am to see you again. We must catch up."

"I'd love nothing better. Come to the teacherage tomorrow for tea." Remembering her manners, Lorena turned to Father. "It's wonderful to see Ella, isn't it, Father?"

With a smile and slight bow, Mr. Wallace squeezed Ella's outstretched hand. "You're a sight for sore eyes, Ella. We're forever in your debt."

The rose in Ella's cheeks deepened. Lorena turned to George who stood to one side watching with interest. "This is one of my dearest friends, Ella Steen. Ella, this is George Curtis, our friend from New York."

Ella turned and the roses faded from her cheeks. Her thick, black lashes blinked. A breath of silence passed as she held out a hand.

"How do you do, Dr. Curtis."

If George noticed the void of emotion in her voice, he didn't show it. With an amiable smile, he took her hand briskly then released it.

"I'm very well, thank you. And you?"

"Quite well."

Beyond them, waiting beside the wagon, stood Earl. Lorena's breath hitched. Almost of their own accord, her feet moved forward, pushing past George and Ella.

She took a few more steps then stopped, suspended in the middle of the yard.

"Earl? It's you." The breeze snatched away the whispered words. Against her will, Lorena filled her eyes with the sight of him.

Watching the commotion at the house, Earl didn't see her. Rigidly, he stood as if ill-at-ease, his hands hanging at his sides. Frustration lined every part of his profile. He tugged at the collar around his neck with a low groan. His broad shoulders shrugged against the suit jacket.

Then he turned and saw her. His face gentled. Once again, Lorena's breath hitched and a bittersweet ache constricted her heart.

His aqua eyes darkened with the same emotion. He made no move toward her, though. Here he was, the one who still haunted her dreams. The man she had loved and lost to cravings that drove him far from her. Though older, he still looked very much the same, still handsome, still commanding. His once turbulent eyes now had a stillness that never rested there in his youth. Strange she had never noticed it in all these weeks, but then, she had resisted everything about him.

She took a step forward, but a touch at her elbow stopped her.

"Lorena, are you ready?" George slipped her arm through his, ignoring Earl.

She tried not to stiffen as her fingers rested on his sleeve, tried not to feel out of place beside him. Tried oh so hard not to feel disloyal in the depths of her spirit.

The light dwindled from Earl's eyes like the dying of a candle deprived of air, the stern lines creeping around his mouth again. Shifting his gaze away, he turned from them and waited for Ella.

Lorena's heart fell. Numbly, she allowed George to lead her to the house.

THE SUPPER TABLE rumbled with conversation from one end to the other. The Mansfields set out quite a spread for everyone, Harley Ray and Edith, Mr. and Mrs. Ray, Andrew, Lorena and Mr. Wallace, Lane, Guy, Jimmy, Earl, and Ella, the vivacious lady with heaps of cinnamon hair and startling violet eyes.

George ventured a sideways look at her laughing with Andrew, a hearty chuckle rather than a simpering giggle. Her scent ... what was it ... a mixture of lemon with just a hint of vanilla tickled his nose. Almost like the lemon cookies his mother used to bake for him when he was a little boy. One of his favorites.

This was Earl's sister. After Mrs. Mansfield had seated her next to him, she had not uttered one syllable to him, even going so far as to look around him and to speak with Mr. Wallace seated on the other side of him.

Mr. Wallace passed George a deep bowl of fried squash. The savory smell hit him in the pit of his stomach. Or was that because Lorena was on the other side of the table across from Earl?

Hiding a frown, George spooned some squash on his plate and offered it to Ella who took it without a glance at him. She instead kept right on talking to Andrew without missing a breath.

George sought Lorena's face but found Lane's eyes upon him instead. Tucking a napkin into her lap, she smiled, but a glare flickered in the depths. Ever since their conversation, Lane had avoided saying much to him. The strain gnawed. Right now, nothing tender showed in her stare no matter how her lips smiled.

Lorena sat between Lane and Edith, seeming more at ease now than she ever had since he picked her up that afternoon. When he had taken her arm to come inside, he felt her stiffen. Her fingers had merely grazed his sleeve and never relaxed.

"George, would you like a roll?" The plate in Mr. Wallace's hands hovered between them. "George?"

Heat spiraled up the back of his neck. "Um. Excuse me, Mr. Wallace." George took the plate and dropped a roll onto his before passing it to an indifferent Ella.

Lorena's eyes were darting everywhere but to the man sitting across the table from her. Craning his neck slightly forward, George glanced at Earl. He, too, was working very hard to look everywhere but at the lovely lady right in front of him.

Could it be that he was fighting a losing battle?

Sitting back, he discovered Edith's dark, honey-colored eyes fastened on him. Curiosity mingled with displeasure settled over her features.

George shifted in his chair, unease crowding in from all sides. Although the talk flowed around and included him, he only caught snatches above his spinning thoughts. What stung most of all was the astonished stares at Earl. Here was this drunk, an outcast, an utter failure looking like a man of means. Even if Earl changed his clothes and parted his hair just right, one fact remained. He was washed up.

"Either the food is not to your liking or your thoughts have soured." Ella's soft, genteel voice elbowed its way into his thoughts.

George wasn't fooled by her guileless expression. "Are you usually this forward with strangers?"

Ella didn't bat an eyelash. "No. Only with interlopers." She lifted a piece of chicken to her lips.

"My dear woman—"

"Miss Steen to you, Dr. Curtis." She sank white teeth into the tender, juicy chicken. George suspected that she wished it were him instead. He skittered a glance around the table, but no one else seemed to have heard. She knew how to hide a well-aimed barb behind a drumstick, the little shrew.

Not to be outdone, George lifted a napkin to his lips. "I'll thank you to mind your own business, *Miss* Steen."

A sugary smile stretched across her heart-shaped lips. "I intend to, Dr. Curtis." With a flick of her wrist, she rotated the drumstick and sank her teeth in once more. She pulled her stare from his and turned her attention elsewhere. For the rest of the evening, he didn't exist in her world.

It was of no consequence. The way that Lorena prudently kept her distance from him was, however.

Their drive home was subdued, the dull thudding of the horse's hooves the only sound breaking the silence most of the time. Above them, the moon peeped in and out of wispy clouds, making her already pale profile even more chalky.

Anger toward his former friend simmered deep in his chest.

When they stopped in front of the teacherage, George turned to Mr. Wallace as he climbed down.

"Would you mind if I have a word with Lorena, sir?"

Mr. Wallace straightened as his feet hit the ground. "No, George. You're both grown. I'm getting too old for such matters." His British accent sounded gravelly in the evening air. "Good night."

To be at odds with a man who was more like his father rankled him further. After all, he didn't come here to lose everyone he cared about.

He watched as Mr. Wallace crossed the small yard and stepped inside. When the door clipped shut, he shifted toward Lorena.

"What happened?"

She didn't pretend to be coy. He knew she was too straightforward for that. "I can't do this, George."

The muscles in his jaw tightened. "You're going to give up even before we've begun?"

"That's precisely it." She clasped her hands in her lap. "How can we begin? Something here, inside, doesn't feel right about this."

"I see." George pulled in a deep breath and let it out slowly. "You're an honorable lady. I don't want to tread on your conscience."

"Going on outings together isn't right. Even if Earl broke his vows, I can't break mine."

The shame filling her countenance pained him. "You could be free."

Lorena closed her eyes. "Earl offered me my freedom."

Shock jolted through him like an electric current. "He did? What did you say?"

"I told him never to bring it up again."

Dread coiled around him as they watched one another. Somewhere in the trees an owl hooted, echoed by another farther away.

"You'd rather be tied to him for the rest of your life? Alone?"

"I don't want to be alone any more than you do, but I can't ignore my vows. It goes against everything I believe. We can't see one another like this."

Swallowing, George nodded. "I understand. But you didn't answer me, Lorena. I asked you if you'd rather be tied to him for the rest of your life. I saw your face when you looked at Earl tonight." He leaned forward, rubbing his chin. "Nothing much scares me, but I'll be honest, that did."

In the air between them, the mist from her breath quivered. "It scared me, too."

Her honesty was almost unbearable. The dread coiled tighter until it was hard to breathe. George leaned back against the seat, wrenching his eyes away from her. He stared at his hands instead.

"I honor you, Lorena. I'll keep my distance and be nothing more than the friend that I've always been. I've nothing but time. I'll wait."

No matter the answer.

"Dr. Curtis is quite taken with your wife."

Dipping behind a translucent cloud, the moon darkened Earl's face but not before Ella glimpsed a spark in his eyes. For a long minute, he said nothing as the wagon creaked and bumped along the road back home. His jaw tensed.

"I know."

"A disagreeable man, if you ask me. He was very rude to you."

"When I was living in New York, he and I were once best friends. I hurt a lot of people in those days. He has a good reason to be angry with me, Ella."

Looking away, she rolled her eyes. Moonlight and starlight silvered the hills, rocks, trees, and grass. The fringe lining the horses' ears. Silver vapor puffed from their nostrils as they plodded ahead.

Ella pulled her coat tighter around her and fastened the top button under her chin. Her fingers brushed the locket brooch underneath the wool cloth. At its cool, metallic touch, her heart nearly twisted the breath from her ribs.

"That's no reason to upset the people around him."

The wagon seat bobbled as Earl turned toward her. "I didn't see anyone else upset."

"Didn't you?" Ella shook her head, crimping her lips together. "Men are so shortsighted. Dr. Curtis would have died if Lane's eyes could kill. Edith barely touched her supper while she watched. Mr. Wallace barely spoke to him. Even Lorena squirmed around as if her corset were too tight."

Her last remark had the desired effect. A deep chuckle rumbled in her brother's chest, the sound alleviating the deep ache closeted inside her.

"I can see where Lane inherited her tongue."

"'The apple doesn't fall far from the tree,' so I've been told." She jutted out a saucy chin.

Earl smiled down at her, then sobered, the amusement wilting on his face. "You've never once asked me why."

His subdued, gentle tone smarted her eyes. Father's and Mother's faces rose unbidden and hovered like fragments of a hazy dream. They never knew why, and she had ceased wondering long ago.

"Is there any point now?"

Seeming surprised, Earl lifted his brows. "I reckon it depends on you."

Ella rubbed her gloved fingers together. "It brought us to our knees, all but Douglas. He refuses to talk about you, and heaven help the person who dares mention you within earshot. Nothing of you remains in sight. He packed everything away in the attic himself. As for Mother and Father, you were the last word on their lips as they breathed their last. And I, I stopped caring why.

"You were the prodigal. I can't tell you how many sunsets our father watched for you to come up that lane, how many times he walked back alone, head down. Or how many late nights I heard Mother walking the floor, praying for you in her room.

"By turns, I was as angry with you as Douglas, hated you for what you'd done to all of us, especially to Lane. As the years rolled by, God taught me an important thing. The *why* no longer mattered. The *who* mattered. You. Lane. That was all that mattered."

Heaving a shaky breath, she ventured a blurred glance at Earl. Silver streaks streamed down his face in silence, washing away a burden she had long carried.

He gulped. "Forgive me, Ella."

Releasing her own tears, she reached over and grasped his hands holding the reins. "My brother, I forgave you long ago when I knelt at the feet of Jesus."

The team knew the way home, all the hills and bends, the shrouded hollows and rocky creek crossings. The whispers of the night were the only voices they heard as they plodded together.

As they neared the barn, Earl stopped them and climbed down. Reaching for Ella, he swung her to the ground then began unhitching the horses. Transfixed, Ella watched while the moonglow smoothed away the years from his face. When he spoke in low tones to the horses, she remembered how he would speak to Dark Cloud, the horse he loved as a young boy. The veil between past and present felt so thin she could almost walk right through.

Almost.

Wistful for things no longer of their world, she turned and entered the house, her footfall a solitary sound in the hollow air. She reached for the box of matches on the table, struck it, then lit the lamp. Though she didn't believe in apparitions, they seemed to swirl around her tonight.

Taking the lamp, she entered the bedroom and unbuttoned her coat. She hung it on a nearby peg. The lamplight glinted across her gold brooch pinned just above her heart. She pulled off her gloves and fumbled with the brooch's catch, releasing the pin.

As she did often, she rubbed a finger over the etched surface nestled in her palm. Another face, another voice came to her mind. She opened the locket.

"Ah, there you are," she whispered. Always, Charles's serious face stared back up at her, yet this time, her eyes studied his features through a different prism. One that stole her breath once more.

"If you had lived, you would look just as Dr. Curtis does."

Whether it delighted or disgusted her, she couldn't tell.

"I JOTTED DOWN THE PROGRAM, but I need you to check over the list and see if it meets with your approval." The paper rustled in Earl's fingers as he held it out to Lorena. Careful not to brush his fingers, she grabbed a corner and took it, not quite meeting his eyes.

Although he wore his plain, blue work shirt and faded overalls, she still couldn't erase the image of him at the Mansfield's out of her thoughts. He looked as though he had stepped right out of her dreams.

She must focus. Rattling the paper, she scanned the works, *Moonlight Sonata*, Liszt's *Consolation No. 3*, Mendelssohn, Debussy's "Clair de Lune," and Grieg's "The Last Spring," among others. Enough for over two hours of entertainment.

"Some of these, are they necessary?"

A pained expression crossed his features. "You have the same sheet music I do. These are the best pieces."

Of course, he was right, and it irked her. "It's just that most of these songs," Lorena ransacked her brain for the right words and, finding none, said, "are significant." She hesitated. "To us."

Puffing out air, Earl swiped the back of his neck. "Have you gone through the stack?"

Lorena shook her head.

"Go through it and tell me which ones aren't significant to us. I tried, but there aren't many, not enough to make a program."

"Father did it knowingly. On purpose." Lorena shook the paper under Earl's nose. And she most certainly would have a word with him tonight.

"At this point, it doesn't matter. There's no time to go looking for different pieces." Earl gently took the paper from her hand. "Even if we had time, do you think we could find any that weren't significant, Lorena?"

Her heart lurched, slicing her breath in half. Of course, he was right again. "No."

"I wouldn't be too hard on your father. He knows good music, and he remembers what worked best for us. I reckon he was also thinking of Valley Creek. This has to work."

Success. The very word shrouded her in weariness. She'd had enough success to last a lifetime or two. Turning away, she forced her feet to move toward the piano bench. She slid into her place.

"It's a perfect program. I don't like it, but it's perfect."

An unexpected grin crept across his mouth and twinkled up into his turquoise eyes. "We could always just ask the Stumptoe Mountain Boys to do a little pickin' and grinnin' for us instead."

Before she could stop it, a laugh bubbled up and echoed through the sanctuary. "Stumptoe?"

Earl bowed, face solemn. "Yes, ma'am. Stumptoe, Arkansas. Best watch your step if you visit."

Covering her face, Lorena's shoulders shook as she laughed as she hadn't in years. Earl's deep chuckle soon joined hers.

"And there's always Hogscald Hollow too."

"Excuse me?"

"Yep." Earl raised his eyebrows with a nod. "You heard me right. I heard tell some of the best music comes from thereabouts."

Unable to contain her laughter, Lorena laid her head on the piano's keylid, her sides aching. What hilarious, mystifying names. And the way Earl said it. She had forgotten his quirky sense of humor and the way he made her laugh. Like discovering a beloved, lost trinket tucked away in an obscure, hidden box of memories.

The hinges on the church door squealed.

They both snapped their heads in that direction. Frozen in mid-step, Edith and Lane hovered in the doorway.

"Mother?" Edith moved first, pulling Lane behind her. "Is everything all right?"

Lorena bobbed her head. "Yes. I, I ..." Laughter snagged her next words into a garbled mess.

"Pa?" Lane's voice brooked no nonsense.

Earl wiped his eyes. "I was educating your mother on some of our town names ... Stumptoe and Hogscald."

Lorena crumpled into giggles once more, slapping her knee in a most unladylike manner.

"Merciful heavens!" Edith waved her hands at nothing in particular.

"Oh, dear, me!" Whipping a handkerchief out of her skirt pocket, Lorena dabbed at her burning forehead then neck.

Choking on a laugh, Earl propped himself against the pulpit.

In the aisle, their daughters stood mesmerized, gaping round-eyed at her, then their father. The sound altogether foreign as well as forgotten in their ears. As the laughter calmed between Lorena and Earl, she realized the girls held no such memories, especially Lane. Once, she had told Lane that she was born into laughter.

For the first time, they were reliving a memory too dim in their minds. Their slow, uncertain smiles wobbled and mingled together. Edith curled an arm around her younger sister's waist.

Their two precious daughters, products of a love that careened far off course.

With a little push off the pulpit, Earl cleared his throat. "What can we do for you girls?"

Both of them blushed as though suddenly shy of them. Lane broke the silence. "We were wondering if we may watch y'all practice."

"If you don't mind." Edith's words tumbled out.

With a silent question, Earl raised his eyebrows at Lorena, clearly leaving the decision up to her.

She nodded, her smile embracing both of them. "Yes, of course." A flurry of butterflies took flight in her stomach as Lane and Edith settled onto the front pew.

"For now, we're only practicing church songs. Just to get used to playing together again. We'll begin practicing scales tomorrow, then the program." Earl lifted the bow and violin from its case and settled the chinrest under his jaw. As usual, he turned his back to the pews and Lorena.

"Father, aren't you supposed to face the audience?"

A crimson flush crawled from Earl's collar to his forehead. His broad chest rose and slowly fell as he twisted around to face their audience of two.

"Yes, Edith. I reckon I should start now as well as later."

Noticing Earl's bow positioned, Lorena knew he was waiting for her to begin. Stiffening her back, she moved her fingers over the keys. "Blessed Assurance."

The melodies of the piano and violin swirled and blended together, their rhythm and timing perfect.

This is my story, this is my song ...

An idea struck Lorena as they started on the final verse. When they practiced years ago, they would test each other to see how well the other would follow. Sometimes at the end of a song, Lorena would move immediately into another one without warning. Earl would often do the same. It was a challenge they once enjoyed. Could he still do it?

They came to the end of the chorus, and Lorena switched without hesitating. "A Mighty Fortress is Our God." A wholly different style and rhythm.

Earl met it without stumbling over the notes, smooth and flawless as though he expected it. Keeping his eyes closed, brow crinkled, he slid into the harmony and enriched the music. Lorena's heart lifted with it. They continued verse after verse.

> We will not fear, for God hath willed
> His truth to triumph through us ...

At last, the final notes receded into the walls and windows around them. Lifting her hands from the keys, Lorena turned.

Hands clasped together, the sisters held onto one another. Their round eyes shimmered, a lovely mix of honey and aqua. Edith, the image of Grandfather's family while Lane carried the mark of Earl's. Light and dark, both beautiful, Lorena realized, just like the path they had trod. This path, at times shadowed and puddled with light, had brought them to this moment together. For the first time, Lorena saw the beauty in those shadows. God's hand had held them all.

"That was stunning," Edith breathed. "It's like finding a piece of childhood. I can remember you both playing together a little."

Lane, however, stayed quiet, no such memories replaying in her eyes. Tattered fragments of a violin playing "Lorena" as Earl sang were the only remains of those days in her mind. Just then, Lane locked eyes with her mother.

Lorena smiled tenderly, silently communicating her understanding. Pulling in a breath, Lane rose, crossed the floor, and wrapped her arms around Lorena. Though she was a grown woman, Lane buried her face on Lorena's shoulder, pressing her nose against her neck. Much as she did when she was a toddler.

The feeling was like a taste of heaven. Lorena's heart overflowed as she returned the embrace. Above Lane's head, Earl filled her gaze. Looking down, he shifted from one foot to the other. Deep regret etched every line on his face, and she saw for the first time, the weight of guilt digging into him.

He caught her stare. Immediately, he yanked his haunted eyes to Edith and pasted on a stiff smile.

"We're getting better. Well, your mother needs no help. I'm still findin' my way."

Edith shook her head. "If that's finding your way, then there's no telling what it will sound like when you do find it."

Lane stiffened, a sharp breath shuddering through her body.

"Quick, Earl! Help her to the door. Lane's getting sick!"

Arm around her waist, Earl whisked Lane outside before the other two ladies could follow. Lorena grimaced at the sounds of gagging as she stood on top of the steps. Beside her, Edith watched, concern furrowing her brow.

Earl clamped a hand on Lane's head as she heaved while the other rested on the small of her stooped back. When Lane had nothing more in her stomach, she clung to Earl's arm as he led her trembling legs inside.

Once she was seated, he dashed outside to the pump and brought back a wrung-out kerchief. He handed it to Lorena.

"We need to get you home now." Lorena swabbed Lane's chalky face with the cool rag.

"I'll be all right in a few minutes, Mother."

"No. It's time you rested. You've been on your feet teaching most of the day."

Lane's eyes closed as she leaned her head against the kerchief. Leaning over her, Edith swept a damp strand of hair from Lane's forehead. "So, how long have you known?"

Lane jerked upright, searching Edith's face. Pressing her lips together, Edith shook her head. "I do know the signs. I've been in a fog, but I'm not blind."

"It hasn't been too long." The pallor deepened on her face. "I'm sorry. I didn't want to make it harder for you." Lane reached over and grasped Edith's hand.

Edith worked her jaw as if steeling herself. "Don't apologize. I want you to be happy. Truly. And I'll be praying for you and the little one."

Lane's knuckles whitened as she squeezed Edith's hand harder. "I'm praying for you too. I want you to be all right." She hesitated. "I don't know what to say."

Skittering her eyes around the room, everywhere but toward them, Edith pressed her free hand against her empty middle. "The Lord giveth and the Lord taketh away. I don't pretend to understand, but He knows all things."

Pain for her daughter pierced underneath Lorena's ribs along with a wave of helplessness. She lifted an inward prayer to the only One who could heal Edith's grief.

Earl laid a hand on Edith's shoulder. "We should get you girls home. The days are getting shorter."

"I picked up Edith after school—"

"Honey, I don't think you need to drive back alone. We'll take Edith home. Your father can meet me at your place and take me back."

Earl widened his eyes. Surely he wasn't frightened? "You're sure?"

Standing, Lorena brushed an imaginary speck of dust from her sleeve. "They're our daughters, after all. If we have to work together, we may as well do it right."

20

A lump wedged in Earl's throat as he offered his hand to help Lorena into the buckboard. Blinking, she curled her fingers together only a moment then reached over to rest them in his. Her eyes focused on the seat behind his shoulder. As soon as she reached it, she snatched her fingers back.

Giving the horse a quick pat, he released his breath, rounded the wagon, and climbed inside. Might as well simmer down. Lane was settled inside, and his job was to see Lorena safely back. Nothing more.

The chilly twilight seeped down into the hollers, sifting through the branches and puddling into shadows around them as he snapped the reins and clucked to his horse. Silence settled between them, tightening the knots in his stomach. Even after all these years, having Lorena so close shook him.

The ruts in the road popped and crunched beneath the wheels. Should he fill the silence? But with what? His tongue felt chained to the roof of his mouth. Besides, what good were words? Just having her near was more than he could've ever hoped. He'd better be satisfied with that.

George's mocking sneer creeped into his thoughts. Anger

bubbled within his chest. *Lord, please take control of these feelings because I'd like to plant a fist right on his jaw and knock that sneer off.* Shaking his head, Earl tried to thrust away the temptation. He'd better steer clear of George. To think of hitting anyone sickened him.

"I invited Ella for tea today, but she didn't come. Was anything wrong?"

Earl shook his head. "I'm sorry. I forgot to tell you when the girls came. Remember how she had those headaches when she was younger? She lay down most of the day with one. She worried because she couldn't send word sooner and asked me to tell you."

"That's all right. Tell her as soon as she feels better to come by. I've missed her." Lorena's voice warmed with fondness.

"She's missed you too." *And so have I.*

Lorena studied her fingernails, first one hand then the other. "How long will it take you to finish the arrangements?"

"Long enough. If I work day and night, and if we work every afternoon together, I think I can finish them in a few weeks. We need to work longer into the evenings too."

Her sigh, though quiet, reached his ears.

"I don't mean to push."

"I know." Again, another sigh. "Whatever we need to do."

"I'm obliged."

Lorena was silent another moment before continuing. "Do you think Lane will be all right?"

"She's always been a strong girl, rarely sick. There's no need to borrow trouble. You were pretty sick when you carried the girls." He ventured a glance at her, but her eyes pointedly avoided his.

"I never was afraid when I carried them. Strange. I don't know why."

"Youth, maybe."

"Maybe." Lorena twisted her fingers together. "I'm surprised you remember."

"I remember a lot of things." It'd be nice to forget a lot of things too.

Though he focused on the road, he felt Lorena's eyes graze the side of his face. "Why did you do it?"

Though she whispered through tight lips, the words shouted at his conscience, making Earl's head vibrate like the pealing of church bells. The truth tasted like iron on his tongue, bitter and harsh.

"Would it make you feel better to hear it?"

"No," she admitted. "But I promised myself if I ever saw you again, I would ask."

Earl took a shuddering breath. For the rest of his days, his past would always be following every step.

No use in sugarcoating it. "I wanted to hurt you for walking out on me." The last day Lorena refused to see him as he pounded on Mr. Wallace's door flashed through his mind. "I never thought you had it in you. We were so close, you and I. I thought you couldn't live without me, since I couldn't live without you."

Shaking her head, Lorena put a hand to her throat. "Things had changed by then. Your drinking tore us apart. You hit me, but when you hit Edith, I couldn't stay another day."

"I know that. I shifted the blame of my actions on you. Everything around me was falling apart. I was dismissed from the orchestra—"

"You showed up drunk at a performance where you had more than one solo. You humiliated everyone there."

"And I blamed you for it, wrongly. It was easy to blame you, Lorena. You had just left me." Earl kneaded his fingers into his forehead as if the rough motion might erase the memories. "You did right. And I retaliated by kidnapping Lane."

"You knew right where to hurt me the most."

"You won't believe me, but at first, I never meant to stay away very long. But then, I figured I lost any chance with you. I'd thrown away everything I worked for, so I just kept running 'til I ran out of money. My last stop was here. Rock bottom, and I wallowed in it for years."

"Very selfish and cruel, Earl."

He saw the tremor in her hands as she balled her fists. He longed to reach over and gather them to his chest. If only tears could wash away those stains and mend the wrongs. He had plenty of those. But no, that was God's doing.

"I've no defense. I was terribly wrong, and I can't fix it. I'm so sorry." He blinked against the burning in his eyes. Did the Apostle Paul ever have bouts of regret for all the wrongs he committed? Did he ever mull over Stephen's murder? Did he mull too much over things he could never change?

The quiet rushed in between them and filled everything like a still pool of water hiding unknown depths. Head bowed, Lorena's chin tucked against her collar, barely moving with the gentle rocking of the wagon. Her long lashes meshed together while her lips slightly moved. A picture of loveliness beyond mere beauty. Earl had never loved her more.

After a while, Lorena lifted her head, staring out at the darkened path.

"I forgive you, Earl."

The reins slipped from his hands as her quiet words settled over him. A burden chained within snapped and tumbled from his soul. Earl drew a breath, testing this new sensation, wondering if it was real or if he was only dreaming.

"You're sure?" His voice cracked.

"Yes, I am. I think I need it as much as you do." Like his voice, hers also wavered.

"I can't tell you how much it means to me, Lorena. I don't deserve it, but I thank you." Earl turned and looked at her, praying she could hear the sincerity in his voice.

When their gazes locked, a thousand unsaid things passed between them, things neither of them knew how to put into words.

Lorena shook her head. "The Lord certainly changed my plans. I always knew if I ever crossed paths with you, I would…" Her eyebrows lifted. "Well, it doesn't matter now. I never thought I'd deal with a saved man. To tell the truth, I don't quite know what to do."

"You can do whatever you want. If you want to hit me, go ahead, or shoot me. You'd be in the right." And he meant every word of it.

Then Lorena did an unexpected thing. She tilted back her head as laughter gushed up like a hidden spring. An altogether lovely sound that swirled around the emptiness of Earl's heart.

It was his undoing.

He took her hands in his and brought them to his lips, first one then another, a lingering scent of the lavender French milled soap on her skin. Ah, he remembered it. She still used it after all this time. He kissed them again, slipping back to another time.

Lorena stilled but didn't withdraw. He lifted his eyes to find hers large and dark almost like a startled doe.

He released her hands and circled his arms around her waist. He drew her so close that the buttons on her blouse brushed his. Lorena gasped, but no fear showed on her face.

Earl shoved back every thought that might intrude on the moment. No past, no future, only this second. His eyes roved her face. Hers, in turn, roved his as if she were seeing him for the first time.

Lorena's lips were but a breath from his. He had only to bend his head if he dared. In his youth, he would've already claimed them. He swallowed, the yearning too strong to overcome. He lowered his head and melded his lips against hers. Soft, trembling, unsure.

He eased her closer, feeling her hands on his shoulders. He tasted the salt of tears. Hers.

"Earl?" she whispered, breathless, against his lips.

Instantly, he snapped his head up. What in blazes was he thinking? Lorena was crying, and it was his fault. Hadn't he promised himself he would never hurt her again? So much for that!

Tenderly, he brushed both of her wet cheeks with his thumbs and slid away. "I'm sorry, Lorena. The very last thing I want to do is make you cry. I've done enough of that."

She said nothing as she wiped her cheeks with the back of her hand, her breathing short.

Gritting his teeth, Earl took the reins and urged the horses to move a little quicker. He'd done enough damage for one night.

Just what had he been thinking? They had no future. He had nothing to offer her. As a matter of fact, he had less than nothing.

Still, the kiss tingled across his lips. He stole a sideways glance. Beside him, Lorena's downcast eyes stared at her lap. She reached up and touched her lips, her fingers lingering there.

Earl knew one thing for certain, and he knew that Lorena had discovered it as well.

Their love hadn't died nor was it one-sided. Rather, it was very much alive, glowing under the ashes of their lives like embers they thought were long dead.

"I'M SO glad you're feeling better, Ella." A slight tremor shook the teapot as Lorena poured the cups between them. The smile stretching across her lips felt as thin as wax paper, and she hoped the dark circles under her eyes didn't tell of the sleepless night she had spent after last evening. The memory of the tender pressure of Earl's lips against hers still made her head swim, warming her heart in ways she didn't expect. Was that really what she wanted? His kiss had stripped away too many years of trying to forget. In truth, her heart had never forgotten.

Setting the teapot down, she tried to look into Ella's direct, too perceptive gaze and felt a flush scorch her cheeks. Lorena's eyes darted away as she sat and lifted the cup to her lips.

Ella rotated the cup between her hands where it sat on the table. "I used to hope I would outgrow those headaches, but now I just hope to out age them." She shrugged. "It's apparently not to be."

"You're still young, only 44. There's time yet."

"Shhhh!" Ella pressed a finger behind grinning lips. "Never speak of a lady's age! May I remind you that you're not far behind?"

"You don't have to remind me. I feel every bit of it today." Though Lorena doubted the ache inside came from age.

Lifting the cup with her smooth, ivory fingers, Ella closed her eyes and inhaled the aroma of orange, lemon, and cloves. "You always made the best tea." She sipped the sweet, spiced liquid. "Some things never change."

The truth, twisting and wrestling inside of Lorena, tightened around her throat as she tried to think of a nonchalant answer. Instead, she also took a sip, but Ella wasn't one to let the silence stretch out too long.

"I can't tell you how glad I am to see you again, Lorena. Seeing you again, seeing Lane and Edith and Earl. Well, I feel like I've come back from the dead. Does that make sense? I feel alive on the inside again."

The smile on Lorena's face became real. "I know exactly what you mean. Ever since I've had my girls together again, I feel it too. Having you here makes it complete. We had some good times, didn't we?"

"The best." Ella's violet eyes perused Lorena's face. "Earl was quiet when he got home."

"Oh?" Lorena struggled to keep her voice even.

"All he said was hello, how are you feeling, and good night. In that order. Then he stayed up the rest of the night writing arrangements. He didn't lie down on his cot until I got up."

Lorena then shared the incident that happened with Lane and how Earl brought her home, leaving out the one detail that had also kept her awake.

Sympathy filled Ella's face as she listened. "I know it couldn't be easy for you, riding back with him."

"I've had enough time to adjust to dealing with Earl. I'll admit, he does try to make it easier, and he stays out of my way when he can. I didn't expect that."

"Is that what you want?"

"What?"

"Do you want him to keep staying out of your way?" Ella raised a russet eyebrow. "I see the way you two try not to look at each other."

Lorena puffed out a breath. "Still as opinionated as always, I see."

"And it doesn't get better with age, my dear. May I offer a bit of insight?"

"Would my answer really matter?"

A droll smile spread across Ella's face. "Probably not."

As she puckered her lips together, Lorena watched Ella's smile seep away into a more thoughtful expression. "Well, fire away."

Ella set the cup on the table with a tiny clink and reached up to release the fastener on her locket brooch. With her thumb, she snapped it open and looked down at Charles's face.

"'Many waters cannot quench love, neither can the floods drown it.' Song of Solomon. I guess that's why I could never love anyone after Charles died."

Lorena watched the grief flood her face, the loneliness clear in her eyes when she glanced up at her. "I've always been sorry for your hurt all these years. To be alone."

"You and I both. The Bible also says, 'Love is strong as death … the coal thereof are coals of fire which hath a most vehement flame.' Death is a powerful force, eternal. Unless a miracle happens, there's no coming back from it. True love can be like that. Forever."

The ache in Lorena's heart sharpened her breath. "Love can also be killed."

"Most certainly. And Earl has done enough to kill it. But that's not what I see between you and him."

"And just what exactly do you see?" Lorena pushed her cup away as if the movement could push away the feelings churning deep within.

Ella's voice grew so soft Lorena scarcely heard it above her thudding heart. "The truth sometimes hurts, Lorena, but only it can free you from your fears. If I had one more chance with Charles, I'd take it no matter what. Life is short, too short to cast real love aside. I've seen the change in Earl. I know it's real." She reached across the table and grasped Lorena's hands. "We can't change the past, but we can let God guide the future. Don't be afraid. Don't hold back. It can slip through your fingers so quickly."

"You make it sound so very simple."

Ella shook her head. "Far from it. Giving forgiveness is hard, putting the past aside even harder." Letting go of Lorena's hands, she lifted the brooch from the table and handed it to her. "And I've been wrong. I've always believed in second chances for others, but never for myself. But now, I wonder." She nodded toward the picture. "What do you see?"

Lorena glanced down at Charles's face and gasped. "He's so like, so like, George. It's remarkable!" Blinking, she shook her head and peered even closer. When she lifted her head, Ella cast her a wistful smile.

"Indeed he does."

A light dawned inside of Lorena like the morning sun breaking over the hills. "Are you interested in George?"

"The question is: are you interested? What do you intend to do?"

Lorena pressed her back against the chair. Once more, the memory of Earl's warm, hungry kiss filled her heart and mind, answering questions that she was still afraid to face. Could she give her heart to him again? What if he went back to his old ways and trampled it? Could she bear it once more? Could her feelings overcome all the bad memories between them? Lorena swallowed.

"Are you merely interested in George because he looks like Charles?"

"I'd be a fool to say it didn't play a part, but I know one thing. George is in no way like Charles. His looks alone wouldn't hold me. But you're standing in the way, my friend. I can't even try if you don't let him go."

Shame flooded Lorena. "I'm sorry. I'm not trying to hold him."

"Then make yourself clear one way or the other. I know I'm being opinionated again, but George isn't for you. And I'm not saying it because of my interest. I want nothing more than for you to be happy. With or without Earl or George."

At the plain, unvarnished honesty in Ella's face, the open vulnerability, tears blurred Lorena's vision.

"You're my dearest friend, Ella. You betrayed your own brother to me so we could find Lane no matter the consequences. I owe you a debt I can never repay. And I want nothing more than your happiness." Lorena placed the brooch in Ella's palm and closed her fingers over it. "No one else deserves a second chance more than you. I give you my word I'll get out of the way."

Strange, it was easy to smile when she said it. A weight lifted from around her heart.

As they shared a smile, a knock thudded on the door. Scooting the chair backwards, Lorena rose and crossed the room. She opened the door and blinked wildly at the person on the step.

Earl.

Hat in hand, he focused on the wall just over her left shoulder as if it took every bit of his concentration. His smooth face was still ruddy from a fresh shave. Lorena struggled not to notice how the breeze twisted one of his unruly auburn waves.

He cleared his throat, shifting on his feet. "Don't mean to interrupt, but I thought I'd let you know we need to postpone our practice this afternoon."

To her surprise, Lorena's heart plunged. He did indeed regret what happened last night.

"Oh?" Lorena lifted her chin, hoping it would somehow lift her heart.

"Congressman Thompson came in on the mornin' train. He's calling for a town meeting later today."

Lorena pulled in a steadying breath, irritated over the relief that Earl wasn't choosing to call it off. What on earth was wrong with her?

"I see. We'll practice tomorrow?"

"Weather permitting, yes." Earl kept his eyes focused on the wall with hardly a blink.

"Ella tells me you worked all night."

Only then did Earl look at her, his clear, blue-green gaze saying more than mere words. "I couldn't sleep, so I figured I might as well work. I'll have to make changes as we practice." He stepped backwards. "Could you let Ella know that I'm headed over to help unload supplies at Huitt's?"

"They've finished his makeshift store?"

Earl nodded. "They finished chinking the last logs this morning. It'll get him through the winter."

"It's good of you to help after all the horrible things he said about you."

Shrugging, Earl took another step back. "He has his reasons, and I can't really blame him."

Amazed, Lorena allowed herself to study him in a way she hadn't dared since setting foot in Valley Creek. No malice in his eyes, no arrogance, no trace of bitterness. Rather she found a quiet, determined set to his firm jaw.

"Perhaps, but he could give you a chance."

For a long moment, Earl stared at her, his look thoroughly warming every spot within her heart. "He doesn't owe me anything, Lorena."

Suddenly she had to know why, to hear from his own lips the reason. "Then why help him?"

Glancing toward Main Street, Earl rubbed the toe of his shoe against the step, looking uneasy. "Everyone here knows Earl Steen the drunk. They know how to deal with him, but they don't know how to deal with me. Huitt doesn't owe me a chance. No one here does. I've got to prove myself, to give what I can. I need to. And I want to."

At his words, something loosened within her soul. Whatever it was, it tasted like freedom. She felt a smile curving her lips, filling her face and radiating toward him. She didn't even try to resist. When Earl turned his head and met her smile, he blinked, the shock plain on his face.

And then a smile, unhurried like the blossoming of new life, crooked the corners of his mouth and radiated back toward her.

21

Voices hummed within the church walls as folks wound their way between pews and over one another's feet. On the platform, Congressman Thompson leaned against the pulpit, smiling and nodding while he waited for the meeting to begin.

Near the door, Earl pressed his back against the wall as more people brushed past him. Someone slammed into his shoulder.

Impatience pinched George's mouth shut as he glanced back at the offender who tripped into him.

"Sorry, Dr. Curtis," sputtered Andrew Ray. "A kid pushed me from behind."

"This place is too small for a town meeting." Then George's eyes flashed into Earl's calm ones.

Earl tipped his head in greeting. "Dr. Curtis."

Without speaking, George shifted away and lumbered through the tight press toward Lorena sitting several pews away.

"I'm sorry, Mr. Steen." Andrew slid into the empty gap beside Earl. "I didn't mean to cause a stir."

Earl smiled. "You didn't, Andrew. No harm done." He watched as George politely squeezed past Edith and Lane, his lips forming words that Earl couldn't distinguish. For a brief second, he felt like the outsider, exiled from what had been rightfully his, but he shook it off. Feelings like that served no purpose.

Beside Lorena, Ella raised her russet eyebrows as she watched George approach. Earl observed the feigned disinterest on her face. The heightened pink in her cheeks was a dead giveaway to no one else but him.

Just as George was about to sit down beside Lorena, she popped out of her seat and motioned for Ella to scoot into her spot. With a smile at George, she settled on the other side of Ella and engaged both of them in conversation.

A mixture of shock and annoyance flashed across his face as George eyed both ladies. Earl rubbed his chin, the prickly stubble from a long, exhausting day scuffing his palm. He was a bit shocked himself and tried to ignore the satisfaction filling him. Why was Lorena putting distance between them?

Just then, Guy pressed through with Jimmy at his heels. "A fellow could get lost in this crowd. I'm coming back here so I can hear myself think."

"You found the best spot in the house." Earl scooted closer to Andrew.

"Papa Guy, can I go outside with the other boys?"

Guy ruffled Jimmy's sandy head. "Do you reckon you can stay out of mischief for an hour?"

Jimmy's head bobbed as he grinned. "I reckon."

"Well, go get some air."

"Thanks!" Jimmy dashed under elbows and into the outdoors with the rest of his playmates.

"I'd like to be that age again." Andrew folded his arms.

"I don't know. I like right where I'm at." Guy grinned, winking at his wife as she glanced back at them.

Just then, Reverend Crandall called the meeting to order. After a short introduction, he stepped aside to allow the congressman to speak. As Thompson stepped behind the pulpit, the late afternoon sun gleamed across the polished wood, adding to the stuffy air in the room. With a short cough, Thompson gripped the edges of the pulpit and smiled. His twinkling eyes swept across the room, taking everyone in with one glance.

"It's good to see y'all here again, my friends. I want to say first that I'm obliged to Mr. Wallace for coming back to Little Rock to talk to folks with me. His words went a long way in helping me secure the venue for the concert free of charge. You owe him a huge debt of thanks. All proceeds will go to the rebuilding of Valley Creek."

Applause thundered through the room mixed with cheers. Nodding, Thompson held up a hand and waited for it to dwindle.

"Word about your plight has spread through Little Rock and beyond. Folks want to help, and I feel more certain than ever that this concert will be a success. So much, in fact, I spoke with Mr. and Mrs. Steen an hour ago about having not just one concert but two. A Friday and a Saturday concert. They have graciously agreed."

More applause followed while others crossed their arms, their dour faces cloudy. Lorena peeped over her shoulder at Earl with a wobbly smile. Dipping his head with a slight nod, Earl hoped his face didn't betray the queasy knot in his stomach, especially as every face turned their focus from Lorena to him. Two days! Could they do it? Of Lorena, he had no doubt. Of himself?

Thompson cleared his throat. "Since they've agreed, I can go back to Little Rock and finalize the dates for November 25th and 26th."

Sweat popped up on Earl's forehead despite having already

agreed to those dates. Barely over a month away. Their practices would have to be longer and harder. Thompson's deep baritone edged into his thoughts.

"I've already arranged for fliers to be distributed starting the first week of November. They'll be circulating the city. Since Thanksgiving is around the corner, I'll be doing everything I can to encourage that spirit of giving. When folks are thankful for their blessings, they tend to open their hearts to help others in need. Y'all have any questions?"

Mr. Watkin, almost recovered from his injuries, stood. "On behalf of Valley Creek, I'd like to thank you, Congressman and Mr. Wallace, for everything. I'm Henry Watkin, owner of Watkin and Sons sawmill. Last time you were here, I was injured and at home."

"Mr. Watkin, glad to see you up and on your feet."

"Thank you, sir. We were wondering how much will two concerts bring in?"

"The venue, Apple Blossom Theatre, seats 850 people. At one dollar a ticket, if we fill every seat both nights, the proceeds could be as much as 1,700 dollars."

Several men whistled while others gasped.

"That's more money than most everyone here has seen in their lives." Doc Brown stood. "It would go a long way to rebuilding the town and buying a sawmill."

Mr. Watkin glanced around the room. "Y'all know my brother-in-law owns a sawmill in Booneville. He'll sell me a used Atlas sawmill for 1,000 dollars. He said it's in good shape and well worth the money. And he's cutting the price because I'm kinfolk."

Murmurs and nods spread across the room as everyone considered the offer.

In the middle of the building, Mr. Huitt stood. "I'd like a word, Congressman." Thompson nodded his consent as the other men sat down. "Now, I'm not tryin' to put a damper on things—"

A few groans interrupted him. Huitt's brows jammed together in a scowl. "It all sounds real good while we're talking it over, but what if Earl gets to Little Rock and goes on a drunk?" He squinted back at Earl who clamped down the fringes of his rising temper. "I still say it ain't right that everything depends on him."

Mr. Mansfield popped from his seat. "See here, Huitt, we've already been over all that!"

Huitt folded his arms. "What if they're not ready? What if the concert flops?"

"It won't!"

All heads shifted toward the voice. Shock rose in Earl's throat as he watched Lane rise, gripping the pew in front of her.

"It won't flop, and they won't fail. Mother and Father have been tirelessly working every day to make sure of it. Your *concern* is unfounded."

"Is it?" The fringes of a sneer played around Huitt's mouth.

"It is. I've watched them practice, and I was amazed." Her voice wobbled as she looked at everyone.

"We're talking about a concert, Mrs. Matthews, not a pickin' and grinnin'."

Dozens of people gasped. Feeling the heat creep up the back of his neck, Earl stepped forward.

Just then, Congressman Thompson held up his hands. "That's not necessary, Huitt. We'll not be tossing insults here." He glanced over his shoulder. "Reverend Crandall, we could use a prayer to help cool us off, I think."

The tension eased in Earl's shoulders as the pastor stepped forward. Scanning the congregation, the pastor called for everyone to bow their heads. As he led them in prayer, murmurs rose around the room, the petitions for wisdom and guidance whispered around him. A quiet knowing, hard to explain or understand, seeped into Earl's heart.

Reverend Crandall lifted his head. "Folks, let's remember that we all have fallen short of God's glory. Everyone here has things they're ashamed of, some known, some not. We've come through hard times before, and with God's help, we've pulled together. He's the One who is in control of our situation, so let's trust Him. And let's not forget to love each other in the meantime."

"Amen." Doc Brown threw a pointed glare at Huitt. As the pastor stepped back, Thompson leaned across the pulpit, a new gleam in his eyes.

"You know what? As we were praying, an idea came to me. Why not have a trial run concert here just for Valley Creek? The Steens could perform, and y'all can see the hard work they're doing, as long as they have no objections."

Smiles, nods, and looks of approval traveled up row after row. Glancing over at Lorena, Earl met her clear, blue eyes. He raised his brows with a silent question, knowing she would understand. A shadow of a smile curved her lips as she nodded.

Earl felt everyone's attention turned to them. He cleared his throat. "Congressman, Mrs. Steen and I are willing."

"Good, good! Now that we've settled—"

The door flew open, the late afternoon sunrays spilling across the floor. A young boy stumbled over the threshold.

"Help us! We was up at the overlook 'an Jimmy Tackett slipped down over the edge!"

Earl was outside before anyone else could react. Behind him, Guy's voice shouted, "Someone bring ropes quick!" Guy mounted a neighbor's horse and sped away.

As Earl jumped into his wagon, someone grabbed the edge of the seat across from him. George.

"Might I come with you?"

"Get in!" Before George could sit, Earl slapped the reins,

and the team sped out of the churchyard. Looking over his shoulder, Earl saw everyone else pouring outside. The rest of the men wouldn't be far behind.

Neither men spoke as the wagon wound its way up the narrow path to the overlook. Earl swallowed down the fear tightening his throat. "Lord," he muttered, "Let Jimmy be all right. Help us get to him quick."

As they twisted around hairpin turns, George clung to the iron armrest. Out of the corner of Earl's eye, he watched his old friend bounce and sway. Strange their friendship had come to this.

Long, hard minutes passed as they climbed higher. Finally, up ahead, Guy burst into the clearing and swung off the horse. Earl pulled into the clearing next, reigned the team to a stop, and set the brake, a billow of dust swirling around them.

"He's about 10 feet down, stuck on a ledge about a foot wide!" Guy yelled.

Earl sprinted toward the edge with George on his heels.

"Just stay calm, Jimmy, and don't move." Guy lay on his belly and peered over the edge. "We'll get you. Everything will be all right." His calming tone belied the alarm in his face as he met Earl's eyes.

Earl glanced to his left. Standing near the trees a group of schoolboys huddled, whispering, the dread etched in their faces. How on earth had Jimmy slipped over the edge? Now wasn't the time to ask. There'd be plenty of time later.

"Lord, help us get him. Give Jimmy strength to hold on longer." The breeze carried his plea upward.

By this time more men, crowded into another wagon, rumbled into the clearing. Harley Ray leaped from the driver's seat.

"How far down is he?"

"About 10 feet." Guy stood. "How much rope do we have?"

"Two, each one about 20 feet long. It'll be just enough."

Harley Ray lowered his voice. "One of the ropes has a weak spot. Dry rot. We didn't notice it until we were almost here. I'll send someone back."

Grimacing, Earl shook his head. "There's no time for that. He's clinging to the rocks and his feet are on a narrow ledge."

Mr. Mansfield joined them. "Someone will have to take the good rope down to Jimmy and put it around him."

"I'm ready." Grim lines dug around Guy's mouth.

A horse whinnied as more wheels clattered onto the overlook. Pulling the reins to a stop, Lorena surveyed the area, her glance ricocheting from one spot to another. Beside her, their girls started climbing down.

Mr. Mansfield raised the rope to slip over Guy's head, but Earl's hand stopped him. "Wait. I'll go."

"He's my boy, Mr. Steen." Guy's face darkened, his voice thick with urgency. "I've got to."

Earl shook his head. "No, son. It's too risky. You have more to lose, and so does Lane. They need you." He clamped a hand on his son-in-law's shoulder. "It'll be all right. The Lord will take care of it."

Without waiting for an answer, Earl reached for the rope. "Mansfield, let's get that boy."

At the edge, Doc Brown called down to Jimmy. "We're sending a rope down, but don't grab it. Mr. Steen is coming down on another rope and will put it around you. Don't move, Jimmy."

Two lines of men poised at the edge, one line ready for Earl's rope and the other holding Jimmy's. As Earl tightened the knot around his waist, he glanced up into Lorena's eyes. White-faced, tight-lipped, she stood rooted to the ground. One arm held Lane close to her side while her other hand pressed against her chest. Beside her, Edith's eyes closed while her lips moved in silent prayer. He might never see them again.

Shifting his eyes back to the knot, he checked it once more. "I'm ready."

A shadow fell at his feet as someone bent down and picked up the other end of the rope. George rose and faced him. Only a flicker of their old affection passed between them.

"We'll get you back safely."

Unable to trust his voice, Earl nodded.

George, Mansfield, and Mr. Wallace were among the men holding Earl's rope as he stepped backwards over the edge.

His feet slowly picked their way over the outcroppings while his hands held the rope. Though Jimmy wasn't far, he tested each rock before placing his full weight on every step. Dirt and smaller pebbles crackled down into the valley below. Earl concentrated on his steps, not the height or the distance to Jimmy.

At last, he stepped onto the narrow ledge holding the boy. Earl could feel the weakness of it through his shoes. The faster Jimmy got off of it, the better.

Earl's rope slackened, his weight and the sharp rocks shredding the rope about five feet above him.

"Here now, Jimmy. Let me tie this rope around you." With swift, deft fingers, Earl circled Jimmy's waist and began tying the knot.

"Mr. Steen!" Tears streaked down his freckled face as he gulped. "I'm sorry."

"Shhhh. There's no need for all of that." Earl tested the knot. The ledge shuddered under their weight.

"Pull Jimmy but leave me!" Earl yelled. "My rope's shredding!"

Jimmy's feet lifted from the ledge as the men above pulled him up.

"Walk your feet up those rocks as they pull, Jimmy!"

Sobbing and clinging to the rope, he obeyed.

Earl felt his rope getting weaker. If only this ledge would

hold, then he could hold on and wait for Jimmy's rope. He dug his fingers into the rocks. He dared not put any more weight onto the rope.

Sweat beaded along his forehead. He licked his lips, tasted the grit and dust. The rocks around the ledge crumbled faster like a stream picking up speed before a waterfall. Holy words from Above whispered within his racing heart.

Yea, though I walk through the valley of the shadow of death, I will fear no evil: for thou art with me.

Earl looked up. Higher Jimmy rose until the men pulled him over the edge. The cheers echoed down to Earl, and he breathed a thanks.

"Hold on, Earl!" Doc Brown's voice reached him.

Jimmy's rope flew over the edge toward him. In a few more feet, he could reach it. Faster the rocks crumbled. The ledge shuddered one last time before giving away.

Earl lunged for the rope. His reach fell only a few inches short. Above him, Earl felt a sickening pop as he slipped away from the hillside, down into nothing but air.

The scream of a woman filled his ears. Then blackness.

22

Through the wall, Doc Brown's clock chimed the half-hour. Lorena flinched, struggling against the fatigue pulsing through every part of her being. Three-thirty. Only three hours since the men had painstakingly hauled Earl up and onto the overlook. Through the dim lights of the lanterns and headlamps, Earl's unconscious, bloodied face appeared void of life even though his chest rose and fell.

Another outcropping, about 12 feet farther down, had caught him. At first, everyone thought he'd gone to the bottom. When Guy and the others searched more closely, they found him sprawled across a ledge wide enough for only two more people. After sending someone for more rope, George and Mr. Ray had gone down to retrieve him.

Everybody thought he was dead. Silence and nightfall shrouded the overlook as the men worked, broken only by murmured commands from Mr. Mansfield. Then came George's voice up through the darkness.

"He's alive!"

Cheers and cries mingled together and filled the valley as they hugged each other. Father had cried, unashamed, huge sobs of relief shaking his sturdy shoulders. The girls had clung to each other.

But then his battered and bruised body came up over the edge.

Blinking away the memory, Lorena shivered and watched Earl's still face, his ruddy hair splayed in all directions across the pillow. Doc and George had cleaned and sewed up a gash in the top of his head. Then Doc had chipped some ice from the icebox, wrapped it in a flour sack towel, and told her to hold it against Earl's eyes.

Gently, she shifted it to the other eye, purple and swelled shut like the other one. A soft touch warmed her shoulder.

"Lorena," whispered Ella. "Why don't you rest a moment and let me?"

She shook her head. "Thank you, no. I'm all right, Ella." With a bracing squeeze, Ella stepped back into the shadows of the room. Her whispered prayers reached Lorena.

The kerosene lamp cast a spectral light across Earl's face. Across from her, George listened to Earl's heartbeat through a stethoscope while checking his pulse. After a minute, he pulled away the earpieces.

"His heartbeat is steady and strong, a little elevated but that's to be expected. Due to the pain." His smile looked eerie in the lamplight. "Waiting is the worst part."

Lorena chewed her lower lip, dreading to ask the question that burned within her for hours. "Will he live?"

Earl shifted his head with a groan. "Lor ..."

Thrusting aside the towel, Lorena gripped Earl's hand and cupped his cheek with the other one.

"Earl. I'm here. Can you hear me?"

Earl nodded, then winced. "What happened?"

"You fell."

"Overlook?"

Lorena squeezed his warm hand. "Yes."

"I'm dead?"

A short laugh, borne of pent up fear, escaped her lips. "No, Earl. You're hurt pretty badly, though. You have a gash in the top of your head."

Earl ran the tip of his tongue over his scabbed lips. "M'head hurts. Thirsty."

Rising from his chair at the foot of the bed, Doc Brown nodded to Ella. "Would you pour him a little water?" He neared and leaned over him. "Earl, this is Doc Brown. You've had a nasty fall, but you'll recover. Like Mrs. Steen said, your head is gashed, eyes swelled shut. You're bruised and will be very sore. As far as George and I can tell, your ribs aren't broken. Your arms and legs aren't. Your right ankle is broken, though. I'm thankful it's not smashed." He glanced at Ella. "Just a little sip. Earl, we're going to give you a little water."

George slipped his arm under Earl's shoulders and pulled him forward. Earl groaned as he sipped.

"More, please."

Doc shook his head at Ella. "That's all for the moment. I don't want you getting sick."

George laid him back against the pillow. "Rest for now, Earl."

Weak from the movement, his voice faltered. "Lorena?" Earl's fingers tightened around hers. With an answering squeeze, she lifted his hand and brushed the back of it against her cheek. Rough and work-worn, it prickled against her smooth skin.

"I'm here."

"My boy, it's good to see you sitting up."

Earl turned his face toward the sound of Mr. Wallace's voice. After two days, he was home, very bruised and sore, and his eyes were still swelled shut. Holding out his hand, he felt Mr. Wallace's strong grasp close around his.

"Thank you, sir. It's good to be sitting up."

Close beside him another man cleared his throat. "Mr. Steen. I can't tell you how glad I am that you're going to be all right." Congressman Thompson took a turn shaking Earl's hand. "We had quite a scare."

Even a smile still hurt the sides of Earl's face. "Congressman, you and I both. I'm just thankful that the Lord saw fit to spare me."

As the men settled into the chairs next to his bed, they commenced small talk for a bit, but Earl sensed they also had something more on their minds. Not being able to see their faces put him at a disadvantage. He might as well plow ahead and broach the subject anyhow.

As the conversation lulled, Earl spoke. "I'm sure you're wondering about how fit I'll be for the concert."

Thompson cleared his throat. "We've discussed it, and it would be better to postpone it awhile. Give you time to recover."

Earl shook his head. "There's time enough. I'd like to go forward as we'd planned."

Silence filled the space. Maybe Mr. Wallace and Thompson were looking at each other while mulling over his words.

"Valley Creek needs the money, and the sooner we can pay for another sawmill, the better. Folks are depending on it. Lorena and I are off to a good start, and I'm confident we can be ready in time."

"But your injuries. Your ankle." Concern laced Mr. Wallace's voice.

"I'll mend." Earl mustered confidence into his words. "Doc says the swelling around my eyes should start going down after today. By next week, Lorena and I should be able to practice."

"My boy, I admire your grit, but you took such a nasty fall.

You should rest awhile." Thompson laid a hand on his shoulder. "We haven't started advertising the concert yet, so don't feel pressured."

Ignoring a stab of pain in his head, Earl pushed himself up straighter in the bed. "I appreciate the concern, but I'd rather move forward with our plans." He hoped he didn't sound too hasty.

Both men chuckled, easing the tension building inside him.

"If that's what you wish, we'll do it."

Relief spread through him. "Thank you, sir." Once more he held out his hand to have it grasped. With God's help, he and Lorena would somehow do this.

A swish of skirts brushed through the doorway. "It's time for our patient's lunch, gentleman, and then a nap." A smile filled Lorena's voice. Taking a breath, Earl's heartbeat ticked up.

"Hear that? I believe your wife is kicking us out." As the chairs scraped across the floor, both men said their goodbyes, leaving them alone.

"Ella made your favorite. Chicken and dumplings, and they look wonderful."

"If they taste as good as they've been smelling all morning, they will be." He dared not mention that she smelled wonderful too.

Lorena sat on the side of the bed and spread a hand towel across his chest. Ever since his fall, she had brought his meals and tended him faithfully. Guilt clenched deep in his stomach. He deserved none of it.

"Are you ready?"

After he nodded, he felt the spoon lightly touch his lips. Taking a bite, he savored the thick, peppery broth as the dumplings almost melted in his mouth. Ella hadn't lost her touch. They tasted exactly like Mother's. The unbidden thought deepened the guilt. He'd never get to tell her how sorry he was.

"Is it good?"

Earl swallowed. "Tastes like home."

"Be sure to tell Ella. That's the best compliment of all."

Quiet settled between them as Lorena spooned bite after bite. Though he couldn't see her, his mind pictured everything. He felt her movements when she clinked the spoon against the side of the bowl, careful not to drip any broth. The spoon scraped any dribbles from his lower lip.

She finally spoke. "This is the last bite."

After taking it, he felt her rise, her weight shifting off the stuffed cotton mattress. The bowl clinked on the bureau. After a moment, he heard water dripping into the washbasin as Lorena wrung out a rag.

The bed sagged once more as Lorena sat. "Now to wash your face."

She swiped the cool rag gently across his forehead, then moved to the sides of his face. Her touch was careful not to cause any pain. Earl hoped she couldn't hear his thudding heart nor notice how he struggled to keep his voice steady.

"Lorena, there's no need. I, I thank you, but you don't have to do this."

The rag brushed across his nose, then across his lips, his chin. Why didn't she answer?

"I want to, Earl." There was no mistaking the catch in her voice. Vulnerable, half-afraid, with other emotions that he would rather ignore for both their sakes.

Shock washed through him when her fingers stroked the hair back from his forehead and lingered. An old, familiar gesture that he'd never forgotten but never expected to feel again. The sweetness made those long, lost years even more acute.

Lifting his hand, he closed it over hers as it threaded through the thick strands. He brought it to the side of his face and pressed it to his cheek. Against his lips. He heard her quick intake of breath, matching his own.

He didn't deserve her. Never could, never would.

Gradually, Earl released her fingers, a pain worse than any physical ache stabbing his heart. He turned his head away. "It's no good, Lorena. I'm ruined."

Saying nothing, she rose. Her footsteps moved almost soundlessly toward the threshold then paused.

"That remains to be seen."

Then she was gone.

THANKFUL SHE HAD WALKED that morning rather than taken the buggy, Lorena lengthened her strides on the road. The cool air clashed against the heat scorching her cheeks. What was wrong with her? And why did she want Earl to be wrong?

She pressed a hand against her chest and felt the hard circle of her ring underneath. His words disappointed her. Lorena clenched a fist, angry with herself rather than him. Just what had she been thinking?

"Lord, please grant me wisdom and guide me," she whispered.

The memory of Earl slipping from the ledge, the rope snapping, her screaming, pulsed through her along with the relief that he was still very much alive. No, it was much more than relief. The feeling terrified her. Elated her.

After they had inched his body over the top of the overlook, she buckled, feeling as though the pieces of her broken world melded back together. Along with her heart.

This wasn't how it was supposed to be.

The past and her heart swirled and tumbled a tug-of-war. She yearned to run and keep on running forever. The swift sound of leaves crackling beneath her feet only fueled her desire.

"Going my way?"

Gasping, Lorena whirled around. "George!"

With chin resting on one hand, he sat on the steps of an old stile almost buried under honeysuckle vines. So troubled by her thoughts, she passed without noticing him. At his feet sat his doctor's bag. Reaching down, he picked it up as he stood.

"I was just coming from Lane's. House call while Doc is making other rounds."

"How is she?" Lorena steadied her voice.

"Doing fine, doing fine." He stepped closer, studying her face. "I patched things up with her."

"I'm glad. She cares a great deal about you."

George nodded. "And I her. Thought I'd walk today, but I'm not used to the distance. I was resting a bit when you came almost running by. Mind if I join you?"

Squelching a sigh, Lorena wished she could say no. All she wanted was to be alone with her thoughts and sort her feelings. With barely a nod, she turned as he fell in step beside her.

"Coming from Earl's?"

"Yes."

A gust of wind rattled the trees while a squirrel barked overhead. Shards of sunlight sliced through the colorful canopy, dappling the ground. Points of light along a shadowed path.

"It's beautiful country here."

Lorena blinked and forced herself into the present. "It's very beautiful."

"Since I've arrived I've learned that the locals call this spot Hainted Holler. At nightfall, the darkness, they say, gets so thick in here you can feel it. Kids like to spin stories about it. I've heard my share." He chuckled.

Sensing George wasn't finished, Lorena remained silent. As she stepped, her toes scattered a layer of leaves in all directions.

"As I was sitting back there, I thought about it. I suppose most of us are haunted by something. We have dark, shadowed valleys to walk through. No way to avoid it. We just have to keep walking. And, eventually, the sun comes up and shines through. Like now. The light doesn't take the valley away. It changes our view instead."

Lorena gazed around her. "It does indeed. I've never thought of it that way."

"Neither have I." George slowed his pace and stopped. "It's time I go."

Feeling the color drain from her face, Lorena faced him. "You're leaving, then?"

"In a few days. I'll send my trunk to the station tomorrow. But I'll say my goodbyes to you here."

"George, I—"

"You know I hate goodbyes." He reached for her hand. "But I'd be an even bigger fool if I stayed any longer. It's no use, Lorena. You love him. You always have and always will. And I might as well stop fighting it."

His words and the strain of the past few days stretched the barriers of her restraint. A vibration quivered in her stomach, spread through her chest and climbed her throat, an earthquake of emotions shaking her. Tears welled up and spilled onto her cheeks. Although she opened her mouth to speak, the words choked her.

"That evening on the overlook, I saw it plainly and every day since. I fought a losing battle. So have you."

Taking a tremulous breath, Lorena sputtered the words out. "I never meant to hurt you, George. If I'd known how you felt all these years, I would have kept my distance."

A grim smile lifted his lips. "All the more reason to hide it from you, my dear. I needed your friendship if nothing else. But now, I can't have either."

Lorena felt at a loss. "I'm so sorry."

Shaking his head, George stroked her knuckles with his thumb. "Don't be. Remember, you tried to warn me, but I wouldn't listen. I could never possess your heart the way Earl does."

"Please don't say that!"

His grip tightened. "You might as well face it too." His breath shuddered. "Goodbye, Lorena." With a swift bend of his head, he brushed his lips quickly against the back of her hand and let go.

Before she could answer, he turned and left her standing in the midst of the road.

"Would you care for a cup of coffee?" Sitting at the table, Earl gestured to the chair across from him. A few days had passed, and he could finally see even though his eyes were still puffy. He blinked against the throb of pain in his head while he waited for George's answer.

Standing stiffly with his hand holding the back of the chair, George nodded. "Thanks." When he sat, Ella brought him a steaming cup and politely excused herself. As she donned her coat and stepped outside, the frosty dawn blushed through the doorway.

George lifted the cup and sipped. Watching him, Earl did likewise. Several long, hushed minutes passed between them as they sipped. On the hearth, the fire popped and crackled, a sound Earl loved. The irony wasn't lost on him. Any outsider looking in would've thought they were friends.

After several more minutes, George set the cup down. "Still having pain in your head?"

"At times, yes."

"That's to be expected. Even for another few weeks." He

chopped the words off one at a time, the strain evident on his face.

"Would you care for another cup?" Earl lifted the pot and poured himself another one.

"Please."

When Earl set aside the pot, George spoke again. "I'm leaving. Today."

Earl kept a calm and steady face, belying the quake within. "I see. And Lorena?"

"She's staying. I didn't bother to ask." The muscles in his jaw knotted. "She wouldn't have me."

He had no right to feel glad, no right at all. Sweeping the room with a glance, Earl tamped down the feeling with a dose of reality.

"I don't know what to say."

"Well, then, that makes two of us." George stared down into his cup.

Earl's heart panged as he watched his old friend. "They told me what you did the other night and how you helped get me off that ledge. I owe you a debt of thanks."

Glancing up, George shook his head. "No need. I'm a doctor. I was only doing my job."

"Either way, I thank you."

For a long moment, George stared, but Earl didn't flinch under it. "You're welcome," he said, the ire in his voice extinguished. "When you left New York, I never expected to see you again. It's been strange watching you in these surroundings."

Earl smiled a little. "I'm used to it. This is my life now, and I'm content with it."

"I envy you that." George pushed back from the table and rose. "Anyhow, I've got to go if I want to catch the train."

Slowly, Earl grabbed his crutches and rose. "Are you walking?"

"I thought I would my last morning here. Doc offered to take me, but I like the quiet." When he reached the door, he turned, hesitating. "Thanks for the coffee."

"Anytime, George." Hobbling closer, Earl held out his hand.

For the first time, George's features relaxed into a slight smile. He reached out and gripped Earl's hand firmly.

Turning away, he opened the door. "What's this?" He stepped back with a confused frown.

A hitched team sat waiting, their foggy breaths swirling together. On the seat, holding the reins, Ella sat as though George expected her to be there.

"Are you ready, Dr. Curtis?"

George opened his mouth, shut it, then opened it again. "What in blazes is she doing?"

"Being Ella."

Muttering something about overbearing spinsters, George picked up his suitcase beside the door and headed down the steps.

When he neared the wagon, George tossed the suitcase in the back and climbed up. With a flick of the reins, they jolted forward.

As he shut the door, Earl chuckled. Whenever his sister made up her mind, nothing could stop her.

"My dear Miss Steen, what is the meaning of this?" Twisting in the seat, George cast the full force of his glare on Ella who didn't even bother peeping his way. Instead, she lifted her chin and glued her eyes on the road.

"I'm not your dear 'Miss Steen.' I'm simply helping you on your way."

"Anxious to see me leave?" The ire in his tone dripped with sarcasm.

Ella seared him with a look then, her brows raised. "Whatever for? You've been such pleasant company."

George blinked. If not for the twinkle lurking in those violet eyes, he would've sworn she was serious. He faced forward and pressed his back against the seat.

"I didn't come here to be pleasant company."

"Well, you certainly succeeded at that."

The serene quiet of that early hour settled around them while the ruddy blush deepened in the sky. The morning stars faded with each passing second, the way memories dwindle with time. Though invisible in the light of day, they never really departed. He sighed.

"This place has a way of getting inside you and not turning loose, doesn't it?" Ella's soft voice drifted over the frosty air.

"You could say that."

The horses nickered to each other, their heads nodding together with each step. Their steps fell in perfect harmony with each other. "A world away from New York," he said more to himself than to her.

"Surely you have friends and family waiting for you?"

"I have nothing except my practice. My only family, my son, lives in Europe."

"I'm sorry."

"What? For me?"

"Why ever not? Don't get me wrong, Dr. Curtis. I don't pity you, but I'm sorry you have no one back at home."

"The Wallace's are my friends, but it won't be the same now." George rubbed an ache in his knee, ignoring a deeper hurt within.

"Without Lorena?"

"Precisely. If nothing else, she was always my friend."

"It is hard to lose a friend."

Something in her voice, perhaps the way it almost hitched,

crumbled the hard edge around George's heart. He glanced at her, but she was staring straight ahead.

"You speak from experience?"

"Precisely."

Despite the heaviness pressing on him, George smiled at the way she imitated his tone and words perfectly. He shook his head. Perplexing lady, that one. Absolutely mystifying.

Eyes roving over the deepening orange and crimson leaves, the hills, and the creek that laughed and gurgled a stone's throw away, George marveled at his pang of leaving it behind. As they rode farther along in silence, George relaxed, grateful that neither of them was ill-at-ease. At least, Miss Steen didn't look uneasy. Did anything perturb the lass?

He heard her take a deep, crisp breath, hold it, then exhale slowly. Almost as though she were relishing the taste of the countryside. If one could taste it. The taste of pine, moist earth, zesty springs, and sweet, mown hay. Indescribable.

The crunch of frost under the horses' hooves soothed George in a way he couldn't explain. Tonight, alone in the train's berth, he would succumb to the burning ache and pain of Lorena's rejection, but for now, he would relish these lasts moments in such an untouched, exquisite place.

At least Miss Steen didn't fill the air with mindless chatter. Her mood almost seemed to match his.

George closed his eyes, and for the first time in years, he thanked God that beauty like this still existed in the world.

The rest of the ride passed wordlessly. Only when they were almost to the station did George speak.

"Miss Steen, I wasn't very gracious when you offered a ride. I thank you."

Only then did Ella turn and look fully at him. Her violet eyes summed up every inch of his face. It heated under her scrutiny.

"You're quite a rude man, Dr. Curtis." Were it not for that

twinkle glimmering behind her unruffled expression, her words would have singed him.

"And you are presumptuous."

"Well, then, I suppose that makes two of us." She chuckled, reining the team to a stop in front of the station.

Frowning, George drew his brows together. "Do you find humor in everything?"

The twinkle dimmed. "No, not everything." She leaned forward. "Dr. Curtis, I know we got off on the wrong foot, but I'd like to make amends. Perhaps we could start again as friends."

George rubbed his jaw. After everything, why would she want to be his friend? He should be the one making amends, not her. If it weren't for his stubborn pride …

She was still speaking, and he hadn't caught a word. He shook his thoughts aside. "What was that?"

Her eyelashes fluttered, cheeks flaming. "I was asking if I could write you."

George would've been less shocked if she had asked if she could hit him. "Write me? Whatever for?"

The rose in her cheeks deepened, burying the faint freckles across her nose while highlighting her lavender eyes. Her throat bobbed. "You said you had no one. It must get lonely."

The future stretched out in front of him like miles of empty track. Long, exhausting days working. A silent house surrounded by a noisy city. No family but his son in Europe. A few friends occupied with their busy lives. And no Lorena. George clenched a hand over his knee.

"I'm sorry." Miss Steen turned away. "It was a silly suggestion."

Here he was staring a hole through her without realizing it. What a dolt he was. "No, Miss Steen, I'm sorry. I was thinking, that's all. I wasn't offended." He swallowed. "Yes, I wouldn't mind getting your letters."

Motionless, Miss Steen only looked straight ahead. Had she heard? George shifted in the creaky seat. Maybe if he tried teasing her a little it would ease her discomfort. "I suppose you want me to write you back?" He even smiled for good measure.

She shook her head. "There's no need for that."

Was she serious? "I would be rude if I didn't answer you."

"Come now, when have we been concerned with that?" That maddening twinkle rippled across her eyes once more at her sideways glance.

George sighed. "Presumptuous lass."

As a smile broke over her face, she extended her hand. "I'm Ella. No friend calls me 'Miss Steen.' It makes me feel like the staid old spinster I am."

At a loss, George reached over and clasped her hand briskly. He chuckled. "And I'm George." Reaching inside his coat pocket, he pulled out a small notepad and pencil. He jotted down his address, tore off the sheet, and handed it to her.

"Thank you."

He shook his head. "No need. I should thank you." Turning, he hopped down and retrieved his suitcase.

"Have a safe journey, George."

He glanced up. With her arm stretched across the back of the seat, Ella watched as the air twiddled with the ginger strands of hair brushing her cheeks. He couldn't decipher her expression.

"It will be a long one."

Ella nodded. "It will at that." With a slight nod, she tucked the address into her skirt pocket and turned. With a slap of the reins, she drove away without a backwards glance.

Inhaling a deep breath, George watched until Ella and the wagon were out of sight. To his surprise, regret settled deep and blinding like a thick fog. What was his purpose anymore? All of it, his goals and dreams, shriveled up and crumbled. New York held nothing for him. If he were a praying man ...

Would Ella write? After the way he behaved, he wouldn't blame her if she didn't. Tightening his grip on the suitcase, George turned on his heel and trudged up the steps to the platform.

His futile time in Valley Creek was over.

24

November 1, 1910

T he sunlight seared a pain through Earl's head as he peered at Lorena sitting in the buggy. Her brow puckered as he held onto the hood's iron brace while Ella laid the crutches inside.

"Are you sure about this?" Lorena asked.

"Yes. I'll be fine." With both hands holding the brace, he swung himself up into the buggy, careful not to hit his foot on anything. On one foot, he turned and lowered himself onto the seat. "There. That's done." He glanced at Lorena with a smile. "Nothing like putting one foot in front of another."

"Doc won't like it."

"It's been a week, and we can't lose any more time. I can see to move around and my fingers are working. That's all we need for now. Although I have no doubt that you could pull off the concert yourself with no problem."

"Earl!" Lorena's lovely eyes widened. "I won't hear of it. You know how I hate performing in public, especially alone."

He chuckled. "Well then, we'd better practice, hadn't we?"

"I'll leave you two to argue your way to the church now." Ella patted Grits's back and turned toward the house.

"If Doc comes, tell him I went for a walk." Earl smirked.

Without a word, Ella shooed them away, fanning a hand behind her.

"You must be feeling better." Lorena urged the horse forward.

"A little. It just feels good to be alive. God has been good to me."

The rest of their ride to church was subdued without the need for words to overtake the quiet. Within Earl's heart, peace brimmed over until he was sure Lorena must have sensed it.

A few miles later, after Lorena set the brake in the churchyard, Edith stepped over the threshold and closed the door behind her. As Lane's morning sickness progressed, Edith took over her teaching duties.

"Another school day finished." Edith smiled shifting her books to the crook of her arm. "So, you're going to practice?"

"We're going to give it our best," Lorena said. "Doc won't like it, but your father insisted."

As Edith approached, she swept her gaze over him. "Your face isn't as bruised or swollen, but you don't need to overdo it, Father."

The concern in her face nearly overwhelmed him. No one deserved it less. He cleared his throat. "No need to worry about that. And how are you faring?" He held out his hand, and her small one grasped it.

Edith's face dimmed a little, but peace hovered across her features. The color of health was returning to her face. "I'm better. Yesterday I went to the graveyard for the first time, and do you know what? There were new crosses on the graves. And the baby's ..." Her chin quivered. "The baby's was the most beautiful of all. Who did it?"

How was he to answer that? As he fumbled for words, Lorena spoke instead.

"Someone who wished to remain unknown, I believe. It's a wonderful gift, isn't it?"

Edith nodded. "As if it were dropped right out of Heaven. For the first time since that day, I felt God's peace, and I knew then He'd never left me. I just couldn't see it."

"The Lord often provides comfort in unexpected ways, darling. You'll meet your wee one again." Reaching across, Lorena cupped Edith's cheek in her hand. "The time for healing has come."

One tear rolled down onto Lorena's hand. She tenderly smoothed it away. Edith held her Mother's gaze.

"For you, too, Mother." Edith turned her dark honey-colored eyes to Earl. For a moment she only stared before finally speaking.

"Thank you, Father."

Earl couldn't trust himself to speak or move. Edith knew. As always, she saw right through him. She squeezed his hand a little harder. "I'm praying for you both." With that, she turned and headed toward home.

"Lorena, you raised an amazing woman."

She shook her head. "I can't take all the credit. The Lord helped her more than I ever could." Rising from the seat, she gathered her skirts and stepped down from the buggy. "Well, are you ready?"

CARRYING THE VIOLIN CASE, Lorena trailed Earl as he maneuvered the crutches down the aisle. Years of working in the sawmill had broadened his shoulders and thickened the muscles in his arms. Though hurt, he remained strong.

As he settled himself on the front pew, Lorena laid the case on the piano bench and opened it. Inside, the shiny face of the violin gleamed up at her. So many memories wrapped up in that little instrument. Pulling it and the bow out, she brought it to Earl.

"Thank you," he said, looking instead at the pew behind her.

"Oh, you'll need your tuning fork and rosin." As she hurried over to the case, she heard Earl snatch his crutches.

"No, Lorena! I'll do it!"

Before he could rise, she had already opened the little compartment within the case. Lorena froze. Beside the rosin lay a folded envelope underneath a folded piece of paper. In another corner lay Earl's wedding ring. Her breathing stilled.

"Lorena. Please. Just close the case."

Turning to him, she read the pleading look in his eyes. "Your ring is there." Silly! Of course, Earl knew that. "The papers. What are they?"

"Those things have been in there ever since I came to Valley Creek. I never thought to take them out." Earl slumped back down on the pew. "Leave them be."

"This envelope has my name on it." Lorena lifted it out and examined the smeared writing. "This was years ago."

Earl's face darkened. "I never mailed it."

She ran a finger along the stained surface. "Was this after you left?"

Lowering his eyes, he stared hard at the floor, gripping the edge of the pew with his hands. "There's no use in digging up what's been buried. I should've burned it a long time ago."

The ache in his voice echoed the ache in her heart. "Earl, will you tell me what it is?"

He rubbed his forehead, keeping his head down. "I wrote it about a year after I left, asking you if I could come back home. I'd tried to stop drinking." He shrugged. "Tried for weeks. I wasn't going to mail it until I was through." A sigh shuddered through him. "But I couldn't stop. So, I put it away in that case along with the ring and found my way to Valley Creek."

All words fled Lorena. What could she say?

Lorena shifted her focus back to the papers. Wasn't the folded piece of paper from her old stationary? Her fingers lifted one rosin-stained corner. Yes, the lily-of-the-valley flowers cascaded down the edges.

"This is my stationary." As she lifted it, the paper crackled between her fingers. "What is this?" She moved toward him until she stood in front of him.

Jerking his head up, Earl's eyes locked with hers. "It's enough, Lorena. Leave the past where it belongs."

"We can't, Earl. We've both tried, but it's always there hovering between us. Maybe we would do better to stop fighting it." She unfolded the paper. When she saw her very own handwriting, the memory flitted into her mind. She clapped a hand over her mouth.

On their third anniversary, she had written that poem. The only poem she had ever written. Her lips quavered. "My poem!"

Earl's eyes never wavered from hers. His voice, low and husky, lapped like quiet waves around her soul.

> "Be there joy or pain
> Laughter or sorrow
> Sunshine or thunder
> Today or tomorrow
> I'll love you no matter
> Though the storms we will weather
> Through life or through death
> Our souls entwine together."

As her breath hitched, the paper shivered between her fingers. He had not forgotten. Every word came from deep within his heart, and Lorena glimpsed, for the first time in ages, the man she fell in love with. Yet he was so different at the same time, humble, without ambition. Peace erased the pride that once drove the wedge between them. Hope flickered like a candle in a gentle breeze. Dared she believe that Earl wouldn't return to his old ways?

Lorena reached out and stroked the side of the fading bruise on his cheek. The afternoon stubble prickled along her fingers. Closing his eyes, Earl leaned his cheek into her hand, nestling it within his own. Lorena's heart thudded.

Earl brought her hand to his lips and brushed it lightly. Once. Then twice. His other hand came around and pressed against the small of her back, urging her closer. The paper drifted to the floor.

Lorena's other hand came up and rested on his shoulder, feeling the strength of hardened muscles from years of work.

Earl lifted his clear, blue-green eyes, his heart and emotions unhidden, burning into hers.

Then a pained, haunted look darkened his face like a sudden cloud sweeping over the sunny mountainside.

"Lorena." He pulled in a steadying breath. "We can't." He loosened his grip on her waist, and the cold sting of loss chilled her.

A loud rap shook the front door, and Lorena jumped back as though burned. Earl's head snapped around. As the door swept open, Mr. Wallace stepped inside. Bending over, Lorena snatched up the paper and folded it.

"I thought I'd drop in and see how it goes, and how you're feeling, Earl." With a brisk stride, Father smiled at them both. "It's good to see you up and around. And in one piece."

While Father clasped Earl's shoulder, Lorena busied herself by stuffing the paper back into the violin case. Her neck and cheeks tingled with heat.

Forcing her voice to be composed, Lorena turned. "If you'll both excuse me, I need a little water." With hardly a glance at either of them, she brushed past them outside. Hurrying over to the pump, she thrust her handkerchief under the spout and pumped until cold water soaked it. Her fingers numbed and tingled as the water splattered over them.

Lorena wrung it out and pressed it to the back of her neck, her forehead, then her cheeks. They couldn't go back. They couldn't go forward.

They were hopelessly stuck.

DRUMMING A PENCIL AGAINST THE TABLE, Earl whooshed air from his lungs and leaned back against the chair. The papers blurred together, and his head ached. Yet it wasn't his injury causing the pain, neither the writing, nor the lack of concentration. As he glanced up through the front window, he saw Ella meander toward Lane's, giving him the solitude he craved.

He needed to clear his head. At his right lay the open violin case. Reaching over, he lifted the violin out and retrieved the bow. He cradled the instrument under his chin, closed his eyes, and drew the bow into a little light-hearted melody, an Irish reel, the music whizzing and swirling through the room.

For several minutes, his fingers flew along the strings before they slowed, as though of their own accord, to the melody closest to his heart.

> The years creep slowly by, Lorena,
> The snow is on the grass again;
> The sun's low down the sky, Lorena,
> The frost gleams where the flow'rs have been.
> But the heart throbs on as warmly now,
> As when the summer days were nigh ...

The bow froze. "Why torture myself?" he murmured, laying it aside. Before replacing the violin, he opened the little compartment within the case and pulled out the letter and his ring.

He fingered the cold metal as it slowly warmed to his touch. He remembered Lorena sliding it onto his finger when she said her vows. Her shy, lovely smile half-hidden beneath her lace veil. He had everything to offer Lorena in those days ... a future, a home. Now he had nothing. Hot, desperate anger seared through him. No one else was to blame. His choices put him in the very spot he was in at that very moment.

"Lord, forgive me, please." The anger eased and melted away, replaced by stinging, unshed tears. "I've no cause to be angry. I can't undo it, Lord. I only ask that You help Lorena and me."

After replacing the ring in the case, he unpeeled the seal of the letter and scanned it. He had written it during one of his sober moments. Fragments of brokenness.

I'm so sorry—I want to change—I'm trying—Will you forgive me?
Lane cries for you—
Can I come back home? I love you.

Earl swiped his eyes and folded the paper. He had tried without God and failed miserably. Casting aside the faith Mother and Father taught him, he sought refuge in the bottle. And found none.

Someone rapped at the door. Earl tucked the letter back into its place and wiped a sleeve over his eyes once more. "Come in!"

"Hullo, brother!" Reverend Crandall stepped inside and shrugged out of his coat.

Earl smiled. "Welcome, Reverend. Hang up your coat and

have a seat." He moved to rise, but the reverend held up his hand.

"Stay put. I know where the coffee pot and cups are."

When the cups sat steaming before them, Reverend Crandall sipped from his and nodded with approval. "Best coffee in these parts. Not bitter at all and smooth going down."

"Ella put it on before going to Lane's. She has a knack for it."

"Give her my compliments." He took another sip. "You're looking better all the time. How are the headaches?"

"They're easing little by little. But I tell you, I'll be glad when this foot heals. I'm tired of sitting around."

"I can imagine." Reverend Crandall glanced at the papers and violin case. "It looks like you're working in other ways, though. It means a lot to me, to the town. I wish there was a way we could repay you and Mrs. Steen."

Earl shook his head. "Thanks, but it's something we want to do. I only hope we raise enough money."

"Jehovah-Jireh. The Lord will provide." Reverend Crandall cleared his throat and straightened, pulling at the cuff of his sleeve. "I'm not here just to see how you're faring. I felt the need to come. While I was praying in the woods, the Lord put you on my heart. I don't know the trouble, but I'm praying. If you need to talk, I'll listen."

Earl sighed, finding it hard to meet the preacher's eyes. "I'm obliged, especially for your prayers. It's a personal matter."

"Even though I'm pretty new here, I'm not new to the talk that goes 'round, if you know what I mean."

"I do. It's not something I'm proud of." Earl wrapped his hands around the cup and stared into the black liquid.

"We all have things we're not proud of. Maybe some more than others, and sometimes those things shadow us."

"Every step I make."

"Brother Earl, how does your shadow get behind you?"

"Pardon?" Squinting, Earl lifted his head.

"Your shadow can be anywhere around you, depending on which way you're facing. In front. Beside you. To get it behind you, you have to face the sun."

Unable to speak, Earl swallowed. Reverend Crandall continued.

"Our past sins are like those shadows. They hound us, torture us at times, but when we face the Son of God, those shadows have to get behind us. When the light of His forgiveness, salvation, and love shine in our hearts, they flee. It's just that sometimes as we're walkin' with the Lord, we forget to face Him."

Considering it, Earl rubbed his chin. "I reckon I've never looked at it quite that way, Reverend, but you're right."

"I think the prophet Malachi said it best. 'But unto you that fear my name shall the Sun of righteousness arise with healing in his wings.' He heals our brokenness and overtakes those shadows."

A grateful smile curved Earl's lips. "Thank you. I needed that."

Reverend Crandall returned the smile then sobered. "Then there's the personal matter. I know a little of the story, so there's no need to rehash it. The Bible also says that love covers a multitude of sins. You and Mrs. Steen have today. You both have the future, if God wills. The past makes a cold, empty companion. Don't be afraid to test the future."

Gesturing his hand at the room, Earl frowned. "You see everything here. I'm a poor man, and Lorena has never known this kind of life. It's not fair to ask her to give up her home and comforts for this. She deserves better than what I offer."

"Don't you think she deserves a chance to decide for herself?"

Not knowing what to say, Earl looked at the ceiling and heaved a sigh.

"If she gives you a chance, brother, then do the same and give her one too. You might be surprised what the Lord will do."

Earl grimaced when he thought of Lorena sharing this house, this life with him. It would be asking too much of her, of God. Wouldn't it?

25

"Fine job! Fine job!" Doc Brown wormed his way through the rumbling crowd and shook Lorena's hand. Even though her arm felt like a pump handle by then, Lorena laughed.

"Thank you, Doc. I'm so glad you enjoyed it."

Doc turned to Earl who was leaning on his crutch beside her. "Never knew you had it in you, Earl. The concert is in great hands."

Lorena watched the flush creep up from Earl's collar all the way to his forehead. "Thanks. I couldn't do it without Lorena or the Lord, for that matter." His humility awed her. Nothing fake or contrived about it.

With a sideways glance, Earl beamed down at her, a hint of something wistful in his eyes. Tonight he wore the suit Father had bought him. His auburn hair was freshly cut, the subtle waves combed to the side. Lorena returned the smile, her heart lifting.

As they stood just below the church steps, folks pressed around them offering congratulations and thanks. Many of them gaped at Earl as if they'd never seen him before. A man who buried a gift God gave him. Earl, in turn, squirmed under all the praise, almost as if he wanted to hide.

Mr. Huitt and his wife approached, their steps lagging. He thrust out his hand almost as if daring Earl to accept it. "Good show, Earl."

"Thank you." Earl accepted the handshake.

With a nod at Lorena, he turned and led his wife to their wagon. Behind them the Mansfields waited. Both of them took their turns giving congratulations.

"Our prayers will be going with you both all the way to Little Rock." Mansfield clasped Earl's shoulder. "Only a week more to go!"

Rather than shaking Lorena's hand, Mrs. Mansfield wrapped her in a tight hug.

"Mrs. Steen, if you only knew how much it means to us! I've never heard such beautiful music!" The tears glistening in her eyes suddenly made Lorena thankful for all the difficult weeks she'd faced with Earl.

"It's a privilege to help."

"This will save Valley Creek and our livelihoods. We can never repay y'all."

Shaking her head, Lorena stepped back and squeezed Mrs. Mansfield's hands. "That's not so. It's the Lord's doing, not ours."

With a furtive glance at Earl, Mrs. Mansfield lowered her voice. "And Earl. I have no words. I never knew he had such a talent. I still can't get over the change in him. I believe that is the greatest miracle of all, don't you?"

Not trusting her voice, Lorena nodded. More people pressed closer, offering their best wishes and prayers. Almost as if they had just been married. Gracious! Warmth infused her cheeks at the unbidden thought.

Her head spun. The excitement buzzing around them dizzied her senses. When the last of everyone climbed into their wagons, Lorena released her pent up breath and pressed her palms against her stomach. Earl turned on his crutches toward her, concern furrowing his forehead.

"Are you ready?"

"Yes. I'll get the buggy."

"Lorena, wait. I wish you'd let your father take me home. It's almost dark, and it's not safe for you to be out alone."

"I'll be fine. I like a nighttime drive. It'll settle my nerves. Besides," she reached inside her pocket and withdrew the end of a derringer. "I carry one of these."

Earl chuckled. "As you wish. Never argue with an armed lady."

As she stepped toward the buggy, she waved at Ella who was climbing into Edith and Harley Ray's wagon to spend the night with them.

"Do you mind if I take charge of the reins?" Earl swung himself into the buggy. "We'd better hurry so you can get back."

"Gladly. I'm still so flustered. It will do me good to sit still." After she handed over the reins, she smoothed her olive skirt.

Neither of them said much as Earl urged Grits down the murky road. While the few miles rolled by, Lorena leaned her head back and closed her eyes, willing her body to relax. Now they only had two more performances, but the audience …

"Do you think I can do it?" The whispered words tripped from her mouth before she could snatch them back.

"What?"

Keeping her eyes shut, she sighed. "I haven't set foot in a theater since we parted. The memories were too much for me, and I lost my taste for public performances. I buried my talent away like you did. Now, I wonder. What if I fail these people? What if I can't do it?"

"You're the strongest person I know. You won't fail, Lorena." Earl's voice, calm and deep, wrapped around and warmed her like a down coverlet. "The Lord didn't bring you this far to let you go. He'll give you what you need when you need it."

"So strange, hearing it from you." Lorena opened her eyes.

The wind rattled the buggy top as leaves whirled across the road like flowing water. Over the hills, lightning flickered a mute warning. Moments later, thunder growled low through the valley.

"A storm's brewing." Earl flicked the reins, urging Grits even faster.

A wet, cold drop of rain spattered Lorena's hand. Then another. "Oh my. Do you think we'll make it to the house in time?"

"I hope so."

Lorena gripped the armrest as wind rammed against the buggy. The drops pelted faster. Whirling into the yard, Earl drove the buggy straight into the barn just as a wall of rain rammed it. Overhead, the wind howled through the rafters.

Wordlessly, Earl clambered down and Lorena followed. Together, they worked to unhitch the horse and put her into a stall. Only after Earl hung the tack and poured feed into the trough did he speak.

"It doesn't sound like it's letting up. We'll have to make a run for it."

Lorena rubbed her chilled arms through her coat. "And how will we do that?"

A slight smirk curved his lips. "This." He plucked a horse blanket from a rack. "A little smelly, but our heads won't get soaked to the skin."

"Well, then. I guess there's no help for it." After she retrieved the violin case from the buggy, Lorena followed him to the doorway. The chilly wind slapped rain across her face. She clutched the handle of the case tighter.

"Here." Drawing her close to his side, Earl draped the blanket over their heads.

"Can you make it?" Lorena lifted her voice against the roar of the storm.

"I'll have to. With you on one side and my crutch on the other, I'll manage." He laid an arm around her shoulders. "I'll be careful not to press my weight on you. Ready?"

Trembling more from his nearness than the storm, Lorena averted her eyes and nodded.

Gingerly, they picked their footsteps across the short distance to the house. Water crept through Lorena's shoes and soaked into her stockings. Rain assailed the exposed part of her skirts, plastering them to her legs. Lorena gritted her teeth. Beside her, Earl's breath heaved as he pulled himself with each step.

Thunder pounded the air. Lorena gasped but kept her steps even with Earl's. When they reached the steps, Earl urged her forward. "You first."

Lorena dashed inside and turned to help him step into safety. While he shut the door, she laid the case on the table and hurried back.

"Whew!" Earl shrugged off the blanket while Lorena took it.

"What a mess!" She grimaced as she draped it across the back of a chair to dry. Her skirts dripped puddles onto the floor.

"Looks like it's here for a while. You'll have to stay for the night." Something gleamed in Earl's eyes. Amusement?

"That's apparent." She jutted a saucy chin at him, and he laughed. The nervous flutter rising in her stomach intensified.

"If you'll go into Ella's room, you'll find something to change into." His tone softened. "I'll change after you're finished."

Her thanks lodged in her throat as his gaze warmed. Turning on her heel, she scurried into the bedroom and shut the door, her skirts trailing water behind her.

❧

Earl rubbed the back of his neck as he stoked the fire. Through the door, the sound of Lorena's movements reached him. The soft thump of wet clothes hitting the floor, the opening and latching of Ella's trunk, the swish of fresh clothes, and the whisk of a brush through Lorena's long hair. His wife so close yet unreachable. He bit back an impatient groan.

After a little while, the door creaked open. Earl jumped. Almost shyly, Lorena stepped into the room, a housecoat wrapped around one of Ella's cotton nightdresses. Looking everywhere but at him, she crossed her arms.

Her hair was down, plaited in a loose braid just as she always wore at the end of the day. Ah, but she was a vision, looking almost like a young girl again. Once more, Earl scraped a hand across the back of his neck. And, then, he saw it.

Just at the hollow of her throat was her wedding ring around a gold chain.

"Your ring." He blinked, unbelieving.

Hand flying to her throat, Lorena paled. "Oh! I forgot!" Her fingers scrambled to tuck the ring under the neckline of her nightdress. "I didn't think. I usually don't ... put it under my nightclothes."

"You still have your ring?" His feet froze to the floor though his fingers itched to touch it.

Taking a breath, Lorena raised her chin and leveled her eyes at him. "Yes." She offered no other explanation.

Words bolted from Earl's mind as his heart churned with emotion too strong to define. Though he knew he was staring, he couldn't move.

Lorena snapped her gaze away. She stepped further into the room toward the fire. "You should go in and change now."

"Oh. Yes." With his crutch jammed under his arm, he limped into the bedroom as quickly as his foot allowed. Though it was now the third week in November, he still couldn't put his full weight on it. The ache did little to clear the fog in his head.

Lorena still wore her ring, albeit around her neck. A mixture of delight, shame, and regret warred within him. He almost regretted seeing it. Almost.

After changing into a plain shirt and clean overalls, he stepped back into the main room. Beside the fire, Lorena sat with a bowed head, tension creasing the lines around her eyes and lips. His chest tightened.

"Lorena, are you afraid?" Earl limped closer yet keeping his distance.

Her head lifted. "I don't know," she sighed.

He detested himself for her vulnerability. Not sure what to do next, he spied the violin case on the table. He shuffled over and brought it to the chair opposite Lorena. Dear heart! Even in her predicament, she thought to bring him a chair by the fire. As he sat, he noticed the firelight threading through the gold in her dark, chestnut hair.

"You don't have anything to fear from me."

Lorena nibbled her bottom lip, taking her time to answer. "I know."

Saying nothing more, Earl pulled out the violin and poised the bow. Nothing romantic, nothing sad, nothing to bring back vivid memories. He played only tunes that brought joy. Some quick that danced around the room, others that flowed peacefully like a deep, quiet stream. Outside the rain pelted the eaves of the little house, but the music bubbled and laughed against it. Little by little, the creases around Lorena's eyes and mouth smoothed away. Peeping from under the edge of her nightdress, her toes tapped in rhythm.

The angst tumbled from Earl's heart.

Lorena's shoulders lifted and fell with her soft sigh. "Everyone seemed to enjoy our performance."

"I'd say so." Earl played softer. He remembered the stunned

hush over the crowd as their opening, Vivaldi's Concerto, "Autumn," filled the building. Within the church, the crush of people packed the pews until folks lined the aisle and walls, even spilling outside. So many crowded around the church that they had to raise the windows. Some families nestled under quilts in their wagons as the ethereal melodies floated through Valley Creek. Most had never heard music like it. Awe filled him all over again as he remembered their faces.

"They were so hopeful. I pray we won't disappoint them."

A rueful smile curved Earl's mouth. Lorena would never disappoint, but he stood little chance. "I expect we'll be doing a lot of extra praying in the meantime." His fingers meandered into "Lavender's Blue," the ancient, magical tune weaving a peaceful calm against the wind rattling the walls.

Resting her head against the back of the chair, Lorena hummed along, the lovely sound almost toppling Earl's concentration. Memories of other evenings such as this edged into his thoughts. The many times they would sit together at the end of the day while he played and she sang or hummed. The bow stiffened in his hand.

Lorena must have sensed it because she halted and darted her eyes at him. "I'm sorry."

Shaking his head, Earl laid aside the instrument. "No need to apologize." He closed the case's lid, careful not to snap it shut. "It sounded lovely. As always."

"I didn't think. It came so easily." A pensive smile played across her lips. "You always had that effect on me."

Not knowing what to say, Earl rubbed his knee and fixed his gaze on the fire. Talk of that sort wouldn't help either of them.

"And what of us?"

He stared harder into the flames, wishing to pretend he hadn't heard. "I don't know what to say, Lorena."

The chair creaked as she shifted. "That evening you fell from the overlook. I thought you were dead."

The sounds, the memory of the rocks crumbling and sliding beneath his feet, surged through him. "Were you the one who screamed? I heard it as I fell."

"You did?"

"Was it you?"

"Yes."

Sheets of rain pummeling the windows filled the silence as Earl kept his eyes trained away from her.

"What is happening between us, Earl?" Her taut voice tugged at his heart.

He rubbed his knuckles. "Nothing can happen between us."

"That's not what I asked, and you well know it."

"It's best to leave it be."

"Perhaps so, but it's not working, is it?"

Shaking his head, Earl let out a heavy breath. "That's why it's best you get back to New York as soon as you can."

Lorena stood, her hands clenched at her sides. "You would say that after ... after all of this? After all these weeks? After learning to ... to be friends again?" Exasperated tears shook her voice. "I don't like it any more than you, but—"

"I didn't say I didn't like it."

"We can't just leave things like this!"

Burrowing his fingers through his hair, Earl stood and faced her, the torrent of his emotions bursting. "What else can we do? Look at me, Lorena! I'm a poor man. Just take a look at this place. Can you live this kind of life? This is all I am now!"

In the flickering light, tears glistened down her cheeks. He groaned. He could never bear to see her cry. Closing the space between them, he gathered her close.

Lorena buried her face into his chest and wept the years away while he held her, one hand stroking the back of her silky hair. Saying nothing, he rested his chin on the top of her head. He would stand there all night if she needed it.

Her tears soaked through his shirt. His own eyes blurred then brimmed over.

Together they stood for a long time. Was it possible, after all, to find their way back to each other?

Finally, a breath shuddered through Lorena as her tears dwindled. "You're wrong, you know," she murmured against his shirt.

"How so?"

"This is all you *have*, not all that you *are*."

Then she lifted her face to his.

Their eyes locked and an age of unspoken words passed between them unhindered, no longer shuttered from each other. Their breathing thinned. They had never forgotten how to read each other's thoughts.

Earl's pulse thundered in his ears. He tightened his hold around her. Though her eyes widened, no dread shone in those blue depths. She made no move to withdraw.

He could wait no longer. He lowered his head and brought his lips to hers. Almost shyly, Lorena met them as their kiss melded together.

Was he dreaming? But no, she was kissing him back, welcoming his caresses. Her arms slid around his neck, drawing him closer as she threaded her fingers into his hair. A joy he'd never known shook him as he responded to her touch like a man long thirsty. If this was all he ever had of her, he would die a happy man.

After another long moment, he lifted his lips a breath away from hers. "Lorena," he whispered, "I don't know what to do. How can we—"

Lorena silenced him with a finger on his lips. "Earl, could we do something we didn't do years ago? Couldn't we give the Lord a chance to work this out His way?"

Earl swallowed. "And if He doesn't?"

"I find it hard to believe that He would bring us all this way and not see this through. Don't you?" Her earnest gaze searched his.

"You amaze me." He feathered a kiss across her brow. "What about all of this? I have nothing to offer you."

With a shaky smile, Lorena ran her fingers along his jaw. "You have more to offer now than you ever did before."

A mixture of awe and humility nearly overwhelmed Earl, his throat constricting, cutting off any answer.

"I'm tired of fighting it, fighting you. And it isn't fair for you to take this decision away from me."

Earl remembered Reverend Crandall's words. "I'm sorry, love. You're right, but are you sure?" He scanned her face for any sign of doubt.

Lorena nodded. "Life is too short, and time is too precious to waste. I want to give us a chance. One step at a time."

Earl wondered if his heart would explode. His trembling hands framed Lorena's face as if she might break. "Far be it from me to argue any longer." He studied her a moment more. "Oh, Lorena!" His lips plunged down to hers.

After a time, Earl loosened his hold to allow Lorena to step back. Her face beamed with the pure joy of a small child. "I'll say good night now."

She was beautiful, radiant as she stood there with the firelight dancing around her feet. And he had never loved her more.

Earl lifted her hand to his lips and kissed it. "Sweet dreams, dear one."

Her lashes fluttered down in a shy smile as he released her hand. Turning, she glided across the floor and clicked the bedroom door shut behind her.

26

From the corner of her eye, Lorena saw Earl tug his collar as he stared out one of the train's windows. He shifted in the seat beside her. Across from them, Lane dozed, her head bobbing on Guy's shoulder while he read a newspaper. Further back, Edith listened to her grandfather and Harley Ray's conversation as she stitched a bonnet for Lane's baby. She caught Lorena's eyes and smiled, the expression brightening her face. Ella, sitting beside Father, tipped back her head and laughed. Lorena's heart warmed. It was like heaven with her family all around her.

Earl shifted again, this time rubbing his knee.

Lorena closed her book. "Is something the matter?"

"I'm sorry." Earl grimaced sheepishly. "I haven't been on a train in years. Haven't been more than fifteen miles from Valley Creek ever since I set foot in it."

"Feeling out of place?"

"You could say that. It's not you or anyone else," he added quickly. "It's hard to say."

"Are you nervous?"

Earl's collar bobbed as he swallowed. Reaching over, he

covered her hand with his and captured it within his grasp. "I'm scared out of my wits."

Lorena's heart sped up both from his touch and his admission. "Well, then, that makes two of us."

Nodding, Earl chuckled a little. "To go from a sawmill to a grand theater. I'm glad it's only this once."

"You mean twice." Her gaze deepened into his, and for a moment, the clacking of the tracks and the gentle rocking of the cars dissolved. His thumb caressed her knuckles. Just as it happened the night of the rainstorm, unsaid words passed between them. One of the many things she had sorely missed about him. They had always been able to understand one another without the need for words.

That same feeling of shyness washed over her, and she looked away feeling the blush heat her cheeks. He squeezed her hand.

Taking a breath, she looked up to discover Lane watching them. Her head still resting on Guy's shoulder, she sat motionless, wonderment filling her face. Her memory held no pictures of the happiness and affection into which she had been born. Lorena's throat tightened.

Earl cleared his throat, and Lorena saw him redden at Lane's silent perusal. The same wonder in their daughter's face mirrored the look on his.

Then he winked at Lane. A slow, sunny smile curved her lips.

The hours passed with few words though Earl kept her hand within his. He had yet to tell her that he loved her. But then, neither had she told him. Truth be known, she wasn't ready for such words just yet. Both of them were giving the matter a lot of prayer. Besides, they had plenty to consider, and she needed this time of healing between them.

Awhile later, the train whistle split the air. Lorena jolted awake.

"We're here." Earl released Lorena's hand, his voice a little gruff.

As Lorena sat up, she craned her neck to see the huge platform as the train neared. A crowd of people gathered on one side, some holding signs and others holding cameras. Earl sat back.

"The Press. I hadn't thought about that."

"You used to love it."

Earl grimaced. "I know, but not so anymore."

Across from them, Lane peered at the crowd as their car rolled past. "It'll be all right, Pa. All you have to do is smile and look smart."

A chuckle pushed past his tight lips, loosening the tension around them. "You're right about that, Lane-girl."

Steam spewed and a white cloud whooshed down the side of the train after it stopped. Mumbles and groans filled the aisle as people stood and stretched. Grabbing the cane that Doc Brown gave him, Earl stood and held out a hand to help Lorena to her feet.

A commotion near the front of the car snagged their attention as a tall, husky man strode toward them. A shaft of sunlight from the window lit his features.

"Congressman Thompson." With a nod, Earl held out his hand to have it heartily shaken in turn.

"Good to see you up and about, my boy! And Mrs. Steen, you're looking as lovely as ever." He bowed slightly.

"It's always a pleasure, Congressman."

After Thompson had greeted the rest of their family, he returned to Lorena and Earl. Raising a bushy eyebrow, he tipped his head toward the crowd.

"I arranged for the press to be here. They may ask you a few questions, but I'll do most of the talking. It will be good publicity for the concert. We've had advertisements and fliers circulating around the city, and I can tell you, people are interested."

Lorena smiled. "That's good. We appreciate everything you're doing."

Thompson shook his head. "Think nothing of it. I was raised in those parts. I'm glad there's something we can do to help them." He gestured a hand toward the front. "Shall we?"

Slipping her hand into the crook of Earl's proffered arm, Lorena felt his muscles beneath her fingers tense. She peeped sideways at him. As they came down the steps and stepped on the platform, he trained his eyes on the newspaper men.

Applause echoed around them. Earl flinched and pulled in a deep breath. Lorena tightened her fingers around his arm. "It's all right, Earl. We'll get through it."

Only then did he look at her. "I hope you're right."

"Remember what Lane said. Just smile and look smart."

A stiff smile curved his mouth but failed to reach his blue-green eyes.

Thompson gave a short speech welcoming them and their family and reminding the journalists of Valley Creek's plight. As Lorena perused them jotting down notes, fingers scurrying, she hardly heard the congressman's words. When the speech ended, the questions began.

A short, bald man with glasses addressed Earl. "How does a renowned violinist end up in Valley Creek, Arkansas?"

Lorena pressed a hand against her stomach trying to squelch the plummeting sensation within.

The stiff smile never faded from Earl's face. His direct gaze met the curious one. "That's a much longer story than you have time for, but Valley Creek has been my home for many years now. I'm glad to help any way I can."

Another reporter waved his hand and wedged his way to the front. "Mrs. Steen, how do you feel about performing after years of retirement?"

Raising her chin, Lorena kept her voice light. "It isn't so much about how I feel. I'm happy to help my friends, many of whom have lost so much."

"Will this be a new start of a career for you, Mr. Steen?"

Lorena felt the muscles in his arm knot up even harder. "No, sir. This is only for the people back home."

Thompson held up his hand. "Thank you all for coming out to meet these good people. We have a busy schedule, and we need to be on our way." A few more reporters clamored with questions, but he turned his attention to Lorena and Earl. "I have two autos waiting. We'll take y'all to your rooms. Come with me."

Turning to glance over her shoulder, Lorena watched her daughters and their husbands follow suit behind them. At the rear, Father offered Ella his arm. Looking up, he met Lorena's eyes and nodded, sending wordless encouragement to bolster her spirit.

The echoing footsteps and droning voices within the station failed to drown out Earl's silence as he led her past ticket counters and the lounge area. His cane tapped the floor, only hammering her anxious thoughts down like a loose shingle in the wind. She'd much rather them blow away. Was Earl going to be all right? Suppose he couldn't go through with it? She had never really doubted it until that moment. If only she could speak with him privately!

Privately. Thompson had mentioned rooms. She hadn't thought about hers and Earl's arrangements. Oh dear! As they stepped outside to meet the waiting cars, a breeze stirred the moisture beading at her forehead.

As Earl stood aside and helped her into the first car, the pulse pounded in Lorena's ears. A moment later, Earl settled beside her, the leather seat creaking against his broad shoulders.

One thing was certain. She would find out soon enough.

CONGRESSMAN THOMPSON, who made arrangements for Lorena and Earl, handed both of them a key.

"Connecting rooms," he commented nodding toward a red-carpeted stairway. "Third floor. The clerk said everything was ready and in order. If you should need anything at all, let them know."

With one gloved hand covering her mouth, Lorena released a pent-up breath. Peeping over at Earl, she found his eyes on her, an amused gleam belying his serious face. Laughing was he! A blush singed her cheeks. Narrowing her eyes, she tugged her gloves tighter.

While Father, who made arrangements for everyone else, collected the keys at the front desk, Lorena busied her thoughts elsewhere.

The polished wood floor boasted a large, flowered rug in the center of the room, a gardened oasis for travelers' feet. Two cracking fires drew several newcomers to the marble fireplaces on each side of the room. Sitting in one of the plush lounge chairs, an elderly gentleman glanced over the top of his newspaper at them. When he caught Lorena's eye, he nodded and raised the paper higher.

After the congressman said his goodbyes, an attendant led the way to their rooms, his lanky stride zipping up the staircase. The polished, chocolate-brown banister reflected the electric lights in the lobby. A very fine place to stay, indeed. Congressman Thompson was generous to host them here for the next several days.

As they reached the top of the stairs, carpet stretched from wall to wall, a woven scroll-work flowing down the corridor. Near the end were Lorena's and Earl's rooms while everyone else's were only down the hallway.

A touch grasped Lorena's sleeve. "Mother, I'm going to lie down for a while, but I'll see you at supper."

Pressing her lips against Lane's forehead, Lorena squeezed her shoulder. "You look pale and exhausted. By all means, dear, sleep as long as you can."

With a hazy smile, Lane slipped her arm around Guy's, and they headed toward their room.

As Lorena slipped the key into the lock of her room, Father approached Earl.

"After you've freshened up, I thought we'd go and get you fitted for that tuxedo. Will that suit you?"

Earl blinked as though clearing his foggy thoughts. "Yes, sir," he answered a bit absently. "I won't be long." While he let himself into his room, Father turned to her.

"What are your plans, Lorena?"

"While Lane is resting, Edith and I are going to shop for that gown I'll be needing for the concert."

"Good, good." Nodding, Father squeezed her elbow, his gray eyes tender and understanding. "Take time to breathe, daughter. And trust." His mustache twitched. "Better get two gowns. You can't wear the same one for each performance."

Sighing, Lorena rolled her eyes. "I'll be glad when this is over."

Father chuckled, the sound warming the chill in the pit of her stomach. "No doubt. But in the meantime, try to enjoy it a little. After all, it's your final performance."

"That's not helping, Father."

Reaching across her, Father unlocked the door and opened it. His chuckle deepened within his chest. "Everything will be all right, Lorena. God hasn't brought you to this moment for nothing."

As the door clicked shut behind her, she sagged against its hard, polished surface while lifting a silent prayer to her Heavenly Father.

Would this concert be successful? Suppose either of them flopped? Or worse, froze on stage? Could they remember how to be the professionals they once were? Would they be able to raise enough money for Valley Creek? Would Earl prove himself to them?

Lorena groaned, shaking her head. If only she could shake her thoughts away!

And what of Earl? Of their future?

The carpet muted her tentative footsteps as she approached the connecting door between their rooms. Her breathing shallowed as she pressed her ear against the door. The solid oak surface muffled Earl's unhurried movements, sounds of drawers opening and shutting, the click of a wardrobe door. No doubt, he was looking everything over. He had very few belongings to put away.

How could they make this work?

Lorena wasn't afraid of being poor, but then again, she realized that she had never faced that reality either. Could she give everything up? Possessions had never filled the empty gap that Earl left behind. Only God had soothed the ache of his betrayal.

In Earl, she once again saw the man she had long loved yet now possessing the qualities he lacked during their careless youth. Neither of them had known the Lord then.

He was the same, yet so very different. Yet one thing had never changed.

She still loved Earl Steen. For always.

Nothing could change it.

Earl's movements silenced. Lorena pressed her ear harder against the door but heard nothing. What was he thinking? Every fiber within her longed to know.

She raised her hand to knock. She paused, hand mid-air.

The next moment she dropped it to her side, hating herself for being a coward.

She was afraid to know.

GASLIGHTS from the chandelier sparkled on the dishes that evening as everyone sat around Congressman Thompson's supper table.

Earl's sleeve grazed Lorena's arm as he reached for his glass of tea. Raising it to his lips, he watched the conversation buzzing around him, his face intent, missing nothing. Lorena sensed his wrestling with the tension coiled in every movement.

Lorena lifted a napkin to her mouth. "Are you all right?"

Earl took another sip before answering. "As all right as I'll be until we're done."

From the head of the table, Congressman Thompson took control of the surrounding conversation. "Earl, I understand you got that tuxedo today."

"I did. It fits very well, thank you."

Thompson waved off his thanks with a grin. "All for a good cause. Are your and Mrs. Steen's rooms to your liking?"

"Yes, very comfortable, much more than I need." Earl turned to Lorena. "And yours?"

Though it pained her to see the anxiety hiding in the depths of his eyes, Lorena kept a placid face and nodded. "Mine is lovely, very restful. As Earl said, much more than we need."

"Piffle tosh. Enjoy it and rest between all the work you'll be doing. If it suits you both, I'll be by at 10 sharp in the morning to give you a tour of the theater and then leave you while you practice."

Two days to prepare for their first concert on Friday. Two days to step back into a world they no longer knew. A world that once brought them grief. An auditorium of people, hundreds of pairs of eyes on them. Her fingers stiffened. No, no. She must keep them loose, relaxed. She flexed them in her lap.

Earl answered, but it sounded like someone jammed cotton in her ears. Clenching her own glass of tea, she let the cool liquid flow over her tongue, refreshing her dry throat.

Focus on the present.

A few seats down from her, Guy cleared his throat. "Could I have a word, Congressman?"

All heads turned toward the handsome young man.

"By all means."

"I know the folks back home thanked you, but I'd like to say again how much we're obliged that you and Mr. Wallace have worked things out." Guy nodded toward Harley Ray. "And Mr. Wallace, we appreciate you providing a way so that our wives could see their mother and father perform."

A tender gleam stole into Father's eyes. "You're welcome, son. It's my gift to them. It's good to remember, to know your beginnings so that you can look back over the path of your life. To find God's hand, His grace in the details. Edith and Lane have never seen their father and mother performing together in a theater. They need this moment as much as Valley Creek. It's a glimpse into their history, a fragment of something they lost."

Tears pricked the back of Lorena's eyelids. Blinking hard, she looked at Earl. He swallowed, a melancholy smile toying with the corners of his mouth. His blue-green eyes swam, their rich aqua glistening with emotions too strong to voice.

"Well said." Thompson puffed out a breath, scarcely covering the waver in his voice.

27

"I must speak with you." The words tripped from Lorena's lips as she unlocked her room door.

Hesitating, Earl opened his mouth then shut it. As he followed her inside, she crossed the room and turned on the lamp. Going over to the fireplace, Earl relaxed his arm along the mantle and waited. Lorena settled on the settee, her back straight and stiff.

"You've hardly spoken since we arrived. What is going on?"

"I've been going over the musical arrangements in my mind."

"I know that, but that's not all, and you know it, Earl."

Earl scrutinized her for a long moment before dropping his glance to his toes. "I no longer fit in this world, Lorena. I'm lost on a city sidewalk. I'd much rather find my way through the woods."

"I know."

"Do you?" he said, his husky voice both gentle and demanding. "When I was being fitted for that tuxedo, I felt like an imposter. When I saw this place, these fine rooms ..." He ran an agitated hand through his hair and grasped the back of his neck. "How can I expect you to give it all up? For nothing? It's asking too much."

"That decision is up to me."

Earl shook his head. "I can't bear to have you live a scant existence. Lorena, we have to face reality. Our time has passed." He curled one hand into a fist. "I squandered it."

Panic quaked Lorena's heart. For several minutes, neither of them said anything. While Earl kept his eyes down, her mind scrambled for an answer. She could not let him just give up.

"I meant our vows. Remember? For richer, for poorer?"

"If it were circumstances beyond our control, but this was my doing. It didn't have to be this way. I won't let you be a part of it."

The despair in his voice ripped through her. And, then, wisdom not belonging to her seeped into her mind. She stood, clasping her hands.

"Pride set you on the path to Valley Creek in the first place. Do you think pride will solve our dilemma?"

Earl's head jerked up, his eyebrows clashing above tear-filled eyes like the rumbling of a cloud before a downpour.

"It's true, we must face reality, but with prayer, not with our wisdom. With faith. You refuse to let me make my decision, and that's a point of pride. Possessions have never meant much to me, especially without Lane and you. The years were empty. I was surrounded with things, yes, but inside I was bereft of everything that mattered. God saved your life, and I believe He isn't through with us."

She stepped toward him, facing him almost toe-to-toe, drawing from a deep well of strength not belonging to her. "I don't know how, but God knows. Isn't that enough for now? Please, Earl."

As his eyes traveled over her face, she failed to read the expression of his thoughts. Without warning, his hands lifted and framed her face. He moved closer. Lorena's heart skipped a quick staccato.

"Dear heart." The old nickname rose up. "You're right. Besides you, pride has always been my weakness. You're giving up far more than I am." His thumbs stroked her jaw, gentle like a whisper. "I don't know how, but if God wills it, then I'll not stand in His way."

Releasing her, Earl stepped back, longing darkening his eyes. "Only if He wills it." He turned on his heel and headed for the door. Pausing, he looked back.

"'Til tomorrow, Lorena."

In his look flamed a kiss more powerful than a mere physical touch. Her short gasp robbed her voice of an answer.

Opening the door, he stepped into the hallway and snapped shut the barrier between them.

Knees wobbling, Lorena moved to the settee and sank onto the cushion. Her fingers, unbidden, pulled the chain from beneath her blouse. Thoughtfully, she fingered the ring, still warm from lying near her heart.

"Quite a building, isn't it?" Mr. Thompson offered Lorena his hand as she stepped from the car.

On either side, cream pillars stretched upward, a decorative parapet of apple blossoms spanning the ridge of the roof between them. A chiseled arch drew the eye to a kaleidoscope of colors glimmering within the round, stained glass window in the center several feet above the ticket booth. Two sets of double glass doors stood on both sides of the booth, reflecting the images of the cars whirling past.

"Yes, indeed. It's very grand!" Wonder and angst mingled on Lorena's face as her eyes scaled the lofty edifice of Apple Blossom Theatre.

Earl wiped clammy palms on his slacks as he climbed out of the two-door Model T touring car. Squinting up at the detailed etchings of apple blossoms, Arkansas's state flower, he shriveled up inside.

The last time he set foot in a concert hall, he was kicked out for showing up intoxicated just before a concert. He cringed, reliving the hazy details. Belligerent and late, he disgraced his family, the orchestra, and himself. Lorena's distressed, mortified face emerged, the only clear thing in that ugly memory.

A tug at his sleeve and her voice called him back to the present. "Earl? Are you ready?"

"I reckon." Turning, he plucked the violin case from the car seat and followed them inside. The cool air swept around him as they entered the elaborate foyer. Their steps rebounded across the marble floor in time with the tap of his cane.

"Welcome to the Apple Blossom." Thompson grinned, hooking his thumbs behind the lapels of his jacket. "I'll give you a brief tour, then I'll leave you to practice. Ask any questions, and I'll do my best to answer."

The ornate fixtures, the chandeliers, and the gilded pictures filled the lobby and swept Earl back to times he struggled to forget.

"Travelers are surprised we have a place like this smack dab in the middle of Arkansas." Thompson laughed as he led them into the grand auditorium. "But why not? We can put on a good show too."

Leaning on the cane, Earl halted, the auditorium yawning wide and deep before him. Row upon row of seats descended gradually until reaching the stage. In the center of the stage, a grand piano gleamed. Earl's gaze lifted to the box seats and balcony surrounding three sides of the room. The gilding shone, the gold-coloring glowing under the lights.

The lights. Once he loved those lights, and that love ruined him. All of the sudden, Earl realized the room was quiet. Ahead of him, Thompson and Lorena watched him take everything in, their conversation suspended like a frozen pendulum.

"Sorry." He hurried forward, ignoring the ache in his foot.

"No rush. It takes one's breath away, doesn't it?" Thompson raised his eyebrows.

"It does at that." What had he gotten himself into? While the congressman shared the brief history, the words only jumbled and reeled in his mind. Only one day more.

"I'll leave y'all to it now." Thompson shook their hands, his pleasant face beaming at both of them. "My driver will be around to pick you up later."

While Thompson's footsteps faded, Lorena gathered her skirts and headed backstage. Earl trudged behind, only too glad to let her take the lead. Almost like walking backwards through time, to another age. Both foreign and familiar at once.

Then they stepped onto the stage.

Lorena's warm fingers wrapped around his. "Did you ever dream we would do this again?"

Earl returned her squeeze, his heart skipping a beat. "Never in a million years."

Surrounded by a world they once knew, they were alone and strangers in it. Audience or no audience.

Lorena squeezed his fingers once more. "I'll go warm up." Like a skiff on tranquil waters, she glided across the polished stage, her skirts rippling around her feet. When she reached the piano, she slid between instrument and bench, then sat, her back straight, her demeanor poised.

She had never been more beautiful to him.

Unaware of his scrutiny, she placed her fingers on the keys and began playing scales. He shook his head. Enough of those thoughts for now. Time to get familiar with the surroundings and focus on the music.

Polished like smooth glass, the stage stretched from one

side of the room to the other, rounding along the front edge. Earl took his time walking the length of it, his eyes soaking in every detail from the molding on the ceiling, the gilded wall sconces, the velvet-red cushioned seats, to the pristine carpet leading to the foyer.

The notes from the piano floated through the space like fine mist, glazing every surface, the melody perfect, its timbre precise, the clarity like fine crystal. Halting near center stage, Earl pulled in a deep breath.

"Lord, help us to get through this and somehow honor You."

In his mind, he heard the orchestra warming up behind them, the humming of the strings, all the sounds that once charmed him.

The notes from the piano ceased. "Earl, are you ready?"

"Do you feel out of place, Lorena?" He turned toward her unable to mask the frown pinching his brows together.

"Like a fish out of water." The fringes of a grin tugged at the corners of her pink lips, easing the frown on his.

Swallowing, Earl allowed himself a wry grin. "Well, then, let's get crackin' before we drown." Laying down the case, he snapped it open and lifted the violin. Next came the bow.

"Shall we?" He quirked an eyebrow and watched with pleasure as a rosy blush crept into her cheeks.

"Let's."

ROLLING UP HIS PANTS LEG, Earl eased his throbbing foot into a basin of steaming Epson salt water prepared by the staff. After five hours of practice, his insides screamed to sit. He laid his head back, easing the pressure both on his foot and his mind. Tomorrow was the beginning of the ending of an unfinished part of his life.

Someone knocked on the door.

"Come in."

Opening it, Lane hovered over the threshold. "I've caught you at a bad time."

"No, not at all." Earl motioned her inside. "I'm just resting my foot."

Hiding a smile, he noticed the very beginnings of her motherhood starting to show at the loosened waist of her dress. After some rest, the purple shadows pooling around her eyes had faded. He prayed her child would live to bring all of them joy.

Lane's eyelashes fluttered downward, almost as though she felt shy while she scooted a footstool next to Earl's chair and sat. Fumbling with a button on her sleeve, she bit her lip, looking at the toes of her shoes.

Even though she was a young lady, Earl still glimpsed traces of the small child he wrenched from Lorena that awful day long ago. A melancholy blend of love and remorse rose and fell within Earl's chest, an ache almost physical.

"What's on your mind, Lane?"

Her gaze dug into him then, clear and direct, examining him the way she always had. Though once it enraged him, now it only sharpened a sadness he would never fully dispel.

"I suppose it's none of my business, but what's going on between you and Mother?"

Earl held her gaze. "It's every bit your business. You're a part of everything we are."

Lane raised her eyebrows, waiting.

"We're finding our way back to one another."

A sheen glazed her eyes, but she stayed silent. A tremor quivered her lips. Whether from unspoken words or emotions, he couldn't tell.

"One thing I need to know. Do you approve?"

"Does my approval mean that much to you?" Awe threaded her voice as she shook her head.

"Very much so." He hoped she believed him. Such small words failed to convey how much her approval meant to him. Fear spread like frost through his insides. And if she didn't?

Then, slowly, Lane nodded. "If God wills it and both of you want it, I heartily approve."

Earl released a breath he didn't realize he was holding. Lane tipped up a saucy chin.

"Afraid, Pa?"

Concentrating on his foot, Earl raised it out of the steaming water then dipped it under again. "Terrified, Lane-girl."

"Are you in earnest? I've never known you to be terrified of anything."

"I was terrified of the truth for years until God showed me how to face it. But this with your mother ..." He grimaced and spread out his hands.

"What?"

"I never expected this. You, more than anyone else, understand my circumstances. Even though we're praying about it, how can I expect your mother to share my life?"

Pinching her lips together, Lane leaned forward, propping her elbows on her knees while resting her chin in her hands.

"I honestly don't know." She crinkled her forehead. "Maybe, if this concert is successful, you could be a violinist again."

"No." Earl shook his head. "I don't want it even if it meant a way to provide for Lorena. That life is over for me."

"Then I'll help pray. Just don't give up."

"Rest assured, I won't. And, Lane?" He reached out, extending his palm. Without hesitation, she rested her hand in his. "Thank you."

She squeezed his hand. "I still can hardly believe the change in you. Sometimes I wake up in the night and wonder if I'm dreaming."

"You know that Bible story about the demoniac in the tombs that Jesus saved. Remember how the town came out and found him clothed and in his right mind? That's how I feel. For the first time in my life, I'm free from the chains that bound me. And I never believed it could happen until I met Jesus." Earl tightened his grip on Lane's hand. "I haven't thought of it until now, but if God can save someone like me, it ought to be a hundred times easier for Him to provide a way for your mother and me."

"I'd say so." Lane's voice grew soft. "Pa, when you were growing up, were you raised to know God? Were your folks Christians?"

Earl tried not to wince. Thoughts of his folks always brought the ache of knowing he could never make things right with them. Not in this life.

"Yes. We rose early every morning before chores and prayed together after Father read a passage of Scripture. Their faith was personal, not a ritual. A daily walk with God. And every night before bed, they would pray with each of us no matter how long the day or how tired they were. I never knew the Lord in those days." His eyes snapped away from Lane's, needing to view the present instead of the past.

"Was it hard breaking away from your home? From them?"

"I loved my folks. I loved our farm. And I had two dreams. One was to farm our place and the other was to play the violin." He rubbed his jaw, his fingers grazing the afternoon stubble. "I was young and had big dreams. The violin and the opportunity to go to New York won. It was hard, at first. With time, I settled in, especially after I met Lorena. It grew harder much later ... after I left everything behind. Trapped in a snare of my own making."

"Growing up, I never imagined there were so many out there who loved us."

"But you knew something was missing."

"I never put my finger on it until Edith came." With her other hand, Lane tapped his arm. "Pa, look at me please."

Crushing his emotions, he forced himself to look at her. In her eyes, unabashed love bridged the remorse and quelled the sting in his heart.

"You don't know what this concert means to me. It's not just about Valley Creek. Watching you and her is like discovering a lost piece of myself. I can't explain how it feels."

Earl covered their clasped hands with his other one. "I understand. Doing this is hard, but I know it's the last piece of myself that needs mending. I have a chance to restore what I ripped apart, my marriage, my family, and my reputation. One thing's certain, though. I couldn't do it without God's help. Or Lorena's."

Lane looked down at their hands, that mix of wonder and awe filling her expression. "There's no one beyond the reach of God, is there?"

"No one."

28

Outside her window below, a wagon clattered past, the horses' hooves clopping against the pavement. A rumbling motor car followed. Lorena lifted her bowed head. Until then, she hadn't realized how much she preferred the quiet of the country. Though daylight was still an hour away, Little Rock was awake and stirring.

Friday, November 25, 1910. What a day ahead!

Rising from her knees, Lorena took the Bible from her bedside table and went to the settee. She switched on the lamp, a flood of light driving the shadows into the corners. Pausing, she switched it off. Darkness engulfed everything like a crashing wave. Nothing untouched.

Once more, she switched on the light and the darkness retreated.

Just so, the light of God's presence in her and Earl's lives had driven the darkness back. Yes, the shadows remained in places, but as long as the light shone, it overtook nothing.

A light flickered to life within Lorena.

Peace pervaded her soul, a sweet invasion against the past, present, and even the future. And in that moment, Lorena knew. Though she and Earl couldn't live apart from the shadows, God's light held them in their proper place. Never out of sight, the shadows accented the light flowing through everything else. Like a masterpiece.

The shadows highlighted the miracle God wrought in them. The intended evil overturned to something good. The light shimmered and danced through a sudden haze of tears. Another accent of God's infinite grace through pain.

Lorena sat and opened her Bible at the bookmark. Her mind soaked up the words as though reading them for the first time.

To every thing there is a season, and a time to every purpose under the heaven...

A time to kill, and a time to heal; a time to break down, and a time to build up; a time to weep, and a time to laugh; a time to mourn, and a time to dance...

A time to get, and a time to lose ... a time to rend, and a time to sew; a time to keep silence, and a time to speak; a time to love, and a time to hate; a time of war, and a time of peace.

Light and shadow melded through the purposes of a loving, ever-present Savior.

A tear puddled on the page. "Thank You, Father," she whispered, as gratitude brimmed over. Reaching around her neck, Lorena unclasped the chain. With nimble fingers, she freed the ring from its cord. The gold metal glinted in the lamplight and warmed to her touch.

She slipped it onto her finger.

THE HUM of the audience seeped through the walls of the dressing room backstage. With a ramrod straight back, Lorena dared not relax against the back of the chair lest she wrinkle the silver gown she wore. In front of her stood Earl, his back to her, motionless, his head bent. Though unaware of her or anything else, she understood. He was with the music.

She glanced down at her ring and covered it with her other hand. Her lips tipped upward. All day Earl failed to notice, but the girls and Ella spied it right away. Their sideways winks and giggles added to the youth spreading through her.

After a light tap on the door, Congressman Thompson entered. "I'll be speaking in two minutes, then I'll introduce you." He patted Earl's shoulder. "It's not a full house tonight. It's about three-quarters of the way full, but it's a good start. If tonight is a success, I expect tomorrow night to be even better."

Earl swallowed, the disappointment clear in the gathering of his brows. "Well, we'd better do the best we can."

"That's the spirit!" Turning on his heel, Thompson opened the door and gestured them through. They remained silent as they neared the stage. Someone was already speaking. After straightening his gloves, Thompson winked at them.

"It's my turn in a moment. Remember to smile. And welcome back." His name was called, and he stepped out into the light amidst applause.

Lorena sensed Earl's eyes on her. As she turned to him, he smiled.

"You look lovely."

The warmth of his gaze sparked a glow deep inside that she allowed to show through her smile. In his tuxedo, Earl resembled very much the handsome gentleman she fell in love with years ago. Only now, not a trace of arrogance touched his features. The Master's touch brought humility and a quiet spirit that appealed to her all the more.

"Are you ready?" she asked, breathless.

"As ready as I'll ever be. The rest is up to the Lord. And you?"

"I'm quivering on the inside like a bowl of jelly." She pressed a hand against her stomach.

Earl crossed the short distance between them and tipped her chin up with his finger.

"I've all the confidence in the world in you. Remember how we used to focus and let the audience melt into the background?"

Unable to trust her voice, she nodded, losing herself in his steady gaze.

"We used to pretend we were performing in the woods, all alone. We'll do it now. Breathe in, breathe out. You can do this, Lorena."

She swallowed and inhaled a deep breath, releasing it slowly.

Earl winked at her. "Just one note, one chord at a time."

Before they knew it, Thompson finished his short speech and called Lorena first. With one last wink, Earl released her and stepped back. Lorena straightened her shoulders and stepped onto the stage.

She glided across the space, her smile unfurling as the audience applauded. Before taking her seat at the piano, she turned, faced the crowd, and curtsied. The only faces clear to her were those in the front row: her family.

Lorena slipped onto the bench, back perfectly straight, and waited for Earl's entrance. Just offstage, his darkened silhouette hid his face. What was he thinking? Feeling? Was he nervous? She saw him reach for his violin and bow. A moment later, Thompson introduced him.

Sixteen years. Earl placed one foot forward and stepped into the lights. Broad shoulders straight, a pleasant expression, he strode with ease across the stage as though he'd never stopped. When he reached the front of the piano, he turned and bowed.

As the clapping died away, Thompson exited the stage. Expectation hovered through the air.

Earl tucked the violin under his chin and raised his bow, a

professional mask enveloping his face. Thus began their two hours.

Breathe in. Breathe out. Their first piece. Strauss's "Roses from the South."

Moving the bow across the strings, Earl began the introduction. The strains, sweet and clear, swept through the room like a wave breaking upon the sand. As her time approached, Lorena poised her fingers on the keys.

As the rhythm evolved into a waltz, she joined him, and together their music danced through the air, swirling around the audience as one. Their focus blended in perfect unison.

When, at last, they finished the piece, the audience applauded, a mixture of interest and curiosity. A good sign.

Once the applause faded, Lorena began the next piece. Tchaikovsky's "Waltz of the Flowers." A few more waltzes followed, the applause building with each piece, and Lorena's heart began to lift.

Then came Beethoven's "Presto Agitato 3rd Movement" led by her. With precision and sharp concentration, her fingers flew along the keys, unaware of anything else. Somewhere, within the notes and the flying of her fingers, Lorena merged with the music in a way she believed was lost to her forever. As the last note died, the thundering applause snapped her back into the present.

She felt reborn.

Then, as planned, Earl slowed the program down a bit. Time to showcase their talents even more deeply with Chopin's "Nocturne No. 20 in C sharp minor." His strings and their harmony cut tenderly into the emotions.

Then came Pachelbel's "Canon in D." More music followed. When the time came for intermission, Lorena ended the first half of the program with Liszt's "Hungarian Rhapsody No. 2." To one side, Earl stood erect holding the violin at his side, his attention trained upon her while she played the solo.

At the ending, as her hands relaxed then lifted from the keys, rigorous clapping vibrated along the walls almost visible with its intensity. Earl stepped forward and held out his hand to her. With grace, she slipped from the bench and stood. Dipping her head, she curtsied as he bowed.

They exited the stage while the clapping continued. Once backstage, the professional mask dissolved. Earl seized her hand and rushed along the narrow hallway to the dressing room. He opened the door and pulled her inside. Latching the door, he set aside his violin and bow, his breath heaving.

He turned to her. Those blue-green eyes sparkled like a creek tumbling over rocks, shining as in old times. His arms circled her waist and drew her close. Before she could speak, Earl lowered his head and crushed his lips against hers. Her arms stole around his neck.

A long moment passed before Earl lifted his head, his lips hovering above hers. "You're wonderful."

Lorena opened her mouth to return the compliment, but a rapping at the door stopped her. Earl stole a swift kiss and turned to open it.

Edith and Lane scurried inside, breathless. Their words tangled and sputtered together as they crowded around them.

"It's glorious!" Edith threw her arms around her father while Lane hugged Lorena.

"I have no words except to say that it's the most beautiful thing I've ever seen or heard!" Lane reached for Earl next. "You should hear everyone outside. They're excited!"

"That's always good." Earl chuckled. "Now we just have to get through the second half."

"You will!" Edith tugged Lane's arm. "We'd better go back now. We just couldn't wait until the end."

Lorena blew them a kiss as the door closed behind them.

"If for no other reason, I'm glad we're doing this for them." Earl's tender perusal swept every inch of her as he closed the short distance between them. He took her chin between his thumb and forefinger. "And you. It's my honor to perform this night with you. It's a dream I never thought I'd live to see again."

A rush of tears clogged Lorena's throat and pushed their way upward. "Earl Steen. You know I can't cry right now."

"Will this help?" He lowered his lips to hers.

This time, his kiss was gentle and full of the tender feelings he left yet unspoken. Full of things that she knew he couldn't say. Lorena returned the kiss in full measure. Would he realize that she didn't dread a future with him? She ached to pour her heart out to him, to have a long talk, but it must wait for now.

Thompson's voice filtered through the door. "Three minute warning!" As his steps echoed down the hall, Earl drew back.

"You go on ahead. I'll be a minute."

He must need a little time to gather his thoughts. Smoothing her gown, Lorena willed her racing heart to calm itself.

As she neared the stage, the murmurs in the auditorium grew louder, a thread of excitement weaving the voices together like colorful tapestry.

Earl soon joined her just as Thompson took the stage to announce them once again. Save for the lingering glimmer in his eyes, the professional mask schooled his features.

They appeared on stage just as they did at first. Only the audience clapped louder this time, ready for more. Once they subsided, Earl cradled the violin under his chin and positioned the bow.

A flash of gold winked at her when he moved his fingers along the bow.

He wore his ring.

A thousand butterflies swarmed within her stomach and took flight.

EASING his aching foot into another steaming basin of Epsom water, Earl relaxed his head against the back of the chair and released the air in his lungs. Standing for over two hours without the aid of his cane made the pain difficult to take. But it was worth it.

His eyes slid closed. A smile played around the corners of his mouth. "Thank You, Lord, for helping us tonight. Thank You for everything."

As their last song ended, the audience stood and clapped for several minutes. Shouts for an encore erupted from one part of the auditorium to another. After bowing, he raised his instrument and played Dvorak's symphony No. 9 in E minor, "From the New World."

After the last notes seeped into silence, Earl thought the clapping would never stop. Their first performance was a success. Only one more to go.

Yet the best part of the evening had nothing to do with the music. When he spied the ring on Lorena's finger, he harnessed every bit of discipline he possessed to focus on their task. Her choice both humbled and frightened him. She deserved so much more than he could give her. Somehow, with God's help, he must find another way to take care of her.

He peeked at the corner clock. After midnight. They decided to wait until after the concert to talk everything over. Just being near one another proved to be distraction enough. For the last half-hour, he hadn't heard Lorena moving around. He hoped she would rest.

A faint tap rapped at the door. "It's me. May I come in?"

Earl raised his head. After toweling off his foot, he let Ella inside. With a wry smile, he raised his eyebrows at her.

"I saw your light underneath the door." Ella headed to the

empty chair across from Earl's. "We haven't had a moment alone since we arrived, and I'd like to talk to you."

Earl settled his foot back in the basin. "So excited you can't sleep?"

Grinning, Ella nodded. "I can't remember the last time I've enjoyed something so much. It was exhilarating! I felt like I was flying the whole time." She leaned forward, her hands on her knees. "Oh, Earl, it was so much like old times!"

"Almost."

Ella eyed the ring on her brother's finger. "I see you and Lorena have an understanding at last."

Earl felt his face warm. "Yes, but we still have matters to discuss."

Sympathy filled Ella's violet eyes. "About that ... I know I'm intruding, but how are you going to provide for her?"

Clamping down on the knot tightening in his chest, Earl ran his palms down the upholstered arms of the chair. "I don't know, but it won't be sawmill work."

"If tomorrow night is as successful as tonight, the bright lights of New York might shine on you again."

"That life isn't for me anymore, Ella. I've thought about working for Mr. Wallace, though."

"That would mean leaving Valley Creek and your daughters."

"I know." He pinched the bridge of his nose. "Lorena and I are praying about it. We'll work something out."

Folding her hands, Ella stared down into her lap a long minute as though mulling over her thoughts. Finally, she lifted her head.

"I can't begin to tell you how proud I am of you. When I first wrote you, asking to come, I had to see for myself if you'd really changed."

"I understand that."

"All these weeks, I've seen it for myself. I confess I've had to ask the Lord to forgive me. I talk so much about how the Lord can save anyone from anything, yet how little I truly believed it for you. I'm sorry for that, Earl."

Uncomfortable, Earl squirmed. "You have nothing to apologize for."

"Oh, but I do." Her voice grew soft, her Georgia drawl almost whispering. "Father and Mother would be so proud, so happy. They were the only ones in the family who never lost hope. No matter how many years passed, Father watched for you to come walking up that road. I told you that you were the last thing he spoke of before he died."

Earl squeezed his eyes shut. "Ella. I'm sorry. I can't think on it now."

"But I have to tell you everything he said. Earl, please look at me."

He couldn't reject her gentle entreaty no matter how much he wanted. He lifted his gaze.

Her chin tremored. "I was holding Father's hand when he turned to me. He said, 'Promise me, you'll do it.' I didn't know what he was talking about, but I promised. He said, 'Earl has gone into a dark place, but I've prayed, and I believe he'll come back. You tell him, Ella, that I always knew. You tell him I knew he would return from that valley of shadows.' In the next breath, he was gone."

With a small groan, Earl covered his eyes as the grief spilled over, flowing down his face. Sliding from the chair, Ella knelt beside his and withdrew his hands, clasping them in hers instead.

"It wasn't the last we heard from Father. After the funeral, when his will was read, he gave you your portion of the inheritance along with your share of the land to be kept in a trust under my control. I was instructed to keep it for you."

Blinking back the blur of tears, Earl jerked his head up. "What?"

Tossing back her head, Ella laughed and cried at once, a watery fountain of mirth. "That's what Father meant by my promise. He didn't trust anyone else to keep your share. He knew Douglas would never do it. Oh, was Douglas furious! He stormed from the house in a rage."

Through the sudden fog that pervaded his senses, Earl wrestled with his muddled thoughts. "Are you certain, Ella?"

"I should say so!" Ella's chest heaved. "Mind you, the money won't make you wealthy, but if you sell the land, you'll have enough to build Lorena a decent, comfortable home, buy a piece of ground to farm, and live on the rest if you manage it wisely. You won't have to leave Valley Creek unless you wish it."

Hardly able to speak, Earl spread his hands across his knees. "I'm not worthy of such a generous gift. My gratitude isn't enough."

"Father and Mother wanted this. They cast their bread upon the waters, and it wasn't in vain. And I can't begin to say how happy I am to turn it over to you."

Unable to speak, Earl pulled his sister close and held her, unashamed of the joy streaming down his face.

29

November 26, 1910

"Do you hear that? It's a full house! We're having to turn people away!" Laughing, Thompson slapped his thigh and whistled.

All Earl could do was grin. With everything that happened during the past day, the joy and delight flowing through him dizzied his thinking.

Thompson hooked his fingers around the suspenders hiding behind his suit jacket. "The sawmill is saved, and there will be enough to help rebuild Valley Creek. I couldn't be more pleased. Don't you see? You're a hero! Y'all did it!"

Sobering, Earl shook his head. "I'm no hero, Congressman. The Lord only used us to work things out. I'm just glad He saw fit to do it."

"Well, He did a fine job!" Thompson whipped out his pocket watch. "It's almost time." Opening the dressing room door, he moved aside to let them pass. As the congressman led them backstage, Earl reached over and captured Lorena's hand. Tonight, instead of the silver gown, she wore a flowing cream one trimmed in gold that accentuated the gold highlights weaving throughout her brown, chestnut hair.

"Time to focus, dear heart." He lifted her hand to his lips and brushed it with a light kiss.

A glow flickered in her eyes. "That doesn't help, Earl."

"I know." He smirked. "It was more for me than you."

As they approached backstage, the electricity hovering in the air thickened with anticipation. Earl sensed the audience's excitement bubbling through the building, rising like vapor from a hot spring.

While Thompson was speaking, Earl turned to Lorena again. "This is it, Lorena. Our final performance."

A little tremor quaked her chin. "Yes, but not our final time. You know, I'm thankful we're finally ending this the right way."

"So am I."

And then, Lorena was called. The crowd erupted into deafening applause as she almost floated across the stage, her gown pooling around her feet. Shedding all thoughts of the future and the past, Earl sucked in a deep breath and exhaled. Focused. Only the music remained.

Thompson called him next. With violin and bow in hand, he veered his mind away from the vibrating air and fixed his thoughts on the first piece.

While he and Lorena played together, time shed away note by note, piece by piece, the way a flower sheds its pedals nearing the end of its beauty. Their music resonated with vibrant clarity, a fusing together of the colors and clouds of a sunrise.

As one. The ending and rebirth of something beautiful.

When the final note of the final piece dwindled, the audience rose and created a thunder lasting several minutes. Earl couldn't hear himself think, but he saw plenty.

He saw his daughters embracing in the front row, pure joy radiating from their tearful smiles. He saw his sons-in-law adding to the thunder. He saw Mr. Wallace pull a handkerchief from his pocket and brush his eyes. Ella, beside him, clapped with abandon like a giddy child.

And Earl saw Lorena. Love radiated from her eyes.

Cries of encore rose above the handclapping, and Earl smiled at her. He didn't know if his heart could contain his gratitude.

Returning to their instruments after the audience settled, Earl began a song that he and Lorena decided on at the last minute. A departure from the classical but a dedication to their future.

> When I survey the wond'rous Cross
> On which the Prince of Glory dy'd,
> My richest Gain I count but Loss,
> And pour Contempt on all my Pride ...

A Presence descended upon the place. A sweetness tinged the air.

> Forbid it, Lord, that I should boast,
> Save in the Death of Christ my God:
> All the vain things that charm me most,
> I sacrifice them to his Blood ...

Mother's and Father's voices drifted across the years and enveloped him the way no earthly embrace could as Earl made music across the strings.

He couldn't ask for a better ending than this.

"Even though our train leaves tomorrow, I'm sure you'll be delaying your return a few days." Mr. Wallace's mustache curved upward as he shook Earl's hand.

A deep crimson flushed Lorena's cheeks as Earl glanced away from her. "Yes, sir. We plan to return to Valley Creek in a few days."

"I'll be waiting." Mr. Wallace embraced his daughter. "God does all things well."

After waiting her turn, Ella hugged them. "I'll miss you both, but home is calling. They'll load my trunk early tomorrow, and I'll be off. Come see me soon."

More goodbyes followed, but everyone soon filtered away to their rooms leaving Earl and Lorena standing alone in the hallway. For the first time that evening, a tremor of nervousness ran along his spine. Lorena watched him with a curious sparkle in her sapphire eyes.

"I reckon I'll say good night." He crammed his hands in his pockets.

Eyelashes fluttering downward, she looked as though she found the carpet suddenly and irresistibly interesting. Earl's heart thrummed in his throat while he awaited her answer. She took a quiet breath.

"Must you?"

Only two words but they almost made his knees wobble. "No." He took her hand. "Lorena, let's talk."

Her eyes darted up. A smile relaxed the tension in her face. "I'd like that."

Relief washing over him at her smile, he squeezed her hand. "Thought you might. So would I. I'll go change while you do the same."

After he changed into his everyday shirt and pants, he knocked at the connecting door. His mouth ran dry as he heard her rustling approach. He steadied himself. She was too precious a treasure to push her in any way.

Lorena opened the door, shyness flitting across her face. She skittered her eyes away. "Would you care to sit?" She motioned to the settee.

Once they were seated, Earl rubbed his chin. "Lorena, nothing has to happen unless you feel right about it. I just want to say that right out."

"Thank you. I feel rather silly at the moment." She laughed a little, rubbing her arms. "I don't know why."

Earl loved her laugh even when it sounded nervous. "I feel the same way." He intertwined his fingers with hers resting on the seat between them. "Did you feel this nervous at the concert?"

"No." The tendrils around her face shook as she laughed again. "Imagine that!"

And then, they began to talk. They discussed the practices, the accident, the weeks leading up to the concert, and the exhausting two days of performing. Earl hardly noticed the progression of the hands around the clock. Time passed as they opened their hearts and their deepest thoughts to each other. They talked of their daughters, of Valley Creek, of finding a new piece of land, and building a house in the coming spring. They spoke of family, the love and generosity of his folks. The provision of their Heavenly Father.

"This is one of the things I missed about us." Lorena stroked the back of his hand with her thumb. "We could always talk about everything. We were such best friends."

Pain wrapped around his joy like a heavy cloak, weighing it down. "Do you think we can be that again, Lorena?" His breath suspended.

"I believe so. Don't you?"

"I pray so. It feels like we're off to a good start, don't you think?"

"Your brow rumples when you frown." With her other

hand, she reached up and smoothed the furrows. "And, yes, I do."

Earl closed his eyes, relishing her touch the way a thirsty man savors a dipper of water at the end of a hot, bone-weary day.

"I love you, Lorena." After spending sixteen years trapped somewhere deep inside, the words broke free.

Her fingers stilled. Her soft intake of air made his insides tremble. Earl dared not open his eyes.

"I love you, too, Earl."

His eyes popped open and beheld the truth shimmering in hers. He was so unworthy.

"You're an amazing lady. You accepted me before we knew about the inheritance. You've had to forgive so much. I'd give everything to return those years back to you."

Sniffing, Lorena shook her head. "We've both needed forgiving. I don't want to spend the rest of my life in the past. I've spent enough years being empty. If God sees fit to fill our lives, why should I fight it?"

Earl's breathing stilled as he lost himself in those blue depths looking at him in a way he never thought possible. He wrapped his arms around her and drew her close. This time, her lips met his first. Joy rose like shafts of a sunrise as he threaded his fingers into her hair. Like silk. The scent of rose water sweetened the air around him.

The clock struck four.

Drawing back, Earl kissed the tip of her nose and released her. He stood, his arms aching to hold her longer. "It's time I said good night ... or good morning." He grinned. Although it took every inch of his will power, he turned toward the door, showing Lorena he wouldn't pressure her. He would wait forever if need be.

"Earl."

He paused without turning around.

"Don't go."

Earl cleared his throat. "You're sure?"

"Very sure." How could her voice sound so shy yet so certain at once?

His heart thundered. When he turned, she stood, happiness cascading over her face like a wave. In two strides, he reached his wife and gathered her close. His hair brushed her forehead as she tipped her chin, waiting while his lips hovered a breath above hers.

"I promise you, Lorena, I'll spend the rest of my life showing you just how much I love you."

Wasting no more time, Earl proceeded to keep his word.

EPILOGUE

Three days later ...

"Y ou young folks ready?" Guy smirked as he heaved their luggage into the wagon.

"You bet." Earl pulled Lorena's coat tighter around her and lifted her onto the seat. Reaching for the quilts stashed underneath, he spread them across her lap and tucked them around her legs. When he glanced up, he met her dancing eyes.

"What is it, Mrs. Steen?"

"You. As if I can't spread a quilt myself."

Earl's mouth quirked to one side. "Well, you know, it takes a certain skill to get it just right."

The wagon seat jiggled as Guy took his seat, reins in hand. "Quit making cow's eyes at the lady and get in."

Earl swung into the back, his hand landing on Guy's shoulder with a good-natured smack. "Boy, you'd best remember who your elders are."

Hooting with laughter, Guy slapped the reins across the team. "At the moment, I feel like the elder around here." Guy turned onto the dirt road, his face sobering. "Welcome home, y'all."

Earl watched as Lorena breathed in the crisp, Ozark air, the morning sunlight lacing threads of gold into her tresses. "It's good to be home, Guy. I've missed this."

"Do you think you'll miss New York City?"

Lorena shook her head. "I'll miss the rest of my family, but that's all. I need this solitude, this beauty here. I don't know when, but somewhere along the way I fell in love with this place, the people, these hills and valleys. It's home." She turned and found Earl's eyes on her. Without words, she spoke things he understood.

As she turned around, awe spread through him. Along the road, warblers sang in the branches on either side, their songs lifting his silent praise heavenward. Their robust singing almost muted the conversation between Lorena and Guy. The wagon jostled in the ruts, but Earl hardly noticed.

What he had shattered, God had mended.

While they wound their way closer to Valley Creek, Earl pondered those years leading up to this serene moment deep within the valley. The first time, he traveled this road an angry man running from the truth. Yet the truth found him anyhow. Always dwelling within the shadows.

Later, as the wagon turned and rolled into the yard, Lorena gasped.

"Earl, look!" Her hand covered her mouth.

As he twisted around, the wind left him as though a mule had kicked him.

All of Valley Creek crowded in his yard. At one time, a yard that no one dared enter.

Cheers and whoops rose along the hillsides. Laughing faces met him at every turn, the Mansfields', Ray's, Reverend Crandall's, Doc Brown's, the Watkins', the Huitt's', sawmill families, farmers, children, his daughters.

With one bound, Jimmy leaped into the wagon, throwing his arms around Earl's neck. "Y'all did it, Mr. Steen! Y'all saved Valley Creek!"

Before Earl could reply, they crowded around the wagon, their words a happy, tumbling jumble of gratitude and kinship for a soul once adrift.

"Get out, man, so we can thank y'all right and proper!" Doc hollered above the commotion.

Harley Ray grabbed his arm and tugged him out while Guy lifted Lorena down. As though in a dream, Earl blinked, overwhelmed. Folks reached out, squeezed his shoulders, and smacked his back. Others grasped his hand and shook it until he thought it might fall off.

Lorena pressed through to his side. She slipped her arm around his waist, laughter illuminating her eyes. More handshakes, cheers, and hugs followed. Though many of the words rattled together like rain on a tin roof, Earl understood the expression of these Ozark people. His people. Lorena's people.

Near the barn, Earl spied tables spread and laden with food and desserts. The offering of their hearts and friendship to them. Hard-fought, hard-won, and least deserved.

"Time to celebrate with these good folks!" Reverend Crandall waved his arms and waited for the crowd to settle. "Let us pray and give thanks!"

One by one, heads bowed though excitement fizzled underneath the hush.

Tugging his wife closer against his side, Earl brushed his lips across her forehead. Deep wells of happiness bubbled up, blurring everything and everyone from his sight.

He was home.

The End

ABOUT THE AUTHOR

Candace West was born in the Mississippi delta to a young minister and his wife. She grew up in small-town Arkansas and is a graduate of the University of Arkansas at Monticello. When she was twelve years old, she wrote her first story, "Following Prairie River." Since then, she has dreamed of writing Christian fiction. Over the years, she has published short stories as well as poems in various magazines. Since her teenage years, she has written many church plays. In 2018, she published her first novel *Lane Steen*. By weaving entertaining, page-turning stories, Candace hopes to share the Gospel and encourage her readers. She currently lives in her beloved Arkansas with her husband Aaron and their son Matthew along with two dogs and three cats.

ALSO BY CANDACE WEST

The Valley Creek Redemption Series

Set in the Arkansas Ozarks, this series is a beautifully written family saga with themes of forgiveness, reconciliation, and redemption.

Book One: Lane Steen

by Candace West

To let go of the past, she must confront it.

When Lane Steen discovers her father kidnapped her years ago, her fractured world shatters. A different world and a new family await to welcome her if she'll only take the chance.

Will they love her? Or will she trade one hostile home for another?

Perhaps the journey will only raise more questions.

Who is her father, really? And what happened to him? Will she ever be able to forgive him so that love can heal her heart?

Valley Creek may be her prison, but perhaps it holds the unexpected. True love, purpose, grace, and redemption.

Join Lane on her search for the truth today!

A shattered heart.

A wounded spirit.

A community in crisis.

Lorena Steen gave up on love years ago. She forgave her long-time estranged husband, but when circumstances bring her to the Ozark town of Valley Creek, she discovers forgiving is far from forgetting.

Haunted by his past acts of betrayal, Earl Steen struggles to grow his reclaimed faith and reinstate himself as an upstanding member of Valley Creek. He soon learns that while God's grace is amazing, that of the small-town gossips is not.

When disaster strikes, the only logical solution is for Earl and Lorena to combine their musical talents in an effort to save the community. But even if they're willing to work together, are they able to? Or will the shadows that descend upon Valley Creek reduce it to a ghost town?

age, she is confronted with the truth about her father's occupation. Burdened with the guilt of her family's sin, she struggles to make a difference in whatever way she can. When she loses her husband in the battle for freedom from England, she makes a difficult decision that will change her life forever.

Sergeant Micah Hughes is too dedicated to serving the fledgling country of America to consider falling in love. When he carries the tragic news to Lydia Saunders about her husband's death, he is appalled by his attraction to the young widow. Micah wrestles with his feelings for Lydia while he tries to focus on helping the cause of freedom. He trains a group of former slaves to become capable soldiers on the battlefield.

Tensions both on the battlefield and on the home front bring hardship and turmoil that threaten to endanger them all. When Lydia and Micah are faced with saving the life of a black infant in danger, can they survive this turning point in their lives?

A groundbreaking book, honest and inspiring, showcasing black soldiers in the American Revolution. *Scarred Vessels* is peopled with flesh and blood characters and true events that not only inspire and entertain but educate. Well done!

~ Laura Frantz, Christy Award-winning author

of *An Uncommon Woman*

The Rancher's Legacy

Homeward Trails

Book One

Matthew Anderson and his father try to help neighbor Bill Maxwell when his ranch is attacked. On the day his daughter Rachel is to return from school back East, outlaws target the Maxwell ranch. After Rachel's world is shattered, she won't even consider the plan her father and Matt's cooked up—to see their two children marry and combine the ranches.

Meanwhile in Maine, sea captain's widow Edith Rose hires a private investigator to locate her three missing grandchildren. The children were abandoned by their father nearly twenty years ago. They've been adopted into very different families, and they're scattered across the country. Can investigator Ryland Atkins find them all while the elderly woman still lives? His first attempt is to find the boy now called Matthew Anderson. Can Ryland survive his trip into the wild Colorado Territory and find Matt before the outlaws finish destroying a legacy?

Books Afloat

Columbia River Undercurrents

Book One

Blaming herself for her childhood role in the Oklahoma farm truck accident that cost her grandfather's life, Anne Mettles is determined to make her life count. She wants to do it all–captain her library boat and resist Japanese attacks to keep America safe. But failing her pilot's exam requires her to bring others onboard.

Will she go it alone? Or will she team with the unlikely but (mostly) lovable characters? One is a saboteur, one an unlikely hero, and one, she discovers, is the man of her dreams.

Stay up-to-date on your favorite books and authors with our free e-newsletters.

ScriveningsPress.com